THE QUEEN IN CRYSTAL

Slowly, Sparhawk raised his eyes to his Queen. She was beautiful. There was almost luminous perfection about her countenance. Her pale blond hair was long and loosely framed her face. She wore her state robes and the heavy gold crown of Elenia. Her slender hands lay upon the arms of her throne, and her eyes were closed. But now she was locked in the semblance of death, embedded in a transparent crystal hexahedron, like some bug frozen in clear amber.

Then he heard and felt it, a regular thudding sound, growing louder by the moment as it announced to any who might enter the throne room that her heart was still beating.

Sparhawk sank to one knee in a move of profound respect, his eyes suddenly filling with tears. "I am here now, Ehlana," he murmured. "Somehow, I'll make everything right again."

The heart beat grew louder, almost as if she had heard.

By David Eddings
Published by Ballantine Books:

THE BELGARIAD

Book One: *Pawn of Prophecy*
Book Two: *Queen of Sorcery*
Book Three: *Magician's Gambit*
Book Four: *Castle of Wizardry*
Book Five: *Enchanters' End Game*

THE MALLOREON

Book One: *Guardians of the West*
Book Two: *King of the Murgos*
Book Three: *Demon Lord of Karanda*
Book Four: *Sorceress of Darshiva*
Book Five: *The Seeress of Kell**

THE ELENIUM

Book One: *The Diamond Throne*
Book Two: *The Ruby Knight**
Book Three: *The Sapphire Rose**

*Forthcoming

Book One
of *The Elenium*

THE
DIAMOND
THRONE

David
Eddings

A Del Rey Book
BALLANTINE BOOKS
NEW YORK

A Del Rey Book
Published by Ballantine Books

Copyright © 1989 by David Eddings

All rights reserved under International and Pan-American Copyright Conventions. Published in the United States of America by Ballantine Books, a division of Random House, Inc., New York, and simultaneously in Canada by Random House of Canada Limited, Toronto.

Library of Congress Catalog Card Number 89-92805

ISBN 0-345-36746-4

Manufactured in the United States of America

First Hardcover Edition: May 1989
First International Edition: February 1990

Cover Art by Keith Parkinson
Maps by Shelly Shapiro
Borders and artwork © 1989 by Holly Johnson

For Eleanor and for Ralph,
for courage and faith.
Trust me.

PROLOGUE

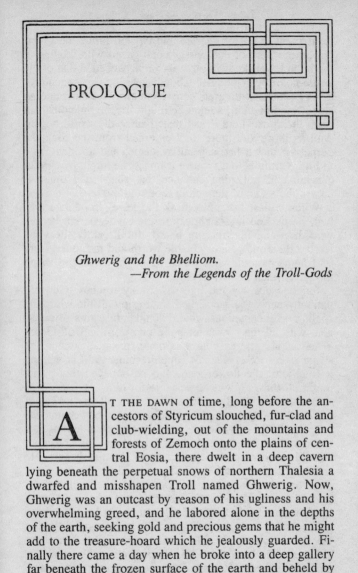

Ghwerig and the Bhelliom.
—From the Legends of the Troll-Gods

A T THE DAWN of time, long before the ancestors of Styricum slouched, fur-clad and
club-wielding, out of the mountains and
forests of Zemoch onto the plains of central Eosia, there dwelt in a deep cavern
lying beneath the perpetual snows of northern Thalesia a
dwarfed and misshapen Troll named Ghwerig. Now,
Ghwerig was an outcast by reason of his ugliness and his
overwhelming greed, and he labored alone in the depths
of the earth, seeking gold and precious gems that he might
add to the treasure-hoard which he jealously guarded. Finally there came a day when he broke into a deep gallery
far beneath the frozen surface of the earth and beheld by
the light of his flickering torch a deep blue gemstone,
larger than his fist, embedded in the wall. Trembling with

1

excitement in all his gnarled and twisted limbs, he squat-
ted on the floor of that passage and gazed with longing at
the huge jewel, knowing that its value exceeded that of the
entire hoard which he had labored for centuries to acquire.
Then he began with great care to cut away the surrounding
stone, chip by chip, so that he might lift the precious gem
from the spot where it had rested since the world began.
And as more and more of it emerged from the rock, he
perceived that it had a peculiar shape, and an idea came
to him. Could he but remove it intact, he might by careful
carving and polishing enhance that shape and thus increase the value of the gem a thousandfold.

When at last he gently took the jewel from its rocky
bed, he carried it straightway to the cave wherein lay his
workshop and his treasure hoard. Indifferently, he shat-
tered a diamond of incalculable worth and fashioned from
its fragments tools with which he might carve and shape
the gem which he had found.

For decades, by the light of smoky torches, Ghwerig
patiently carved and polished, muttering all the while the
spells and incantations which would infuse this priceless
gem with all the power for good or ill of the Troll-Gods.
When at last the carving was done, the gem was in the
shape of a rose of deepest sapphire blue. And he named
it Bhelliom, the flower-gem, and he believed that by its
might all things might be possible for him.

But though Bhelliom was filled with all the power of
the Troll-Gods, it would not yield up that power unto its
misshapen and ugly owner, and Ghwerig pounded his fists
in rage upon the stone floor of his cavern. He consulted
with his Gods and made offerings to them of heavy gold
and bright silver, and his Gods revealed to him that there
must be a key to unlock the power of Bhelliom, lest its
might be unleashed by the whim of any who came upon
it. Then the Troll-Gods told Ghwerig what he must do to
gain mastery over the gem which he had wrought. Taking
the shards which had fallen unnoticed in the dust about
his feet as he had labored to shape the sapphire rose, he
fashioned a pair of rings. Of finest gold were the rings,
and each was mounted with a polished oval fragment of
Bhelliom itself. When it was done, he placed the rings one

on each of his hands and then lifted the sapphire rose. The deep, glowing blue of the stones mounted in his rings fled back into Bhelliom itself, and the jewels that adorned his twisted hands were now as pale as diamond. And as he held the flower-gem, he felt the surge of its power and he rejoiced in the knowledge that the jewel he had wrought had consented to yield to him.

As the uncounted centuries rolled by, great were the wonders Ghwerig wrought by the power of Bhelliom. But the Styrics came at last into the land of the Trolls. When the Elder Gods of Styricum learned of Bhelliom, each in his heart coveted it by reason of its power. But Ghwerig was cunning and he sealed up the entrances to his cavern with enchantments to repel their efforts to wrest Bhelliom from him.

Now at a certain time, the Younger Gods of Styricum took counsel with each other, for they were disquieted about the power which Bhelliom would confer upon whichever God came to possess it, and they concluded that such might should not be unloosed in the earth. They resolved then to render the stone powerless. Of their number they selected the nimble Goddess Aphrael for the task. Then Aphrael journeyed to the north, and, by reason of her slight form, she was able to wriggle her way through a crevice so small that Ghwerig had neglected to seal it. Once she was within the cavern, Aphrael lifted her voice in song. So sweetly she sang that Ghwerig was all bemused by her melody and he felt no alarm at her presence. So it was that Aphrael lulled him. When, with dreamy smile, the Troll-Dwarf closed his eyes, she tugged the ring from off his right hand and replaced it with a ring set with a common diamond. Ghwerig started up when he felt the tug; but when he looked at his hand, a ring still encircled his finger, and he sat him down again and took his ease, delighting in the song of the Goddess. When once again, in sweet reverie, his eyes drooped shut, the nimble Aphrael tugged the ring from off his left hand, replacing it with yet another ring mounted with yet another diamond. Again Ghwerig started to his feet and looked with alarm at his left hand, but he was reassured by the presence there of a ring which looked for all the world like one of the pair which he had fashioned from the shards of the flower-gem. Aphrael continued to sing for him until at last he lapsed into deep slumber. Then the Goddess stole away on silent feet, bearing with her the rings which were the keys to the power of Bhelliom.

Now, upon a later day, Ghwerig lifted Bhelliom from the crystal case wherein it lay that he might perform a task by its power, but Bhelliom would not yield to him, for he no longer possessed the rings which were the keys to its power. The rage of Ghwerig was beyond measure, and he went up and down in the land seeking the Goddess Aphrael that he might wrest his rings from her, but he found her not, though for centuries he searched.

Thus it was for as long as Styricum held sway over the mountains and plains of Eosia. But there came a time when the Elenes rode out of the east and intruded themselves into this place. After centuries of random wandering to and fro in the land, some of their number came at last into far northern Thalesia and dispossessed the Styrics and their Gods. And when the Elenes heard of Ghwerig and his Bhelliom, they sought the entrances to the Troll-Dwarf's cavern throughout the hills and valleys of Thalesia, all hot with their lust to find and own the fabled gem by reason of its incalculable worth, for they knew not of the power locked in its azure petals.

It fell at last to Adian of Thalesia, mightiest and most crafty of the heroes of antiquity, to solve the riddle. At peril of his soul, he took counsel with the Troll-Gods and made offering to them, and they relented and told him that Ghwerig went abroad in the land at certain times in search of the Goddess Aphrael of Styricum that he might reclaim a pair of rings which she had stolen from him, but of the true meaning of those rings they told him not. And Adian journeyed to the far north and there he awaited each twilight for a half-dozen years the appearance of Ghwerig.

When at last the Troll-Dwarf appeared, Adian went up to him in a dissembling guise and told him that he knew where Aphrael might be found and that he would reveal her location for a helmet full of fine yellow gold. Ghwerig was deceived and straightaway led Adian to the hidden mouth of his cavern and he took the hero's helm and went into his treasure chamber and filled it to overflowing with fine gold. Then he emerged again, sealing the entrance to his cavern behind him. And he gave Adian the gold, and Adian deceived him again, saying that Aphrael might be found in the district of Horset on the western coast of Thalesia. Ghwerig hastened to Horset to seek out the God-dess. And once again Adian imperiled his soul and im-plored the Troll-Gods to break Ghwerig's enchantments that he might gain entrance to the cavern. The capricious Troll-Gods consented and the enchantments were broken.

As rosy dawn touched the ice fields of the north into flame, Adian emerged from Ghwerig's cavern with Bhel-liom in his grasp. He journeyed straightway to his capital at Emsat and there he fashioned a crown for himself and surmounted it with Bhelliom.

The chagrin of Ghwerig knew no bounds when he re-turned empty-handed to his cavern to find that not only had he lost the keys to the power of Bhelliom, but that the flower-gem itself was no longer in his possession. There-after he usually lurked by night in the fields and forests about the city of Emsat, seeking to reclaim his treasure, but the descendants of Adian protected it closely and pre-vented him from approaching it.

Now as it happened, Azash, an Elder God of Styricum, had long yearned in his heart for possession of Bhelliom and of the rings which unlocked its power and he sent forth his hordes out of Zemoch to seize the gems by force of arms. The kings of the west took up arms to join with the knights of the Church to face the armies of Otha of Zemoch and of his dark Styric God, Azash. And King Sarak of Thalesia took ship with some few of his vassals and sailed south from Emsat, leaving behind the royal command that his earls were to follow when the mobili-zation of all Thalesia was complete. As it happened, how-ever, King Sarak never reached the great battlefield on the plains of Lamorkand, but fell instead to a Zemoch spear in an unrecorded skirmish near the shores of Lake Venne in Pelosia. A faithful vassal, though mortally wounded, took up his fallen lord's crown and struggled his way to the marshy eastern shore of the lake. There, hard-pressed and dying, he cast the Thalesian crown into the murky, peat-clouded waters of the lake, even as Ghwerig, who had followed his lost treasure, watched in horror from his place of concealment in a nearby peat bog.

The Zemochs who had slain King Sarak immediately began to probe the brown-stained depths, that they might find the crown and carry it in triumph to Azash, but they were interrupted in their search by a column of Alcione Knights sweeping down out of Deira to join the battle in Lamorkand. The Alciones fell upon the Zemochs and slew them to the last man. The faithful vassal of the Thalesian king was given an honorable burial, and the Alciones rode on, all unaware that the fabled crown of Thalesia lay beneath the turbid waters of Lake Venne.

It is sometimes rumored in Pelosia, however, that on moonless nights the shadowy form of the immortal Troll-Dwarf haunts the marshy shore. Since, by reason of his malformed limbs, Ghwerig dares not enter the dark waters of the lake to probe its depths, he must creep along the marge, alternately crying out his longing to Bhelliom and dancing in howling frustration that it will not respond to him.

PART ONE

CIMMURA

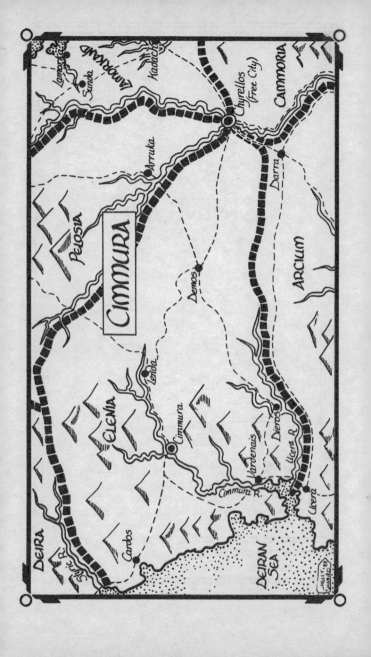

CHAPTER
ONE

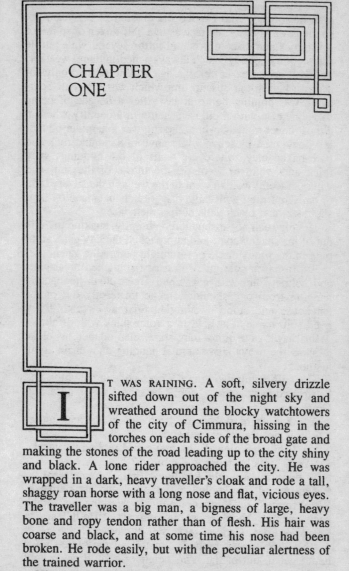

T WAS RAINING. A soft, silvery drizzle sifted down out of the night sky and wreathed around the blocky watchtowers of the city of Cimmura, hissing in the torches on each side of the broad gate and making the stones of the road leading up to the city shiny and black. A lone rider approached the city. He was wrapped in a dark, heavy traveller's cloak and rode a tall, shaggy roan horse with a long nose and flat, vicious eyes. The traveller was a big man, a bigness of large, heavy bone and ropy tendon rather than of flesh. His hair was coarse and black, and at some time his nose had been broken. He rode easily, but with the peculiar alertness of the trained warrior.

His name was Sparhawk, a man at least ten years older

than he looked, who carried the erosion of his years not so much on his battered face as in a half-dozen or so minor infirmities and discomforts and in the several wide purple scars upon his body which always ached in damp weather. Tonight, however, he felt his age and he wished only for a warm bed in the obscure inn which was his goal. Sparhawk was coming home at last after a decade of being someone else with a different name in a country where it almost never rained—where the sun was a hammer pounding down on a bleached white anvil of sand and rock and hard-baked clay, where the walls of the buildings were thick and white to ward off the blows of the sun, and where graceful women went to the wells in the silvery light of early morning with large clay vessels balanced on their shoulders and black veils across their faces.

The big roan horse shuddered absently, shaking the rain out of his shaggy coat, and approached the city gate, stopping in the ruddy circle of torchlight before the gatehouse.

An unshaven gate guard in a rust-splotched breastplate and helmet, and with a patched green cloak negligently hanging from one shoulder, came unsteadily out of the gatehouse and stood swaying in Sparhawk's path. "I'll need your name," he said in a voice thick with drink.

Sparhawk gave him a long stare, then opened his cloak to show the heavy silver amulet hanging on a chain about his neck.

The half-drunk gate guard's eyes widened slightly, and he stepped back a pace. "Oh," he said, "sorry, my Lord. Go ahead."

Another guard poked his head out of the gatehouse. "Who is he, Raf?" he demanded.

"A Pandion Knight," the first guard replied nervously.

"What's his business in Cimmura?"

"I don't question the Pandions, Bral," the man named Raf answered. He smiled ingratiatingly up at Sparhawk. "New man," he said apologetically, jerking his thumb back over his shoulder at his comrade. "He'll learn in time, my Lord. Can we serve you in any way?"

"No," Sparhawk replied, "thanks all the same. You'd better get in out of the rain, neighbor. You'll catch cold out here." He handed a small coin to the green-cloaked guard and rode on into the city, passing up the narrow, cobbled street beyond the gate with the slow clatter of the big roan's steel-shod hooves echoing back from the buildings.

The district near the gate was poor, with shabby, run-down houses standing tightly packed beside each other with their second floors projecting out over the wet, littered street. Crude signs swung creaking on rusty hooks in the night wind, identifying this or that tightly shuttered shop on the street-level floors. A wet, miserable-looking cur slunk across the street with his ratlike tail between his legs. Otherwise, the street was dark and empty.

A torch burned fitfully at an intersection where another street crossed the one upon which Sparhawk rode. A sick young whore, thin and wrapped in a shabby blue cloak, stood hopefully under the torch like a pale, frightened ghost. "Would you like a nice time, sir?" she whined at him. Her eyes were wide and timid, and her face gaunt and hungry.

He stopped, bent in his saddle, and poured a few small coins into her grimy hand. "Go home, little sister," he told her in a gentle voice. "It's late and wet, and there'll be no customers tonight." Then he straightened and rode on, leaving her to stare in grateful astonishment after him. He turned down a narrow side street clotted with shadow and heard the scurry of feet somewhere in the rainy dark ahead of him. His ears caught a quick, whispered conversation in the deep shadows somewhere to his left.

The roan snorted and laid his ears back.

"It's nothing to get excited about," Sparhawk told him. The big man's voice was very soft, almost a husky whisper. It was the kind of voice people turned to hear. Then he spoke more loudly, addressing the pair of footpads lurking in the shadows. "I'd like to accommodate you, neighbors," he said, "but it's late, and I'm not in the mood for casual entertainment. Why don't you go rob some drunk young nobleman instead, and live to steal another day?" To emphasize his words, he threw back his damp cloak to reveal the leather-bound hilt of the plain broadsword belted at his side.

There was a quick, startled silence in the dark street, followed by the rapid patter of fleeing feet.

The big roan snorted derisively.

"My sentiments exactly," Sparhawk agreed, pulling his cloak back around him. "Shall we proceed?"

They entered a large square surrounded by hissing torches where most of the brightly colored canvas booths had their fronts rolled down. A few forlornly hopeful enthusiasts remained open for business, stridently bawling their wares to indifferent passersby hurrying home on a late, rainy evening. Sparhawk reined in his horse as a group of rowdy young nobles lurched unsteadily from the door of a seedy tavern, shouting drunkenly to each other as they crossed the square. He waited calmly until they vanished into a side street and then looked around, not so much wary as alert.

Had there been but a few more people in the nearly empty square, even Sparhawk's trained eye might not have noticed Krager. The man was of medium height and he was rumpled and unkempt. His boots were muddy, and his maroon cape carelessly caught at the throat. He slouched across the square, his wet, colorless hair plastered down on his narrow skull and his watery eyes blinking nearsightedly as he peered about in the rain. Sparhawk drew in his breath sharply. He hadn't seen Krager since that night in Cippria, almost ten years ago, and the man had aged considerably. His face was grayer and more pouchy-looking, but there could be no question that it was Krager.

Since quick movements attracted the eye, Sparhawk's reaction was studied. He dismounted slowly and led his big horse to a green canvas food vendor's stall, keeping the animal between himself and the nearsighted man in the maroon cape. "Good evening, neighbor," he said to the brown-clad food vendor in his deadly quiet voice. "I have some business to attend to. I'll pay you if you'll watch my horse."

The unshaven vendor's eyes came quickly alight.

"Don't even think it," Sparhawk warned. "The horse won't follow you, no matter what you do—but I *will*, and you wouldn't like that at all. Just take the pay and forget about trying to steal the horse."

The vendor looked at the big man's bleak face, swallowed hard, and made a jerky attempt at a bow. "Whatever you say, my Lord," he agreed quickly, his words tumbling over each other. "I vow to you that your noble mount will be safe with me."

"Noble what?"

"Noble mount—your horse."

"Oh, I see. I'd appreciate that."

"Can I do anything else for you, my Lord?"

Sparhawk looked across the square at Krager's back. "Do you by chance happen to have a bit of wire handy—about so long?" He measured out perhaps three feet with his hands.

"I may have, my Lord. The herring kegs are bound with wire. Let me look."

Sparhawk crossed his arms and leaned them on his saddle, watching Krager across the horse's back. The past years, the blasting sun, and the women going to the wells in the steely light of early morning fell away, and quite suddenly he was back in the stockyards outside Cippria with the stink of dung and blood on him, the taste of fear and hatred in his mouth, and the pain of his wounds making him weak as his pursuers searched for him with their swords in their hands.

He pulled his mind away from that, deliberately concentrating on this moment rather than the past. He hoped that the vendor could find some wire. Wire was good. No noise, no mess, and with a little time it could be made to look exotic—the kind of thing one might expect from a Styric or perhaps a Pelosian. It wasn't so much Krager, he thought as the tense excitement built in him. Krager had never been more than a dim, feeble adjunct to Martel—an extension, another set of hands, just as the other man, Adus, had never been more than a weapon. It was what Krager's death would do to Martel—that was what mattered.

"This is the best I could find, my Lord," the greasy-aproned food vendor said respectfully, coming out of the back of his canvas booth and holding out a length of rusty, soft-iron wire. "I'm sorry. It isn't much."

"It's just fine," Sparhawk replied, taking the wire. He snapped the rusty strand taut between his hands. "It's perfect, in fact." Then he turned to his horse. "Stay here, Faran," he said.

The horse bared his teeth at him. Sparhawk laughed softly and moved out into the square, some distance behind Krager. If the nearsighted man were found in some shadowy doorway, bowed tautly backward with the wire knotted about his neck and ankles and with his eyes popping out of a blackened face, or face down in the trough of some back-alley public urinal, that would unnerve Martel, hurt him, perhaps even frighten him. It might be enough to bring him out into the open, and Sparhawk had been waiting for years for a chance to catch Martel out in the open. Carefully, his hands concealed beneath his cloak, he began to work the kinks out of his length of wire, even as he stalked his quarry.

His senses had become preternaturally alert. He could clearly hear the guttering of the torches along the sides of the square and see their orange flicker reflected in the puddles of water lying among the cobblestones. That reflected glow seemed for some reason very beautiful. Sparhawk felt good—better perhaps than he had for ten years.

"Sir Knight? Sir Sparhawk? Can that be you?"

Startled, Sparhawk turned quickly, swearing under his breath. The man who had accosted him had long, elegantly curled blond hair. He wore a saffron-colored doublet, lavender hose, and an apple-green cloak. His wet maroon shoes were long and pointed, and his cheeks were rouged. The small, useless sword at his side and his broad-brimmed hat with its dripping plume marked him as a courtier, one of the petty functionaries and parasitic hangers-on who infested the palace like vermin.

"What are you doing back here in Cimmura?" the fop demanded, his high-pitched, effeminate voice startled. "You were banished."

Sparhawk looked quickly at the man he had been following. Krager was nearing the entrance to a street that opened into the square, and in a moment he would be out of sight. It was still possible, however. One quick, hard blow would put this overdressed butterfly before him to sleep, and Krager would still be within reach. Then a hot disappointment filled Sparhawk's mouth as a detachment of the watch marched into the square with lumbering tread. There was no way now to dispose of this interfering popinjay without attracting their attention. The look he directed at the perfumed man barring his path was flat with anger.

The courtier stepped back nervously, glancing quickly at the soldiers who were moving along in front of the booths, checking the fastenings on the rolled-down canvas fronts. ''I insist that you tell me what you're doing back here,'' he said, trying to sound authoritative.

''Insist? You?'' Sparhawk's voice was full of contempt.

The other man looked quickly at the soldiers again, seeking reassurance, then he straightened boldly. ''I'm taking you in charge, Sparhawk. I demand that you give an account of yourself.'' He reached out and grasped Sparhawk's arm.

''Don't touch me.'' Sparhawk spat out the words, striking the hand away.

''You hit me!'' the courtier gasped, clutching at his hand in pain.

Sparhawk took the man's shoulder in one hand and pulled him close. ''If you ever put your hands on me again, I'll rip out your guts. Now get out of my way.''

''I'll call the watch,'' the fop threatened.

''And how long do you think you'll continue to live after you do that?''

''You can't threaten me. I have powerful friends.''

''But they're not here, are they? I *am*, however.'' Sparhawk pushed him away in disgust and turned to walk on across the square.

''You Pandions can't get away with this highhanded behavior any more. There are laws in Elenia now,'' the overdressed man called after him shrilly. ''I'm going straight to Baron Harparin. I'm going to tell him that you've come back to Cimmura and about how you hit me and threatened me.''

''Good,'' Sparhawk replied without turning. ''Do that.''

He continued to walk away, his irritation and disappointment rising to the point where he had to clench his teeth tightly to keep himself under control. Then an idea came to him. It was petty—even childish—but for some reason it seemed quite appropriate. He stopped and straightened his shoulders, muttering under his breath in the Styric tongue, even as his fingers wove intricate designs in the air in front of him. He hesitated slightly, groping for the word for carbuncle. He finally settled for boils instead and completed the incantation. He turned slightly, looked at his tormentor, and released the spell. Then he turned back and continued on across the square, smiling slightly to himself. It was, to be sure, quite petty, but Sparhawk was like that sometimes.

He handed the food vendor a coin for minding Faran, swung up into his saddle, and rode across the square in the misty drizzle, a big man shrouded in a rough wool cloak, astride an ugly-faced roan horse.

Once he was past the square, the streets were dark and empty again, with guttering torches hissing in the rain at intersections and casting their dim, sooty orange glow. The sound of Faran's hooves was loud in the empty street. Sparhawk shifted slightly in his saddle. The sensation he felt was very faint, a kind of prickling of the skin across his shoulders and up the back of his neck, but he recognized it immediately. Someone was watching him, and the watcher was not friendly. Sparhawk shifted again, carefully trying to make the movement appear to be no more than the uncomfortable fidgeting of a saddle-weary traveller. His right hand, however, was concealed beneath his cloak and it sought the hilt of his sword. The oppressive sense of malevolence increased, and then, in the shadows beyond the flickering torch at the next intersection, he saw a figure robed and hooded in a dark gray garment that blended so well into the shadows and wreathing drizzle that the watcher was almost invisible.

The roan tensed his muscles, and his ears flicked.

"I see him, Faran," Sparhawk replied very quietly.

They continued on along the cobblestone street, passing through the pool of orange torchlight and on into the shadowy street beyond. Sparhawk's eyes readjusted to the dark, but the hooded figure had already vanished up some alley-way or through one of the narrow doors along the street. The sense of being watched was gone, and the street was no longer a place of danger. Faran moved on, his hooves clattering on the wet stones.

The inn which was Sparhawk's destination was on an unobtrusive back street. It was gated at the front of its central courtyard with stout oaken planks. Its walls were peculiarly high and thick, and a single, dim lantern glowed beside a much-weathered wooden sign that creaked mournfully as it swung back and forth in the rain-filled night breeze. Sparhawk pulled Faran close to the gate, leaned back in his saddle, and kicked the rain-blackened planks solidly with one spurred foot. There was a peculiar rhythm to the kicks.

He waited.

Then the gate creaked inward and the shadowy form of a porter, hooded in black, looked out. He nodded briefly, then pulled the gate wider to admit Sparhawk. The big knight rode into the rain-wet courtyard and slowly dismounted. The porter swung the gate shut and barred it, then he pushed his hood back from his steel helm, turned, and bowed. "My Lord," he greeted Sparhawk respectfully.

"It's too late at night for formalities, Sir Knight," Sparhawk responded, also with a brief bow.

"Formality is the very soul of gentility, Sir Sparhawk," the porter replied ironically. "I try to practice it whenever I can."

"As you wish." Sparhawk shrugged. "Will you see to my horse?"

"Of course. Your man, Kurik, is here."

Sparhawk nodded, untying the two heavy leather bags from the skirt of his saddle.

"I'll take those up for you, my Lord," the porter offered.

"There's no need. Where's Kurik?"

"First door at the top of the stairs. Will you want supper?"

Sparhawk shook his head. "Just a bath and a warm bed." He turned to his horse, who stood dozing with one hind leg cocked slightly so that his hoof rested on its tip. "Wake up, Faran," he told the animal.

Faran opened his eyes and gave him a flat, unfriendly stare.

"Go with this knight," Sparhawk instructed firmly. "Don't try to bite him, or kick him, or pin him against the side of the stall with your rump—and don't step on his feet, either."

The big roan briefly laid back his ears and then sighed.

Sparhawk laughed. "Give him a few carrots," he instructed the porter.

"How can you tolerate this foul-tempered brute, Sir Sparhawk?"

"We're perfectly matched," Sparhawk replied. "It was a good ride, Faran," he said then to the horse. "Thank you, and sleep warm."

The horse turned his back on him.

"Keep your eyes open, Sir Knight," Sparhawk cautioned the porter. "Someone was watching me as I rode here, and I got the feeling that it was a little more than idle curiosity."

The knight porter's face hardened. "I'll tend to it, my Lord," he said.

"Good." Sparhawk turned and crossed the wet, glistening stones of the courtyard and mounted the steps leading to the roofed gallery on the second floor of the inn.

The inn was a well-kept secret that few in Cimmura knew about. Though ostensibly no different from any of dozens of others, this particular establishment was owned and operated by the Pandion Knights and it provided a safe haven for any of their number who, for one reason or another, were reluctant to avail themselves of the facilities of their chapterhouse on the eastern outskirts of the city.

At the top of the stairs, Sparhawk stopped and tapped his fingertips lightly on the first door. After a moment, the door opened. The man inside was burly and he had iron-gray hair and a coarse, short-trimmed beard. His hose and boots were of black leather, and his long vest was of the same material. A heavy dagger hung from his belt, steel cuffs encircled his wrists, and his heavily muscled arms and shoulders were bare. He was not a handsome

man, and his eyes were as hard as agates. "You're late,"
he said flatly.

"A few interruptions along the way," Sparhawk replied
laconically, stepping into the warm, candlelit room. The
bare-shouldered man closed the door behind him and slid
the bolt with a solid clank. Sparhawk looked at him. "I
trust you've been well, Kurik?" he said to the man he had
not seen for ten years.

"Passable. Get out of that wet cloak."

Sparhawk grinned, dropped his saddlebags to the floor,
and undid the clasp of his dripping wool cloak. "How are
Aslade and the boys?"

"Growing," Kurik grunted, taking the cloak. "My sons
are getting taller and Aslade's getting fatter. Farm life
agrees with her."

"You like plump women, Kurik," Sparhawk reminded
his squire. "That's why you married her."

Kurik grunted again, looking critically at his lord's lean
frame. "You haven't been eating, Sparhawk," he accused.

"Don't mother me, Kurik." Sparhawk sprawled in a
heavy oak chair. He looked around. The room had a stone
floor and stone walls. The ceiling was low, with heavy
black beams supporting it. A fire crackled in an arched
fireplace, filling the room with dancing light and shadows.
Two candles burned on the table, and two narrow cots
stood, one against either wall. It was to the heavy rack
beside the single blue-draped window that Sparhawk's eyes
went first, however. Hanging on that rack was a full suit
of armor, enameled shiny black. Leaning against the wall
beside it was a large black shield with the emblem of his
family, a hawk with flared wings and with a spear in its
talons, worked in silver upon its face. Beside the shield
stood a massive, sheathed broadsword with a silver-bound
hilt.

"You forgot to oil it when you left," Kurik accused.
"It took me a week to get the rust off. Give me your
foot." He bent and worked off one of Sparhawk's riding
boots and then the other. "Why do you always have to
walk in the mud?" he growled, tossing the boots over
beside the fireplace. "I've got a bath ready for you in the

next room," he said then. "Strip. I want to see those wounds of yours anyway."

Sparhawk sighed wearily and stood up. With his gruff squire's peculiarly gentle help, he undressed.

"You're wet clear through," Kurik noted, touching his lord's clammy back with one rough, calloused hand.

"Rain does that to people sometimes."

"Did you ever see a surgeon about these?" the squire demanded, lightly touching the wide purple scars on Sparhawk's shoulders and left side.

"A physician looked at them. There wasn't a surgeon handy, so I left them to heal by themselves."

Kurik nodded. "It shows," he said. "Go get in the tub. I'll fetch something for you to eat."

"I'm not hungry."

"That's too bad. You look like a skeleton. Now that you're back, I'm not going to let you walk around in that condition."

"Why are you bullying me, Kurik?"

"Because I'm angry. You frightened me half to death. You've been gone for ten years, and there's been little news—and all of it bad." The gruff man's eyes grew momentarily soft, and he roughly grasped Sparhawk's shoulders in a grip that might have brought a lesser man to his knees. "Welcome home, my Lord," he said in a thick voice.

Sparhawk roughly embraced his friend. "Thank you, Kurik," he said, his voice also thick. "It's good to be back."

"All right," Kurik said, his face hard again. "Now go bathe. You stink." And he turned on his heel and went to the door.

Sparhawk smiled and walked into the next room. He stepped into the wooden tub and sank gratefully down into the steaming water. He had been another man with another name—a man called Mahkra—for so long now that he knew that no simple bath would wash that other identity away, but it was good to relax and let the hot water and coarse soap rinse the dust of that dry, sunblasted coast from his skin. In a kind of detached reverie as he washed his lean, scarred limbs, he remembered the life he had led as Mahkra in the city of Jiroch in Rendor. He remembered the small, cool shop where, as an untitled commoner, Mahkra had sold brass ewers, candied sweetmeats, and exotic perfumes while the bright sunlight reflected blindingly from the thick, white walls across the street. He remembered the hours of endless talk in the little wine shop on the corner, where Mahkra had sipped sour, resinous Rendorish wine by the hour and had delicately, subtly, probed for the information which was then passed on to his friend and fellow Pandion, Sir Voren—information concerning the reawakening of Eshandist sentiment in Rendor, of secret caches of arms hidden in the desert and of the activities of the agents of Emperor Otha of Zemoch. He remembered the soft, dark nights filled with the clinging perfume of Lillias, Mahkra's sulking mistress, and of the beginning of each day when he had arisen and gone to the window to watch the women going to the wells in the steel-gray light of sunless dawn. He sighed. "And who are you now, Sparhawk?" he asked himself softly. "No longer a merchant in brass and candied dates and perfumes, certainly, but once again a Pandion Knight? A magician? The Queen's Champion? Perhaps not. Perhaps no more than a battered and tired man with a few too many years and scars and far too many skirmishes behind him."

"Didn't it occur to you to cover your head while you were in Rendor?" Kurik asked sourly from the doorway. The burly squire held a robe and a rough towel. "When a man starts talking to himself, it's a sure sign that he's been out in the sun too long."

"Just musing, Kurik. I've been a long time away from home, and it's going to take a while to get used to it again."

"You may not have a while. Did anyone recognize you when you rode in?"

Sparhawk remembered the fop in the square and nodded. "One of Harparin's toadies saw me in the square near the west gate."

"That's it, then. You're going to have to present yourself at the palace tomorrow, or Lycheas will have Cimmura taken apart stone by stone searching for you."

"Lycheas?"

"The prince regent—bastard son to Princess Arissa and whatever drunken sailor or unhanged pickpocket got him on her."

Sparhawk sat up quickly, his eyes hardening. "I think you'd better explain a few things, Kurik," he said. "Ehlana's the queen. Why does her kingdom need a prince regent?"

"Where have you been, Sparhawk? On the moon? Ehlana fell ill a month ago."

"Not dead?" Sparhawk demanded with a sudden sinking in his stomach and a wrench of unbearable loss at the memory of the pale, beautiful girl-child with the grave, serious gray eyes whom he had watched throughout her childhood and whom, in a peculiar way, he had come to love, though she had been but eight years old when King Aldreas had sent him into his exile in Rendor.

"No," Kurik replied, "not dead, though she might as well be." He picked up the large, rough towel. "Come out of the tub," he ordered. "I'll tell you about it while you eat."

Sparhawk nodded and stood up. Kurik roughly toweled him off and then draped the soft robe about him. The table in the other room was laid with a platter of steaming slices of meat swimming in gravy, a half loaf of rough, dark peasant bread, a wedge of cheese, and a pitcher of chilled milk. "Eat," Kurik said.

"What's been going on here?" Sparhawk demanded as he seated himself at the table and started to eat. He was surprised to find that he was suddenly ravenous. "Start at the beginning."

"All right," Kurik agreed, drawing his dagger and starting to carve thick slices of bread from the loaf. "You knew that the Pandions were confined to the motherhouse at Demos after you left, didn't you?"

Sparhawk nodded. "I heard about it. King Aldreas was never really very fond of us."

"That was your father's fault, Sparhawk. Aldreas was *very* fond of his sister, and then your father forced him to marry someone else. That sort of soured his attitude toward the Pandion Order."

"Kurik," Sparhawk said, "it's not proper to talk about the king that way."

Kurik shrugged. "He's dead now, so it doesn't hurt him, and the way he felt about his sister was common knowledge anyway. The palace pages used to take money from anyone who wanted to watch Arissa walk mother-naked through the upper halls to her brother's bedchamber. Aldreas was a weak king, Sparhawk. He was totally under the control of Arissa and the Primate Annias. With the Pandions confined at Demos, Annias and his underlings had things pretty much the way they wanted them. You were lucky not to have been here during those years."

"Perhaps," Sparhawk murmured. "What did Aldreas die from?"

"They say that it was the falling-sickness. My guess would be that the whores Annias used to slip into the palace for him after his wife died finally wore him out."

"Kurik, you gossip worse than an old woman."

"I know," Kurik admitted blandly. "It's a vice I have."

"And then Ehlana was crowned queen?"

"Right. And then things started to change. Annias was certain that he'd be able to control her the same way that he'd been able to control Aldreas, but she brought him up short. She summoned Preceptor Vanion from the motherhouse at Demos and made him her personal advisor. Then she told Annias to make preparations to retire to a monastery to meditate on the virtues proper to a churchman. Annias was livid, of course, and he started to scheme immediately. The messengers were as thick as flies on the road between here and the cloister where the Princess Arissa has been confined. They're old friends, and they had certain common interests. At any rate, Annias suggested that Ehlana should marry her bastard cousin, Lycheas, but she laughed in his face."

"That sounds fairly characteristic," Sparhawk smiled. "I raised her myself and I taught her what was appropriate. What is this illness of hers?"

"It appears to be the same one that killed her father. She had a seizure and never regained consciousness. The court physicians all maintained that she wouldn't live out the week, but then Vanion took steps. He appeared at court with Sephrenia and eleven other Pandions—all in full armor and with their visors down. They dismissed the queen's attendants, took her from her bed, clothed her in her state robes, and put the crown on her head. Then they carried her to the great hall and set her on the throne and locked the door. Nobody knows what they did in there, but when they opened the door again, Ehlana sat on her throne encased in crystal.''

"What?'' Sparhawk exclaimed.

"It's as clear as glass. You can see every freckle on the queen's nose, but you can't get near her. The crystal's harder than diamond. Annias had workmen hammering on it for five days, and they couldn't even chip it.'' Kurik looked at Sparhawk. "Could you do something like that?'' he asked curiously.

"Me? Kurik, I wouldn't even know where to start. Sephrenia taught us the basics, but we're like babies compared to her.''

"Well, whatever it was that she did, it's keeping the queen alive. You can hear her heart beating. It echoes through the throne room like a drum. For the first week or so, people were flocking in there just to listen to it. There was even talk that it was some kind of miracle and that the throne room ought to be made a shrine. But Annias locked the door and summoned Lycheas the bastard to Cimmura and set him up as prince regent. That was about two weeks ago. Since then Annias has had the church soldiers rounding up all his enemies. The dungeons under the cathedral are bulging with them. That's where things stand right now. You picked a good time to come back.'' He paused, looking directly into his lord's face. "What happened in Cippria, Sparhawk?'' he asked. "The news we got here was pretty sketchy.''

Sparhawk shrugged. "It wasn't much. Do you remember Martel?''

"The renegade Vanion stripped of his knighthood? The one with white hair?''

Sparhawk nodded. "He came to Cippria with a couple of underlings, and they hired fifteen or twenty cutthroats to help them. They waylaid me in a dark street.''

"Is that where you got the scars?''

"Yes."

"But you got away."

"Obviously. Rendorish murderers are a trifle squeamish when the blood on the cobblestones and splashed all over the walls happens to be theirs. After I cut down a dozen or so of them, the rest sort of lost heart. I got clear of them and made my way to the edge of town. I hid in a monastery until the wounds healed, then I took Faran and joined a caravan for Jiroch."

Kurik's eyes were shrewd. "Do you think there's any possibility that Annias might have been involved in it?" he asked. "He hates your family, you know, and it's fairly certain that he was the one who persuaded Aldreas to exile you."

"I've had the same thought from time to time. Annias and Martel have had dealings before. At any rate, I think the good primate and I have several things to discuss."

Kurik looked at him, recognizing the tone in his voice. "You're going to get in trouble," he warned.

"Not as much as Annias will if I find out that he had a hand in that attack." Sparhawk straightened. "I'm going to need to talk with Vanion. Is he still here in Cimmura?"

Kurik nodded. "He's at the chapterhouse on the east edge of town, but you can't get there right now. They lock the east gate at sundown. I think you'd better present yourself at the palace right after the sun comes up, though. It won't take Annias long to come up with the idea of declaring you outlaw for breaking your exile, and it's better to appear on your own, rather than be dragged in like a common criminal. You're still going to have to do some fast talking to stay out of the dungeon."

"I don't think so," Sparhawk disagreed. "I've got a document with the queen's seal on it authorizing my return." He pushed back his plate. "The handwriting's a little childish, and there are tearstains on it, but I think it's still valid."

"She cried? I didn't think she knew how."

"She was only eight at the time, Kurik, and quite fond of me, for some reason."

"You have that effect on a few people." Kurik looked at Sparhawk's plate. "Have you had all of that you want?"

Sparhawk nodded.

"Then get you to bed. You've got a busy day ahead of you tomorrow."

IT WAS MUCH later. The room was faintly lit with the orange coals of the banked fire, and Kurik's regular breathing came from the cot on the other side of the room. The insistent, nagging bang of an unlatched shutter swinging freely in the wind several streets over had set some brainless dog to barking, and Sparhawk lay, still half-bemused by sleep, patiently waiting for the dog to grow wet enough or weary enough of his entertainment to seek his kennel again.

Since it had been Krager he had seen in the square, there was no absolute certainty that Martel was in Cimmura. Krager was an errand boy and was frequently half a continent away from Martel. Had it been the brutal Adus who had crossed that rainy square, there would be no question of Martel's presence in the city. Of necessity, Adus had to be kept on a short leash.

Krager would not be hard to find. He was a weak man with the usual vices and the usual predictability of weak men. Sparhawk smiled bleakly into the darkness. Krager would be easy to find and Krager would know where Martel could be found. It would be a simple matter to drag that information out of him.

Moving quietly to avoid waking his sleeping squire, Sparhawk swung his legs out of the bed and crossed silently to the window to watch the rain slant past into the deserted, lantern-lit courtyard below. Absently he wrapped his hand about the silver-bound hilt of the broadsword standing beside his formal armor. It felt good—like taking the hand of an old friend.

Dimly, as always, there was the remembered sound of the bells. It had been the bells he had followed that night in Cippria. Sick and hurt and alone, stumbling through the dung-reeking night in the stockyards, he had half crawled toward the sound of the bells. He had come at last to the wall and had followed it, his good hand on the ancient stones, until he had come finally to the gate, and there he had fallen.

Sparhawk shook his head. That had been a long time ago. It was strange that he could still remember the bells so clearly. He stood with his hand on his sword, looking out at the tag end of night, watching it rain and remembering the sound of the bells.

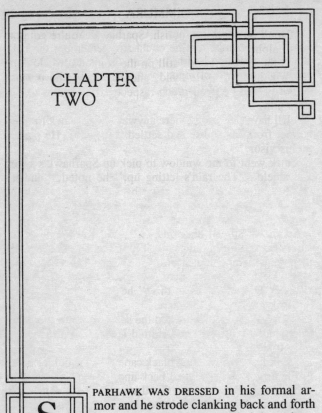

CHAPTER TWO

SPARHAWK WAS DRESSED in his formal armor and he strode clanking back and forth in the candlelit room to settle it into place. "I'd forgotten how heavy this is," he said.

"You're getting soft," Kurik told him. "You need a month or two on the practice field to toughen you up. Are you sure you want to wear it?"

"It's a formal occasion, Kurik, and formal occasions demand formal dress. Besides, I don't want any confusion in anybody's mind when I get there. I'm the Queen's Champion, and I'm supposed to wear armor when I present myself to her."

"They won't let you in to see her," Kurik predicted, picking up his lord's helmet.

"Won't let?"

"Don't do anything foolish, Sparhawk. You're going to be all alone."

"Is the Earl of Lenda still on the council?"

Kurik nodded. "He's old, and he doesn't have much authority, but he's too much respected for Annias to dismiss him."

"I'll have one friend there anyway." Sparhawk took his helmet from his squire and settled it in place. He pushed up his visor.

Kurik went to the window to pick up Sparhawk's sword and shield. "The rain's letting up," he noted, "and it's starting to get light." He came back, laid the sword and shield on the table, and picked up the silver-colored surcoat. "Hold out your arms," he instructed.

Sparhawk spread his arms wide, and Kurik draped the surcoat over his shoulders, then he laced up the sides. He then took up the long sword belt and wrapped it twice about his lord's waist. Sparhawk picked up his sheathed sword. "Did you sharpen this?" he asked.

Kurik gave him a flat stare.

"Sorry." Sparhawk locked the scabbard onto the heavy steel studs on the belt and shifted it around into place on his left side.

Kurik fastened the long black cape to the shoulder plates of the armor, then stepped back and looked Sparhawk up and down appraisingly. "Good enough," he said. "I'll bring your shield. You'd better hurry. They rise early at the palace. It gives them more time for mischief."

They went out of the room and on down the stairs to the innyard. The rain for the most part had passed, with only a few last intermittent sprinkles slanting into the yard in the gusty morning wind. The dawn sky, however, was still covered with tattered cloud, although there was a broad band of pale yellow off to the east.

The knight porter led Faran out of the stable, and he and Kurik boosted Sparhawk up into his saddle.

"Be careful when you get inside the palace, my Lord," Kurik warned in the formal tone he used when they were not alone. "The regular palace guards are probably neutral, but Annias has a troop of church soldiers there as

well. Anybody in red livery is likely to be your enemy."
He handed up the embossed black shield.

Sparhawk buckled the shield into place. "You're going
to the chapterhouse to see Vanion?" he asked his squire.

Kurik nodded. "Just as soon as they open the east gates
of the city."

"I'll probably go there when I'm through at the palace,
but you come back here and wait for me." He grinned.
"We may have to leave town in a hurry."

"Don't go out of your way to force the issue, my Lord."

Sparhawk took Faran's reins from the porter. "All right
then, Sir Knight," he said. "Open the gate and I'll go
present my respects to the bastard Lycheas."

The porter laughed and swung open the gate.

Faran moved out at a proud, rolling trot, lifting his steel-
shod hooves exaggeratedly and bringing them down in a
ringing staccato on the wet cobblestones. The big horse
had a peculiar flair for the dramatic and he always pranced
outrageously when Sparhawk was mounted on his back in
full armor.

"Aren't we both getting a little old for exhibitionism?"
Sparhawk asked drily.

Faran ignored that and continued his prancing.

There were few people abroad in the city of Cimmura
at that hour—rumpled artisans and sleepy shopkeepers for
the most part. The streets were wet, and the gusty wind
set the brightly painted wooden signs over the shops to
swinging and creaking. Most of the windows were still
shuttered and dark, although here and there golden candlelight marked the room of some early riser.

Sparhawk noted that his armor had already begun to
smell—that familiar compound of steel, oil, and the leather
harness that had soaked up his sweat for years. He had
nearly forgotten that smell in the sun-blasted streets and
spice-fragrant shops of Jiroch; almost more than the familiar sights of Cimmura, it finally convinced him that he
was home.

An occasional dog came out into the street to bark at
them as they passed, but Faran disdainfully ignored them
as he trotted through the cobblestone streets.

The palace lay in the center of town. It was a very

grandiose sort of building, much taller than those around it, with high, pointed towers surmounted by damply flapping colored pennons. It was walled off from the rest of the city, and the walls were surmounted by battlements. At some time in the past, one of the kings of Elenia had ordered the exterior of those walls sheathed in white limestone. The climate and the pervasive pall of smoke that lay heavy over the city in certain seasons, however, had turned the sheathing a dirty, streaked gray.

The palace gates were broad and patrolled by a half-dozen guards wearing the dark blue livery that marked them as members of the regular palace garrison.

"Halt!" one of them barked as Sparhawk approached. He stepped into the center of the gateway, holding his pike slightly advanced. Sparhawk gave no indication that he had heard, and Faran bore down on the man. "I said to halt, Sir Knight!" the guard commanded again. Then one of his fellows jumped forward, seized his arm, and pulled him out of the roan's path. "It's the Queen's Champion," the second guard exclaimed. "Don't *ever* stand in his way."

Sparhawk reached the central courtyard and dismounted, moving a bit awkwardly because of the weight of his armor and the encumbrance of his shield. A guard came forward, his pike at the ready.

"Good morning, neighbor," Sparhawk said to him in his quiet voice.

The guard hesitated.

"Watch my horse," the knight told him then. "I shouldn't be too long." He handed the guard Faran's reins and started up the broad staircase toward the heavy double doors that opened into the palace.

"Sir Knight," the guard called after him.

Sparhawk did not turn, but continued on up the stairs. There were two blue-liveried guards at the top, older men, he noted, men he thought he recognized. One of the guard's eyes widened, then he suddenly grinned. "Welcome back, Sir Sparhawk," he said, pulling the door open for the black-armored knight.

Sparhawk gave him a slow wink and went on inside, his mail-shod feet and his spurs clinking on the polished flagstones. Just beyond the door, he encountered a palace functionary with curled and pomaded hair and wearing a maroon-colored doublet. "I will speak with Lycheas," Sparhawk announced in a flat tone. "Take me to him."

"But—" The man's face had gone slightly pale. He drew himself up, his expression growing lofty. "How did you—"

"Didn't you hear me, neighbor?" Sparhawk asked him.

The man in the maroon doublet shrank back. "A-at once, Sir Sparhawk," he stammered. He turned then and led the way down the broad central corridor. His shoulders were visibly trembling. Sparhawk noted that the functionary was not leading him toward the throne room, but rather toward the council chamber where King Aldreas had customarily met with his advisors. A faint smile touched the big man's lips as he surmised that the presence of the young queen sitting encased in crystal on the throne might have had a dampening effect on her cousin's attempts to usurp her crown.

They reached the door to the council chamber and found it guarded by two men wearing the red livery of the church—the soldiers of the Primate Annias. The two automatically crossed their pikes to bar entry to the chamber.

"The Queen's Champion to see the prince regent," the functionary said to them, his voice shrill.

"We have had no orders to admit the Queen's Champion," one of them declared.

"You have now," Sparhawk told him. "Open the door."

The man in the maroon doublet made a move as if to scurry away, but Sparhawk caught his arm. "I haven't dismissed you yet, neighbor," he said. Then he looked at the guards. "Open the door," he repeated.

It hung there for a long moment, while the guards looked first at Sparhawk and then nervously at each other. Then one of them swallowed hard and, fumbling with his pike, he reached for the door handle.

"You'll need to announce me," Sparhawk told the man whose arm he still held firmly in his gauntleted fist. "We wouldn't want to surprise anyone, would we?"

The man's eyes were a little wild. He stepped into the

open doorway and cleared his throat. "The Queen's Champion," he blurted with his words tumbling out over each other. "The Pandion Knight, Sir Sparhawk."

"Thank you, neighbor," Sparhawk said. "You can go now."

The functionary bolted.

The council chamber was very large and was carpeted and draped in blue. Large candelabra lined the walls, and there were more candles on the long, polished table in the center of the room. Three men sat at the table with documents before them, but the fourth had half risen from his chair.

The man on his feet was the Primate Annias. The churchman had grown leaner in the ten years since Sparhawk had last seen him, and his face looked gray and emaciated. His hair was tied back from his face and was now shot with silver. He wore a long black cassock, and the bejeweled pendant of his office as primate of Cimmura hung from a thick gold chain about his neck. His eyes were wide with surprised alarm as Sparhawk entered the room.

The Earl of Lenda, a white-haired man in his seventies, was dressed in a soft gray doublet and he was grinning openly, his bright blue eyes sparkling in his lined face. The Baron Harparin, a notorious pederast, sat with an astonished expression on his face. His clothing was a riot of conflicting colors. Seated next to him was a grossly fat man in red, whom Sparhawk did not recognize.

"Sparhawk!" Annias said sharply, recovering from his surprise, "what are you doing here?"

"I understand that you've been looking for me, your Grace," Sparhawk replied. "I thought I'd save you some trouble."

"You've broken your exile, Sparhawk," Annias accused angrily.

"That's one of the things we need to talk about. I'm told that Lycheas the bastard is functioning as prince regent until the queen regains her health. Why don't you send for him so we won't have to go through all this twice?"

Annias's eyes widened in shock and outrage.

"That's what he is, isn't it?" Sparhawk said. "His origins are hardly a secret, so why tiptoe around them? The bell pull, as I recall, is right over there. Give it a yank, Annias, and send some toady to fetch the prince regent."

The Earl of Lenda chuckled openly.

Annias gave the old man a furious look and went to the pair of bell pulls hanging down the far wall. His hand hesitated between the two.

"Don't make any mistakes, your Grace," Sparhawk warned him. "All sorts of things could go terribly wrong if a dozen soldiers come through that door instead of a servant."

"Go ahead, Annias," the Earl of Lenda urged. "My life is almost over anyway, and I wouldn't mind going out with a bit of excitement."

Annias clenched his teeth and yanked the blue bell pull instead of the red one. After a moment the door opened, and a liveried young man entered. "Yes, your Grace?" he said, bowing to the primate.

"Go tell the prince regent that we require his presence here at once."

"But—"

"*At once!*"

"Yes, your Grace." The servant scurried out.

"There, you see how easy that was?" Sparhawk said to Annias. Then he went over to the white-haired Earl of Lenda, removed his gauntlet, and took the old man's hand. "You're looking well, my Lord," he said.

"Still alive, you mean?" Lenda laughed. "How was Rendor, Sparhawk?"

"Hot, dry, and very dusty."

"Always has been, my boy. Always has been."

"Are you going to answer my question?" Annias demanded.

"Please, your Grace," Sparhawk responded piously, holding up one hand, "not until the bastard regent arrives. We must mind our manners, mustn't we?" He lifted one eyebrow. "Tell me," he added, almost as an afterthought, "how's his mother—her health, I mean? I wouldn't expect a churchman to be able to testify to the carnal talents of the Princess Arissa—although just about everybody else in Cimmura could.''

''You go too far, Sparhawk.''

''You mean you didn't know? My goodness, old boy, you really should try to stay abreast of things.''

''How *rude*!'' Baron Harparin exclaimed to the fat man in red.

''It's not the sort of thing you'd understand, Harparin,'' Sparhawk told him. ''I hear that your inclinations lie in other directions.''

The door opened and a pimpled young man with muddy blond hair and a slack-lipped mouth entered. He wore a green, ermine-trimmed robe and a small gold coronet. ''You wanted to see me, Annias?'' His voice had a nasal, almost whining quality to it.

''A state matter, your Highness,'' Annias replied. ''We need to have you pass judgment in a case involving high treason.''

The young man blinked stupidly at him.

''This is Sir Sparhawk, who has deliberately violated the command of your late uncle, King Aldreas. Sparhawk here was ordered to Rendor, not to return unless summoned back by royal command. His very presence in Elenia convicts him.''

Lycheas recoiled visibly from the bleak-faced knight in black armor, his eyes going wide and his loose mouth gaping. ''Sparhawk?'' he quailed.

''The very same,'' Sparhawk told him. ''The good primate, however, has slightly overstated the case, I'm afraid. When I assumed my position as hereditary champion of the crown, I took an oath to defend the king—or the queen—whenever the royal life was endangered. That oath takes precedence over any command—royal or otherwise—and the queen's life is clearly in danger.''

''That's merely a technicality, Sparhawk,'' Annias snapped.

''I know,'' Sparhawk replied blandly, ''but technicalities are the soul of the law.''

The Earl of Lenda cleared his throat. ''I have made a study of such matters,'' he said, ''and Sir Sparhawk has correctly cited the law. His oath to defend the crown does in fact take precedence.''

Prince Lycheas had gone around to the other side of the table, giving Sparhawk a wide berth. ''That's absurd,'' he declared. ''Ehlana's sick. She's not in any physical danger.'' He sat down in the chair next to the primate.

''The queen,'' Sparhawk corrected him.

''What?''

''Her proper title is 'her Majesty'—or at the least, 'Queen Ehlana.' It's extremely discourteous simply to call her by name. Technically, I suppose, I'm obliged to protect her from discourtesy as well as physical danger. I'm a little vague on that point of law, so I'll defer to the judgment of my old friend, the Earl of Lenda, on the matter before I have my seconds deliver my challenge to your Highness.''

Lycheas went pasty white. ''Challenge?''

''This is sheer idiocy,'' Annias declared. ''There will be no challenges delivered or accepted.'' His eyes narrowed then. ''The prince regent's point is well taken, however,'' he said. ''Sparhawk has simply seized this flimsy excuse to violate his banishment. Unless he can present some documentary evidence of having been summoned, he stands convicted of high treason.'' The primate's smile was thin.

''I thought you'd never ask, Annias,'' Sparhawk said. He reached under his sword belt and drew out a tightly folded parchment tied with a blue ribbon. He untied the ribbon and opened the parchment, the blood-red stone on his ring flashing in the candlelight. ''This all seems to be in order,'' he said, perusing the document. ''It has the queen's signature on it and her personal seal. Her instructions to me are quite explicit.'' He stretched out his arm, offering the parchment to the Earl of Lenda. ''What's your opinion, my Lord?''

The old man took the parchment and examined it. ''The seal is the queen's,'' he confirmed, ''and the handwriting is hers. She commands Sir Sparhawk to present himself to her immediately upon her ascension to the throne. It's a valid royal command, my Lords.''

''Let me see that,'' Annias snapped.

Lenda passed it on down the table to him.

The primate read the document quickly, his teeth tightly clenched. "It's not even dated," he accused.

"Excuse me, your Grace," Lenda pointed out, "but there is no legal requirement that a royal decree or command be dated. Dating is merely a convention."

"Where did you get this?" the primate asked Sparhawk, his eyes narrowing.

"I've had it for quite some time."

"It was obviously written before the queen ascended the throne."

"It does appear that way, doesn't it?"

"It has no validity." The primate took the parchment in both hands as if he would tear it in two.

"What's the penalty for destroying a royal decree, my Lord of Lenda?" Sparhawk asked mildly.

"Death."

"I rather thought it might be. Go ahead and rip it up, Annias. I'll be more than happy to carry out the sentence myself—just to save time and the expense of all the tiresome legal proceedings." His eyes locked with those of Annias. After a moment, the primate threw the parchment on the table in disgust.

Lycheas had watched all of this with a look of growing chagrin. Then he seemed to notice something for the first time. "Your ring, Sir Sparhawk," he said in his whining voice. "That is your badge of office, is it not?"

"In a manner of speaking, yes. Actually the ring—and the queen's ring—are symbolic of the link between my family and hers."

"Give it to me."

"No."

Lycheas's eyes bulged. "I just gave you a royal command!" he shouted.

"No. It was a personal request, Lycheas. You can't give royal commands, because you're not the king."

Lycheas looked uncertainly at the primate, but Annias shook his head slightly. The pimpled young man flushed.

"The prince regent merely wished to examine the ring, Sir Sparhawk," the churchman said smoothly. "We have sought its mate, the ring of King Aldreas, but it seems to be missing. Would you have any idea where we might find it?''

Sparhawk spread his hands. "Aldreas had it on his finger when I left for Cippria," he replied. "The rings are not customarily taken off, so I assume he was still wearing it when he died."

"No. He was not."

"Perhaps the queen has it, then."

"Not so far as we're able to determine."

"I want that other ring," Lycheas insisted, "as a symbol of my authority."

Sparhawk looked at him, his face amused. "What authority?" he asked bluntly. "The ring belongs to Queen Ehlana, and if someone tries to take it from her, I imagine that I'll have to take steps." He suddenly felt a faint prickling of his skin. It seemed that the candles in their gold candelabra lowered slightly and the blue-draped council chamber grew perceptibly dimmer. Instantly, he began to mutter under his breath in the Styric tongue, carefully weaving the counterspell even as he searched the faces of the men sitting around the council table for the source of the rather crude attempt at magic. When he released the counterspell, he saw Annias flinch and he smiled bleakly. Then he drew himself up. "Now," he said, his voice crisp, "let's get down to business. Exactly what happened to King Aldreas?"

The Earl of Lenda sighed. "It was the falling-sickness, Sir Sparhawk," he replied sadly. "The seizures began several months ago, and they grew more and more frequent. The king grew weaker and weaker, and finally—" He shrugged.

"He didn't have the falling-sickness when I left Cimmura," Sparhawk said.

"The onset was sudden," Annias said coldly.

"So it seems. It's rumored that the queen fell ill with the same affliction."

Annias nodded.

"Didn't that strike any of you as odd? There's never been a history of the disease in the royal family, and isn't it peculiar that Aldreas didn't develop symptoms until he was in his forties, and his daughter fell ill when she was little more than eighteen?''

"I have no medical background, Sparhawk," Annias told him. "You may question the court physicians if you wish, but I doubt that you're going to unearth anything that we haven't already discovered."

Sparhawk grunted. He looked around the council chamber. "I think that covers everything we need to discuss here," he said. "I'll see the queen now."

"Absolutely not!" Lycheas said.

"I'm not *asking* you, Lycheas," the big knight said firmly. "May I have that?" He pointed at the parchment still lying on the table in front of the primate.

They passed it down to him, and he ran through it quickly. "Here it is," he said, picking out the sentence he wanted. " 'You are commanded to present yourself to me immediately upon your return to Cimmura.' That doesn't leave any room for argument, does it?"

"What are you up to, Sparhawk?" the primate asked suspiciously.

"I'm just obeying orders, your Grace. I'm commanded by the queen to present myself to her and I'm going to do precisely that."

"The door to the throne room is locked," Lycheas snapped.

The smile Sparhawk gave him was almost benign. "That's all right, Lycheas," he said. "I've got a key." He put his hand suggestively on the silver-bound hilt of his sword.

"You wouldn't!"

"Try me."

Annias cleared his throat. "If I may speak, your Highness?" he said.

"Of course, your Grace," Lycheas replied quickly. "The crown is always open to the advice and counsel of the church."

"Crown?" Sparhawk asked.

"A formula, Sir Sparhawk," Annias told him. "Prince Lycheas speaks for the crown for so long as the queen is incapacitated."

"Not to me, he doesn't."

Annias turned back toward Lycheas. "It is the advice of the church that we accede to the somewhat churlish request of the Queen's Champion," he said. "Let no one accuse *us* of incivility. Moreover, the church advises that the prince regent and all of the council accompany Sir Sparhawk to the throne room. He is reputed to be adept at certain forms of magic, and—to protect the queen's life—we must not permit him to employ precipitously those arts without full consultation with the court physicians."

Lycheas made some pretence of thinking it over. Then he rose to his feet. "It shall be as you advise, then, your Grace," he declared. "You are directed to accompany us, Sir Sparhawk."

"Directed?"

Lycheas ignored that and swept regally toward the door.

Sparhawk let Baron Harparin and the fat man in red pass, then fell in beside Primate Annias. He was smiling in a relaxed fashion, but there was little in the way of good humor in the low voice that came from between his teeth. "Don't ever try that again, Annias," he said.

"What?" The primate sounded startled.

"Your magic. You're not very good at it in the first place, and it irritates me to have to waste the effort of countering the work of amateurs. Besides, churchmen are forbidden to dabble in magic, as I recall."

"You have no proof, Sparhawk."

"I don't need proof, Annias. My oath as a Pandion Knight would be sufficient in any civil or ecclesiastical court. Why don't we just leave it there? But don't mutter any more incantations in my direction."

With Lycheas in the lead, the council and Sparhawk went down a candlelit corridor to the broad double doors of the throne room. When they reached the doors, Lycheas took a key from inside his doublet and unlocked them. "All right," he said to Sparhawk. "It's open. Go present yourself to your queen—for all the good it's going to do you."

Sparhawk reached up and took a burning candle from a silver sconce jutting from the wall of the corridor and went into the dark room beyond the doors.

It was cool, almost clammy inside the throne room, and

the air smelled musty and stale. Methodically, Sparhawk went along the walls, lighting candles. Then he went to the throne and lighted the ones standing in the candelabra flanking it.

"You don't need *that* much light, Sparhawk," Lycheas said irritably from the doorway.

Sparhawk ignored him. He put out his hand, tentatively touched the crystal which encased the throne, and felt Sephrenia's familiar aura permeating the crystal. Then slowly he raised his eyes to look into Ehlana's pale young face. The promise that had been there when she had been a child had been fulfilled. She was not simply pretty as so many young girls are pretty; she was beautiful. There was an almost luminous perfection about her countenance. Her pale blonde hair was long and loosely framed her face. She wore her state robes, and the heavy gold crown of Elenia encircled her head. Her slender hands lay upon the arms of her throne, and her eyes were closed.

He remembered that at first he had bitterly resented the command of King Aldreas that had made him the young girl's caretaker. He had quickly found, however, that she was no giddy child, but rather was a serious young lady with a quick, retentive mind and an overwhelming curiosity about the world. After her initial shyness had passed, she had begun to question him closely about palace affairs and thus, almost by accident, had begun her education in statecraft and the intricacies of palace politics. After a few months they had grown very close, and he had found himself looking forward to their daily private conversations during which he had gently molded her character and had prepared her for her ultimate destiny as queen of Elenia.

To see her as she was now, locked in the semblance of death, wrenched at his heart, and he swore to himself that he would take the world apart if need be to restore her to health and to her throne. For some reason it made him angry to look at her, and he felt an irrational desire to lash out at things, as if by sheer physical force he could return her to consciousness.

And then he heard and felt it. The sound appeared to grow more pronounced, and it grew louder moment by moment. It was a regular, steady thudding sound, not quite like the beating of a drum, and it did not change nor falter, but echoed through the room, its volume steadily increasing as it announced to any who might enter that Ehlana's heart was still beating.

Sparhawk drew his sword and saluted his queen with it. Then he sank to one knee in a move of profoundest respect and a peculiar form of love. He leaned forward and gently kissed the unyielding crystal, his eyes suddenly filling with tears. "I am here now, Ehlana," he murmured, "and I'll make everything all right again."

The heartbeat grew louder, almost as if in some peculiar way she had heard him.

From the doorway he heard Lycheas snicker derisively and he promised himself that should the opportunity arise, he would do a number of unpleasant things to the queen's bastard cousin. Then he rose and went toward the door again.

Lycheas stood smirking at him, still holding the key to the throne room in his hand. As Sparhawk passed the prince, he reached out and took the key. "You won't need this any more," he said. "I'm here now, so I'll take care of it."

"Annias," Lycheas said in a voice shrill with protest.

Annias, however, took one look at the bleak face of the Queen's Champion and decided not to press the issue. "Let him keep it," he said shortly.

"But—"

"I said to let him keep it," the primate snapped. "We don't need it anyway. Let the Queen's Champion hold the key to the room in which she sleeps." There was a vile innuendo in the churchman's voice, and Sparhawk clenched his still-gauntleted left fist.

"Will you walk with me as we return to the council chamber, Sir Sparhawk?" the Earl of Lenda said, placing a lightly restraining hand on Sparhawk's armored forearm. "My steps sometimes falter, and it's comforting to have a strong young person at my side."

"Certainly, my Lord," Sparhawk replied, unclenching his fist. When Lycheas had led the members of the council back down the corridor toward their meeting room, Sparhawk closed the door and locked it. Then he handed the key to his old friend. "Will you keep this for me, my Lord?" he asked.

"Gladly, Sir Sparhawk."

"And if you can, keep the candles burning in the throne room. Don't leave her sitting there in the dark."

"Of course."

They started down the corridor.

"Do you know something, Sparhawk?" the old man said, "they left a great deal of bark on you when they were giving you the last polishing touches."

Sparhawk grinned at him.

"You can be *truly* offensive when you set your mind to it." Lenda chuckled.

"I can but try, my Lord."

"Be very careful here in Cimmura, Sparhawk," the old man cautioned seriously in a low voice. "Annias has a spy on every street corner. Lycheas won't even sneeze without his permission, so the primate is the real ruler here in Elenia and he hates you."

"I'm not overly fond of him, either." Sparhawk thought of something. "You've been a good friend here today, my Lord. Is that going to put you in danger?"

The Earl of Lenda smiled. "I doubt it. I'm too old and powerless to be any kind of threat to Annias. I'm hardly more than an irritation, and he's far too calculating to take action against me for that."

The primate awaited them at the door to the council chamber. "The council has discussed the situation here, Sir Sparhawk," he said coldly. "The queen is quite obviously in no danger. Her heartbeat is strong, and the crystal which encloses her is quite impregnable. She has no real need of a protector at this particular time. It is the command of the council, therefore, that you return to the chapterhouse of your order here in Cimmura and remain there until you receive further instructions." A chill smile touched his lips. "Or until the queen herself summons you, of course."

"Of course," Sparhawk replied distantly. "I was about to suggest that myself, your Grace. I'm just a simple knight and I'll be far more at ease in the chapterhouse with my brothers than here in the palace.'' He smiled. ''I'm really quite out of place at court.''

''I noticed that.''

''I thought you might have.'' Sparhawk briefly clasped the hand of the Earl of Lenda by way of farewell. Then he looked directly at Annias. ''Until we meet again, then, your Grace.''

''*If* we meet again.''

''Oh, we will, Annias. Indeed we will.'' Then Sparhawk turned on his heel and walked on down the corridor.

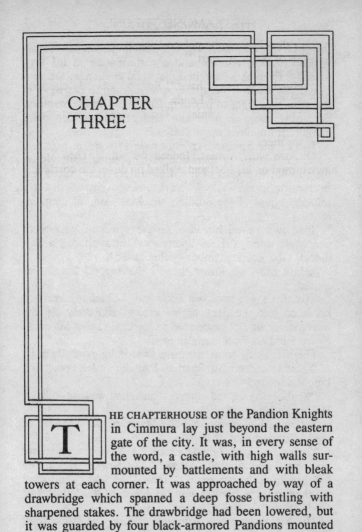

CHAPTER THREE

T HE CHAPTERHOUSE OF the Pandion Knights in Cimmura lay just beyond the eastern gate of the city. It was, in every sense of the word, a castle, with high walls surmounted by battlements and with bleak towers at each corner. It was approached by way of a drawbridge which spanned a deep fosse bristling with sharpened stakes. The drawbridge had been lowered, but it was guarded by four black-armored Pandions mounted on war horses.

Sparhawk reined Faran in at the outer end of the bridge and waited. There were certain formalities involved in gaining entry into a Pandion chapterhouse. Oddly, he found that he did not chafe at those formalities. They had been a part of his life for all the years of his novitiate, and the observance of these age-old ceremonies seemed somehow to mark a renewal and a reaffirmation of his very identity. Even as he awaited the ritual challenge, the sunbaked city of Jiroch and the women going to the wells in the steel-gray light of morning faded back in his memory, becoming more remote and taking their proper place among all his other memories.

Two of the armored knights rode forward at a stately pace, the hooves of their chargers booming hollowly on the foot-thick planks of the drawbridge. They halted just in front of Sparhawk. "Who art thou who entreateth entry into the house of the Soldiers of God?" one of them intoned.

Sparhawk raised his visor in the symbolic gesture of peaceable intent. "I am Sparhawk," he replied, "a Soldier of God and a member of this order."

"How may we know thee?" the second knight inquired.

"By this token may you know me." Sparhawk reached his hand into the neck of his surcoat and drew out the heavy silver amulet suspended on the chain about his neck. Every Pandion wore such an amulet.

The pair made some pretence of looking carefully at it.

"This is indeed Sir Sparhawk of our order," the first knight declared.

"Truly," the second agreed, "and shall we then—uh—" He faltered, frowning.

" 'Grant him entry into the house of the Soldiers of God,' " Sparhawk prompted.

The second knight made a face. "I can never remember that part," he muttered. "Thanks, Sparhawk." He cleared his throat and began again. "Truly," he said, "and shall we then grant him entry into the house of the Soldiers of God?"

The first knight was grinning openly. "It is his right freely to enter this house," he said, "for he is one of us. Hail, Sir Sparhawk. Prithee, come within the walls of this house, and may peace abide with thee beneath its roof."

"And with thee and thy companion as well, wheresoever you may fare," Sparhawk replied, concluding the ceremony.

"Welcome home, Sparhawk," the first knight said warmly then. "You've been a long time away."

"You noticed," Sparhawk answered. "Did Kurik get here?"

The second knight nodded. "An hour or so ago. He talked with Vanion and then left again."

"Let's go inside," Sparhawk suggested. "I need a large dose of that peace you mentioned earlier, and I've got to see Vanion."

The two knights turned their horses, and the three rode together back across the drawbridge.

"Is Sephrenia still here?" Sparhawk asked.

"Yes," the second knight replied. "She and Vanion came from Demos shortly after the Queen fell ill, and she hasn't gone back to the motherhouse yet."

"Good. I need to talk with her as well."

The three of them halted at the castle gate. "This is Sir Sparhawk, a member of our order," the first knight declared to the two who had remained at the gate. "We have confirmed his identity and vouch for his right to enter the house of the Knights Pandion."

"Pass then, Sir Sparhawk, and may peace abide with thee whilst thou remain within this house."

"I thank thee, Sir Knight, and may peace also be thine."

The knights drew their mounts aside, and Faran moved forward without any urging.

"You know the ritual as well as I do, don't you?" Sparhawk murmured.

Faran flicked his ears.

In the central courtyard, an apprentice knight who had not yet been vested with his ceremonial armor or spurs hurried forward and took Faran's reins. "Welcome, Sir Knight," he said.

Sparhawk hooked his shield to his saddlebow and swung down from Faran's back with his armor clinking. "Thank you," he replied. "Do you have any idea of where I might find Lord Vanion?"

"I believe he's in the south tower, my Lord."

"Thanks again." Sparhawk started across the courtyard, then stopped. "Oh, be careful of the horse," he warned. "He bites."

The novice looked startled and then cautiously stepped away from the big, ugly roan, though still firmly holding the reins.

The horse gave Sparhawk a flat, unfriendly stare.

"It's more sporting this way, Faran," Sparhawk explained. He started up the worn steps that led into the centuries-old castle.

The inside of the chapterhouse was cool and dim, and the few members of the order Sparhawk met in those halls wore cowled monk's robes, as was customary inside a secure house, although an occasional steely clink betrayed the fact that, beneath their humble garb, the members of this order wore chain mail and were inevitably armed. There were no greetings exchanged, and the cowled brothers of Pandion went resolutely about their duties with bowed heads and shadowed faces.

Sparhawk put the flat of his hand out in front of one of the cowled men. Pandions seldom touched each other. "Excuse me, brother," he said. "Do you know if Vanion is still in the south tower?"

"He is," the other knight replied.

"Thank you, brother. Peace be with you."

"And with you, Sir Knight."

Sparhawk went on along the torchlit corridor until he came to a narrow stairway which wound up into the south tower between walls of massive, unmortared stones. At the top of the stairs there was a heavy door guarded by two young Pandions. Sparhawk did not recognize either of them. "I need to talk with Vanion," he told them. "The name is Sparhawk."

"Can you identify yourself?" one of them asked, trying to make his youthful voice sound gruff.

"I just did."

It hung there while the two young knights struggled to find a graceful way out of the situation. "Why not just open the door and tell Vanion that I'm here?" Sparhawk suggested. "If he recognizes me, fine. If he doesn't, the two of you can try to throw me back down the stairs." He laid no particular emphasis on the word *try*.

The two looked at each other, then one of them opened the door and looked inside. "A thousand pardons, my Lord Vanion," he apologized, "but there's a Pandion here who calls himself Sparhawk. He says that he wants to talk with you."

"Good," a familiar voice replied from inside the room. "I've been expecting him. Send him in."

The two knights looked abashed and stepped out of Sparhawk's way.

"Thank you, my brothers," Sparhawk murmured to them. "Peace be with you." And then he went on through the door. The room was large, with stone walls, dark green drapes at the narrow windows, and a carpet of muted brown. A fire crackled in the arched fireplace at one end, and there was a candlelit table surrounded by heavy chairs in the center. Two people, a man and a woman, sat at the table.

Vanion, the Preceptor of the Pandion Knights, had aged somewhat in the past ten years. His hair and beard were iron gray now. There were a few more lines in his face, but there were no signs of feebleness there. He wore a mail shirt and a silver surcoat. As Sparhawk entered the room, he rose and came around the table. "I was about to send a rescue party to the palace for you," he said, grasping Sparhawk's armored shoulders. "You shouldn't have gone there alone, you know."

"Maybe not, but things worked out all right." Sparhawk removed his gauntlets and helmet, laying them on the table. Then he unfastened his sword from its studs and laid it beside them. "It's good to see you again, Vanion," he said, taking the older man's hand in his. Vanion had always been a stern teacher, tolerating no shortcomings in the young knights he had trained to take their places in Pandion ranks. Although Sparhawk had come close to hating the man during his novitiate, he now regarded the blunt-spoken preceptor as one of his closest friends, and their handclasp was warm, even affectionate.

Then the big knight turned to the woman. She was small and had that peculiar neat perfection one sometimes sees in small people. Her hair was as black as night, though her eyes were a deep blue. Her features were obviously not Elene, but had that strangely foreign cast that marked her as a Styric. She wore a soft, white robe, and there was a large book on the table in front of her. "Sephrenia," he greeted her warmly, "you're looking well." He took both of her hands in his and kissed her palms in the ritual Styric gesture of greeting.

"You have been long away, Sir Sparhawk," she replied. Her voice was soft and musical and had an odd, lilting quality to it.

"And will you bless me, little mother?" he asked, a smile touching his battered face. He knelt before her. The form of address was Styric, reflecting that intimate personal connection between teacher and pupil which has existed since the dawn of time.

"Gladly." She lightly touched her hands to his face and spoke a ritual benediction in the Styric tongue.

"Thank you," he said simply.

Then she did something she rarely did. With her hands still holding his face, she leaned forward and lightly kissed him. "Welcome home, dear one," she murmured.

"It's good to be back," he replied. "I've missed you."

"Even though I scolded you when you were a boy?" she asked with a gentle smile.

"Scoldings don't hurt that much." He laughed. "I even missed those, for some reason."

"I think that perhaps we did well with this one, Vanion," she said to the preceptor. "Between us, we've made a good Pandion."

"One of the best," Vanion agreed. "I think Sparhawk's what they had in mind when they formed the order."

Sephrenia's position among the Pandion Knights was a peculiar one. She had appeared at the gates of the order's motherhouse at Demos upon the death of the Styric tutor who had been instructing the novices in what the Styrics referred to as the secrets. She had neither been selected nor summoned, but had simply appeared and taken up her predecessor's duties. Generally, Elenes despised and feared Styrics. They were a strange, alien people who lived in small, rude clusters of houses deep in the forests and mountains. They worshipped strange Gods and practiced magic. Wild stories about hideous rites involving the use of Elene blood and flesh had circulated among the more gullible in Elene society for centuries, and periodically mobs of drunken peasants would descend on unsuspecting Styric villages, bent on massacre. The Church vigorously denounced such atrocities. The Church Knights, who had come to know and respect their alien tutors, went perhaps a step further than the Church, letting it be generally known that unprovoked attacks on Styric settlements would result in swift and savage retaliation. Despite such organized protection, however, any Styric who entered an Elene village or town could expect taunts and abuse and, not infrequently, showers of stones and offal. Thus, Sephrenia's appearance at Demos had not been without personal risk. Her motives for coming had been unclear, but over the years she had served faithfully; to a man the Pandions had come to love and respect her. Even Vanion, the preceptor of the order, frequently sought her counsel.

Sparhawk looked at the volume lying on the table before her. "A book, Sephrenia?" he said in mock amazement. "Has Vanion finally persuaded you to learn how to read?"

"You know my beliefs about that practice, Sparhawk," she replied. "I was merely looking at the pictures." She pointed at the brilliant illuminations on the page. "I was ever fond of bright colors."

Sparhawk drew up a chair and sat, his armor creaking.

"You saw Ehlana?" Vanion asked, resuming his seat across the table.

"Yes." Sparhawk looked at Sephrenia. "How did you do that?" he asked her. "Seal her up like that, I mean?"

"It's a bit complex." Then she stopped and gave him a penetrating look. "Perhaps you're ready, at that," she murmured. She rose to her feet. "Come over here, Sparhawk," she said, moving toward the fireplace.

Puzzled, he rose and followed her.

"Look into the flames, dear one," she said softly, using that odd Styric form of address she had used when he was her pupil.

Compelled by her voice, he stared at the fire. Faintly, he heard her whispering in Styric, and then she passed her hand slowly across the flames. Unthinking, he sank to his knees and stared into the fireplace.

Something was moving in the fire. Sparhawk leaned forward and stared hard at the little bluish curls of flame dancing along the edge of a charred oak log. The blue color expanded, growing larger and larger, and within that nimbus of coruscating blue, he seemed to see a group of figures that wavered as the flame flickered. The image grew stronger, and he realized that he was looking at the semblance of the throne room in the palace, many miles away. Twelve armored Pandions were crossing the flagstone floor bearing the slight figure of a young girl. She was borne, not upon a litter, but upon the flat sides of a dozen gleaming sword blades held rock-steady by the twelve black-armored and visored men. They stopped before the throne, and Sephrenia's white-robed figure stepped out of the shadows. She raised one hand, seeming to say something, though all Sparhawk could hear was the crackling flames. With a dreadful jerking motion, the young girl sat up. It was Ehlana. Her face was distorted and her eyes wide and vacant.

Without thinking, Sparhawk reached toward her, thrusting his hand directly into the flames.

"No," Sephrenia said sharply, pulling his hand back. "You may watch only."

The image of Ehlana, trembling uncontrollably, jerked to its feet, following, it seemed, the unspoken commands of the small woman in the white robe. Imperiously, Sephrenia pointed at the throne, and Ehlana stumbled, even staggered, up the steps of the dais to assume her rightful place.

Sparhawk wept. He tried once again to reach out to his queen, but Sephrenia held him back with a gentle touch that was strangely like an iron chain. "Continue to watch, dear one," she told him.

The twelve knights then formed a circle around the enthroned queen and the white-robed woman standing at her side. Reverently, they extended their swords so that the two women on the dais were ringed in steel. Sephrenia raised her arms and spoke. Sparhawk could clearly see the strain on her face as she uttered the words of an incantation he could not even begin to imagine.

The point of each of the twelve swords began to glow

and grew brighter and brighter, bathing the dais in intense silvery-white light. The light from those sword tips seemed to coalesce around Ehlana and her throne. Then Sephrenia spoke a single word, bringing her arm down as she did so in a peculiar cutting motion. In an instant the light around Ehlana solidified, and she became as she had been when Sparhawk had seen her in the throne room that morning. The image of Sephrenia, however, wilted and collapsed on the dais beside the crystal-encased throne.

The tears were streaming openly down Sparhawk's face, and Sephrenia gently enfolded his head in her arms, holding him to her. "It is not easy, Sparhawk," she comforted him. "To look thus into the fire opens the heart and allows what we really are to emerge. You are gentler far more than you would have us believe."

He wiped at his eyes with the back of his hand. "How long will the crystal sustain her?" he asked.

"For so long as the thirteen of us who were there continue to live," Sephrenia replied. "A year at most, as you Elenes measure time."

He stared at her.

"It is our life force that keeps her heart alive. As the seasons turn, we will one by one drop away, and one of us who was there will then have to assume the burden of the fallen. Eventually—when we have each and every one given all we can—your queen will die."

"No!" he said fiercely. He looked at Vanion. "Were you there, too?"

Vanion nodded.

"Who else?"

"It wouldn't serve any purpose for you to know that, Sparhawk. We all went willingly and we knew what was involved."

"Who's going to take up the burden you mentioned?" Sparhawk asked Sephrenia.

"I will."

"We're still arguing that point," Vanion disagreed. "Any one of us who was there can do it, actually."

"Not unless we modify the spell, Vanion," she told him just a bit smugly.

"We'll see," he said.

"But what good does it do?" Sparhawk demanded. "All you've done is to give her a year more of life at a dreadful cost—and she doesn't even know."

"If we can isolate the cause of her illness and find a cure, the spell can be reversed," Sephrenia replied. "We have suspended her life to give us time."

"Are we making any progress?"

"I've got every physician in Elenia working on it," Vanion said, "and I've summoned others from various parts of Eosia. Sephrenia's looking into the possibility that the illness may not be of natural origin. We're encountering some resistance, though. The court physicians refuse to cooperate."

"I'll go back to the palace then," Sparhawk said bleakly. "Perhaps I can persuade them to be more helpful."

"We thought of that already, but Annias has them all closely guarded."

"What *is* Annias up to?" Sparhawk burst out angrily. "All we want to do is to restore Ehlana. Why is he putting all these stumbling blocks in our path? Does he want the throne for himself?"

"I think he has his eyes on a bigger throne," Vanion said. "The Archprelate Cluvonus is old and in poor health. I wouldn't be at all surprised if Annias believes that the miter of the archprelacy might fit him."

"Annias? Archprelate? Vanion, that's an absurdity."

"Life is filled with absurdities, Sparhawk. The militant orders are all opposed to him, of course, and our opinion carries a great deal of weight with the Church Hierocracy, but Annias has his hands in the treasury of Elenia up to the elbows and he's very free with his bribes. Ehlana would have been able to cut off his access to that money, but she fell ill. That may have something to do with his lack of enthusiasm about her recovery."

"And he wants to put Arissa's bastard on the throne to replace her?" Sparhawk was growing angrier by the minute. "Vanion, I've just seen Lycheas. He's weaker—and stupider—than King Aldreas was. Besides, he's illegitimate."

Vanion spread his hands. "A vote of the royal council could legitimize him, and Annias controls the council."

"Not all of it, he doesn't," Sparhawk grated. "Technically, I'm *also* a member of the council, and I think I might just want to sway a few votes if that ever came up. A public duel or two might change the minds of the council."

"You're rash, Sparhawk," Sephrenia told him.

"No, I'm angry. I feel a powerful urge to hurt some people."

Vanion sighed. "We can't make any decisions just yet," he said. Then he shook his head and turned to another matter. "What's *really* going on in Rendor?" he asked. "Voren's reports were all rather carefully worded in the event they fell into unfriendly hands."

Sparhawk rose and went to one of the embrasured windows with his black cape swirling about his ankles. The sky was still covered with dirty-looking cloud, and the city of Cimmura seemed to crouch beneath that scud as if clenched to endure yet another winter. "It's hot there," he mused, almost as if to himself, "and dry and dusty. The sun reflects back from the walls and pierces the eye. At first light, before the sun rises and the sky is like molten silver, veiled women in black robes with clay vessels on their shoulders pass in silence through the streets on their way to the wells."

"I've misjudged you, Sparhawk," Sephrenia said in her melodic voice. "You have the soul of a poet."

"Not really, Sephrenia. It's just that you need to get the feel of Rendor to understand what's happening there. The sun is like the blows of a hammer on the top of your head, and the air is so hot and dry that it leaves no time for thought. Rendors seek simplistic answers. The sun doesn't give them time for pondering. That might explain what happened to Eshand in the first place. A simple shepherd with his brains half baked out isn't the logical receptacle for any kind of profound epiphany. It's the aggravation of the sun, I think, that gave the Eshandist Heresy its impetus in the first place. Those poor fools would have accepted *any* idea, no matter how absurd, just for the chance to move around—and perhaps find some shade."

"That's a novel explanation for a movement that plunged all of Eosia into three centuries of warfare," Vanion observed.

"You have to experience it," Sparhawk told him, returning to his seat. "Anyway, one of those sun-baked enthusiasts arose at Dabour about twenty years ago."

"Arasham?" Vanion surmised. "We've heard of him."

"That's what he calls himself," Sparhawk replied. "He was probably born with a different name, though. Religious leaders tend to change their names fairly often to fit the prejudices of their followers. From what I understand, Arasham is an unlettered, unwashed fanatic with only a tenuous grip on reality. He's about eighty or so and he sees things and hears voices. His followers have less intelligence than their sheep. They'd gladly attack the kingdoms of the north—if they could only figure out which way north is. That's a matter of serious debate in Rendor. I've seen a few of them. These heretics that send the members of the Hierocracy in Chyrellos trembling to their beds every night are little more than howling desert dervishes, poorly armed and with no military training. Frankly, Vanion, I'd worry more about the next winter storm than any kind of resurgence of the Eshandist Heresy in Rendor."

"That's blunt enough."

"I've just wasted ten years of my life on a nonexistent danger. I'm sure you'll forgive a certain amount of discontent about the whole thing."

"Patience will come to you, Sparhawk." Sephrenia smiled. "Once you have reached maturity."

"I thought that I already had."

"Not by half."

He grinned at her then. "Just how old are you, Sephrenia?" he asked.

Her look was filled with resignation. "What is it about you Pandions that makes you all ask that same question? You *know* I'm not going to answer you. Can't you just accept the fact that I'm older than you are and let it go at that?"

"You're also older than I am," Vanion added. "You were my teacher when I was no older than those boys who guard my door."

"And do I look so very, very old?"

"My dear Sephrenia, you're as young as spring and as wise as winter. You've ruined us all, you know. After we've known you, the fairest of maidens have no charm for us."

"Isn't he nice?" She smiled at Sparhawk. "Surely no other man alive has so beguiling a tongue."

"Try him sometime when you've just missed a pass with the lance," Sparhawk replied sourly. He shifted his shoulders under the weight of his armor. "What else is afoot? I've been gone a long time and I'm hungry for news."

"Otha's mobilizing," Vanion told him. "The word that's coming out of Zemoch is that he's looking eastward toward Daresia and the Tamul Empire, but I've got a few doubts about that."

"And I have more than a few," Sephrenia agreed. "The kingdoms of the west are suddenly awash with Styric vagabonds. They camp at crossroads and hawk the rude goods of Styricum, but no local Styric band acknowledges them as members. For some reason the Emperor Otha and his cruel master have innundated us with watchers. Azash has driven the Zemochs to attack the west before. Something lies hidden here that he desperately wants, and he's not going to find it in Daresia."

"There have been Zemoch mobilizations before," Sparhawk said, leaning back. "Nothing ever came of it."

"I think that this time might be a bit more serious," Vanion disagreed. "When he gathered his forces before, it was always on the border; as soon as the four militant orders moved into Lamorkand to face him, he disbanded his armies. He was testing us, nothing more. This time, though, he's massing his troops back behind the mountains—out of sight, so to speak."

"Let him come," Sparhawk said bleakly. "We stopped him five hundred years ago and we can do it again if we have to."

Vanion shook his head. "We don't want a repetition of what happened after the battle at Lake Randera—a century of famine, pestilence, and complete social collapse. No, my friend, *that* we don't want."

"*If* we can avoid it," Sephrenia added. "I am Styric,

and I know even better than you Elenes just how totally evil the Elder God Azash is. If he comes west again, he *must* be stopped—no matter what the cost.''

"That's what the Church Knights are here for," Vanion said. "Right now, about all we can do is keep our eyes on Otha.''

"I just remembered something," Sparhawk said. "When I was riding into town last night, I saw Krager.''

"Here in Cimmura?" Vanion asked, sounding surprised. "Do you think Martel could be with him?''

"Probably not. Krager's usually Martel's errand boy. Adus is the one who has to be kept on a short chain.'' He squinted his eyes. "How much did you hear about the incident in Cippria?" he asked them.

"We heard that Martel attacked you," Vanion replied. "That's about all.''

"There was a bit more to it than that," Sparhawk told him. "When Aldreas sent me to Cippria, I was supposed to report to the Elenian consul there—a diplomat who just *happens* to be the cousin of the Primate Annias. Late one night, he summoned me. I was on my way to his house when Martel, Adus, and Krager—along with a fair number of local cutthroats—came charging out of a side street. There's no way that they could have known that I'd be passing that way unless someone had told them. Put that together with the fact that Krager's back in Cimmura, where there's a price on his head, and you start to come up with some interesting conclusions.''

"You think that Martel is working for Annias?''

"It's a possibility, wouldn't you say? Annias wasn't very happy about the way my father forced Aldreas to give up the notion of marrying his own sister, and it's entirely possible that he felt that he'd have a freer hand here in Elenia if the family of Sparhawk became extinct in a back alley in Cippria. Of course, Martel has his *own* reasons for disliking me. I really think you made a mistake, Vanion. You could have saved us all a lot of trouble if you hadn't ordered me to withdraw my challenge.''

Vanion shook his head. "No, Sparhawk," he said. "Martel had been a brother in our order, and I didn't want you two trying to kill each other. Besides, I couldn't be entirely sure who'd win. Martel is very dangerous.''

"So am I.''

"I'm not taking any unnecessary chances with you, Sparhawk. You're too valuable.''

"Well, it's too late to worry about it now.''

"What are your plans?''

"I'm *supposed* to stay here in the chapterhouse, but I think I'll drift around the city a bit and see if I can run across Krager again. If I can connect him with anybody who's working for Annias, I'll be able to answer a few burning questions.''

"Perhaps you should wait a bit,'' Sephrenia advised. "Kalten's on his way back from Lamorkand.''

"Kalten? I haven't seen him in years.''

"She's right, Sparhawk,'' Vanion agreed. "Kalten's a good man in tight quarters, and the streets of Cimmura can be just as dangerous as the alleys of Cippria.''

"When's he likely to arrive?''

Vanion shrugged. "Soon, I think. It could even be today.''

"I'll wait until he gets here.'' An idea came to Sparhawk then. He smiled at his teacher and rose to his feet.

"What are you doing, Sparhawk?'' she asked him suspiciously.

"Oh, nothing,'' he replied. He began to speak in Styric, weaving his fingers in the air in front of him as he did so. When he had built the spell, he released it and held out his hand. There came a humming vibration, followed by a dimming of the candles and a lowering of the flames in the fireplace. When the light came up again, he was holding a bouquet of violets. "For you, little mother,'' he said, bowing slightly and offering the flowers to her, "because I love you.''

"Why, thank you, Sparhawk.'' She smiled, taking them. "You were always the most thoughtful of my pupils. You mispronounced *staratha*, though,'' she added critically. "You came very close to filling your hand with snakes.''

"I'll practice,'' he promised.

"Do.''

There was a respectful knock at the door.

"Yes?" Vanion called.

The door opened and one of the young knights stepped inside. "There's a messenger from the palace outside, Lord Vanion. He says that he has been commanded to speak with Sir Sparhawk."

"*Now* what do they want?" Sparhawk muttered.

"You'd better send him in," Vanion told the young knight.

"At once, my Lord." The knight bowed slightly and went out again.

The messenger had a familiar face. His blond hair was still elegantly curled. His saffron-colored doublet, lavender hose, maroon shoes, and apple-green cloak still clashed horribly. The young fop's face, however, sported an entirely new embellishment. The very tip of his pointed nose was adorned with a large and extremely painful-looking boil. He was trying without much success to conceal the excrescence with a lace-trimmed handkerchief. He bowed elegantly to Vanion. "My Lord Preceptor," he said, "the prince regent sends his compliments."

"And please, convey mine back to him," Vanion replied.

"Be assured that I shall, my Lord." The elegant fellow then turned to Sparhawk. "My message is for you, Sir Knight," he declared.

"Say on then," Sparhawk answered with exaggerated formality. "My ears hunger for your message."

The fop ignored that. He removed a sheet of parchment from inside his doublet and read grandly from it. " 'By royal decree, you are commanded by his Highness to journey straightway to the motherhouse of the Pandion Knights at Demos, there to devote yourself to your religious duties until such time as he sees fit to summon you once again to the palace.' "

"I see," Sparhawk replied.

"Do you understand the message, Sir Sparhawk?" the fop asked, handing over the parchment.

Sparhawk did not bother to read the document. "It was quite clear. You have completed your mission in a fashion which does you credit." Sparhawk peered at the perfumed young fellow. "If you don't mind some advice, neighbor, you ought to have that boil looked at by a surgeon. If it isn't lanced soon, it's going to keep growing to the point where you won't be able to see around it.''

The fop winced at the word *lanced*. ''Do you really think so, Sir Sparhawk?'' he asked plaintively, lowering his handkerchief. ''Wouldn't a poultice, perhaps—''

Sparhawk shook his head. ''No, neighbor,'' he said with false sympathy. ''I can almost guarantee you that a poultice won't work. Be brave, my man. Lancing is the only solution.''

The courtier's face grew melancholy. He bowed and left the room.

''Did *you* do that to him, Sparhawk?'' Sephrenia asked suspiciously.

''Me?'' He gave her a look of wide-eyed innocence.

''*Somebody* did. That eruption is not natural.''

''My, my,'' he said. ''Imagine that.''

''Well?'' Vanion said. ''Are you going to obey the bastard's orders?''

''Of course not,'' Sparhawk snorted. ''I've got too many things to do here in Cimmura.''

''You'll make him very angry.''

''So?''

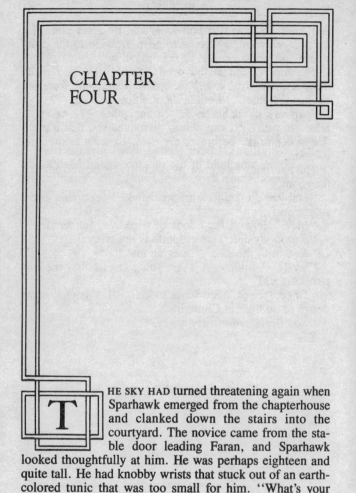

CHAPTER FOUR

T HE SKY HAD turned threatening again when Sparhawk emerged from the chapterhouse and clanked down the stairs into the courtyard. The novice came from the stable door leading Faran, and Sparhawk looked thoughtfully at him. He was perhaps eighteen and quite tall. He had knobby wrists that stuck out of an earth-colored tunic that was too small for him. "What's your name, young man?" Sparhawk asked him.

"Berit, my Lord."

"What are your duties here?"

"I haven't been assigned anything specific as yet, my Lord. I just try to make myself useful."

"Good. Turn around."

"My Lord?"

"I want to measure you."

Berit looked puzzled, but he did as he was told. Sparhawk measured him across the shoulders with his hands. Although he looked bony, Berit was actually a husky youth. "You'll do fine," Sparhawk told him.

Berit turned, his face baffled.

"You're going to be making a trip," Sparhawk told him. "Gather up what you'll need while I go get the man who's going to go with you."

"Yes, my Lord," Berit replied, bowing respectfully.

Sparhawk took hold of the saddlebow and hauled himself up onto Faran's back. Berit handed him the reins, and Sparhawk nudged the big roan into a walk. They crossed the courtyard, and Sparhawk responded to the salutes of the knights at the gate. Then he rode on across the drawbridge and through the east gate of the city.

The streets of Cimmura were busy now. Workmen carrying large bundles wrapped in muddy-colored burlap grunted their way through the narrow lanes, and merchants dressed in conventional blue stood in the doorways of their shops with their brightly colored wares piled around them. An occasional wagon clattered along the cobblestones. Near the intersection of two narrow streets, a squad of church soldiers in their scarlet livery marched with a certain arrogant precision. Sparhawk did not give way to them, but instead bore down on them at a steady trot. Grudgingly, they separated and stood aside as he passed. "Thank you, neighbors," Sparhawk said pleasantly.

They did not answer him.

He reined Faran in. "I said, thank you, neighbors."

"You're welcome," one of them replied sullenly.

Sparhawk waited.

". . . my Lord," the soldier added grudgingly.

"Much better, friend." Sparhawk rode on.

The gate to the inn was closed, and Sparhawk leaned over and banged on its timbers with his gauntleted fist. The porter who swung it open for him was not the same knight who had admitted him the evening before. Sparhawk swung down from Faran's back and handed him the reins.

"Will you be needing him again, my Lord?" the knight asked.

"Yes. I'll be going right back out. Would you saddle my squire's horse, Sir Knight?"

"Of course, my Lord."

"I appreciate that." Sparhawk laid one hand on Faran's neck. "Behave yourself," he said.

Faran looked away, his expression lofty.

Sparhawk clinked up the stairs and rapped on the door of the room at the top.

Kurik opened the door for him. "Well? How did it go?"

"Not bad."

"You came out alive, anyway. Did you see the queen?"

"Yes."

"That's surprising."

"I sort of insisted. Do you want to get your things together? You're going back to Demos."

"You didn't say 'we,' Sparhawk."

"I'm staying here."

"I suppose there are good reasons."

"Lycheas has ordered me back to the motherhouse. I more or less plan to ignore him, but I want to be able to move around Cimmura without being followed. There's a young novice at the chapterhouse who's about my size. We'll put him in my armor and mount him on Faran. Then the two of you can ride to Demos with a grand show of obedience. As long as he keeps his visor down, the primate's spies will think I'm obeying orders."

"It's workable, I suppose. I don't like the idea of leaving you here alone, though."

"I won't be alone. Kalten's coming in either today or tomorrow."

"That's a little better. Kalten's steady." Kurik frowned. "I thought that he'd been exiled to Lamorkand. Who ordered him back?"

"Vanion didn't say, but you know Kalten. Maybe he just got bored with Lamorkand and took independent action."

"How long do you want me to stay at Demos?" Kurik asked as he began to gather up his things.

"A month or so at least. The road's likely to be watched. I'll get word to you. Do you need any money?"

"I always need money, Sparhawk."

"There's some in the pocket of that tunic." Sparhawk pointed at his travel clothes draped across the back of a chair. "Take what you need."

Kurik grinned at him.

"Leave me a *little*, though."

"Of course, my Lord," Kurik said with a mocking bow. "Do you want me to pack up your things?"

"No. I'll be coming back here when Kalten arrives. It's a little hard to get in and out of the chapterhouse without being seen. Is the back door to that tavern still open?"

"It was yesterday. I drop in there from time to time."

"I thought you might."

"A man needs a few vices, Sparhawk. It gives him something to repent when he goes to chapel."

"If Aslade hears that you've been drinking, she'll set fire to your beard."

"Then we'll just have to make sure that she doesn't hear about it, won't, we, my Lord?"

"Why do I always get mixed up in your domestic affairs?"

"It keeps your feet planted in reality. Get your own wife, Sparhawk. Then other women won't feel obliged to take special note of you. A married man is safe. A bachelor is a constant challenge to any woman alive."

About half an hour later, Sparhawk and his squire went down the stairs into the courtyard, mounted their horses, and rode out through the gate. They clattered along the cobblestone streets toward the east gate of the city.

"We're being watched, you know," Kurik said quietly.

"I certainly *hope* so," Sparhawk replied. "I'd hate to have to ride around in circles until we attract somebody's attention."

They went through the ritual again at the drawbridge of the chapterhouse and then rode on into the courtyard. Berit was waiting for them.

"This is Kurik," Sparhawk told him as he dismounted.

"The two of you will be going to Demos. Kurik, the young man's name is Berit."

The squire looked the acolyte up and down. "He's the right size," he noted. "I might have to shorten a few straps, but your armor should come close to fitting him."

"I thought so myself."

Another novice came out and took their reins.

"Come along then, you two," Sparhawk said. "Let's go tell Vanion what we're going to do, and then we'll put my armor on our masquerader here."

Berit looked startled.

"You're being promoted, Berit," Kurik told him. "You see how quickly one can move up in the Pandions? Yesterday a novice; today Queen's Champion."

"I'll explain it to you when we see Vanion," Sparhawk told Berit. "It's not so interesting a story that I want to go over it more than once."

It was midafternoon when the three of them emerged from the chapterhouse door again. Berit walked awkwardly in the unaccustomed armor, and Sparhawk was dressed in a plain tunic and hose.

"I think it's going to rain," Kurik said, squinting at the sky.

"You won't melt," Sparhawk told him.

"I'm not worried about that," the squire replied. "It's just that I'll have to scour the rust off your armor again."

"Life is hard."

Kurik grunted, and then the two of them boosted Berit up into Faran's saddle. "You're going to take this young man to Demos," Sparhawk told his horse. "Try to behave as if it were me on your back."

Faran gave him an inquiring look.

"It would take much too long to explain. It's entirely up to you, Faran, but he's wearing my armor, so if you try to bite him, you'll probably break your teeth." Sparhawk turned to his squire. "Say hello to Aslade and the boys for me," he said.

"Right," Kurik nodded. Then he swung up into his saddle.

"Don't make *too* big a show when you leave," Sparhawk added, ''but make sure that you're seen—and make sure that Berit keeps his visor down.''

''I know what I'm doing, Sparhawk. Come along then, my Lord,'' Kurik said to Berit.

''My Lord?''

''You might as well get used to it, Berit.'' Kurik pulled his horse around. ''I'll see you, Sparhawk.'' Then the two of them rode out of the courtyard toward the drawbridge.

The rest of the day passed quietly. Sparhawk sat in the cell which Vanion had assigned to him, reading a musty old book. At sundown he joined the other brothers in the refectory for the simple evening meal, then marched in quiet procession with them to chapel. Sparhawk's religious convictions were not profound, but there was again that sense of renewal involved in the return to the practices of his novitiate. Vanion conducted the services that evening and spoke at some length on the virtue of humility. In keeping with his long-standing practice, Sparhawk fell into a doze about halfway through the sermon.

He was awakened at the end of the sermon by the voice of an angel. A young knight with hair the color of butter and a neck like a marble column lifted his clear tenor voice in a hymn of praise. His face shone, and his eyes were filled with adoration.

''Was I really all that boring?'' Vanion murmured, falling in beside Sparhawk as they left the chapel.

''Probably not,'' Sparhawk replied, ''but I'm not really in any position to judge. Did you do the one about the simple daisy being as beautiful in the eyes of God as the rose?''

''You've heard it before?''

''Frequently.''

''The old ones are the best.''

''Who's your tenor?''

''Sir Parasim. He just won his spurs.''

''I don't want to alarm you, Vanion, but he's too good for this world.''

''I know.''

''God will probably call him home very soon.''

''That's God's business, isn't it, Sparhawk?''

"Do me a favor, Vanion. Don't put me in a situation where I'm the one who lets him get killed."

"That's also God's business. Sleep well, Sparhawk."

"You, too, Vanion."

IT WAS PROBABLY about midnight when the door to Sparhawk's cell banged open. He rolled quickly out of his narrow cot and came to his feet with his sword in his hand.

"*Don't* do that," the big blond-haired man in the doorway said in disgust. He was holding a candle in one hand and a wineskin in the other.

"Hello, Kalten," Sparhawk greeted his boyhood friend. "When did you get in?"

"About a half-hour ago. I thought I was going to have to scale the walls there for a while." He looked disgusted. "It's peacetime. Why do they raise the drawbridge every night?"

"Probably out of habit."

"Are you going to put that down?" Kalten asked, pointing at the sword in Sparhawk's hand, "or am I going to have to drink this whole thing by myself?"

"Sorry," Sparhawk said. He leaned his plain sword against the wall.

Kalten set his candle on the small table in the corner, tossed the wineskin onto Sparhawk's bed, and then caught his friend in a huge bear hug. "It's good to see you," he declared.

"And you, too," Sparhawk replied. "Have a seat." He pointed at the stool by the table and sat down on the edge of his cot. "How was Lamorkand?"

Kalten made an indelicate sound. "Cold, damp, and nervous," he replied. "Lamorks are not my favorite people in the world. How was Rendor?"

Sparhawk shrugged. "Hot, dry, and probably just as nervous as Lamorkand."

"I heard a rumor that you ran into Martel down there. Did you give him a nice funeral?"

"He got away."

"You're slipping, Sparhawk." Kalten unfastened the collar of his cloak. A great mat of curly blond hair protruded out of the neck of his mail coat. "Are you going to sit on that wineskin all night?" he asked pointedly.

Sparhawk grunted, unstoppered the skin and lifted it to his lips. "Not bad," he said. "Where did you get it?" He handed the skin to his friend.

"I picked it up in a wayside tavern about sundown," he replied. "I remembered that all there is to drink in Pandion chapterhouses is water—or tea, if Sephrenia happens to be around. Stupid custom."

"We *are* a religious order, Kalten."

"There are a half-dozen patriarchs in Chyrellos who get drunk as lords every night." Kalten lifted the wineskin and took a long drink. Then he shook the skin. "I should have picked up two," he observed. "Oh, by the way, Kurik was in the tavern with some young puppy wearing your armor."

"I should have guessed that," Sparhawk said wryly.

"Anyway, Kurik told me that you were here. I was going to spend the night there, but when I heard that you'd come back from Rendor, I rode on the rest of the way."

"I'm touched."

Kalten laughed and handed back the wineskin.

"Were Kurik and the novice staying out of sight?" Sparhawk asked.

Kalten nodded. "They were in one of the back rooms, and the young fellow was keeping his visor down. Have you ever seen anybody try to drink through his visor? Funniest thing I ever saw. There were a couple of local whores there, too. Your young Pandion might be getting an education along about now."

"He's due," Sparhawk observed.

"I wonder if he'll try to do that with his visor down as well."

"Those girls are usually adaptable."

Kalten laughed. "Anyhow, Kurik told me about the situation here. Do you really believe you can sneak around Cimmura without being recognized?"

"I was thinking along the lines of a disguise of some sort."

"Better come up with a false nose," Kalten advised.

"That broken beak of yours makes you fairly easy to pick out of a crowd."

"You should know," Sparhawk said. "You're the one who broke it."

"We were only playing," Kalten said, sounding a bit defensive.

"I've gotten used to it. We'll talk with Sephrenia in the morning. She should be able to come up with something in the way of disguises."

"I'd heard that she was here. How is she?"

"The same. Sephrenia never changes."

"Truly." Kalten took another drink from the wineskin and wiped his mouth with the back of his hand. "You know, I think I was always a big disappointment to her. No matter how hard she tried to teach me the secrets, I just couldn't master the Styric language. Every time I tried to say *'ogeragekgasek,'* I almost dislocated my jaw."

"Okeragukasek," Sparhawk corrected him.

"However you say it. I'll just stick to my sword and let others play with magic." He leaned forward on his stool. "They say that the Eshandists are on the rise again in Rendor. Is there any truth to that?"

"It's no particular danger." Sparhawk shrugged, lounging back on his cot. "They howl and spin around in circles out in the desert and recite slogans to each other. That's about as far as it goes. Is anything very interesting going on in Lamorkand?"

Kalten snorted. "All the barons there are involved in private wars with each other," he reported. "The whole kingdom reeks with the lust for revenge. Would you believe that there's actually a war going on over a bee sting? An earl got stung and declared war on the baron whose peasants owned the hive. They've been fighting each other for ten years now."

"That's Lamorkand for you. Anything else happening?"

"The whole countryside east of Motera is crawling with Zemochs."

Sparhawk sat up quickly. "Vanion did say that Otha was mobilizing."

"Otha mobilizes every ten years." Kalten handed his

friend the wineskin. "I think he does it just to keep his people from getting restless."

"Are the Zemochs doing anything significant in Lamorkand?"

"Not that I was able to tell. They're asking a lot of questions—mostly about old folklore. You can find two or three of them in almost every village. They question old women and buy drinks for the loafers in the village taverns."

"Peculiar," Sparhawk murmured.

"That's a fairly accurate description of just about anybody from Zemoch," Kalten said. "Sanity has never been particularly prized there." He stood up. "I'll go find a cot someplace," he said. "I can drag it in here and we can talk old times until we both fall asleep."

"All right."

Kalten grinned. "Like the time your father caught us in that plum tree."

Sparhawk winced. "I've been trying to forget about that for almost thirty years now."

"Your father *did* have a very firm hand, as I recall. I lost track of most of the rest of that day—and the plums gave me a bellyache besides. I'll be right back." He turned and went out the door of Sparhawk's cell.

It was good to have Kalten back. The two of them had grown up together in the house of Sparhawk's parents at Demos after Kalten's family had been killed and before the pair of boys had entered their novitiate training at the Pandion motherhouse. In many ways, they were closer than brothers. To be sure, Kalten had some rough edges to him, but their close friendship was one of the things Sparhawk valued more than anything else.

After a short time, the big blond man returned, dragging a cot behind him, and then the two of them lay in the dim candlelight reminiscing until quite late. All in all, it was a very good night.

Early the following morning, they rose and dressed themselves, covering their mail coats with the hooded robes Pandions wore when they were inside their chapterhouses. They rather carefully avoided the morning procession to chapel and went in search of the woman who had trained whole generations of Pandion Knights in the intricacies of what were called the secrets.

They found her seated with her morning tea before the fire high up in the south tower.

"Good morning, little mother," Sparhawk greeted her from the doorway. "Do you mind if we join you?"

"Not at all, Sir Knights."

Kalten went to her, knelt, and kissed both her palms. "Will you bless me, little mother?" he asked her.

She smiled and put one hand on each side of his face. Then she spoke her benediction in Styric.

"That always makes me feel better for some reason," he said, rising to his feet again. "Even though I don't understand all the words."

She looked at them critically. "I see that you chose not to attend chapel this morning."

"God won't miss us all that much." Kalten shrugged. "Besides, I could recite all of Vanion's sermons from memory."

"What other mischief are you two planning for today?" she asked.

"Mischief, Sephrenia?" Kalten asked innocently.

Sparhawk laughed. "Actually, we weren't even contemplating any mischief. We just have a fairly simple errand in mind."

"Out in the city?"

He nodded. "The only problem is that we're both fairly well known here in Cimmura. We thought you might be able to help us with some disguises."

She looked at them, her expression cool. "I'm getting a strong sense of subterfuge in all this. Just exactly what is this errand of yours?"

"We thought we'd look up an old friend," Sparhawk replied. "A fellow named Krager. He has some information he might want to share with us."

"Information?"

"He knows where Martel is."

"Krager won't tell you that."

Kalten cracked his big knuckles, the sound unpleasantly

calling to mind the sharp noise of breaking bones. "Would you care to phrase that in the form of a wager, Sephrenia?" he asked.

"Won't you two ever grow up? You're a pair of eternal children."

"That's why you love us so much, isn't it, little mother?" Kalten grinned.

"What sort of disguise would you recommend?" Sparhawk asked her.

She pursed her lips and looked at them. "A courtier and his squire, I think."

"No one could ever mistake me for a courtier," he objected.

"I was thinking of it the other way around. I can make you look *almost* like a good honest squire, and once we dress Kalten in a satin doublet and curl that long blond hair of his, he can pass for a courtier."

"I *do* look good in satin," Kalten murmured modestly.

"Why not just a couple of common workmen?" Sparhawk asked.

She shook her head. "Common workmen cringe and fawn when they encounter a nobleman. Could either of you manage a cringe?"

"She's got a point," Kalten said.

"Besides, workmen don't carry swords, and I don't imagine that either of you would care to go into Cimmura unarmed."

"She thinks of everything, doesn't she?" Sparhawk observed.

"All right," she said. "Let's see what we can do."

Several acolytes were sent scurrying to various places in the chapterhouse for a number of articles. Sephrenia considered each one of them, selecting some and discarding others. What emerged after about an hour were two men who only faintly resembled the pair of Pandions who had first entered the room. Sparhawk now wore a plain livery not unlike Kurik's, and he carried a short sword. A fierce black beard was glued to his face, and a purple scar ran across his broken nose and up under a black patch that covered his left eye.

"This thing itches," he complained, reaching up to scratch at the false beard.

"Keep your fingers off of it until the glue dries," she told him, lightly slapping his knuckles. "And put on a glove to cover that ring."

"Do you actually expect me to carry this toy?" Kalten demanded, flourishing a light rapier. "I want a sword, not a knitting needle."

"Courtiers don't carry broadswords, Kalten," she reminded him. She looked at him critically. His doublet was bright blue, gored and inset with red satin. His hose matched the goring, and he wore soft half boots, since no pair of the pointed shoes currently in fashion could be found to fit his huge feet. His cape was of pale pink, and his freshly curled blond hair spilled down over the collar. He also wore a broad-brimmed hat adorned with a white plume. "You look beautiful, Kalten," she complimented him. "I think you might pass—once I rouge your cheeks."

"Absolutely not!" He backed away from her.

"Kalten," she said quite firmly, "sit down." She pointed at a chair and reached for a rouge pot.

"Do I have to?"

"Yes. Now sit."

Kalten looked at Sparhawk. "If you laugh, we're going to fight, so don't even think about it."

"Me?"

Since the chapterhouse was watched at all times by the agents of the Primate Annias, Vanion came up with a suggestion that was part subterfuge and part utilitarian. "I need to transfer some things to the inn anyway," he explained. "Annias knows that the inn belongs to us, so we're not giving anything away. We'll hide Kalten in the wagon bed and turn this good, honest fellow into a teamster." He looked pointedly at the patch-eyed, bearded Sparhawk. "Where on earth did you find so close a match to his real hair?" he asked Sephrenia curiously.

She smiled. "The next time you go into the stables, don't look too closely at your horse's tail."

"*My* horse?"

"He was the only black horse in the stable, Vanion, and I didn't take all that much, really."

"*My* horse?" he repeated, looking injured.

"We must all make sacrifices now and then," she told him. "It's a part of the Pandion oath, remember?"

CHAPTER FIVE

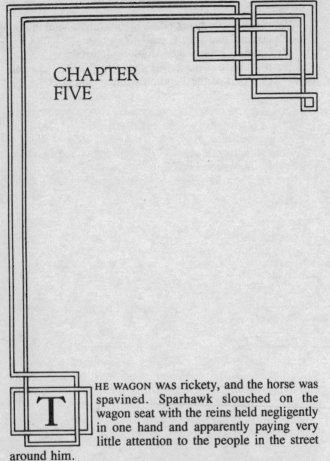

T HE WAGON WAS rickety, and the horse was spavined. Sparhawk slouched on the wagon seat with the reins held negligently in one hand and apparently paying very little attention to the people in the street around him.

The wheels wobbled and creaked as the wagon jolted over a rutted place in the stone-paved street. "Sparhawk, do you have to hit every single bump?" Kalten's muffled voice came from under the boxes and bales loosely piled around him in the back of the wagon.

"Keep quiet," Sparhawk muttered. "Two church soldiers are coming this way."

Kalten grumbled a few choice oaths, then fell silent.

The church soldiers wore red livery and disdainful expressions. As they walked through the crowded streets, the workmen and blue-clad merchants stepped aside for them. Sparhawk reined in his nag, stopping the wagon in the exact center of the street so that the soldiers would be forced to go around him. '' 'Morning, neighbors,'' he greeted them.

They glared at him, then walked on around the wagon.

"Have a pleasant day," he called after them.

They ignored him.

"What was that all about?" Kalten demanded in a low voice from the wagon bed.

"Just checking my disguise," Sparhawk replied, shaking the reins.

"Well?"

"Well what?"

"Does it work?"

"They didn't give me a second glance."

"How much farther to the inn? I'm suffocating under all this."

"Not too much farther."

"Give me a big surprise, Sparhawk. Miss a bump or two—just for the sake of variety."

The wagon creaked on.

At the barred gate of the inn, Sparhawk climbed down from the wagon and pounded the rhythmic signal on its stout timbers. After a moment the knight porter opened the gate. He looked at Sparhawk carefully. "Sorry, friend," he said. "The inn's all full."

"We won't be staying, Sir Knight," Sparhawk told him. "We just brought a load of supplies from the chapter-house."

The porter's eyes widened and he peered more closely at the big man. "Is that you, Sir Sparhawk?" he asked incredulously. "I didn't even recognize you."

"That was sort of the idea. You aren't supposed to."

The knight pushed the gate open, and Sparhawk led the weary horse into the courtyard. "You can get out now," he said to Kalten as the porter closed the gate.

"Help get all this off me."

Sparhawk moved a few of the boxes, and Kalten came squirming out.

The knight porter gave the big blond man an amused look.

"Go ahead and say it," Kalten said in a belligerent tone.

"I wouldn't dream of it, Sir Knight."

Sparhawk took a long, rectangular box out of the wagon bed and hoisted it up onto his shoulder. "Get somebody to help you with these supplies," he told the porter. "Preceptor Vanion sent them. And take care of the horse. He's tired."

"Tired? Dead would be closer." The porter eyed the disconsolate-looking nag.

"He's old, that's all. It happens to all of us sooner or later. Is the back door to the tavern open?" He looked across the courtyard at a deeply inset doorway.

"It's always open, Sir Sparhawk."

Sparhawk nodded and he and Kalten crossed the courtyard.

"What have you got in the box?" Kalten asked.

"Our swords."

"That's clever, but won't they be a little hard to draw?"

"Not after I throw the box down on the cobblestones, they won't." He opened the inset door. "After you, my Lord," he said, bowing.

They passed through a cluttered storeroom and came out into a shabby-looking tavern. A century or so of dust clouded the single window, and the straw on the floor was moldy. The room smelled of stale beer and spilled wine and vomit. The low ceiling was draped with cobwebs, and the rough tables and benches were battered and tired-looking. There were only three people in the place, a sour-looking tavern keeper, a drunken man with his head cradled in his arms on a table by the door, and a blowsy-looking whore in a red dress dozing in the corner.

Kalten went to the door and looked out into the street. "It's still a little underpopulated out there," he grunted. "Let's have a tankard or two while we wait for the neighborhood to wake up."

"Why not have some breakfast instead?"

"That's what I just said."

They sat at one of the tables, and the tavern keeper

came over, giving no hint that he recognized them as Pandions. He made an ineffective swipe at a puddle of spilled beer on the table with a filthy rag. "What would you like?" His voice had a sullen, unfriendly tone.

"Beer," Kalten replied.

"Bring us a little bread and cheese, too," Sparhawk added.

The tavern keeper grunted and left them.

"Where was Krager when you saw him?" Kalten asked quietly.

"In that square near the west gate."

"That's a shabby part of town."

"Krager's a shabby sort of person."

"We could start there, I suppose, but this might take a while. Krager could be down just about any rat hole in Cimmura."

"Did you have anything else more pressing to do?"

The whore in the red dress hauled herself wearily to her feet and shuffled across the straw-covered floor to their table. "I don't suppose either of you fine gentlemen would care for a bit of a frolic?" she asked in a bored-sounding voice. One of her front teeth was missing, and her red dress was cut very low in front. Perfunctorily she leaned forward to offer them a view of her flabby-looking breasts.

"It's a bit early, little sister," Sparhawk said. "Thanks all the same."

"How's business?" Kalten asked her.

"Slow. It's always slow in the morning." She sighed. "I don't suppose you could see your way clear to offer a girl something to drink?" she asked hopefully.

"Why not?" Kalten replied. "Tavern keeper," he called, "bring the lady one, too."

"Thanks, my Lord," the whore said. She looked around the tavern. "This is a sorry place," she said with a certain amount of resignation in her voice. "I wouldn't even come in here—except that I don't like to work the streets." She sighed. "Do you know something?" she said. "My feet hurt. Isn't that a strange thing to happen to someone in my profession? You'd think it would be my back. Thanks again, my Lord." She turned and shuffled back to the table where she had been sitting.

"I like talking with whores," Kalten said. "They've got a nice, uncomplicated view of life."

"That's a strange hobby for a Church Knight."

"God hired me as a fighting man, Sparhawk, not as a monk. I fight whenever He tells me to, but the rest of my time is my own."

The tavern keeper brought them tankards of beer and a plate with bread and cheese on it. They sat eating and talking quietly.

After about an hour the tavern had attracted several more customers—sweat-smelling workmen who had slipped away from their chores and a few of the keepers of nearby shops. Sparhawk rose, went to the door, and looked out. Although the narrow back street was not exactly teeming with traffic, there were enough people moving back and forth to provide some measure of concealment. Sparhawk returned to the table. "I think it's time to be on our way, my Lord." he said to Kalten. He picked up his box.

"Right," Kalten replied. He drained his tankard and rose to his feet, swaying slightly and with his hat on the back of his head. He stumbled a few times on the way to the door and he was reeling just a bit as he led the way out into the street. Sparhawk followed him with the box once again on his shoulder. "Aren't you overdoing that just a little?" he muttered to his friend when they turned the corner.

"I'm just a typical drunken courtier, Sparhawk. We just came out of a tavern."

"We're well past it now. If you act too drunk, you'll attract attention. I think it's time for a miraculous recovery."

"You're taking all the fun out of this, Sparhawk," Kalten complained. He stopped staggering and straightened his white-plumed hat.

They moved on through the busy streets with Sparhawk trailing respectfully behind his friend as a good squire would.

When they reached another intersection, Sparhawk felt a familiar prickling of his skin. He set down his wooden box and wiped at his brow with the sleeve of his smock.

"What's the matter?" Kalten asked, also stopping.

"The case is heavy, my Lord," Sparhawk explained in a voice loud enough to be heard by passersby. Then he spoke in a half whisper. "We're being watched," he said as his eyes swept the sides of the street.

The robed and hooded figure was in a second floor window, partially concealed behind a thick green drape. It looked very much like the one that had watched him in the rain-wet streets the night he had first arrived back in Cimmura.

"Have you located him?" Kalten asked quietly, making some show of adjusting the collar of his pink cloak.

Sparhawk grunted, raising the box to his shoulder again. "Second floor window—over the chandler's shop."

"Let's be off then, my man," Kalten said in a louder voice. "The day's wearing on." As he started on up the street, he cast a quick, furtive glance at the green-draped window.

They rounded another corner. "Odd-looking sort, wasn't he?" Kalten noted. "Most people don't wear hoods when they're indoors."

"Maybe he's got something to hide."

"Do you think he recognized us?"

"It's hard to say. I'm not positive, but I think he was the same one who was watching me the night I came into town. I didn't get a good look at him, but I could feel him, and this one feels just about the same."

"Would magic penetrate these disguises?"

"Easily. Magic sees the man, not the clothes. Let's go down a few alleys and see if we can shake him off in case he decides to follow us."

"Right."

It was nearly noon when they reached the square near the west gate where Sparhawk had seen Krager. They split up there. Sparhawk went in one direction and Kalten the other. They questioned the keepers of the brightly colored booths and the more sedate shops closely, describing Krager in some detail. On the far side of the square, Sparhawk rejoined his friend. "Any luck?" he asked.

Kalten nodded. "There's a wine merchant over there who says that a man who looks like Krager comes in three or four times a day to buy a flagon of Arcian red."

"That's Krager's drink, all right." Sparhawk grinned. "If Martel finds out that he's drinking again, he'll reach down his throat and pull his heart out."

"Can you actually do that to a man?"

"You can if your arm's long enough, and if you know what you're looking for. Did your wine merchant give you any sort of hint about which way Krager usually comes from?"

Kalten nodded. "That street there." He pointed.

Sparhawk scratched at his horse-tail beard, thinking.

"If you pull that loose, Sephrenia's going to turn you over her knee and paddle you."

Sparhawk took his hand away from his face. "Has Krager picked up his first flagon of wine this morning?" he asked.

Kalten nodded. "About two hours ago."

"He's likely to finish that first one fairly fast. If he's drinking the way he used to, he'll wake up in the mornings feeling a bit unwell." Sparhawk looked around the busy square. "Let's go on up that street a ways where there aren't quite so many people and wait for him. As soon as he runs out of wine, he'll come out for more."

"Won't he see us? He knows us both, you know."

Sparhawk shook his head. "He's so shortsighted that he can barely see past the end of his nose. Add a flagon of wine to that, and he wouldn't be able to recognize his own mother."

"Krager's got a mother?" Kalten asked in mock amazement. "I thought he just crawled out from under a rotten log."

Sparhawk laughed. "Let's go find someplace where we can wait for him."

"Can we skulk?" Kalten asked eagerly. "I haven't skulked in years."

"Skulk away, my friend," Sparhawk said.

They walked up the street the wine merchant had indicated. After a few hundred paces, Sparhawk pointed toward the narrow opening of an alley. "That ought to do it," he said. "Let's go do our skulking in there. When Krager goes by, we can drag him into the alley and have our little chat in private."

"Right," Kalten agreed with an evil grin.

They crossed the street and entered the alley. Rotting garbage lay heaped along the sides, and some way farther on was a reeking public urinal. Kalten waved one hand in front of his face. "Sometimes your decisions leave a lot to be desired, Sparhawk," he said. "Couldn't you have picked someplace a little less fragrant?"

"You know," Sparhawk said, "that's what I've missed about not having you around, Kalten—that steady stream of complaints."

Kalten shrugged. "A man needs something to talk about." He reached under his azure doublet, took out a small, curved knife, and began to strop it on the sole of his boot. "I get him first," he said.

"What?"

"Krager. I get to start on him first."

"What gave you that idea?"

"You're my friend, Sparhawk. Friends always let their friends go first."

"Doesn't that work the other way around, too?"

Kalten shook his head. "You like me better than I like you. It's only natural, of course. I'm a lot more likable than you are."

Sparhawk gave him a long look.

"That's what friends are for, Sparhawk," Kalten said ingratiatingly, "to point out our little shortcomings to us."

They waited, watching the street from the mouth of the alley. It was not a particularly busy street, for there were but few shops along its sides. It seemed rather to be given over largely to storehouses and private dwellings.

An hour dragged by, and then another.

"Maybe he drank himself to sleep," Kalten said.

"Not Krager. He can hold more than a regiment. He'll be along."

Kalten thrust his head out of the opening of the alleyway and squinted at the sky. "It's going to rain," he predicted.

"We've both been rained on before."

Kalten plucked at the front of his gaudy doublet and rolled his eyes. "But *Thpar*hawk," he lisped outrageously. "You *know* how thatin thpotth when it getth wet."

Sparhawk doubled over with laughter, trying to muffle the sound.

They waited once more, and another hour dragged by.

"The sun's going to go down before long," Kalten said. "Maybe he found another wine shop."

"Let's wait a little longer," Sparhawk replied.

The rush came without warning. Eight or ten burly fellows in rough clothing came charging down the alley with swords in their hands. Kalten's rapier came whistling out of its sheath even as Sparhawk's hand flashed to the hilt of his short sword. The man leading the charge doubled over and gasped as Kalten smoothly ran him through. Sparhawk stepped past his friend as the blond man recovered from his lunge. He parried the sword stroke of one of the attackers and then buried his sword in the man's belly. He wrenched the blade as he jerked it out to make the wound as big as possible. "Get that box open!" he shouted at Kalten as he parried another stroke.

The alleyway was too narrow for more than two of them to come at him at once; even though his sword was not as long as theirs, he was able to hold them at bay. Behind him he heard the splintering of wood as Kalten kicked the rectangular box apart. Then his friend was at his shoulder with his broadsword in his hand. "I've got it now," Kalten said. "Get your sword."

Sparhawk spun and ran back to the mouth of the alley. He discarded the short sword, jerked his own weapon out of the wreckage of the box, and whirled back again. Kalten had cut down two of the attackers, and he was beating the others back step by step. He did, however, have his left hand pressed tightly to his side, and there was blood coming out from between his fingers. Sparhawk rushed past him, swinging his heavy sword with both hands. He split one fellow's head open and cut the sword arm off another. Then he drove the point of his sword deep into the body of yet a third, sending him reeling against the wall with a fountain of blood gushing from his mouth.

The rest of the attackers fled.

Sparhawk turned and saw Kalten coolly pulling his sword out of the chest of the man with the missing arm. "Don't leave them behind you like that, Sparhawk," the blond man said. "Even a one-armed man can stab you in the back. Besides, it isn't tidy. Always finish one job before you go on to the next." He still had his left hand tightly pressed to his side.

"Are you all right?" Sparhawk asked him.

"It's only a scratch."

"Scratches don't bleed like that. Let me have a look."

The gash in Kalten's side was sizable, but it did not appear to be too deep. Sparhawk ripped the sleeve off the smock of one of the casualties, wadded it up, and placed it over the cut in Kalten's side. "Hold that in place," he said. "Push in on it to slow the bleeding."

"I've been cut before, Sparhawk. I know what to do."

Sparhawk looked around at the crumpled bodies littering the alley. "I think we ought to leave," he said. "Somebody in the neighborhood might get curious about all the noise." Then he frowned. "Did you notice anything peculiar about these men?" he asked.

Kalten shrugged. "They were fairly inept."

"That's not what I mean. Men who make a living by waylaying people in alleys aren't usually very interested in their personal appearance, and these fellows are all clean-shaven." He rolled one of the bodies over and ripped open the front of his canvas smock. "Isn't *that* interesting?" he observed. Beneath the smock the dead man wore a red tunic with an embroidered emblem over the left breast.

"Church soldier," Kalten grunted. "Do you think that Annias might possibly dislike us?"

"It's not unlikely. Let's get out of here. The survivors might have gone for help."

"The chapterhouse then—or the inn?"

Sparhawk shook his head. "Somebody's seen through our disguises, and Annias would expect us to go to one of those places."

"You could be right about that. Any ideas?"

"I know of a place. It's not too far. Are you all right to walk?"

"I can go as far as you can. I'm younger, remember?"

"Only by six weeks."

"Younger is younger, Sparhawk. Let's not quibble about numbers."

They tucked their broadswords under their belts and walked out of the mouth of the alley. Sparhawk supported his wounded friend as they moved out into the open.

The street along which they walked grew progressively shabbier, and they soon entered a maze of interconnecting lanes and unpaved alleys. The buildings were large and run-down, and they teemed with roughly dressed people who seemed indifferent to the squalor around them.

"It's a rabbit warren, isn't it?" Kalten said. "Is this place much farther? I'm getting a little tired."

"It's just on the other side of that next intersection."

Kalten grunted and pressed his hand more tightly to his side.

They moved on. The looks directed at them by the inhabitants of this slum were unfriendly, even hostile. Kalten's clothing marked him as a member of the ruling class, and these people at the very bottom of society had little use for courtiers and their servants.

When they reached the intersection, Sparhawk led his friend up a muddy alley. They had gone about halfway when a thick-bodied man with a rusty pike in his hands stepped out of a doorway to bar their path. "Where do you think you're going?" he demanded.

"I need to talk to Platime," Sparhawk replied.

"I don't think he wants to hear anything you have to say. If you're smart, you'll get out of this part of town before nightfall. Accidents happen here after dark."

"And sometimes even before dark," Sparhawk said, drawing his sword.

"I can have a dozen men here in two winks."

"And my broken-nosed friend here can have your head off in one," Kalten told him.

The man stepped back, his face apprehensive.

"What's it to be, neighbor?" Sparhawk asked. "Do you take us to Platime, or do you and I play for a bit?"

"You've got no right to threaten me."

Sparhawk raised his sword so that the fellow could get a good look at it. "This gives me all sorts of rights, neighbor. Lean your pike against that wall and take us to Platime—now!"

The thick-bodied man flinched and then carefully set

his pike against the wall, turned, and led them on up the alley. It came to a dead end a hundred paces farther on, and a stone stairway ran down to what appeared to be a cellar door.

"Down there," the man said, pointing.

"Lead the way," Sparhawk told him. "I don't want you behind me, friend. You look like the sort who might make errors in judgment."

Sullenly, the fellow went down the mud-coated stairs and rapped twice on the door. "It's me," he called. "Sef. There are a couple of nobles here who want to talk to Platime."

There was a pause followed by the rattling of a chain. The door opened and a bearded man thrust his head out. "Platime doesn't like noblemen," he declared.

"I'll change his mind for him," Sparhawk said. "Step back out of the way, neighbor."

The bearded man looked at the sword in Sparhawk's hand, swallowed hard, and opened the door wider.

"Press right along, Sef," Kalten said to their guide.

Sef went through the door.

"Join us, friend," Sparhawk told the bearded man when he and Kalten were inside. "We like lots of company."

The stairs continued down between moldy stone walls that wept moisture. At the bottom, the stair opened out into a very large cellar with a vaulted stone ceiling. There was a fire burning in a pit in the center of the room, filling the air with smoke, and the walls were lined with roughly constructed cots and straw-filled pallets. Two dozen or so men and women in a wide variety of garments sat on those cots and pallets drinking and playing at dice. Just beyond the firepit a huge man with a fierce black beard and a vast paunch sprawled in a large chair with his feet thrust out toward the flames. He wore a satin doublet of a faded orange color, spotted and stained down the front, and he held a silver tankard in one beefy hand.

"That's Platime," Sef said nervously. "He's a little drunk, so you should be careful, my Lords."

"We can deal with it," Sparhawk told him. "Thanks for your help, Sef. I don't know how we'd have managed without you." Then he led Kalten on around the firepit.

"Who are all these people?" Kalten asked in a low voice, looking around at the men and women lining the walls.

"Thieves, beggars, a few murderers probably—that sort of thing."

"You've got some very nice friends, Sparhawk."

Platime was carefully examining a necklace with a ruby pendant attached to it. When Sparhawk and Kalten stopped in front of him, he raised his bleary eyes and looked them over, paying particular attention to Kalten's finery. "Who let these two in here?" he roared.

"We sort of let ourselves in, Platime," Sparhawk told him, thrusting his sword back under his belt and turning up his eye patch so that it no longer impaired his vision.

"Well, you can sort of let yourselves back out again."

"That wouldn't be convenient right now, I'm afraid," Sparhawk told him.

The gross man in the orange doublet snapped his fingers, and the people lining the walls stood up. "You're badly outnumbered, my friend." Platime looked around suggestively at his cohorts.

"That's been happening fairly often lately," Kalten said with his hand on the hilt of his broadsword.

Platime's eyes narrowed. "Your clothes and that sword don't exactly match," he said.

"And I try so hard to coordinate my attire," Kalten sighed.

"Just who are you two?" Platime asked suspiciously. "This one is dressed like a courtier, but I don't think he's really one of those walking butterflies from the palace."

"He sees right to the core of things, doesn't he?" Kalten said to Sparhawk. He looked at Platime. "Actually, we're Pandions," he said.

"Church Knights? I thought it might be something like that. Why the fancy clothes, then?"

"We're both fairly well known," Sparhawk told him. "We wanted to be able to move around without being recognized."

Platime looked meaningfully at Kalten's blood-stained doublet. "It looks to me as if *somebody* saw through your disguises," he said, "or maybe you just frequent the wrong taverns. Who stabbed you?"

"A church soldier." Kalten shrugged. "He got in a lucky thrust. Do you mind if I sit down? I'm feeling a little shaky for some reason."

"Somebody bring him a stool," Platime shouted. Then he looked back at the two of them. "Why would Church Knights and church soldiers be fighting?" he asked.

"Palace politics." Sparhawk shrugged. "They get a little murky sometimes."

"That's God's own truth. What's your business here?"

"We need a place to stay for a while," Sparhawk told him. He looked around. "This cellar of yours ought to work out fairly well."

"Sorry, friend. I can sympathize with a man who's just had a run-in with the church soldiers, but I'm conducting a business here, and there's no room for outsiders." Platime looked at Kalten, who had just sunk down on a stool that a ragged beggar had brought him. "Did you kill the man who stabbed you?"

"He did." Kalten pointed at Sparhawk. "I killed a few others, but my friend here did most of the fighting."

"Why don't we get down to business?" Sparhawk said. "I think you owe my family a debt, Platime."

"I don't have any dealings with nobles," Platime replied, "except to cut a few of their throats from time to time—so it's unlikely that I owe your family a thing."

"This debt has nothing to do with money. A long time ago, some church soldiers were hanging you. My father stopped them."

Platime blinked. "You're Sparhawk?" he said in surprise. "You don't look that much like your father."

"It's his nose," Kalten said. "When you break a man's nose, you change his whole appearance. Why were the soldiers hanging you?"

"It was all a misunderstanding. I knifed a fellow. He wasn't wearing his uniform, so I didn't know he was an officer in the primate's guard." He looked disgusted. "And all he had in his purse were two silver coins and a handful of copper."

"Do you acknowledge the debt?" Sparhawk pressed.

Platime pulled at his coarse black beard. "I guess I do," he admitted.

"We'll stay here, then."

"That's all you want?"

"Not quite. We're looking for a man—a fellow named Krager. Your beggars are all over town, and I want them to look for him."

"Fair enough. Can you describe him?"

"I can do better than that. I can show him to you."

"That doesn't exactly make sense, friend."

"It will in a minute. Have you got a basin of some kind—and some clean water?"

"I think I can manage that. What have you got in mind?"

"He's going to make an image of Krager's face in the water," Kalten said. "It's an old trick."

Platime looked impressed. "I've heard that you Pandions are all wizards, but I've never seen anything like that before."

"Sparhawk's better at it than I am," Kalten admitted.

One of the beggars furnished a chipped basin filled with slightly cloudy water. Sparhawk set the basin on the floor and concentrated for a moment, muttering the Styric words of the spell under his breath. Then he passed his hand slowly over the basin, and Krager's puffy-looking face appeared.

"Now *that* is really something to see," Platime marveled.

"It's not too difficult," Sparhawk said modestly. "Have your people here look at it. I can't keep it there forever."

"How long can you hold it?"

"Ten minutes or so. It starts to break up after that."

"Talen!" the fat man shouted. "Come here."

A grubby-looking boy of about ten slouched across the room. His tunic was ragged and dirty, but he wore a long, red satin vest that had been fashioned by cutting the sleeves off a doublet. There were several knife-holes in the vest. "What do you want?" he asked insolently.

"Can you copy that?" Platime asked, pointing at the basin.

"Of course I can, but why should I?"

"Because I'll box your ears if you don't."

Talen grinned at him. "You'd have to catch me first, fat man, and I can run faster than you can."

Sparhawk dug a finger into a pocket of his leather jerkin and took out a small silver coin. "Would this make it worth your while?" he asked, holding up the coin.

Talen's eyes brightened. "For that, I'll give you a masterpeice," he promised.

"All we want is accuracy."

"Whatever you say, my patron." Talen bowed mockingly. "I'll go get my things."

"Is he really any good?" Kalten asked Platime after the boy had scurried over to one of the cots lining the wall.

Platime shrugged. "I'm not an art critic," he said. "He spends all his time drawing pictures, though—when he isn't begging or stealing."

"Isn't he a little young for your line of work?"

Platime laughed. "He's got the nimblest fingers in Cimmura," he said. "He could steal your eyes right out of their sockets, and you wouldn't even miss them until you went to look closely at something."

"I'll keep that in mind," Kalten said.

"It could be too late, my friend. Weren't you wearing a ring when you came in?"

Kalten blinked, then raised his blood-stained left hand and stared at it. There was no ring on the hand.

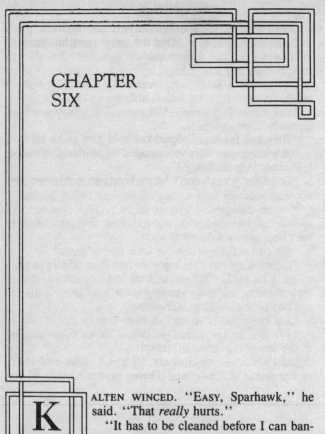

CHAPTER
SIX

KALTEN WINCED. "EASY, Sparhawk," he said. "That *really* hurts."

"It has to be cleaned before I can bandage it," Sparhawk replied, continuing to wipe the cut on his friend's side with a wine-soaked cloth.

"But do you have to do it so hard?"

Platime waddled around the smoky firepit and stood over the cot where Kalten lay. "Is he going to be all right?" he asked.

"Probably," Sparhawk replied. "He's had the blood let out of him a few times before, and he usually recovers." He laid aside the cloth and picked up a long strip of linen. "Sit up," he told his friend.

92

Kalten grunted and pushed himself into a sitting position. Sparhawk began to wind the strip about his waist.

"Not so tight," Kalten said. "I have to be able to breathe."

"Quit complaining."

"Were those church soldiers after you for any particular reason?" Platime asked, "or were they just amusing themselves?"

"They had reasons," Sparhawk told him as he knotted Kalten's bandage. "We've managed to be fairly offensive to Primate Annias lately."

"Good for you. I don't know how you noblemen feel about him, but the common people all hate him."

"We moderately despise him."

"That's one thing we all have in common then. Is there any chance that Queen Ehlana might recover?"

"We're working on that."

Platime sighed. "I think she's our only hope, Sparhawk. Otherwise Annias is going to run Elenia to suit himself, and that would really be too bad."

"Patriotism, Platime?" Kalten asked.

"Just because I'm a thief and a murderer doesn't mean that I'm disloyal. I respect the crown as much as any man in the kingdom. I even respected Aldreas, weak as he was." Platime's eyes grew sly. "Did his sister ever really seduce him?" he asked. "There were all kinds of rumors."

Sparhawk shrugged. "That's sort of hard to say."

"She went absolutely wild after your father forced Aldreas to marry Queen Ehlana's mother, you know." Platime sniggered. "She was totally convinced that she was going to marry her brother and get control of the throne."

"Isn't that sort of illegal?" Kalten asked.

"Annias said that he'd found a way around the law. Anyway, after Aldreas got married, Arissa ran away from the palace. They found her a few weeks later in that cheap brothel over by the river. Just about everybody in Cimmura had tried her before they dragged her out of the place." He squinted at them. "What did they finally do with her anyway? Chop off her head?"

"No," Sparhawk told him. "She's cloistered in the nunnery at Demos. They're very strict there."

"At least she's getting some rest. From what I hear, the Princess Arissa was a very busy young woman." He straightened and pointed at a nearby cot. "You can use that one," he told Sparhawk. "I've got every thief and beggar in Cimmura out looking for this Krager fellow of yours. If he sets foot in the streets, we'll know about it within an hour. In the meantime, you might as well get some sleep."

Sparhawk nodded and rose to his feet. "Are you all right?" he asked Kalten.

"I'm fine."

"Do you need anything?"

"How about some beer—just to restore all the blood I lost, of course."

"Of course."

It was impossible to tell what time it was since the cellar had no windows. Sparhawk felt a light touch and came awake immediately, catching the hand that had touched him.

The grubby-looking boy, Talen, made a sour face. "Never try to pick a pocket when you're shivering," he said. He mopped the rain out of his face. "It's really a miserable morning out there," he added.

"Were you looking for anything in particular in my pockets?"

"No, not really—just anything that might turn up."

"Would you like to give me back my friend's ring?"

"Oh, I suppose so. I only took it to keep in practice anyway." Talen reached inside his wet tunic and drew out Kalten's ring. "I cleaned the blood off it for him," he said, admiring it.

"He'll appreciate that."

"Oh, by the way, I found that fellow you were looking for."

"Krager? Where?"

"He's staying in a brothel in Lion Street."

"A brothel?"

"Maybe he needs affection."

Sparhawk sat up. He touched his horsehair beard to make sure it was still in place. "Let's go talk to Platime."

"Do you want me to wake your friend?"

"Let him sleep. I'm not going to take him out in the rain in his condition anyway."

Platime was snoring in his chair, but his eyes opened instantly when Talen touched his shoulder.

"The boy found Krager," Sparhawk told him.

"You're going after him, I suppose?"

Sparhawk nodded.

"Do you think the primate's soldiers are still looking for you?"

"Probably."

"And they know what you look like?"

"Yes."

"You won't get very far then."

"I'll have to chance it."

"Platime," Talen said.

"What?"

"Do you remember that time when we had to get Weasel out of town in a hurry?"

Platime grunted, scratching at his paunch and looking speculatively at Sparhawk. "How much are you attached to that beard?" he asked.

"Not too much. Why?"

"If you'd be willing to shave it off, I know a way you might be able to move around Cimmura without being recognized."

Sparhawk began pulling off chunks of the false beard.

Platime laughed. "You really *aren't* attached to it, are you?" He looked at Talen. "Go get what he'll need out of the bin."

Talen went to a large wooden box in the corner of the cellar and started rummaging around inside as Sparhawk finished removing the beard. When the boy came back, he was carrying a ragged-looking cloak and a pair of shoes that were little more than rotting leather bags.

"How much of the rest of your face will come off?" Platime asked.

Sparhawk took the ragged cloak from Talen and poured some of Platime's wine on one corner. Then he vigorously scrubbed his face, removing the remnants of Sephrenia's glue and the purple scar.

"The nose?" Platime asked.

"No. That's real."

"How did it get broken?"

"It's a long story."

Platime shrugged. "Take off your boots and those leather breeches. You'll wear the cloak and those shoes."

Sparhawk pulled off his boots and peeled off the leather hose. Talen draped the cloak around him, then pulled one corner across the front and fastened it to the opposite shoulder so that it covered Sparhawk's body and reached about halfway to his knees.

Platime squinted at him. "Put on the shoes and rub some dirt on your legs. You look a bit too clean." Talen went back to the bin and returned with a scuffed leather cap, a long, slender stick and a length of dirty sackcloth.

"Put on the cap and tie the rag across your eyes," Platime instructed.

Sparhawk did that.

"Can you see well enough through the bandage?"

"I can make things out, but that's about all."

"I don't want you to see too well. You're supposed to be blind. Get him a begging bowl, Talen." Platime turned back to Sparhawk. "Practice walking around a bit. Swing the stick in front of you, but bump into things from time to time and don't forget to stumble."

"It's an interesting idea, Platime, but I know exactly where I'm going. Won't that make people suspicious?"

"Talen will lead you. You'll just be a pair of ordinary beggars."

Sparhawk hitched up his belt and shifted his broadsword around.

"You're going to have to leave that here," Platime told him. "You can hide a dagger under the cloak, but a broadsword's a little too obvious."

"I suppose you're right." Sparhawk pulled out his sword and handed it to the fat man in the orange doublet. "Don't lose it," he said. Then he began to practice the blind man's groping walk, tapping the long, slender stick Talen had given him on the floor as he went.

"Not too bad," Platime said after several minutes.
"You pick things up fast, Sparhawk. It ought to be good
enough to get you by. Talen can teach you how to beg as
you go along."

Talen came back from the large wooden storage box.
His left leg looked grotesquely twisted, and he limped
along with the aid of a crutch. He had removed his gaudy
vest, and he was now dressed in rags.

"Doesn't that hurt?" Sparhawk asked, pointing at the
boy's leg with his stick.

"Not much. All you have to do is walk on the side of
your foot and turn your knee in."

"It looks very convincing."

"Naturally. I've had a lot of practice."

"Are you both ready then?" Platime asked.

"Probably as ready as we'll ever be," Sparhawk replied. "I don't think I'll be very good at begging,
though."

"Talen can teach you the basics. It's not too hard. Good
luck, Sparhawk."

"Thanks. I might need it."

It was the middle of a gray rainy morning when Sparhawk and his young guide emerged from the cellar and
started back down the muddy alleyway. Sef was once again
standing watch in a recessed doorway. He did not speak
to them as they passed.

When they reached the street, Talen took hold of the
corner of Sparhawk's cloak and led him along by it. Sparhawk groped his way behind him, his stick tapping the
cobblestones.

"There are several ways to beg," the boy said after they
had gone a short distance. "Some prefer just to sit and
hold out the begging bowl. That doesn't bring in too many
coins, though—unless you do it outside a church on a day
when the sermon's been about charity. Some people like
to shove the bowl into the face of everybody who walks
by. You get more coins that way, but sometimes it irritates
people, and every so often you'll get punched in the face.
You're supposed to be blind, so we'll have to work out
something a little different."

"Do I have to say anything?"

Talen nodded. "You've got to get their attention. 'Charity' is usually good enough. You don't have time for long speeches, and people don't like to talk with beggars anyway. If somebody decides to give you something, he wants to get it over with as quickly as possible. Make your voice sound hopeless. Whining isn't all that good, but try to put a little catch in your voice—as if you were just about to cry."

"Begging's quite an art, isn't it?"

Talen shrugged. "It's just selling something, that's all. But you've got to do all the selling with just one or two words, so put your heart in it. Do you have any coppers with you?"

"Unless you've stolen them already. Why?"

"When we get to the brothel, you'll need to bait the bowl. Drop in a couple of coppers to make it look as if you've already gotten something."

"I don't quite follow what you've got in mind."

"You want to wait for this Krager to come out, don't you? If you go in after him, you're likely to run into the bruisers who keep order in the place." He looked Sparhawk up and down. "You might be able to deal with them at that, but that sort of thing gets noisy, and the madame would probably send for the watch. It's usually better just to wait outside."

"All right. I suppose we'll wait then."

"We'll station ourselves outside the door and beg until he shows up." The boy paused. "Are you going to kill him?" he asked. "And if you are, can I watch?"

"No. I just want to ask him a few questions."

"Oh." Talen's voice sounded a little disappointed.

It was raining harder now, and Sparhawk's cloak had begun to drip down the backs of his bare legs.

They reached Lion Street and turned left. "The brothel's just up ahead," Talen said, tugging Sparhawk along by the corner of his dripping cloak. Then he stopped suddenly.

"What's the matter?" Sparhawk asked him.

"Competition," Talen replied. "There's a one-legged man leaning against the wall beside the door."

"Begging?"

"What else?"

"Now what?"

"It's no particular problem. I'll just tell him to move on."

"Will he do it?"

Talen nodded. "He will when I tell him that we've rented the spot from Platime. Wait here. I'll be right back."

The boy crutched his way up the rainy street to the red-painted brothel door and spoke briefly with the one-legged beggar stationed there. The man glared at him for a moment, then his leg miraculously unfolded out from under his rough smock and he stalked off, carrying his crutch and muttering to himself. Talen came back down the street and led Sparhawk to the door of the brothel. "Just lean against the wall and hold the bowl out when anybody comes by. Don't hold it right in front of them, though. You're not supposed to be able to see them, so sort of stick it off to one side."

A prosperous-looking merchant came by with his head down and his dark cloak wrapped tightly about him. Sparhawk thrust out his bowl. "Charity," he said in a pleading tone of voice.

The merchant ignored him.

"Not too bad," Talen said. "Try to put that little catch I mentioned in your voice, though."

"Is that why he didn't put anything in the bowl?"

"No. Merchants never do."

"Oh."

Several workmen dressed in leather smocks came along the street. They were talking loudly and were a bit unsteady on their feet.

"Charity," Sparhawk said to them.

Talen sniffled, wiping his nose on his sleeve. "Please, good masters," he said in a choked voice. "Can you help my poor blind father and me?"

"Why not?" one of the workmen said good-humoredly. He fished around in one of his pockets, drew out a few coins, and looked at them. Then he selected one small copper and dropped it into Sparhawk's bowl.

One of the others sniggered. "He's trying to get enough together to go in and visit the girls," he said.

"That's his business, isn't it?" the generous one replied as they went on down the street.

"First blood," Talen said. "Put the copper in your pocket. We don't want the bowl to have *too* many coins in it."

In the next hour, Sparhawk and his youthful instructor picked up about a dozen more coins. It became challenging after the first few times, and Sparhawk felt a small surge of triumph each time he managed to wheedle a coin out of a passerby.

Then an ornate carriage drawn by a matched pair of black horses came up the street and stopped in front of the red door. A liveried young footman jumped down from the back, lowered a step from the side of the vehicle, and opened the door. A nobleman dressed all in green velvet stepped out. Sparhawk knew him.

"I may be a while, love," the nobleman said, fondly touching the footman's boyish face. "Take the carriage up the street and watch for me." He giggled girlishly. "Someone might recognize it, and I certainly wouldn't want people to think I was frequenting a place like *this*." He rolled his eyes and then minced toward the red door.

"Charity for the blind," Sparhawk begged, thrusting out his bowl.

"Out of my way, knave," the nobleman said, fluttering one hand as if shooing away a bothersome fly. He opened the door and went inside as the carriage moved off.

"Peculiar," Sparhawk murmured.

"Wasn't he, though?" Talen grinned.

"Now that's a sight I thought I'd never see—the Baron Harparin going into a brothel."

"Noblemen get urges, too, don't they?"

"Harparin gets urges, all right, but I don't think the girls inside would satisfy them. He might find *you* interesting, though."

Talen flushed. "Never mind *that*," he said.

Sparhawk frowned. "Why would Harparin go into the same brothel where Krager's staying?" he mused.

"Do they know each other?"

"I wouldn't think so. Harparin's a member of the council and a close friend of the Primate Annias. Krager's a third-rate toad. If they're meeting in there, I'd give a great deal to hear what they're saying."

"Go on in, then."

"What?"

"It's a public place, and blind men need affection, too. Just don't start any fights." Talen looked around cautiously. "Once you get inside, ask for Naween. She works for Platime on the side. Tell her that he sent you. She'll get you to someplace where you can eavesdrop."

"Does Platime control the whole city?"

"Only the underside of it. Annias runs the top half."

"Are you going in with me?"

Talen shook his head. "Shanda's got a twisted sense of morality. She doesn't allow children inside—not male ones, anyway."

"Shanda?"

"The madame of this place."

"I probably should have guessed. Krager's mistress is named Shanda—Thin woman?"

Talen nodded. "With a very sour mouth?"

"That's her."

"Does she know you?"

"We met once about twelve years ago."

"The bandage hides most of your face, and the light inside isn't too good. You should be able to get by if you change your voice a bit. Go on in. I'll stay out here and keep watch. I know every policeman and spy in Cimmura by sight."

"All right."

"Have you got the price for a girl? I can lend you some if you need it. Shanda won't let you see any of her whores unless you pay her first."

"I can manage it—unless you've picked my pocket again."

"Would I do that, my Lord?"

"Probably, yes. I might be in there for a while."

"Enjoy yourself. Naween's very frisky—or so I've been told."

Sparhawk ignored that. He opened the red-painted door and went inside.

The hallway he entered was dim and filled with the cloyingly sweet scent of cheap perfume. Maintaining his pose as a blind man, Sparhawk swung his stick from side to side, tapping the walls. "Hello," he called in a squeaky voice. "Is anybody here?"

The door at the far end of the hall opened, and a thin woman in a yellow velvet dress emerged. She had limp, dirty-blonde hair, a disapproving expression, and eyes as hard as agates. "What do you want?" she demanded. "You can't beg in here."

"I'm not here to beg," Sparhawk replied. "I'm here to buy—or at least rent."

"Have you got money?"

"Yes."

"Let's see it."

Sparhawk reached inside his ragged cloak and took several coins out of a pocket. He held them out on the palm of his hand.

The thin woman's eyes narrowed shrewdly.

"Don't even think about it," he told her.

"You're not blind," she accused him.

"You noticed."

"What's your pleasure, then?" she asked.

"A friend told me to ask for Naween."

"Ah, Naween. She's been very popular lately. I'll send for her—just as soon as you pay."

"How much?"

"Ten coppers—or a silver half crown."

Sparhawk gave her a small silver coin, and she went back through the door. She came back a moment later with a buxom brunette girl of about twenty. "This is Naween," Shanda said. "I hope you enjoy yourselves." She simpered briefly at Sparhawk, then the smile seemed to drain off her face. She turned and went back into the room at the end of the hall.

"You're not really blind, are you?" Naween asked coquettishly. She was wrapped in a sleazy-looking dressing gown of bright red, and her cheeks were dimpled.

"No," Sparhawk admitted, "not really."

"Good. I've never done a blind man before, so I wouldn't know what to expect. Let's go upstairs, shall we?" She led him to a stairway that climbed into the upper parts of the house. "Anything in particular that you'd like?" She asked, smiling back over her shoulder at him.

"At the moment, I'd like to listen," he told her.

"Listen? To what?"

"Platime sent me. Shanda's got a friend staying here—a fellow named Krager."

"Mousy-looking little man with bad eyes?"

"That's him. A nobleman dressed in green velvet just came in here, and I think that he and Krager might be talking. I'd like to hear what they're saying. Can you arrange it?" He reached up and took the bandage off his eyes.

"Then you don't really want to. . . ?" She left it hanging, and her generous lower lip took on a slight pout.

"Not today, little sister," he told her. "I've got other things on my mind."

She sighed. "I like your looks, friend," she said. "We could have had a very nice time."

"Some other day, maybe. Can you take me someplace where I can hear what Krager and his friend are saying?"

She sighed again. "I suppose so," she said. "It's on up the stairs. We can use Feather's room. She's visiting her mother."

"Her mother?"

"Whores have mothers, too, you know. Feather's room is right next to the one where Shanda's friend is staying. If you put your ear to the wall, you should be able to hear what's going on."

"Good. Let's go. I don't want to miss anything."

The room near the far end of the upper hallway was small, and its furnishings were sparse. A single candle burned on the table. Naween closed the door, then she removed the dressing gown and lay down on the bed. "Just for the sake of appearances," she whispered archly, "in case someone looks in on us. *Or* in case you change your mind later." She gave him a suggestive little leer.

"Which wall is it?" he asked in a low voice.

"That one." She pointed.

He crossed the room and put the side of his head to the wall's grimy surface.

". . . to my Lord Martel," a familiar voice was saying. "I need something that proves that you're really from Annias and that what you tell me comes from him."

It was Krager. Sparhawk grinned exultantly and continued to listen.

CHAPTER
SEVEN

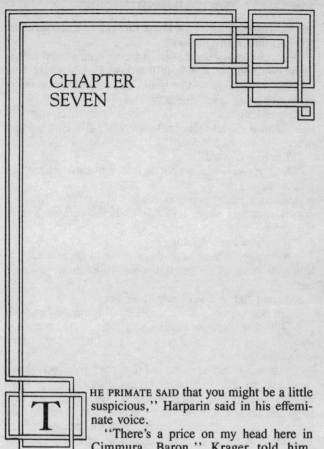

T HE PRIMATE SAID that you might be a little suspicious," Harparin said in his effeminate voice.

"There's a price on my head here in Cimmura, Baron," Krager told him. "Under those circumstances, a certain amount of caution seems to be in order."

"Would you recognize the primate's signature—and his seal—if you saw them?"

"I would," Krager replied.

"Good. Here's a note from him that will identify me. Destroy it after you've read it."

"I don't think so. Martel might want to see the proof with his own eyes." Krager paused. "Why didn't Annias just write down his instructions?"

"Be sensible, Krager," Harparin said. "A message can fall into unfriendly hands."

"So can a messenger. Have you ever seen what the Pandions do to people who have information they want?"

"We would assume that you'd take steps to keep yourself from being questioned."

Krager laughed derisively. "Not a chance, Harparin," he said in a slightly slurred voice. "My life isn't all that much, but it's all I've got."

"You're a coward."

"And you're—whatever it is that you are. Let me see that note."

Sparhawk heard paper rustling. "All right," Krager's mushy-sounding voice said. "This is the primate's seal, I'll agree."

"Have you been drinking?"

"Naturally. What else is there to do in Cimmura? Unless you have other entertainments—like some I could name."

"I don't like you very much, Krager."

"I'm not fond of you either, Harparin, but we can both live with that, can't we? Just give me the message and go away. That perfume you're wearing is beginning to turn my stomach."

There was a stiff silence, and then the baron spoke very precisely, as if to a child or a simpleton. "This is what the Primate Annias wants you to say to Martel: Tell him to gather up as many men as he'll need and to dress them all in black armor. They are to carry the banners of the Pandion Knights—any seamstress can counterfeit them for you, and Martel knows what they look like. They are then to ride with great show to the castle of Count Radun, uncle of King Dregos of Arcium. Do you know the place?"

"It's on the road between Darra and Sarrinium, isn't it?"

"Precisely. Count Radun is a pious man and he'll admit the Church Knights without question. Once Martel is inside the walls, his men are to kill the inhabitants. There shouldn't be much resistance, because Radun doesn't maintain a large garrison. He has a wife and a number of unmarried daughters. Annias wants them all repeatedly raped.''

Krager laughed. ''Adus would do that anyway.''

''Good, but tell him not to be self-conscious about it. Radun has several churchmen in his castle. We want them to witness it all. After Adus and the others finish with the women, cut their throats. Radun is to be tortured and then beheaded. Take his head with you when you leave, but leave enough personal jewelry and clothing on the body so that it can be identified. Butcher everybody else in the castle, *except* for the churchmen. After they've witnessed everything, let them go.''

''Why?''

''To report the outrage to King Dregos at Larium.''

''The idea then is that Dregos will declare war on the Pandions?''

''Not quite, no—although that's possible, too. As soon as the business is finished, dispatch a man on a fast horse to me here in Cimmura to tell me that it's been done.''

Krager laughed again. ''Only an idiot would carry that kind of message. He'd have a dozen knives in him as soon as he finished talking.''

''You *are* suspicious, aren't you, Krager?''

''Better suspicious than dead, and the people Martel will hire are likely all to feel pretty much the same way. You'd better tell me a little more about this scheme, Harparin.''

''You don't need to know any more.''

''Martel will. He won't be a cat's-paw for anybody.''

Harparin muttered an oath. ''All right then. The Pandions have been interfering with the primate's activities. This atrocity will give him an excuse to confine them in their motherhouse at Demos again. Then he will personally carry a report of the affair to Chyrellos to lay before the Church Hierocracy and the archprelate himself. They will have no choice but to disband the Pandion Order. The leaders—Vanion, Sparhawk, and the others—will be imprisoned in the dungeons beneath the Basilica of Chyrellos. No man has ever come out of those dungeons alive.''

''Martel will like that idea.''

"Annias thought that he might. The Styric woman, Se-phrenia, will be burned as a witch, of course."

"We'll be well rid of her." There was another pause. "There's more, isn't there?" Krager added.

Harparin did not answer.

"Don't be coy, Harparin," Krager told him. "If *I* can see through all this, you can be sure that Martel will, too. Let's have the rest of it."

"All right." Harparin's voice was sullen. "The Pandions are likely to resist confinement and they'll certainly try to protect their leaders. At that point, the army will move against them. That will give Annias and the royal council an excuse to declare a state of emergency and to suspend certain laws."

"Which laws are those?"

"The ones having to do with the succession to the throne. Elenia will technically be in a state of war, and Ehlana is obviously in no condition to deal with that. She'll abdicate in favor of her cousin, the Prince Regent Lycheas."

"Arissa's bastard—the sniveler?"

"Legitimacy can be bestowed by a decree of the council, and I'd really watch what I say about Lycheas, Krager. Disrespect for the king is high treason and it *can* be made retroactive, you know."

There was an apprehensive silence. "Wait a minute," Krager said then. "I've heard that Ehlana's unconscious— and sealed in some kind of crystal."

"That's no particular problem."

"How can she sign the instrument of abdication?"

Harparin laughed. "There's a monk at the monastery near Lenda. He's been practicing the queen's signature for a month now. He's very good."

"Clever. What happens to her after she abdicates?"

"As soon as Lycheas is crowned king, we'll give her a splendid funeral."

"But she's still alive, isn't she?"

"So? If need be, we'll entomb her throne and all."

"There's only one problem then, isn't there?"

"I don't see any problem."

"That's because you're not looking, Harparin. The pri-

mate is going to have to move very fast. If the Pandions
find out about this before he can get to the Hierocracy in
Chyrellos, they'll take steps to counter his accusations.''

"We're aware of that. That's why you have to send the
message to me as soon as the count and his people are
dead.''

"The message would never reach you. Any man we
send will realize that he'll be killed as soon as he delivers
it—and he'll find an excuse to go to Lamorkand or Pelosia
instead.'' Krager paused. "Let me see that ring of yours,''
he said.

"My ring? Why?''

"It's a signet, isn't it?''

"Yes—with the coat of arms of my family.''

"All noblemen have rings like that, don't they?''

"Of course.''

"Good. Tell Annias to pay close attention to the collection plate in the cathedral of Cimmura here. One of these
days a ring will show up among the pennies. The ring will
bear the coat of arms of Count Radun's family. He'll understand the message, and the messenger can slip away
unharmed.''

"I don't think Annias will like that.''

"He doesn't have to like it. All right, how much?''

"How much what?''

"Money. What is Annias willing to pay Martel for his
assistance? He's getting the crown for Lycheas and absolute control of Elenia for himself. What's it worth to him?''

"He told me to mention the sum of ten thousand gold
crowns.''

Krager laughed. "I think Martel might want to negoti-
ate that point just a bit.''

"Time is important here, Krager.''

"Then Annias probably won't be too stubborn about the
price, will he? Why don't you go back to the palace and
suggest to him that a bit more generosity might be in order? I could wind up spending the whole winter riding
back and forth between Annias and Martel carrying pro-
posals and counterproposals.''

"There's only so much money in the treasury, Krager.''

"Simplicity in itself, my dear Baron. Just increase taxes—or have Annias dip into church funds."

"Where is Martel now?"

"I'm not at liberty to say."

Sparhawk swore under his breath and took his ear away from the wall.

"Was it interesting?" Naween asked. She still lounged on the bed.

"Very."

She stretched voluptuously. "Are you sure that you won't change your mind?" she asked. "Now that you've taken care of your business?"

"Sorry, little sister," Sparhawk declined. "I've got a great deal left to do today. Besides, I've already paid Shanda your price. Why work if you don't have to?"

"Professional ethics, I suppose. Besides, I sort of like you, my big broken-nosed friend."

"I'm flattered." He reached into his pocket, took out a gold coin, and gave it to her. She stared at him in amazed gratitude. "I'll slip out the front door before Krager's friend gets ready to leave," he told her. He went to the door.

"Come back sometime when your mind's not so occupied," she whispered.

"I'll think about it," he promised. He tied the bandage over his eyes again, opened the door, and stepped quietly into the hall. Then he went on down into the dimly lit lower hall and back out to the street.

Talen was leaning against the wall beside the door, trying to stay out of the rain. "Did you have fun?" he asked.

"I found out what I needed to know."

"That's not what I meant. Naween's supposed to be the best in Cimmura."

"I really wouldn't know about that. I was there on business."

"I'm disappointed in you, Sparhawk." Talen grinned impudently, "But probably not nearly so much as Naween was. They say that she's a girl who likes her work."

"You've got a nasty mind, Talen."

"I know, and you've got no idea how much I enjoy it." His young face grew serious, and he looked around cautiously. "Sparhawk," he said, "is somebody following you?"

"It's possible, I suppose."

"I'm not talking about a church soldier. There was a man at the far end of the street—at least I think it was a man. He was wearing a monk's habit, and the hood covered his face, so I couldn't be sure."

"There are a lot of monks in Cimmura."

"Not like this one. It made me cold all over just to look at him."

Sparhawk looked at him sharply. "Have you ever had this kind of feeling before, Talen?"

"Once. Platime had sent me to the west gate to meet somebody. Some Styrics were coming into the city, and after they passed, I couldn't even keep my mind on what I was supposed to be doing. It was two days before I could shake off the feeling."

There was not really any point in telling the boy the truth about the matter. Many people were sensitives, and it seldom went any further. "I wouldn't worry about it," Sparhawk advised. "We all get these peculiar feelings now and then."

"Maybe," Talen said dubiously.

"We're finished here," Sparhawk said. "Let's go back to Platime's place."

The rainy streets of Cimmura were a bit more crowded now, filled with nobles wearing brightly colored cloaks and with workmen dressed in plain brown or gray. Sparhawk was obliged to grope his way along, swinging his blindman's stick in front of him to avoid suspicion. It was noon by the time he and Talen descended the steps into the cellar again.

"Why didn't you wake me up?" Kalten demanded crossly. He was sitting on the edge of his cot holding a bowl of thick stew.

"You needed your rest." Sparhawk untied the bandage from his eyes. "Besides, it's raining out there."

"Did you see Krager?"

"No, but I heard him, which is just as good." Sparhawk went on around the firepit to where Platime sat. "Can you get me a wagon and a driver?" he asked.

"If you need one." Platime lifted his silver tankard and drank noisily, spilling beer on the front of his spotted orange doublet.

"I do," Sparhawk said. "Kalten and I have to get back to the chapterhouse. The primate's soldiers are probably still looking for us, so I thought that we could hide in the back of a wagon to stay out of sight."

"Wagons don't move very fast. Wouldn't a carriage with the curtains drawn be faster?"

"Do you have a carriage?"

"Several, actually. God's been good to me lately."

"I'm delighted to hear it." Sparhawk turned. "Talen," he called.

The boy came over to where he was standing.

"How much money did you steal from me this morning?"

Talen's face grew cautious. "Not too much. Why?"

"Be more specific."

"Seven coppers and one silver piece. You're a friend, so I put the gold coins back in your pocket."

"I'm touched."

"You want the money back, I suppose."

"Keep it—as payment for your services."

"You're generous, my Lord."

"I'm not finished yet. I want you to keep an eye on Krager for me. I think I'm going to be out of town for a while and I want to keep track of him. If he leaves Cimmura, go to the inn on Rose Street. Do you know it?"

"The one that's run by the Pandions?"

"How did you find out about that?"

"Everybody knows about it."

Sparhawk let that pass. "Knock on the gate three times, then pause. Then knock twice more. A porter will open the gate. Be polite to him because he's a knight. Tell him that the man Sparhawk was interested in has left town. Try to give him the direction Krager took. Can you remember all that?"

"Do you want me to recite it back to you?"

"That won't be necessary. The knight porter at the inn will give you half a crown for the information."

Talen's eyes brightened.

Sparhawk turned back to Platime. "Thank you, my friend," he said. "Consider your debt to my father paid."

"I've already forgotten it." The fat man grinned.

"Platime's very good at forgetting debts," Talen said. "The ones he owes, anyway."

"Someday your mouth is going to get you in serious trouble, boy."

"Nothing that my feet can't carry me away from."

"Go tell Sef to hitch the gray team to the carriage with the blue wheels and to bring it to the alley door."

"What's in it for me?"

"I'll postpone the thrashing I'm just about to give you."

"That sounds fair." The boy grinned and scampered away.

"That's a very clever young man," Sparhawk said.

"He's the best," Platime agreed. "It's my guess that he'll replace me when I retire."

"He's the crown prince, then."

Platime laughed uproariously. "The crown prince of thieves. It has a nice ring to it, doesn't it? You know, I like you, Sparhawk." Still laughing, the fat man clapped the big knight on the shoulder. "If there's ever anything else I can do for you, let me know."

"I will, Platime."

"I'll even give you a special rate."

"Thanks," Sparhawk said drily. He picked up his sword from beside Platime's chair and went back to his cot to change back into his own clothes.

"How are you feeling?" he asked Kalten.

"I'm fine."

"Good. You'd better get ready to leave."

"Where are we going?"

"Back to the chapterhouse. I found out something that Vanion needs to know."

The carriage was not new, but it was soundly constructed and well maintained. The windows were draped with heavy curtains which effectively hid the passengers from prying eyes. The team which drew the carriage was a pair of matched grays, and they moved out at a brisk trot.

Kalten leaned back against the leather cushion. "Is it

my imagination, or does thieving pay better than knighting?''

"We didn't go into the business for the money, Kalten," Sparhawk reminded him.

"That's painfully obvious, my friend." Kalten stretched out his legs and crossed his arms contentedly. "You know," he said, "I could get to like this sort of thing."

"Try not to," Sparhawk advised him.

"You have to admit that it's a great deal more comfortable than pounding your backside on a hard saddle."

"Discomfort's good for the soul."

"My soul's just fine, Sparhawk. It's my behind that's starting to wear out."

The carriage moved rapidly through the streets, and they soon passed through the east gate of the city and pulled up at the drawbridge of the chapterhouse. Sparhawk and Kalten stepped out into the drizzly afternoon, and Sef immediately turned the carriage around and clattered back toward the city.

Following the ritual which gained them entrance into the fortified house, Sparhawk and Kalten went immediately to the preceptor's study in the south tower.

Vanion was seated at the large table in the center of the room with a stack of documents in front of him, and Sephrenia sat by the crackling fire with her ever-present teacup in her hand. She was looking into the dancing flames, her eyes a mystery.

Vanion looked up and saw the bloodstains on Kalten's doublet. "What happened?" he asked.

"Our disguises didn't work." Kalten shrugged. "A group of church soldiers waylaid us in an alley. It's not serious."

Sephrenia rose from her chair and came over to them. "Did you have it tended?" she asked.

"Sparhawk put a bandage on it."

"Why don't you let me look at it? Sometimes Sparhawk's bandages are a little rudimentary. Sit down and open your doublet."

Kalten grumbled a bit, but did as he was told.

She untied the bandage and looked at the cut in his side

with pursed lips. "Did you clean it at all?" she asked Sparhawk.

"I wiped it down with some wine."

She sighed. "Oh, Sparhawk." She rose, went to the door, and sent one of the young knights outside for the things she would need.

"Sparhawk picked up some information," Kalten told the preceptor.

"What kind of information?" Vanion asked.

"I found Krager," Sparhawk told him, drawing up a chair. "He's staying in a brothel near the west gate."

One of Sephrenia's eyebrows shot up. "What were you doing in a brothel, Sparhawk?"

"It's a long story," he replied, flushing slightly. "Someday I'll tell you all about it. Anyway," he continued, "the Baron Harparin came to the brothel, and—"

"Harparin?" Vanion looked startled. "In a brothel? He had less business there than you did."

"He was there to meet with Krager. I managed to get inside and into the room next to the one where they were meeting." He quickly sketched out the details of the involuted scheme of the Primate Annias.

Vanion's eyes were narrow as Sparhawk finished his report. "Annias is even more ruthless than I'd imagined," he said. "I never thought that he'd stoop to mass murder."

"We're going to stop them, aren't we?" Kalten asked as Sephrenia began to cleanse his wound.

"Of course we are," Vanion replied absently. He stared up at the ceiling, his eyes lost in thought. "I think I see a way to turn this around." He looked at Kalten. "Are you fit to ride?" he asked.

"This is hardly more than a scratch," Kalten assured him as Sephrenia laid a compress over the cut.

"Good. I want you to go to the motherhouse at Demos. Take every man you can get your hands on and start out for Count Radun's castle in Arcium. Stay off the main roads. We don't want Martel to know you're coming. Sparhawk, I want you to lead the knights from here in Cimmura. Join Kalten down there in Arcium someplace."

Sparhawk shook his head. "If we ride out in a body, Annias will know that we're up to something. If he gets suspicious, he could postpone the whole thing and then attack the count's castle some other time when we aren't around.''

Vanion frowned. "That's true, isn't it? Maybe you could sneak your men out of Cimmura a few at a time."

"It would take too long that way," Sephrenia told him, winding a clean bandage around Kalten's waist, "and sneaking attracts more attention than riding out openly." She pursed her lips in thought. "Does the order still own that cloister on the road to Cardos?" she asked.

Vanion nodded. "It's in total disrepair, though."

"Wouldn't this be an excellent time to restore it?"

"I don't quite follow you, Sephrenia."

"We need to find some excuse for most of the Pandions here in Cimmura to ride out of town together. If you were to go to the palace and tell the council that you're going to take all your knights and go repair that cloister, Annias would think you're playing right into his hands. Then you could take wagonloads of tools and building materials to make it look genuine and leave town with them. Once you're out of Cimmura, you can change direction with no one the wiser.''

"It sounds workable, Vanion," Sparhawk said. "Will you be coming with us?"

"No," Vanion replied. "I'm going to have to ride to Chyrellos and alert a few friendly members of the Church Hierocracy to what Annias has planned."

Sparhawk nodded; then he remembered something. "I'm not entirely positive about this," he said, "but I think there's someone here in Cimmura who's been watching me, and I don't think he's an Elene." He smiled at Sephrenia. "I've been trained to recognize the subtle touch of a Styric mind. Anyway, this watcher seems to be able to pick me out no matter what kind of disguise I wear. I'm almost certain that he's the one who set the church soldiers on Kalten and me, and that means that he has ties to Annias.''

"What does he look like?" Sephrenia asked him.

"I can't really say. He wears a hooded robe and keeps his face hidden."

"He can't report to Annias if he's dead," Kalten

shrugged. "Lay an ambush for him somewhere on the road to Cardos."

"Isn't that a little direct?" Sephrenia asked disapprovingly, tying the bandage firmly in place.

"I'm a simple man, Sephrenia. Complications confuse me."

"I want to work out a few more details," Vanion said. He looked at Sephrenia. "Kalten and I will be riding together as far as Demos. Do you want to return to the motherhouse?"

"No," she replied. "I'll go with Sparhawk just in case this Styric who's been watching him tries to follow us. I should be able to deal with that without resorting to murder."

"All right, then," Vanion said, rising to his feet. "Sparhawk, you and Kalten go see to the wagons and the building materials. I'll go to the palace and lie a little bit. As soon as I get back, we'll all leave."

"And what would you like to have me do, Vanion?" Sephrenia asked him.

He smiled. "Why don't you have another cup of tea, Sephrenia?"

"Thank you, Vanion. I believe I will."

CHAPTER EIGHT

T HE WEATHER HAD turned cold, and the sullen afternoon sky was spitting pellets of hard-frozen snow. A hundred cloaked and black-armored Pandion Knights rode at a jingling trot through the heavily forested region near the Arcian border with Sparhawk and Sephrenia in the lead. They had been travelling for five days.

Sparhawk glanced up at the sky and reined in the black horse he was riding. The horse reared, pawing at the air with his front hooves. "Oh, stop that," Sparhawk told him irritably.

"He's very enthusiastic, isn't he?" Sephrenia said.

"He's also not very bright. I'll be glad when we catch up with Kalten and I can get Faran back."

"Why are we stopping?"

"It's close to evening, and that grove over there seems to be fairly clear of undergrowth. We may as well set up our night's encampment here." He raised his voice then, calling back over his shoulder. "Sir Parasim," he shouted.

The young knight with the butter-colored hair rode forward. "Yes, my Lord Sparhawk?" he said in his light tenor voice.

"We'll stop for the night here," Sparhawk told him. "As soon as the wagons get here, set up Sephrenia's tent for her and see to it that she has everything she needs."

"Of course, my Lord."

The sky had turned a chill purple by the time Sparhawk had overseen the setting up of their encampment and had posted sentries. He walked past the tents and the flickering cook fires to join Sephrenia at the small fire before her tent, which was set slightly apart from the rest of the camp. He smiled when he saw her ever-present teakettle hanging from a metal tripod which she had set over the flames.

"Something amusing, Sparhawk?" she asked.

"No," he said. "Not really." He looked back toward the youthful knights moving around their cook fires. "They all seem so young," he said almost as if to himself, "hardly more than boys."

"That's the nature of things, Sparhawk. The old make the decisions, and the young carry them out."

"Was I ever that young?"

She laughed. "Oh yes, dear Sparhawk," she told him. "You couldn't begin to believe how young you and Kalten were when you came to me for your first lessons. I felt as if a pair of babies had been placed in my care."

He made a rueful face. "I guess that answers that question, doesn't it?" He held out his hands to the warmth of her fire. "It's a cold night. I think my blood thinned out while I was in Jiroch. I haven't been really warm since I came back to Elenia. Did Parasim bring you your supper?"

"Yes. He's a very nice boy, isn't he?"

Sparhawk laughed. "He'd probably be offended if he heard you say that."

"It's the truth, isn't it?"

"Of course, but he'd be offended all the same. Young knights are always sensitive."

"Have you ever heard him sing?"

"Once. In chapel."

"He has a glorious voice, doesn't he?"

Sparhawk nodded. "I don't think he really belongs in a militant order. A regular monastery would probably suit his temperament a little better." He looked around, then stepped outside the circle of firelight, dragged a log to the side of the fire, and covered it with his cloak. "It's not exactly an easy chair," he apologized, "but it's better than sitting on the ground."

"Thank you, Sparhawk." She smiled. "That was very thoughtful of you."

"I do have a few manners, I suppose." He looked at her gravely. "This is going to be a hard journey for you, I'm afraid."

"I can endure it, my dear."

"Perhaps, but don't go out of your way to be unnecessarily brave. If you get tired or cold, don't hesitate to say something to me."

"I'll be just fine, Sparhawk. Styrics are a hardy people."

"Sephrenia," he said then, "how long will it be until the twelve knights who were in the throne room with you begin to die?"

"That's really impossible to say, Sparhawk."

"Will you know—each time it happens, I mean?"

"Yes. At the moment, I'm the one to whom their swords will be delivered."

"Their swords?"

"The swords were the instruments of the spell, and they symbolize the burden that must be passed on."

"Wouldn't it have been wiser to have distributed that responsibility?"

"I chose not to."

"That might have been a mistake."

"Perhaps, but it was mine to make."

He began to pace angrily. "We should be working on a cure instead of riding halfway across Arcium," he burst out.

"This is important, too, Sparhawk."

"I couldn't bear to lose you and Ehlana," he said, "and Vanion, too."

"There's still time, dear one."

He sighed. "Are you all settled in, then?" he asked her.

"Yes. I have everything I need."

"Try to get a good night's sleep. We'll be starting early. Good night, Sephrenia."

"Sleep well, Sparhawk."

HE AWOKE AS daybreak had begun to spread its light through the wood. He strapped on his armor, shivering at the touch of the cold plate. He emerged from the tent he shared with five other knights and looked around the sleeping camp. Sephrenia's fire was flickering in front of her tent again, and her white robe gleamed in the steely light of dawn and the glow of her fire.

"You're up early," he said as he approached her.

"So are you. How far is it to the border?"

"We should cross into Arcium today."

And then from somewhere out in the forest they heard a strange, flutelike sound. The melody was in a minor key, but it was not sad; rather it seemed filled with an ageless joy.

Sephrenia's eyes grew wide, and she made a peculiar gesture with her right hand.

"A shepherd maybe?" Sparhawk said.

"No," she replied. "Not a shepherd." She stood up. "Come with me, Sparhawk," she said, and then she led him away from the fire.

The sky was growing lighter as they moved out into the meadow lying just to the south of their encampment, following the flutelike sound. They approached the sentry Sparhawk had stationed there.

"You heard it, too, my Lord Sparhawk?" the black-armored knight asked.

"Yes. Can you see who it is or where it's coming from?"

"I can't make out who it is yet, but it seems to be

coming from that tree out in the center of the meadow. Do you want me to come along with you?''

"No. Stay here. We'll investigate.''

Sephrenia had already gone on ahead, moving directly toward the tree that seemed to be the source of the strange melody.

"You'd better let me go first,'' Sparhawk said when he caught up with her.

"There's no danger, Sparhawk.''

When they reached the tree, Sparhawk peered up through the shadowy limbs and saw the mysterious musician. It was a little girl of six or so. Her long hair was black and glossy, and her large eyes were as deep as night. A headband of plaited grass encircled her brow, holding her hair back. She was sitting on a limb breathing sound into a simple, many-chambered set of pipes such as a goatherd might play. Although it was quite cold, she wore only a short, belted linen smock that left her arms and legs bare. Her grass-stained, unshod feet were crossed, and she perched on the limb with a sedate sureness.

"What's she doing here?'' Sparhawk asked, puzzled. "There aren't any houses or villages around.''

"I think she's been waiting for us,'' Sephrenia replied.

"That doesn't make any sense.'' He looked up at the child. "What's your name, little girl?'' he asked.

"Let me question her, Sparhawk,'' Sephrenia said. "She's a Styric child, and they tend to be shy.'' She pushed back her hood and spoke to the little girl in a dialect Sparhawk did not understand.

The child lowered her rude pipe and smiled. Her lips were like a small, pink bow.

Sephrenia asked her another question in a strange, gentle tone.

The little girl shook her head.

"Does she live in some house back in the forest?'' Sparhawk asked.

"She has no home nearby,'' Sephrenia said.

"Doesn't she talk?''

"She chooses not to.''

Sparhawk looked around. "Well, we can't leave her

here." He reached up his arms to the child. "Come down, little girl," he said.

She smiled at him and slipped off the limb into his hands. Her weight was very slight, and her hair smelled of grass and trees. She confidently put her arms about his neck and then wrinkled her nose at the smell of his armor.

He set her down on her feet, and she immediately went to Sephrenia, took the small woman's hands in hers, and kissed them. Something peculiarly Styric seemed to pass between the woman and the little girl, something that Sparhawk could not understand. Sephrenia lifted the child into her arms and held her close. "What will we do with her, Sparhawk?" she asked in a strangely intent tone. For some reason it seemed very important to her.

"We'll have to take her with us, I guess—at least until we find some people to leave her with. Let's go back to camp and see if we can find something for her to wear."

"And some breakfast, I think."

"Would you like that, Flute?" Sparhawk asked the child.

The little girl smiled and nodded.

"Why did you call her that?" Sephrenia asked him.

"We have to call her something, at least until we find out her real name—if she has one. Let's go back to the fire where it's warm." He turned and led the way back across the meadow toward the camp.

They crossed the border into Arcium near the city of Dieros, once again avoiding contact with the local inhabitants. They paralleled the road leading eastward, staying well back from that heavily travelled highway. The countryside of the kingdom of Arcium was noticeably different from that of Elenia. Unlike its northern neighbor, Arcium seemed to be a kingdom of walls. They stretched along the roads or cut across open pastureland, often for no apparent reason. The walls were thick and high, and Sparhawk was frequently obliged to lead his knights on long detours to go around them. Wryly he remembered the words of a twenty-fourth century patriarch of the Church who, after travelling from Chyrellos to Larium, had referred to Arcium as "God's rock garden."

The following day they entered a large forest of winter-bare birch trees. As they rode deeper into the chill wood, Sparhawk began to smell smoke and he soon saw a dark pall lying low among the stark white tree trunks. He halted the column and rode on ahead to investigate.

He had gone perhaps a mile when he came to a cluster of rudely built Styric houses. They were all on fire, and bodies littered the open area around the houses. Sparhawk began to swear. He wheeled the young black horse and galloped back to where he had left his troops.

"What is it?" Sephrenia asked him, looking at his bleak expression. "Where's the smoke coming from?"

"There was a Styric village up ahead," he replied darkly. "We both know what the smoke means."

"Ah." She sighed.

"You'd better keep the little girl back here until I can get a burial detail up there."

"No, Sparhawk. This sort of thing is a part of her heritage, too. All Styrics know that it happens. Besides, I might be able to help the survivors—if there are any."

"Have it your own way," he said shortly. A huge rage had descended upon him, and he curtly motioned the column forward.

There was some evidence that the hapless Styrics had made an attempt to defend themselves, but that they had been swarmed under by people carrying only the crudest of weapons. Sparhawk put his men to work—some of them digging graves and others extinguishing the fires.

Sephrenia came across the littered field, her face deathly pale. "There are only a few women among the dead," she reported. "I'd guess that the rest fled back into the woods."

"See if you can persuade them to come back," he said. He looked over at Sir Parasim, who was weeping openly as he spaded dirt out of a grave. The young knight was obviously not emotionally suited for this kind of work. "Parasim," Sparhawk ordered, "go with Sephrenia."

"Yes, my Lord," Parasim sobbed, dropping his spade.

The dead were finally all committed to the earth, and Sparhawk briefly murmured an Elene prayer over the graves. It was probably not appropriate for Styrics, but he didn't really know what else to do.

After about an hour, Sephrenia and Parasim returned. "Any luck?" Sparhawk asked her.

"We found them," she replied, "but they won't come out of the woods."

"I can't really blame them very much," he said. "We'll see if we can fix up at least a few of these houses for them to keep them out of the weather."

"Don't waste your time, Sparhawk. They won't come back to this place. That's a part of the Styric religion."

"Did they give you some idea of which way the Elenes who did this went?"

"What are you planning, Sparhawk?"

"Chastisement. That's a part of the Elene religion."

"No. I won't tell you which way they went, if that's what you've got in mind."

"I'm not going to let this pass, Sephrenia. You can tell me or not, whichever you choose. I can find their trail by myself if I need to."

She looked at him helplessly. Then her eyes became shrewd. "A bargain, Sparhawk?" she suggested.

"I'll listen."

"I'll tell you where to find them if you promise not to kill anybody."

"All right," he agreed grudgingly, his face still black with anger. "Which way did they go?"

"I'm not done yet," she said. "You'll stay here with me. I know you, and you sometimes go to extremes. Send someone else to do it."

He glared at her, then turned. "Lakus!" he bellowed.

"No," she said, "not Lakus. He's as bad as you are."

"Who, then?"

"Parasim, I think."

"Parasim?"

"He's a gentler person. If we tell him not to kill anybody, he won't make any mistakes."

"All right, then," he said from between clenched teeth. "Parasim," he said to the young knight standing sorrowfully nearby, "take a dozen men and run down the animals who did this. Don't kill anybody, but make them all very, very sorry that they ever came up with the idea."

"Yes, my Lord," Parasim said, his eyes suddenly glinting like steel. Sephrenia gave him directions, and he started back to where the other knights were gathered. On his way, he stopped and uprooted a thorn bush. He seized it in one gauntleted fist and swung it very hard at an unoffending birch tree, ripping off a fair-sized chunk of white bark.

"Oh, dear," Sephrenia murmured.

"He'll do just fine." Sparhawk laughed mirthlessly. "I have great hopes for that young man and great faith in his sense of the appropriate."

Some distance away, Flute was standing over the scattered graves. She was playing her pipes softly, and her melody seemed to convey eons of sorrow.

The weather continued cold and unpleasant, though no significant amounts of snow fell. After a week of steady travel, they reached a ruined castle some six or eight leagues west of the city of Darra. Kalten and the main body of the Pandion Knights awaited them there.

"I thought you'd got lost," the blond man said as he reined up in front of Sparhawk. He looked curiously at Flute, who sat in front of Sparhawk's saddle, her bare feet both on one side of the black horse's neck and with Sparhawk's cloak wrapped around her. "Isn't it a little late for you to be starting a family?"

"We found her along the way," Sparhawk replied. He took the little girl and handed her across to Sephrenia.

"Why didn't you put some shoes on her?"

"We did. She keeps losing them. There's a nunnery on the other side of Darra. We'll drop her off there." Sparhawk looked at the ruin crouched on the hill above them. "Is there any kind of shelter in there?"

"Some. It breaks the wind, at least."

"Let's get inside, then. Did Kurik bring Faran and my armor?"

Kalten nodded.

"Good. This horse is a little unruly, and Vanion's old armor has rubbed me raw in more places than I care to count."

They rode up into the ruin and found Kurik and the young novice, Berit, waiting for them. "What took you so long?" Kurik asked bluntly.

"It's a long way, Kurik," Sparhawk replied a bit defensively, "and the wagons can only move so fast."

"You should have left them behind."

"They were carrying the food and extra equipment."

Kurik grunted. "Let's get in out of the weather. I've got a fire going in what's left of that watchtower over there." He looked rather peculiarly at Sephrenia, who carried Flute in her arms. "Lady," he greeted her respectfully.

"Dear Kurik," she said warmly. "How are Aslade and the boys?"

"They're well, Sephrenia," he replied. "Very well indeed."

"I'm so glad to hear it."

"Kalten said you'd be coming along," he said to her. "I have water boiling for your tea." He looked at Flute, who had her face nestled against Sephrenia's. "Have you been keeping secrets from us?"

She laughed, a rippling cascade of a laugh. "That's what Styrics do best, Kurik."

"Let's get you all inside where it's warm." He turned and led the way across the rubble-strewn courtyard of the ruin, leaving Berit to care for the horses.

"Was it a good idea to bring him along?" Sparhawk asked, jerking his thumb back over his shoulder in the direction of the novice. "He's a little young for an all-out battle."

"He'll be all right, Sparhawk," Kurik said. "I took him to the practice field at Demos a few times and gave him some instruction. He handles himself well and he learns fast."

"All right, Kurik," Sparhawk said, "but when the fighting starts, stay close to him. I don't want him getting hurt."

"I never let *you* get hurt, did I?"

Sparhawk grinned at his friend. "No. As I recall, you didn't."

They stayed the night in the ruin and rode out early the following morning. Their combined forces numbered just over five hundred men, and they rode south under a still-threatening sky. Just beyond Darra stood a nunnery with yellow sandstone walls and a red tile roof. Sparhawk and

Sephrenia turned aside from the road and crossed a winter-browned meadow toward the building.

"And what is the child's name?" the black-robed mother superior asked when they were admitted into her presence in a severely simple room with only a small brazier to warm it.

"She doesn't talk, Mother," Sparhawk replied. "She plays those pipes all the time, so we call her Flute."

"That is an unseemly name, my son."

"The child doesn't mind, Mother Superior," Sephrenia told her.

"Did you make some effort to find her parents?"

"There was no one in the vicinity when we found her," Sparhawk explained.

The mother superior looked gravely at Sephrenia. "The child is Styric," she pointed out. "Would it not perhaps be better to put her with a family of her own race and her own faith?"

"We have pressing business," Sephrenia said, "and Styrics can be very difficult to find when they choose to be."

"You know, of course, that if she stays with us, we will raise her in the Elene faith."

Sephrenia smiled. "You will *try*, Mother Superior. I think you will find that she's not amenable to conversion, however. Coming, Sparhawk?"

They rejoined the column and rode south under clearing skies, moving first at a rolling trot and then at a thunderous gallop. They crossed a knoll, and Sparhawk reined Faran in sharply, staring in astonishment at Flute, who sat cross-legged on a large white rock playing her pipes. "How did you—" he began, then broke off. "Sephrenia," he called, but the white-robed woman had already dismounted. She approached the child, speaking gently to her in that strange Styric dialect.

Flute lowered her pipes and gave Sparhawk an impish little grin. Sephrenia laughed and took the child in her arms.

"How did she get ahead of us?" Kalten asked, his face baffled.

"Who knows?" Sparhawk replied. "I guess I'd better take her back."

"No, Sparhawk," Sephrenia said firmly. "She wants to go with us."

"That's too bad," he said bluntly. "I'm not going to take a little girl into battle."

"Don't concern yourself with her, Sparhawk. I'll care for her." She smiled at the child nestled in her arms. "I'll care for her as if she were my own." She laid her cheek against Flute's glossy black hair. "In a way, she is."

He gave up. "Have it your own way," he said. Just as he began to wheel Faran around, he felt a sudden chill accompanied by the sense of an implacable hatred. "Sephrenia!" he said sharply.

"I felt it, too!" she cried, drawing the little girl closer to her. "It's directed at the child!"

Flute struggled briefly, and Sephrenia, looking surprised, set her down. The little girl's face was set, looking more annoyed than angered or frightened. She set her pipes to her lips and began to play. The melody this time was not that light air in a minor key which she had played before. It was sterner and peculiarly ominous.

Then from some distance away they heard a sudden howl of pain and surprise. The howl immediately began to fade, as if whoever or whatever had made it were fleeing at an unimaginable rate.

"What was that?" Kalten exclaimed.

"An unfriendly spirit," Sephrenia replied calmly.

"What drove it away?"

"The child's song. It seems that she has learned to protect herself."

"Do you understand any of what's going on here?" Kalten asked Sparhawk.

"No more than you do. Let's keep moving. We've still got a couple of days hard riding ahead of us."

THE CASTLE OF Count Radun, the uncle of King Dregos, was perched atop a high, rocky promontory. Like so many of the castles in this southern kingdom, it was surrounded by massive walls. The weather had cleared off, and the noonday sun was very bright as Sparhawk, Kalten, and

Sephrenia, who still carried Flute in front of her saddle, rode across a broad meadow of yellow grass toward the fortress.

They were admitted without question; in the courtyard they were met by the count, a blocky man with heavy shoulders and silver-shot hair. He wore a dark green doublet trimmed in black and surmounted by a heavily starched white ruff of a collar. It was a style which had gone out of fashion in Elenia decades ago. "My house is honored to welcome the Knights of the Church," he declared formally after they had introduced themselves.

Sparhawk swung down off Faran's back. "Your hospitality is legendary, my Lord," he said, "but our visit is not entirely social. Is there someplace private where we can talk? We have a matter of some urgency to discuss with you."

"Of course," the count replied. "If you will all be so good as to come with me." They followed him through the broad doors of his castle and along a candlelit corridor strewn with rushes. At the end of the corridor, the count produced a brass key and unlocked a door. "My private study," he said modestly. "I'm rather proud of my collection of books. I have almost two dozen."

"Formidable," Sephrenia murmured.

"Perhaps you might care to read some of them, madame?"

"The lady doesn't read," Sparhawk told him. "She's a Styric and an initiate in the secrets. She feels that reading might somehow interfere with her abilities."

"A witch?" the count said, looking at the small woman. "Truly?"

"We prefer to use other terms, my Lord," she replied mildly.

"Please, sit down," the count said, pointing at a large table standing in a chill patch of wintery sunlight coming through a heavily barred window. "I'm curious to hear about this urgent matter."

Sparhawk removed his helmet and gauntlets and laid them on the table. "Are you familiar with the name of Annias, primate of Cimmura, my Lord?"

The count's face hardened. "I've heard of him," he said shortly.

"You know his reputation then?"

"I do."

"Good. Quite by accident, Sir Kalten and I unearthed a plot hatched by the primate. Fortunately, he isn't aware of the fact that we know about it. Is it your common practice so freely to admit Church Knights?"

"Of course. I revere the Church and honor her knights."

"Within a few days—a week at most—a sizable group of men in black armor and bearing the standards of Pandion Knights will ride up to your gates. I strongly advise you not to admit them."

"But—"

Sparhawk held up one hand. "They will *not* be Pandions, my Lord. They're mercenaries under the command of a renegade named Martel. If you let them in, they will kill everyone within your walls—excepting only a churchman or two who will spread word of the outrage."

"Monstrous!" the count gasped. "What reason could the primate of Cimmura have to bear me such hatred?"

"The plot isn't directed at you, Count Radun," Kalten told him. "Your murder is designed to discredit the Pandion Knights. Annias hopes that the Hierocracy of the Church will be so infuriated that they'll disband the order."

"I must send word to Larium at once," the count declared, coming to his feet. "My nephew can have an army here in a few days."

"That won't be necessary, my Lord," Sparhawk said. "I have five hundred fully armed Pandions—real ones— concealed in the woods just to the north of your castle. With your permission, I'll bring a hundred of them inside your walls to reinforce your garrison. When the mercenaries arrive, find some excuse not to admit them."

"Won't that seem strange?" Radun asked. "I have a reputation for hospitality—for the Knights of the Church in particular."

"The drawbridge," Kalten said.

"I beg your pardon?"

"Tell them that the windlass that operates your drawbridge is broken. Then tell them that you have men working on it and ask them to be patient.''

"I will not lie," the count said stiffly.

"That's all right, my Lord," Kalten assured him. "I'll break the windlass for you myself, so you won't really be lying."

The count stared at him for a moment, then burst out laughing.

"The mercenaries will be outside the castle," Sparhawk went on, "and your walls will give them very little room for maneuvering. That's when we'll attack them from behind."

Kalten grinned broadly. "It should be almost like a cheese grater when we start to grind them up against your walls."

"And I can drop some interesting things on them from my battlements as well," the count added, also grinning. "Arrows, large rocks, burning pitch—that sort of thing."

"We're going to get on splendidly, my Lord," Kalten told him.

"I will, of course, make arrangements to lodge this lady and the little girl here in safety," the count said.

"No, my Lord," Sephrenia disagreed. "I will accompany Sir Sparhawk and Sir Kalten back to our hiding place. This Martel Sparhawk mentioned is a former Pandion and he has delved deeply into secret knowledge that is forbidden to honest men. It may be necessary to counter him, and I'm best equipped to do that."

"But surely the child—"

"The child must stay with me," Sephrenia said firmly. She looked over at Flute, who was in the act of curiously opening a book. "No!" she said, probably more sharply than she had intended. She rose and took the book away from the little girl.

Flute sighed, and Sephrenia spoke briefly to her in that dialect Sparhawk did not understand.

SINCE THERE WAS no way to know when Martel's mercenaries might arrive, the Pandions built no fires that night, and when the next morning dawned clear and cold, Sparhawk unrolled himself from his blankets and looked with some distaste at his armor, knowing that it would take at least an hour for the heat of his body to take the clammy chill out of it. He decided that he was not ready to face that just yet, so he belted on his sword, pulled his stout cloak around his shoulders, and walked down through the sleeping camp toward a small brook that trickled through the woods where he and his knights lay hidden.

He knelt beside the brook and drank from his cupped hands, then braced himself and splashed icy water on his face. Then he rose, dried his face with the hem of his cloak, and stepped across the brook. The just-risen sun streamed golden into the leafless wood, slanting between the dark trunks and touching fire into the dewdrops collected like strings of beads along the stems of the grass about his feet. Sparhawk walked on through the woods.

He had gone perhaps half a mile when he saw a grassy meadow through the trees. As he approached the meadow, he heard the thudding of hooves. Somewhere ahead, a single horse was loping across the turf at a canter. And then he heard the sound of Flute's pipes rising in the morning air.

He pushed his way to the edge of the meadow, parted the bushes, and peered out.

Faran, his roan coat glistening in the morning sun, cantered easily in a wide circular course around the meadow. He wore no saddle nor bridle, and there was something almost joyful about his stride. Flute lay face-up on his back with her pipes at her lips. Her head was nestled comfortably on his surging front shoulders, her knees were crossed, and she was beating time on Faran's rump with one little foot.

Sparhawk gaped at them, then stepped out into the meadow to stand directly in the big roan's path. He spread his arms wide, and Faran slowed to a walk and then stopped in front of his master.

"What do you think you're doing?" Sparhawk barked at him.

Faran's expression grew lofty and he looked away.

"Have you completely taken leave of your senses?"

Faran snorted and flicked his tail even as Flute continued to play her song. Then the little girl slapped her grass-stained foot imperiously on his rump several times, and he neatly sidestepped the fuming Sparhawk and cantered on with Flute's song soaring above him.

Sparhawk swore and ran after them. After a few yards, he knew it was hopeless and he stopped, breathing hard.

"Interesting, wouldn't you say?" Sephrenia said. She had come out from among the trees and stood at the edge of the meadow with her white robe gleaming in the morning sun.

"Can you make them stop?" Sparhawk asked her. "She's going to fall off and get hurt."

"No, Sparhawk," Sephrenia disagreed, "she will not fall." She said it in that strange manner into which she sometimes lapsed. Despite the decades she had spent in Elene society, Sephrenia remained a Styric to her fingertips, and Styrics had always been an enigma to Elenes. The centuries of close association between the militant orders of the Elene Church and their Styric tutors, however, had taught the Church Knights to accept the words of their instructors without question.

"If you're sure," Sparhawk said a bit dubiously as he looked across the turf at Faran, who seemed somehow to have lost his normally vicious temperament.

"Yes, dear one," she said, laying an affectionate hand on his arm in reassurance. "I'm absolutely sure." She looked out at the great horse and his tiny passenger joyously circling the dew-drenched meadow in the golden morning sunlight. "Let them play a while longer," she advised.

ABOUT MIDMORNING KALTEN returned from the vantage point to the south of the castle where he and Kurik had been keeping watch over the road coming up from Sarrinium. "Nothing yet," he reported as he dismounted, his armor clinking. "Do you think Martel might just try to come across country and avoid the roads?"

"It's not very likely," Sparhawk replied. "He *wants* to be seen, remember? He needs lots of witnesses."

"I suppose I hadn't thought of that," Kalten admitted. "Have you got the road coming down from Darra covered?"

Sparhawk nodded. "Lakus and Berit are watching it."

"Berit?" Kalten sounded surprised. "The apprentice? Isn't he a little young?"

"He'll get over it. He's steady and he's got good sense. Besides, Lakus can keep him out of trouble."

"You're probably right. Is there any of that roast ox the count sent us left?"

"Help yourself. It isn't hot, though."

Kalten shrugged. "Better cold meat than no meat."

The day dragged on, as days spent only in waiting will do; by evening, Sparhawk was pacing the camp with his impatience gnawing at him. Finally Sephrenia emerged from the rough little tent she shared with Flute. She placed herself directly in front of the big knight in black armor with her hands on her hips. "*Will* you stop that?" she demanded crossly.

"Stop what?"

"Pacing. You jingle at every step, and the noise is very distracting."

"I'm sorry. I'll go jingle on the other side of camp."

"Why not just go sit down?"

"Nerves, I guess."

"Nerves? You?"

"I get twinges now and then."

"Well, go twinge someplace else."

"Yes, little mother," he replied obediently.

It was cold again the following morning. Kurik rode quietly into camp just before sunrise. He carefully picked his way past the sleeping knights wrapped in their black cloaks to the place where Sparhawk had spread his blankets. "You'd better get up." he said, lightly touching Sparhawk's shoulder. "They're coming."

Sparhawk sat up quickly. "How many?" he asked, throwing off his blankets.

"I make it about two hundred and fifty."

Sparhawk stood up. "Where's Kalten?" he asked as Kurik began to buckle the black armor over his lord's padded tunic.

"He wanted to make sure that there wouldn't be any surprises, so he joined the end of their column."

"He did *what*?"

"Don't worry, Sparhawk. They're all wearing black armor, so he blends right in."

"Do you want to tie this on?" Sparhawk handed his squire the length of bright ribbon that each knight was to wear as a means of identification during a battle in which both sides would be dressed in black.

Kurik took the red ribbon. "Kalten's wearing a blue one," he noted. "It matches his eyes." He tied the ribbon around Sparhawk's upper arm, then stepped back and looked at his lord appraisingly. "Adorable," he said, rolling his eyes.

Sparhawk laughed and clapped his friend on the shoulder. "Let's go wake the children," he said, looking across the encampment of generally youthful knights.

"I've got some bad news for you, Sparhawk," Kurik said as the two of them moved out through the camp, shaking the sleeping Pandions awake.

"What's that?"

"The man leading the column isn't Martel."

Sparhawk felt a hot surge of disappointment. "Who is it?" he asked.

"Adus. He had blood all over his chin. I think he's been eating raw meat again."

Sparhawk swore.

"Look at it this way. At least the world's going to be a cleaner place without Adus, and I'd imagine that God would like to have a long talk with him anyway."

"We'll have to see what we can do to arrange that."

Sparhawk's knights were assisting each other into their armor when Kalten rode into camp. "They've pulled up just beyond that hill to the south of the castle," he reported, not bothering to dismount.

"Is Martel possibly lurking around somewhere among them?" Sparhawk asked hopefully.

Kalten shook his head. "I'm afraid not." He stood up in his stirrups, shifting his sword around. "Why don't we just go ahead and attack them?" he suggested. "I'm getting cold."

"I think Count Radun would be disappointed if we didn't let him take part in the fight."

"That's true, I suppose."

"Is there anything unusual about the mercenaries?"

"Run of the mill—except that about half of them are Rendors."

"Rendors?"

"They don't smell very good, do they?"

Sephrenia, accompanied by Parasim and Flute, came up to join them.

"Good morning, Sephrenia," Sparhawk greeted her.

"Why all the bustle?" she asked.

"We have company coming. We thought we'd ride out to greet them."

"Martel?"

"No. I'm afraid it's only Adus—and a few friends." He shifted the helmet he was holding under his left arm. "Since Martel isn't leading them, and since Adus can barely speak Elenic, much less Styric, there isn't anybody out there who could stir up enough magic to knock a fly off the wall. I'm afraid that means that you've made the trip for nothing. I want you to stay back here in the woods, well hidden and out of danger. Sir Parasim will stay with you."

The young knight's face filled with disappointment.

"No, Sparhawk," Sephrenia replied. "I need no guard, and this is Parasim's first battle. We won't deprive him of it."

Parasim's face shone with gratitude.

Kurik came back through the woods from the place where he had been keeping watch. "The sun's coming up," he reported, "and Adus is leading his men over the top of that hill."

"We'd better mount up, then," Sparhawk said.

The Pandions swung up into their saddles and moved cautiously through the wood until they reached the edge of the broad meadow that surrounded the count's castle. Then they waited, watching the black-armored mercenaries riding down the hill in the golden dawn sunlight.

Adus, who normally spoke in grunts and belches, rode up to the gate of Count Radun's castle and read haltingly from a piece of paper which he held in front of him at arm's length.

"Can't he extemporize?" Kalten asked quietly. "He's only asking for permission to enter the castle."

"Martel doesn't take chances," Sparhawk replied, "and Adus usually has trouble remembering his own name."

Adus continued to read his request. He had some trouble with the word *admission*, since it had more than one syllable.

Then Count Radun appeared on the battlements to announce regretfully that the windlass which raised and lowered the drawbridge was broken and to beg them to be patient until it was repaired.

Adus mulled that over. It took him quite a while. The mercenaries dismounted and lounged about on the grass at the foot of the castle wall.

"This is going to be almost too easy," Kalten muttered.

"Let's just make sure that none of them get away," Sparhawk told him. "I don't want anybody riding to Annias with word of what *really* happens today."

"I still think Vanion's trying to be too clever about this."

"Maybe that's why he's the preceptor and we're only knights."

A red banner appeared atop the count's walls.

"There's the signal," Sparhawk said. "Radun's forces are ready." He put on his helmet, gathered his reins, and rose in his stirrups, firmly holding Faran in. Then he raised his voice. "Charge!" he roared.

CHAPTER NINE

NY CHANCE AT all?'' Kalten asked.

"No," Sparhawk replied with deep regret as he lowered Sir Parasim to the ground. "He's gone." He smoothed the young knight's hair with his hand, then gently closed the vacant eyes.

"He wasn't ready to come up against Adus," Kalten said.

"Did that animal get completely away?"

"I'm afraid so. After he cut down Parasim, he rode off to the south with about a dozen other survivors."

"Send some people after him," Sparhawk said bleakly as he straightened the fallen Sir Parasim's limbs. "Tell them to run him into the sea if necessary."

"Do you want me to do it?"

"No. You and I have to go to Chyrellos." He raised his voice then. "Berit," he shouted.

The novice approached at a half run. He was wearing an old mail shirt splashed with blood and a dented foot soldier's helmet with no visor. He carried a grim, long-handled battle-axe.

Sparhawk looked closely at the blood on the rangy youth's mail shirt. "Is any of that yours?" he asked.

"No, my Lord," Berit answered. "All theirs." He looked pointedly at the mercenary dead littering the field.

"Good. What's your feeling about a long ride?"

"As my Lord commands."

"He's got good manners, at least," Kalten observed. "Berit," he said then, "ask 'Where?' before you agree so quickly."

"I'll remember that, my Lord Kalten."

"I want you to come with me," Sparhawk said to the novice. "We need to talk with Count Radun before you leave." He turned to Kalten. "Get a group of men to chase Adus," he said. "Push him hard. I don't want him to have time to send one of his people to Cimmura to report all of this to Annias. Tell the rest of the men to bury our dead and care for the wounded."

"What about these?" Kalten pointed at the dead bodies of the mercenaries heaped in front of the castle walls.

"Burn them."

Count Radun met Sparhawk and Berit in the courtyard of his castle. He was wearing full armor and held his sword in his hand. "I see that the reputation of the Pandions is well deserved," he said.

"Thank you, my Lord," Sparhawk replied. "I have a favor—no, two favors—to ask of you."

"Anything, Sir Sparhawk."

"Are you known to any members of the Hierocracy in Chyrellos?"

"Several, actually, and the patriarch of Larium is a distant cousin of mine."

"Very good. I know it's a bad season for travel, but I'd like for you to join me in a little ride."

"Of course. Where are we going?"

"To Chyrellos. The next favor is a bit more personal. I'll need your signet ring."

"My ring?" The count lifted his hand and looked at the heavy gold ring bearing his coat of arms.

Sparhawk nodded. "And worse yet, I can't guarantee that I'll be able to return it."

"I'm not sure that I understand."

"Berit here is going to take the ring to Cimmura and drop it in the collection plate during services in the cathedral there. The Primate Annias will take that to mean that his scheme has succeeded and that you and your family have all been murdered. He will then rush to Chyrellos to lay charges against the Pandions before the Hierocracy."

Count Radun grinned broadly. "But then you and I will step forward and refute those charges, right?"

Sparhawk grinned back. "Exactly," he said.

"That might cause the primate a certain amount of embarrassment," the count said as he tugged the ring off his finger.

"That was sort of what we had in mind, my Lord."

"The ring is well lost, then," Radun said, handing his signet to Berit.

"All right," Sparhawk said to the young novice. "Don't kill any horses on your way to Cimmura. Give us time to get to Chyrellos before Annias does." He squinted thoughtfully. "Morning service, I think."

"My Lord?"

"Drop the count's ring in the collection plate during morning services. Let's give Annias a whole day to gloat before he starts out for Chyrellos. Wear ordinary clothes when you go into the cathedral and pray a bit—just to make it look convincing. Don't go near the chapterhouse or the inn on Rose Street." He looked at the young novice, feeling a renewed pang at the loss of Sir Parasim. "I can't assure you that your life won't be in danger, Berit," he said soberly, "so I can't order you to do this."

"There's no need to order me to do it, my Lord Sparhawk," Berit replied.

"Good man," Sparhawk said. "Now go get your horse. You've got a long ride ahead of you."

It was nearly noon when Sparhawk and Count Radun

emerged from the castle. "How long do you think it's going to take for Primate Annias to reach Chyrellos?" the count asked.

"Two weeks at least. Berit has to get to Cimmura before Annias can even start for Chyrellos."

Kurik came riding up to them. "Everything's ready," he told Sparhawk.

Sparhawk nodded. "You'd better go get Sephrenia," he said.

"Is that really a good idea, Sparhawk? Things might get a little chancy when we get to Chyrellos."

"Do *you* want to be the one to tell her that she has to stay behind?"

Kurik winced. "I see what you mean," he said.

"Where's Kalten?"

"Over there at the edge of the woods. He's building a bonfire for some reason."

"Maybe he's cold."

The winter sun was very bright in the cold blue sky as Sparhawk and his party set out. "Surely, madame," Count Radun objected to Sephrenia, "the child would have been quite safe within the walls of my castle."

"She would not have stayed there, my Lord," Sephrenia replied in a small voice. She laid her cheek against Flute's hair. "Besides," she added, "I take great comfort in having her with me." Her voice sounded weak somehow, and she looked very pale and tired. In one hand she carried Sir Parasim's sword.

Sparhawk pulled Faran in beside her white palfrey. "Are you all right?" he asked her quietly.

"Not really," she answered.

"What's the matter?" He felt a sudden alarm.

"Parasim was one of the twelve knights in the throne room in Cimmura." She sighed. "I've just been obliged to shoulder his burden as well as my own." She gestured slightly with the sword.

"You're not ill, are you?"

"Not in the way that you mean, no. It's just that it's going to take a little while to adjust to the additional weight."

"Is there any way that I could carry it for you?"

"No, dear one."

He drew in a deep breath. "Sephrenia," he said, "is what happened to Parasim today a part of what you told me was going to happen to the twelve knights?"

"There's no way to know, Sparhawk. The compact we made with the Younger Gods was not that specific." She smiled wanly. "If another of the knights dies this moon, though, we'll know that it was merely an accident and had nothing to do with the compact."

"We're going to lose them one every month?"

"Moon," she corrected. "Twenty-eight days. Most probably yes. The Younger Gods tend to be methodical about such things. Don't concern yourself about me, Sparhawk. I'll be all right in a little while."

It was some sixty leagues from the count's castle to the city of Darra, and on the morning of the fourth day of their journey, they crested a hill and looked down upon the red tile roofs and the hundreds of chimneys sending pale blue columns of smoke straight up into the windless air. A black-armored Pandion Knight awaited them on the hilltop. "Sir Sparhawk," the knight said, raising his visor.

"Sir Olven," Sparhawk replied, recognizing the knight's scarred face.

"I have a message for you from Preceptor Vanion. He instructs you to proceed directly to Cimmura with all possible speed."

"Cimmura? Why the change in plans?"

"King Dregos is there, and he's invited Wargun of Thalesia and Obler of Deira to join him. He wants to investigate the illness of Queen Ehlana—and the justification for the appointment of the bastard Lycheas as prince regent. Vanion believes that Annias will level his charges against our order at that council in order to deflect an inquiry that might be embarrassing."

Sparhawk swore. "Berit's a good way ahead of us by now," he said. "Have all the kings gathered in Cimmura yet?"

Olven shook his head. "King Obler is too old to travel very fast, and it's likely to take a week to sober King Wargun up before he can make the voyage from Emsat."

"Let's not gamble on that," Sparhawk said. "We'll cut

across country to Demos and then ride directly to Cimmura. Is Vanion still at Chyrellos?''

"No. He came through Demos on his way to Cimmura. The Patriarch Dolmant was with him.''

"Dolmant?'' Kalten said. "That's a surprise. Who's running the Church?''

"Sir Kalten,'' Count Radun said stiffly. "The guidance of the Church is in the hands of the archprelate.''

"Sorry, my Lord,'' Kalten apologized. "I know how much Arcians revere the Church, but let's be honest. Archprelate Cluvonus is eighty-five years old and he sleeps a great deal. Dolmant doesn't make an issue of it, but most of the decisions that come out of Chyrellos are his.''

"Let's ride,'' Sparhawk said.

It took them four days of hard travelling to reach Demos, where Sir Olven left them to return to the Pandion motherhouse, and it was three more days before they arrived at the gates of the chapterhouse in Cimmura.

"Do you know where we can find Lord Vanion?'' Sparhawk asked the novice who came out into the courtyard to take their horses.

"He's in his study in the south tower, my Lord—with the Patriarch Dolmant.''

Sparhawk nodded and led the way inside and up the narrow stairs.

"Thank God you arrived in time,'' Vanion greeted them.

"Did Berit deliver the count's ring yet?'' Sparhawk asked him.

Vanion nodded. "Two days ago. I had men inside the cathedral watching.'' He frowned slightly. "Was it altogether wise to entrust that kind of mission to a novice, Sparhawk?''

"Berit's a solid young man,'' Sparhawk explained, "and he isn't widely known here in Cimmura. Most of the full-fledged knights are.''

"I see. It was your command, Sparhawk. The decision was yours. How did things go in Arcium?''

"Adus led the mercenaries,'' Kalten replied. "We didn't see a sign of Martel. Otherwise, things went more or less as planned. Adus got away, though.''

Sparhawk drew in a deep breath. "We lost Parasim," he said sadly. "I'm sorry, Vanion. I tried to keep him out of the fight."

Vanion's eyes clouded with sudden grief.

"I know," Sparhawk said, touching the older man's shoulder. "I loved him, too." He saw the quick look that passed between Vanion and Sephrenia. She nodded slightly as if to advise the preceptor that Sparhawk knew that Parasim had been one of the twelve. Then Sparhawk straightened and introduced Count Radun and Vanion to each other.

"I owe you my life, Lord Vanion," Radun said as they shook hands. "Please tell me how I can repay you."

"Your presence here in Cimmura is ample repayment, my Lord."

"Have the other kings joined my nephew as yet?" the count asked.

"Obler has," Vanion replied. "King Wargun is still at sea, though."

A thin man dressed in a severe black cassock sat near the window. He appeared to be in his late fifties and had silvery hair. His face was ascetic and his eyes were very keen. Sparhawk crossed the room and knelt respectfully before him. "Your Grace," he greeted the patriarch of Demos.

"You're looking well, Sir Sparhawk," the churchman told him. "It's good to see you again." Then he looked over Sparhawk's shoulder. "Have you been going to chapel, Kurik?" he asked the squire.

"Uh—whenever there's opportunity, your Grace," Kurik answered, flushing slightly.

"Excellent, my son," Dolmant said. "I'm sure that God is always glad to see you. How are Aslade and the boys?"

"Well, your Grace. Thank you for asking."

Sephrenia had been looking critically at the patriarch. "You haven't been eating properly, Dolmant," she told him.

"Sometimes I forget," he said. Then he smiled slyly at her. "My overwhelming concern with the conversion of the heathens fills all my waking thoughts. Tell me, Sephrenia, are *you* ready at last to put aside your pagan ways and embrace the true faith?''

"Not yet, Dolmant," she replied, also smiling. "It was nice of you to ask, though."

He laughed. "I thought I'd get the question out of the way early so we can converse without having it hanging over our heads." He looked curiously at Flute, who was walking about the room examining the furnishings. "And who is this beautiful child?" he asked.

"She's a foundling, your Grace," Sparhawk replied. "We came across her near the Arcian border. She doesn't talk, so we call her Flute."

Dolmant looked at the little girl's grass-stained feet. "And was there no time to bathe her?" he asked.

"That would not be appropriate, your Grace," Sephrenia replied.

The patriarch looked puzzled at that. Then he looked again at Flute. "Come over here, child," he said.

Flute approached him warily.

"And will you not speak—even to me?"

She raised her pipes and blew a questioning little note.

"I see," Dolmant said. "Well, then, Flute, will you accept my blessing?"

She looked at him gravely, then shook her head.

"She is a Styric child, Dolmant," Sephrenia explained. "An Elene blessing would have no meaning for her."

Flute then reached out and took the patriarch's thin hand and placed it over her heart. Dolmant's eyes grew suddenly very wide and his expression troubled.

"She will give you *her* blessing, however," Sephrenia told him. "And will *you* accept it?"

Dolmant's eyes were still wide. "I think perhaps that I should not," he said, "but God help me, I will—and gladly."

Flute smiled at him and then kissed both of his palms. Then she pirouetted away, her black hair flying and her pipes sounding joyously. The patriarch's face was filled with wonder.

"I expect that I'll be summoned to the palace as soon as King Wargun arrives," Vanion said. "Annias wouldn't want to miss the chance to confront me personally." He looked at Count Radun. "Did anyone see you arrive, my Lord?" he asked.

Radun shook his head. "I had my visor down, my Lord Vanion, and at Sparhawk's suggestion, I had covered the crest on my shield. I'm positive that no one knows that I'm in Cimmura."

"Good." Vanion grinned suddenly. "We wouldn't want to spoil the surprise for Annias, would we?"

The expected summons from the palace arrived two days later. Vanion, Sparhawk, and Kalten put on the simple robes Pandions customarily wore inside the chapterhouse, though beneath them they wore mail coats and their swords. Dolmant and Radun wore the cowled black robes of monks. Sephrenia wore her usual white. She had spoken at some length with Flute, and it appeared that the little girl had agreed to remain behind. Kurik belted on a sword. "Just in case there's trouble," he grunted to Sparhawk before the party left the chapterhouse.

The day was cold and raw. The sky was leaden, and a chill wind whistled through the streets of Cimmura as Vanion led them toward the palace. There were few people abroad in the streets. Sparhawk could not be sure if the citizens were staying inside because of the weather or because some rumors had leaked out about the possibility of trouble.

Not too far from the palace gate, Sparhawk saw a familiar figure. A lame beggar boy wrapped in a ragged cloak crutched his way out from the corner where he had been sheltering himself. "Charity, my Lords, charity," he begged in a brokenhearted voice.

Sparhawk reined Faran in and reached inside his robe for a few coins.

"I need to talk with you, Sparhawk," the boy said quietly after the others had ridden out of earshot.

"Later," Sparhawk replied, bending to his saddle to place the coins in the boy's begging bowl.

"Not too much later, I hope," Talen said, shivering. "I'm freezing out here."

There was a brief delay at the palace gate where the guards tried to deny entrance to Vanion's escort. Kalten resolved the problem by pulling open his robe and putting his hand meaningfully on his sword hilt. The discussion ended abruptly at that point, and the party rode on into the palace courtyard and dismounted.

"I *love* doing that," Kalten said blithely.

"It doesn't take very much to make you happy, does it?" Sparhawk said.

"I'm a simple man, my friend—with simple pleasures."

They proceeded directly to the blue-draped council chamber where the kings of Arcium, Deira, and Thalesia sat on thronelike chairs, flanking the slack-lipped Lycheas. Behind each king stood a man in formal armor. The crests of the three other militant orders were emblazoned on their surcoats. Abriel, preceptor of the Cyrinic Knights in Arcium, stood sternly behind King Dregos; Darellon, preceptor of the Alcione Knights of Deira had taken up a similar position behind the aged King Obler; and the big-boned Komier, leader of the Genidian Knights stood behind King Wargun of Thalesia. Although it was early in the day, Wargun was already bleary-eyed. He held a large silver cup in a hand that was visibly shaking.

The Royal Council of Advisors sat to one side of the room. The face of the Earl of Lenda was troubled, while that of the Baron Harparin was smug.

The Primate Annias wore a purple satin cassock, and the expression on his emaciated face was coldly triumphant as Vanion entered. When he saw the rest of them accompanying the Pandion preceptor, however, his eyes flashed angrily. "Who authorized this entourage of yours, Lord Vanion?" he demanded. "The summons did not mention an escort."

"I require no authorization, your Grace," Vanion answered coldly. "My rank is all the authority I need."

"That's true," the Earl of Lenda said. "Law and custom support the preceptor's position."

Annias gave the old man a look filled with hate. "What a comfort it is to have the advice of one so versed in the law," he said in a sarcastic voice. Then his eyes fell on Sephrenia. "Remove that Styric witch from my presence," he demanded.

"No," Vanion said. "She stays."

Their eyes locked for a long moment, and Annias finally looked away. "Very well, then, Vanion," he said. "Because of the seriousness of the matter I am about to present to their majesties, I will control my natural revulsion at the presence of a heathen sorceress."

"You're too kind," Sephrenia murmured.

"Just get on with it, Annias," King Dregos said irritably. "We're gathered here to examine certain irregularities involving the throne of Elenia. What is this burning matter that is important enough to delay our inquiry?"

Annias straightened. "The matter concerns you directly, your Majesty. Last week a body of armed men attacked a castle in the eastern part of your kingdom."

King Dregos's eyes blazed. "Why was I not informed?" he demanded.

"Forgive me, your Majesty," Annias apologized. "I myself learned of the incident only recently and I felt it wiser to present the matter to this council rather than to advise you in advance. Although this outrage occurred within the boundaries of your kingdom, the implications of it spread beyond your borders to all four western kingdoms."

"Get on with it, Annias," King Wargun growled. "Save the flowery language for your sermons."

"As your Majesty wishes," Annias said, bowing. "There are witnesses to this criminal act, and I think perhaps it were best that your Majesties hear their accounts directly rather than at secondhand from me." He turned and gestured to one of the red-liveried church soliders who lined both walls of the council chamber. The soldier stepped to a side door and admitted a nervous-looking man whose face went visibly pale when he saw Vanion.

"Don't be afraid, Tessera," Annias told him. "So long as you tell the truth, no harm will come to you."

"Yes, your Grace," the nervous man mumbled.

"This is Tessera," Annias introduced him, "a merchant of this city who has recently returned from Arcium. Tell us what you saw there, Tessera."

"Well, your Grace, it was as I told you before. I was in Sarrinium on business. I was returning from there when I was overtaken by a storm and I took shelter in the castle

of Count Radun, who was kind enough to take me in.''
Tessera's voice had the singsong quality some people assume when they are reciting something previously committed to memory. "Anyway," he went on, "after the
weather cleared, I was preparing to leave and I was in the
count's stables seeing to my horse. I heard the sounds of
many men in the courtyard, so I peered out the stable door
to see what was happening. It was a sizable body of Pandion Knights.''

"Are you certain that they were Pandions?" Annias
prompted him.

"Yes, your Grace. They were wearing black armor and
carrying Pandion banners. The count is well known to be
most respectful of the Church and her knights, so he had
admitted them without challenge. As soon as they were
inside the walls, however, they all drew their swords and
began to kill everyone in sight.''

"My uncle!" King Dregos exclaimed.

"The count tried to fight them, of course, but they
quickly disarmed him and tied him to a stake in the center
of the courtyard. They killed all the men inside the castle,
and then—''

"*All* the men?" Annias interrupted him, his face suddenly stern.

"They killed all the men inside the castle, and then—''
Tessera faltered. "Oh, I almost forgot that part. They
killed all the men inside the castle—*except* for the churchmen—and then they brought out the count's wife and
daughters. They were all stripped naked and then violated
before the count's eyes.''

A sob escaped the king of Arcium. "My aunt and my
cousins," he cried.

"Steady, Dregos," King Wargun said, putting his hand
on the other king's shoulder.

"Then," Tessera continued, "after the count's wom-
enfolk had all been repeatedly raped, they were dragged
one by one to a spot directly before where the count was
tied and their throats were cut. The count wept and tried
to tear his hands free, but his bonds were too tight. He
pleaded with the Pandions to stop, but they only laughed
and continued their butchery. Finally, when his wife and

daughters were all dead and lying in their own blood, he asked them why they were doing this. One of them, the leader, I think, replied that it was on the orders of Lord Vanion, the preceptor of the Pandions.''

King Dregos leaped to his feet. He was weeping openly and clawing at his sword hilt. Annias stepped in front of him. ''I share your outrage, your Majesty, but a quick death for this monstrous Vanion would be far too merciful. Let us hear this good, honest man out. Go on with your account, Tessera.''

''There isn't much more to tell, your Grace,'' Tessera replied. ''Once the Pandions had killed all the women, they tortured the count to the point of death and then they beheaded him. After that, they drove the churchmen out of the castle and looted the place.''

''Thank you, Tessera,'' Annias said. He motioned to another of his soldiers, and the guard went to the same side door to admit a man dressed in a peasant smock. The peasant had a slightly furtive look and he was trembling noticeably.

''Say your name, fellow,'' Annias ordered.

''I am Verl, your Grace, an honest serf from the estate of Count Radun.''

''And why are you in Cimmura? A serf may not leave the estate of his lord without permission.''

''I fled, your Grace, after the murder of the count and all his family.''

''Can you tell us what happened? Did you witness this atrocity?''

''Not directly, your Grace. I was working in a field near the count's castle when I saw a large group of men dressed in black armor and carrying the banners of the Pandion Knights ride out of the castle. One of them had the count's head on the point of his spear. I hid myself and I could hear them talking and laughing as they rode by.''

''What were they saying?''

''The one who was carrying the count's head said, 'We must carry this trophy to Demos to prove to Lord Vanion that we have carried out his orders.' After they had gone past, I ran to the castle and found everyone inside dead. I was afraid that the Pandions might come back, so I ran away.''

"Why did you come to Cimmura?"

"To report the crime to you, your Grace, and to place myself under your protection. I was afraid that if I stayed in Arcium, the Pandions would hunt me down and kill me.''

"Why did you do this?" Dregos demanded of Vanion. "My uncle has never given any offense to your order."

The other kings were also glaring at the Pandion preceptor accusingly.

Dregos wheeled to glare at Prince Lycheas. "I insist that this murderer be placed in chains!''

Lycheas tried without much success to look like a king. "Your demand is reasonable, your Majesty," he said in his nasal voice. He cast a quick look at Annias, seeking reassurance. "We therefore command that this miscreant Vanion be placed—"

"Um, excuse me, your Majesties," the Earl of Lenda interposed, "but by law, Lord Vanion is entitled to present his defense.''

"What defense can there possibly be?" Dregos asked in a sick voice.

Sparhawk and the others had remained at the back of the council chamber. Sephrenia made a small gesture, and Sparhawk leaned toward her. "Someone here is using magic," she whispered. "That's why the kings are so willing to accept the infantile charges against Vanion. The spell induces belief.''

"Can you counter it?" he whispered back.

"Only if I know who's doing it.''

"It's Annias. He tried a spell on me when I first came back to Cimmura.''

"A churchman?" she looked surprised. "All right. I'll take care of it." Her lips began to move, and she concealed her hands in her sleeves to hide their gesturing.

"Well, Vanion," Annias sneered, "what have you to say for yourself?''

"These men are obviously lying," Vanion replied scornfully.

"Why would they lie?" Annias turned to the kings

seated at the front of the room. "As soon as I received the reports of these witnesses, I dispatched a troop of church soldiers to the count's castle to verify the details of this crime. I expect their report within the next week. In the meantime, it is my recommendation that the Pandion Knights all be disarmed and confined within their chapterhouses to prevent any further atrocities."

King Obler stroked his long gray beard. "Under the circumstances, that would be the prudent course," he said sagely. He turned to Darellon of the Alcione Knights. "My Lord Darellon," he said. "Dispatch a rider to Deira. Tell him to bring your knights to Elenia. They are to assist the civil authorities here in disarming and confining the Pandions."

"It shall be as your Majesty commands," Darellon replied, glaring at Vanion.

The aged king of Deira looked at King Wargun and King Dregos. "I would strongly advise that the Cyrinics and Genidians also send forces," he said. "Let us seal up these Pandions until we can separate the innocent from the guilty."

"See to it, Komier," King Wargun said.

"Send your knights as well, Abriel," King Dregos commanded the preceptor of the Cyrinics. He glared at Vanion with hate-filled eyes. "I pray that your underlings attempt to resist," he said fiercely.

"A splendid idea, your Majesties," Annias said, bowing. "I would further suggest that as soon as we receive confirmation of the murders, your Majesties travel with me and these two honest witnesses to Chyrellos. There we can lay the entire affair before the Hierocracy of the Church and the archprelate himself with our strong recommendation that the Pandion Order be disbanded. Strictly speaking, that order is under Church authority, and only the Church can make the final decision."

"Truly," Dregos grated. "Let us rid ourselves of this Pandion infection once and for all."

A thin smile touched the primate's lips. Then he flinched, and his face went deathly pale as Sephrenia released her counterspell.

It was at that point that Dolmant stepped forward, pushing back the hood of his monk's robe to reveal his face. "May I speak, your Majesties?" he asked.

"Y—your Grace," Annias stammered in surprise, "I didn't know that you were in Cimmura."

"I didn't think you did, Annias. As you've so correctly pointed out, the Pandions are under Church authority. As the ranking churchman present, I think it's proper for me to take charge of this inquiry. You are to be commended for the way in which you have conducted things thus far, however."

"But—"

"That will be all, Annias," Dolmant dismissed him. He turned then to the kings and to Lycheas, who was staring open-mouthed at him.

"Your Majesties," the patriarch began, pacing back and forth with his hands clasped behind him as if deep in thought. "This is indeed a serious accusation. Let us, however, consider the character of the accusers. On the one hand, we have an untitled merchant, and on the other, a runaway serf. The accused is the preceptor of an order of Church Knights, a man whose honor has always been above question. Why would a man of Lord Vanion's stature commit such a crime? Indeed, we have as yet received no substantiation that the crime *did* in fact take place. Let us not move in haste."

"As I mentioned, your Grace," Annias injected, "I have dispatched church soldiers to Arcium to view the scene of the crime with their own eyes. I have also ordered them to seek out the churchmen who were in the castle of Count Radun and witnessed this horror and to return with them to Cimmura. Their reports should leave no doubts whatsoever."

"Ah, yes," Dolmant agreed. "None whatsoever. I think, however, that I might be able to save us a bit of time. As it happens, I myself have with me a man who witnessed what happened at the castle of Count Radun and I don't think his testimony can be questioned by any man here." He looked at the robed and cowled Count Radun, who had remained unobtrusively at the rear of the chamber. "Would you be so good as to step forward, brother?" he said.

Annias was gnawing on a fingernail. His expression clearly showed his chagrin at having the proceedings taken out of his grasp and at the appearance of Dolmant's unexpected witness.

"Would you reveal your identity to us, brother?" Dolmant asked mildly as the count joined him before the kings.

There was a tight grin on Radun's face as he pushed back his hood.

"Uncle!" King Dregos gasped in astonishment.

"Uncle?" King Wargun exclaimed, coming to his feet and spilling his wine.

"This is Count Radun—my uncle," Dregos told him, his eyes still wide with amazement.

"You seem to have made an astonishing recovery, Radun," Wargun laughed. "My congratulations. Tell me, how did you stick your head back on?"

Annias had gone very pale. He stared in stunned disbelief at Count Radun. "How did you—" he blurted. Then he recovered. He looked around wildly for an instant as if seeking a way to escape. Then he seemed to get hold of himself. "Your Majesties," he stammered, "I have been misled by false witnesses. Please forgive me." He was visibly sweating now. Then he spun about. "Seize those two liars!" He pointed at Tessera and Verl, who were both cringing in terror. Several red-liveried guards quickly rushed the pair from the room.

"Annias thinks very fast on his feet, doesn't he?" Kalten murmured to Sparhawk. "How much would you care to wager that those two will manage somehow to hang themselves before the sun goes down—with a certain amount of help, of course?"

"I'm not a betting man, Kalten," Sparhawk replied. "Not on a proposition like that, anyway."

"Why don't you tell us what *really* happened at your castle, Count Radun?" Dolmant suggested.

"It was really fairly simple, your Grace," Radun replied. "Sir Sparhawk and Sir Kalten arrived at my gates some time ago and warned me that a group of men dressed in the armor of Pandion Knights were planning to gain entry by subterfuge and murder me and my family. They had a number of *real* Pandions with them. When the imposters arrived, Sir Sparhawk led his knights against them and drove them off.''

''Fortuitous,'' King Obler observed. ''Which of these stalwarts is Sir Sparhawk?''

Sparhawk stepped forward. ''I am, your Majesty.''

''How did you become aware of this plot?''

''It was quite by accident, your Majesty. I happened to overhear a conversation concerning it. I immediately informed Lord Vanion, and he ordered Kalten and me to take preventive steps.''

King Dregos rose to his feet and came down from the dais. ''I have wronged you, Lord Vanion,'' he said in a thick voice. ''Your motives were the very best, and I accused you. Can you forgive me?''

''There is nothing to forgive, your Majesty,'' Vanion replied. ''Under the circumstances, I'd have done exactly the same.''

The Arcian king took the preceptor's hand and clasped it warmly.

''Tell me, Sir Sparhawk,'' King Obler asked, ''could you by chance identify the plotters?''

''I couldn't see their faces, your Majesty.''

''A shame, really,'' the old king sighed. ''It would appear that the plot was fairly widespread. The two who came before us to testify would also seem to have been a part of it, and at some prearranged signal were to have stepped forward with their obviously well-coached lies.''

''That same thought had occurred to me, your Majesty,'' Sparhawk agreed.

''But who was behind it? And against whom was it really directed? Count Radun, perhaps? Or King Dregos? Or even Lord Vanion?''

''That might be impossible to determine—unless the so-called witnesses can be persuaded to identify their fellow plotters.''

''Excellent point, Sir Sparhawk.'' King Obler looked sternly at the Primate Annias. ''It lies upon you, your Grace, to insure that the merchant Tessera and the serf Verl are available for questioning. We would all be most

distressed should anything of a permanent nature happen
to either of them.''

Annias's face grew stiff. ''I shall have them both closely
guarded, your Majesty,'' he assured the king of Deira. He
gestured to one of his soldiers and muttered some instructions to the man, who blanched slightly, then hurried from
the room.

''Sir Sparhawk,'' Lycheas blustered, ''you were ordered to Demos and told to remain there until you received
permission to leave. Why is it that you—''

''Be still, Lycheas,'' Annias snapped at him.

A slow flush crept up the pimpled young man's face.

''I would say that you owe Lord Vanion an apology,
Annias,'' Dolmant said pointedly.

Annias paled and then turned stiffly to the Pandion chief.
''Please accept my apologies, Lord Vanion,'' he said
shortly. ''I was misled by liars.''

''Of course, my dear Primate,'' Vanion replied. ''We
all blunder from time to time, don't we?''

''I believe that more or less concludes this matter then,''
Dolmant said. He cast a sidelong glance at Annias, who
was obviously making a great effort to control his emotions. ''Be assured, Annias,'' the patriarch of Demos said
to him, ''I will cast this entire matter in as charitable a
light as I can when I make my report to the Hierocracy in
Chyrellos. I'll try my very best not to make you look like
a *complete* idiot.''

Annias bit his lip.

''Tell us, Sir Sparhawk,'' King Obler said, ''could you
in any way identify the people who approached the count's
castle?''

''The man who was leading them is named Adus, your
Majesty,'' Sparhawk told him. ''He's a thick-witted sav-
age who does the bidding of a renegade Pandion named
Martel. Many of his men were just ordinary mercenaries.
The rest were Rendors.''

''Rendors?'' King Dregos said, his eyes narrowing.
''There *have* been tensions of late between my kingdom
and Rendor, but this plot seems a bit involuted for the
Rendorish mind.''

''We could spend hours in speculation, Dregos,'' King

Wargun said, holding his empty wine cup out for a serving man to refill. "An hour or so on the rack should persuade the merchant and the serf down in the dungeon to tell us what they know about their fellow plotters."

"The Church does not approve of such methods, your Majesty," Dolmant said.

Wargun snorted derisively. "The dungeons beneath the Basilica of Chyrellos are reputed to employ the most expert interrogators in the world," he said.

"That practice is being discontinued."

"Perhaps," Wargun said, "but this is a civil matter. We're not constrained by churchly delicacy, and I for one don't propose to wait while you pray an answer out of those two."

Lycheas, who had been smarting from the almost absentminded rebuke Annias had delivered to him, straightened on his thronelike chair. "We are delighted that this matter has been resolved so amicably," he announced, "and we rejoice that the reports concerning the death of Count Radun have proved to be unfounded. I agree with the patriarch of Demos that we can consider this inquiry concluded—unless Lord Vanion's excellent witnesses can shed further light on just who might have been behind this monstrous conspiracy."

"No, your Highness," Vanion told him. "We are not prepared at this time to do so."

Lycheas turned to the kings of Thalesia, Deira, and Arcium, trying with scant success to look regal. "Our time, your Majesties, is short," he said. "We each have kingdoms to rule, and there are other matters requiring our attention. I suggest that we tender Lord Vanion our appreciation for his aid in clarifying this situation and give him permission to withdraw so that we may turn to state matters."

The kings nodded their agreement.

"You and your friends may leave now, Lord Vanion," Lycheas said grandly.

"Thank you, your Highness," Vanion replied with a stiff bow. "We are all happy to have been of service to you." He turned and started toward the door.

"A moment, Lord Vanion," Darellon, the slightly built

preceptor of the Alcione Knights said. Then he stepped
forward. "Since your Majesties' conversations will now
turn on state matters, I think that I, Lord Komier, and
Lord Abriel will also withdraw. We are little versed in
statecraft and could contribute nothing of value to your
discussions. The matter that has come to light this morning, however, requires some consultation among the militant orders. Should conspiracies of this nature recur, we
must make preparations to meet them."

"Well said," Komier agreed.

"A splendid idea, Darellon," King Obler assented.
"Let's not be caught asleep again. Keep me advised of
the thrust of your discussions."

"You may rely upon me, your Majesty."

The preceptors of the other three orders marched down
from the dais and joined Vanion, who led the way from
the ornate audience chamber. Once they were out in the
corridor, Komier, the hulking preceptor of the Genidian
Knights, grinned openly. "Very neat, Vanion," he said.

"I'm glad you liked it." Vanion grinned back.

"My head must have been packed in wool this morning," Komier confessed. "Would you believe I almost
accepted all that tripe?"

"It was not entirely your fault, Lord Komier," Sephrenia told him.

He gave her a questioning look.

"Let me think my way through it a bit more," she said,
frowning.

The big Thalesian looked at Vanion. "It was Annias,
wasn't it?" he guessed shrewdly as they progressed down
the hall. "The scheme was his, I take it?"

Vanion nodded. "The Pandion presence in Elenia is
hindering his operations. He saw this as a way to remove
us."

"Elenian politics get a bit dense sometimes. We're much
more direct in Thalesia. Just how powerful is the primate
of Cimmura?"

Vanion shrugged. "He controls the royal council. That
makes him more or less the ruler of the kingdom."

"Does he want the throne for himself?"

"No, I don't think so. He prefers to manipulate things

from behind the scenes. He's trying to groom Lycheas for the throne.''

"Lycheas is a bastard, isn't he?''

Vanion nodded again.

"How can a bastard be king? Nobody knows who his father is.''

"Annias probably believes he can get around that problem. Until Sparhawk's father intervened, our good primate had very nearly convinced King Aldreas that it was perfectly legitimate for him to marry his own sister.''

"That's disgusting,'' Komier shuddered.

"I've heard that Annias has certain ambitions involving the archprelate's throne in Chyrellos,'' Abriel, the gray-haired preceptor of the Cyrinic Knights, said to Patriarch Dolmant.

"I've heard some of the same rumors myself,'' Dolmant replied blandly.

"This humiliation is going to be quite a setback for him, isn't it? The Hierocracy's likely to look with some disfavor on a man who makes a total ass of himself in public.''

"That thought had crossed my mind as well.''

"And your report will be quite detailed, I expect?''

"That is my obligation, Lord Abriel,'' Dolmant said piously. "As a member of the Hierocracy myself, I could hardly conceal any of the facts, could I? I will have to present the *whole* truth to the high councils of the Church.''

"We wouldn't have it any other way, your Grace.''

"We're going to need to talk, Vanion,'' Darellon, the preceptor of the Alcione Knights, said seriously. "This scheme was directed at you and your order this time, but it concerns us all. It could be any one of us the next time. Is there someplace secure where we can discuss this matter?''

"Our chapterhouse is on the eastern edge of the city,'' Vanion replied. "I can guarantee that none of the primate's spies are inside its walls.''

As they rode out through the palace gates, Sparhawk remembered something and slowed to ride with Kurik at the rear of the column.

"What's the matter?" Kurik asked.

"Let's drop behind a little bit. I want to talk with that beggar boy."

"That's hardly good manners, Sparhawk," Kurik said. "A meeting of the preceptors of all four orders happens about once in a lifetime, and they're going to have some questions for you."

"We can catch up with them before they get to the chapterhouse."

"What do you want to talk to a beggar for?" Kurik sounded more than a little irritated.

"He's working for me." Sparhawk gave his friend an appraising look. "What's bothering you, Kurik?" he asked. "Your face looks like a rain cloud."

"Never mind," Kurik replied shortly.

Talen was still huddled in the angle between two intersecting walls. He had his ragged cloak wrapped about him and he was shivering.

Sparhawk dismounted a few feet from the boy and made some pretense of checking his saddle girth. "What did you want to tell me?" he said quietly.

"That man you had me watching," Talen began. "Krager, wasn't that his name? He left Cimmura about the same time you did, but he came back a week or so later. There was another man with him—a fellow with white hair. It sort of stands out because he's not really that old. Anyway, they went to the house of that baron who's so fond of little boys. They stayed there for several hours, then they rode out of town again. I got close enough to them at the east gate to hear them talking with the gate guards. When the guard asked their destination, they said they were going to Cammoria."

"Good lad," Sparhawk congratulated him, dropping a gold crown into the begging bowl.

"Child's play," Talen shrugged. He bit the coin and then tucked it inside his tunic. "Thanks, Sparhawk."

"Why didn't you tell the porter at the inn on Rose Street?"

"The place is being watched. I decided to play it safe." Then Talen looked over the big knight's shoulder. "Hello, Kurik," he said. "I haven't seen you for a long time."

"You two know each other?" Sparhawk was a bit surprised.

Kurik flushed, looking embarrassed.

"You wouldn't believe how far back our friendship goes, Sparhawk," Talen said with a sly little smile at Kurik.

"That's enough, Talen," Kurik said sharply. Then his expression softened slightly. "How's your mother?" he asked. There was a strange, wistful note in his voice.

"She's doing quite well, actually. When you add what I make to what you give her from time to time, she's comfortably off."

"Am I missing something here?" Sparhawk asked mildly.

"It's a personal matter, Sparhawk," Kurik told him. Then he turned to the boy. "What are you doing out here in the streets, Talen?" he demanded.

"I'm begging, Kurik. You see?" Talen held out his bowl. "That's what this is for. Would you like to drop something in for old times' sake?"

"I put you in a very good school, boy."

"Oh, it was very good indeed. The headmaster used to tell us how good it was three times a day—at mealtimes. He and the other teachers ate roast beef. The students got porridge. I don't like porridge all that much, so I enrolled in a different school." He gestured extravagantly at the street. "This is my classroom now. Do you like it? The lessons I learn here are much more useful than rhetoric or philosophy or all that tiresome theology. If I pay attention, I can earn enough to buy my own roast beef—or anything else, for that matter."

"I ought to thrash you, Talen," Kurik threatened.

"Why, father," the boy replied, wide-eyed, "what a thing to suggest!" He laughed. "Besides, you'd have to catch me first. That's the first lesson I learned in my new school. Would you like to see how well I learned it?" He took up his crutch and begging bowl and ran off down the street. He was, Sparhawk noted, very fast on his feet.

Kurik started to swear.

"Father?" Sparhawk asked.

"I told you that this is none of your business, Sparhawk."

"We don't keep any secrets from each other, Kurik."

"You're going to push this, aren't you?"

"Me? I'm just curious, that's all. This is a side of you I've never seen before."

"I was indiscreet some years ago."

"That's a delicate way to put it."

"I can do without the clever remarks, Sparhawk."

"Does Aslade know about this?"

"Of course not. It would only make her unhappy if I told her. I kept quiet about it to spare her feelings. A man owes that to his wife, doesn't he?"

"I understand perfectly, Kurik," Sparhawk assured him. "And was Talen's mother so very beautiful?"

Kurik sighed, and his face grew oddly soft. "She was eighteen and like a spring morning. I couldn't help myself, Sparhawk. I love Aslade, but . . ."

Sparhawk put his arm about his friend's shoulder. "It happens sometimes, Kurik," he said. "Don't beat yourself over the head about it." Then he straightened. "Why don't we see if we can catch up with the others?" he suggested, as he swung back up into his saddle.

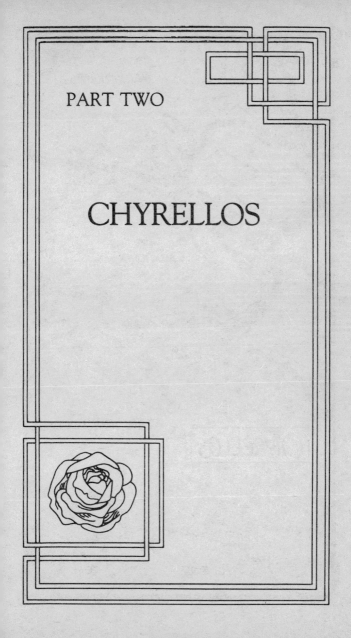

PART TWO

CHYRELLOS

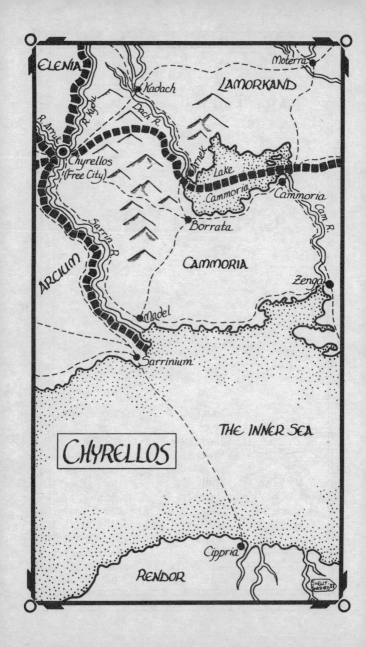

CHAPTER TEN

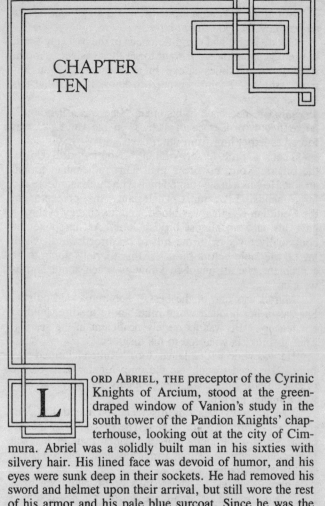

ORD ABRIEL, THE preceptor of the Cyrinic Knights of Arcium, stood at the green-draped window of Vanion's study in the south tower of the Pandion Knights' chapterhouse, looking out at the city of Cimmura. Abriel was a solidly built man in his sixties with silvery hair. His lined face was devoid of humor, and his eyes were sunk deep in their sockets. He had removed his sword and helmet upon their arrival, but still wore the rest of his armor and his pale blue surcoat. Since he was the eldest of the four preceptors, the others deferred to him. "I'm sure that we're all aware of most of what's been happening here in Elenia," he began, "but there are a few things that need a little clarification, I think. Would you mind if we asked you some questions, Vanion?"

"Not at all," Vanion replied. "We'll all try our best to answer any that you might have."

"Good. We've had our differences in the past, my Lord, but in this situation we'll want to set those aside." Abriel, like all the Cyrinics spoke in a considered, even formal, fashion. "I think we need to know more about this Martel person."

Vanion leaned back in his chair. "He was a Pandion," he replied with a trace of sadness in his voice. "I was forced to expel him from the order."

"That's a little terse, Vanion," Komier said. Unlike the others, Komier wore a mail shirt rather than formal armor. He was a heavy-boned man with thick shoulders and large hands. Like most Thalesians, the preceptor of the Genidian Knights was blond, and his shaggy eyebrows gave his face an almost brutish look. As he spoke, he continually toyed with the hilt of his broadsword, which lay on the table before him. "If this Martel's going to be a problem, we all ought to know as much about him as we can."

"Martel was one of the best," Sephrenia said quietly. She sat in her hooded white robe before the fire, holding her teacup. "He was extremely proficient in the secrets. That, I think, is what led to his disgrace."

"He was good with a lance, too," Kalten admitted ruefully. "He used to unhorse me on a regular basis on the practice field. Sparhawk was probably the only one who was a match for him."

"Exactly what was this disgrace you mentioned, Sephrenia?" Lord Darellon asked. The preceptor of the Alcione Knights of Deira was a slender man in his late forties. His massive Deiran armor looked almost too heavy for his slight frame.

Sephrenia sighed. "The secrets of Styricum are myriad," she replied. "Some are fairly simple—common spells and incantations. Martel mastered those very quickly. Beyond commonplace magic, however, lies a deeper and far more dangerous realm. Those of us who instruct the Knights of the Church in the secrets do not introduce our pupils to that level of magic. It serves no practical purpose and it involves things that imperil the souls of Elenes.''

Komier laughed. "Many things imperil the souls of Elenes, my Lady," he said. "I felt a certain wrench in mine the first time I contacted the Troll-Gods. I gather that this Martel of yours dabbled in things he should not have?''

Sephrenia sighed again. "Yes," she admitted. "He came to me asking that I instruct him in the forbidden secrets. He was very intense about it. That's one of Martel's characteristics. I refused him, of course, but there are renegade Styrics, even as there are renegade Pandions. Martel came from a wealthy family, so he could afford to pay for the instruction he wanted.''

"Who found him out?" Darellon asked.

"I did," Sparhawk said. "I was riding from Cimmura to Demos. That was shortly before King Aldreas sent me into exile. There's a patch of woods three leagues this side of Demos. It was just about dusk when I passed those woods, and I saw a strange light back among the trees. I went to investigate and saw Martel. He'd raised some kind of glowing creature. Its light was very bright—so bright that I couldn't make out its face.''

"I don't think you'd have wanted to see its face, Sparhawk," Sephrenia told him.

"Perhaps not," he agreed. "Anyway, Martel was speaking to the creature in Styric, commanding it to do his bidding.''

"That doesn't seem like anything out of the ordinary," Komier said. "We've all raised spirits or ghosts of one kind or another from time to time.''

"This was not precisely a spirit, Lord Komier," Sephrenia told him. "It was a Damork. The Elder Gods of Styricum created them to serve as slaves to their will. The Damorks have extraordinary powers, but they are soulless. A God can summon them from that unimaginable place where they dwell and control them. For a mortal to attempt that, however, is sheer folly. No mortal can control a Damork. What Martel had done is absolutely forbidden by all of the Younger Gods.''

"And the Elder Gods?" Darellon asked.

"The Elder Gods have no rules, my Lord—only whims and desires."

"Sephrenia," Dolmant pointed out, "Martel is an Elene. Perhaps he felt no obligation to observe the prohibitions of the Gods of Styricum."

"So long as one is practicing the arts of Styricum, one is subject to the Styric Gods, Dolmant," she replied.

"I wonder if perhaps it might have been a mistake to arm the Church Knights with Styric magic as well as conventional weapons," Dolmant mused. "We seem to be dabbling in an area best left untapped."

"That decision was made over nine hundred years ago, your Grace," Abriel reminded him, coming back to the table, "and if the Knights of the Church had not been proficient in magic, the Zemochs would have won that battle on the plains of Lamorkand."

"Perhaps," Dolmant said.

"Go on with your story, Sparhawk," Komier suggested.

"There's not too much more, my Lord. I didn't know what the Damork was until Sephrenia told me about it later, but I knew that it was something we were forbidden to contact. After a while, the thing vanished, and I rode in to talk with Martel. We were friends, and I wanted to warn him that what he was doing was prohibited, but he seemed almost mad somehow. He shrieked at me and told me to mind my own business. That didn't leave me any choice. I rode on to our motherhouse at Demos and reported what I'd seen to Vanion and Sephrenia. She told us what the creature was and how dangerous it was to have it loose in the world. Vanion ordered me to take a number of men and to apprehend Martel and to bring him to the motherhouse for questioning. He went completely wild when we approached him and he went to his sword. Martel's very good to begin with, and his madness made him all the more savage. I lost a couple of very close friends that day. We finally managed to overpower him and we dragged him back to the motherhouse in chains."

"By the ankles, as I recall," Kalten added. "Sparhawk can be very direct when he's irritated." He smiled at his friend. "You didn't endear yourself to him by doing it that way, Sparhawk," he said.

"I wasn't trying to. He'd just killed two of my friends, and I wanted to give him plenty of reasons to accept my challenge when Vanion was finished with him."

"Anyway," Vanion took up the story, "when they brought Martel back to Demos, I confronted him. He didn't even try to deny what he'd been doing. I ordered him to stop practicing the forbidden secrets, and he defied me. I had no choice but to expel him from the order at that point. I stripped him of his knighthood and his armor and turned him out the front gate."

"That could have been a mistake," Komier grunted. "I'd have had him killed. Did he raise that thing again?"

Vanion nodded. "Yes, but Sephrenia appealed to the Younger Gods of Styricum, and they exorcized it. Then they stripped Martel of the most significant of his powers. He went away weeping and swearing revenge upon us all. He's still dangerous, but at least he can't summon up horrors anymore. He left Elenia and he's been hiring his sword out to the highest bidder in other parts of the world for the past ten or twelve years."

"He's just a common mercenary then?" Darellon asked. The slender Alcione preceptor had an intent look on his narrow face.

"Not quite common, my Lord," Sparhawk disagreed. "He's had Pandion training. He could have been the very best of us and he's very clever. He has wide contacts with mercenaries all over Eosia. He can raise an army at a moment's notice and he's totally ruthless. I don't believe that Martel believes in anything anymore."

"What does he look like?" Darellon asked.

"A little bigger than medium size," Kalten replied. "He's about the same age as Sparhawk and me, but he's got white hair—he has had it since he was in his twenties."

"I think we might all want to keep an eye out for him," Abriel suggested. "Who's the other one—Adus?"

"Adus is an animal," Kalten told him. "After Martel was expelled from the Pandions, he recruited Adus and a man named Krager to help him in his activities. Adus is a

Pelosian, I think—or maybe a Lamork. He can barely talk, so his accent is a little hard to identify. He's a total savage, devoid of human feelings. He enjoys killing people— slowly—and he's very good at it.''

''And the other one?'' Komier asked. ''Krager?''

''Krager's fairly intelligent,'' Sparhawk replied. ''Basically, he's a criminal—false coins, extortion, fraud, that sort of thing—but he's weak. Martel trusts him to perform tasks that Adus wouldn't be able to understand.''

''What's the link between Annias and Martel?'' Count Radun asked.

''Probably nothing more than money, my Lord.'' Sparhawk shrugged. ''Martel is for hire and he has no strong convictions about anything. There are rumors that he has about half a ton of gold hidden somewhere.''

''I was right,'' Komier said bluntly. ''You should have killed him, Vanion.''

''I made the offer,'' Sparhawk said, ''but Vanion said no.''

''I had reasons,'' Vanion said.

''Was there anything significant about the fact that there were Rendors in the party that attacked Count Radun's house?'' Abriel asked then.

''Probably not,'' Sparhawk replied. ''I've just come back from Rendor. There's a pool of mercenaries there in the same way that there is in Pelosia, Lamorkand, and Cammoria. Martel draws on those people whenever he needs men. Rendorish mercenaries have no particular religious convictions, Eshandist or otherwise.''

''Do we have enough evidence against Annias to take before the Hierocracy in Chyrellos?'' Darellon asked.

''I don't think so,'' Patriarch Dolmant said. ''Annias has bought many voices in the higher councils of the Church. Any charges we might bring against him would have to be supported by overwhelming proof. All we have now is an overheard conversation between Krager and Baron Harparin. Annias could wriggle out of that rather easily—or simply buy his way out of it.''

Komier leaned back in his chair, tapping at his chin with one finger. ''I think the patriarch has just put his finger on the key to the whole affair. As long as Annias has his hands on the Elenian treasury, he can finance these schemes of his and continue to buy support in the Hierocracy. If we aren't careful, he'll bribe his way to the archprelacy. We've all stood in his path from time to time, and I'd guess that his first act as archprelate would be to disband all four militant orders. Is there any way we can cut off his access to those funds?''

Vanion shook his head. ''He controls the Royal Council—except for the Earl of Lenda. They vote him all the money he needs.''

''What about your queen?'' Darellon asked. ''Did he control her, too—before she fell ill, I mean?''

''Not even a little,'' Vanion replied. ''Aldreas was a weak king who did anything Annias told him to do. Ehlana's an altogether different matter and she despises Annias.'' He shrugged. ''But she's ill, and Annias will have a free hand until she recovers.''

Abriel began to pace up and down, his lined face deep in thought. ''That would seem to be our logical course then, gentlemen. We must bend all of our efforts to finding a cure for Queen Ehlana's illness.''

Darellon leaned back, his fingers tapping on the polished table. ''Annias is very cunning,'' he observed. ''He will easily guess what our course is likely to be and he's certain to try to block us. Even if we succeed in finding a cure, won't that immediately put the queen's life in danger?''

''Sparhawk is her champion, my Lord,'' Kalten told him. ''He can cope—particularly if I'm there to back him up.''

''Are you making any progress on a cure, Vanion?'' Komier asked.

''The local physicians are all baffled,'' Vanion replied. ''I've sent out requests for others, though, but most of them haven't arrived as yet.''

''Physicians don't always respond to requests,'' Abriel noted. ''This might be particularly true in a situation where the head of the royal council has a certain interest in *not* seeing the queen recover.'' He considered the problem. ''The Cyrinics have many contacts in Cammoria,'' he said. ''Have you considered taking your queen to the medical faculty at the University of Borrata in that kingdom? They're reputed to be experts in obscure ailments.''

"I don't think we dare dissolve the encasement that surrounds her," Sephrenia said. "At the moment it's all that sustains her life. She could not survive a trip to Borrata."

The preceptor of the Cyrinic Knights nodded thoughtfully. "Perhaps you're right, madame," he said.

"Not only that," Vanion added. "Annias would never let us take her out of the palace."

Abriel nodded bleakly. He considered it for a moment. "There's an alternative. It's not as good as having the physician actually look at the patient, but sometimes it works—or so I've been told. A skilled physician can learn a great deal from a detailed description of symptoms. That would be my suggestion, Vanion. Write down everything you know about Queen Ehlana's illness and send someone to Borrata with the documents.''

"I'll take it," Sparhawk said quietly. "I have certain personal reasons for wanting the queen restored to health. Besides, Martel's in Cammoria—or at least he's reputed to be—and he and I have a few things to discuss.''

"That raises another point," Abriel said. "There's a great deal of turmoil in Cammoria right now. Someone's been stirring up civil unrest there. It's not the safest place in the world.''

Komier leaned back again. "What would you gentlemen say to a little show of unity?" he said to the other preceptors.

"What did you have in mind?" Darellon asked.

"I'd say that we all have a stake in this," Komier replied. "Our common goal is to keep Annias off the archprelate's throne. We all have champions who stand above their comrades in skill and bravery. I think it might be a good idea for us each to select one of those champions and send him to join Sparhawk in Cammoria. The assistance couldn't hurt, and the sending of men from all four orders would convince the world that the Church Knights stand as one in this matter.''

"Very good, Komier," Darellon agreed. "The militant orders have had their differences in the past few centuries, and too many people still think that we're divided." He turned to Abriel. "Have you any idea who's behind the trouble in Cammoria?" he asked.

"Many believe that it's Otha," the Cyrinic replied. "He's been infiltrating the central kingdoms for the past six months or so."

"You know," Komier said, "I've got a strong feeling that someday we're going to have to do something about Otha—something fairly permanent."

"That would involve coming up against Azash," Sephrenia said, "and I'm not sure we want to do that."

"Can't the Younger Gods of Styricum do something about him?" Komier asked her.

"They choose not to," she replied. "The wars of men are bad enough, but a war between the Gods would be dreadful beyond imagining." She looked at Dolmant. "The God of the Elenes is reputed to be all-powerful," she said. "Couldn't the Church appeal to Him to confront Azash?"

"It's possible, I suppose," the patriarch said. "The only problem is that the Church does not admit the existence of Azash—or any other Styric God. It's a matter of theology."

"How very shortsighted."

Dolmant laughed. "My dear Sephrenia," he said. "I thought you knew that was the nature of the ecclesiastical mind. We're all like that. We find one truth and embrace it. Then we close our eyes to everything else. It avoids confusion." He looked at her curiously. "Tell me, Sephrenia, which heathen God do *you* worship?"

"I'm not permitted to say," she answered gravely. "I *can* tell you that it's not a God, though. I serve a Goddess."

"A female deity? What an absurd idea."

"Only to a man, Dolmant. Women find it very natural."

"Is there anything else you think we ought to know, Vanion?" Komier asked.

"I think we've just about covered everything, Komier." Vanion looked at Sparhawk. "Anything you want to add?" he asked.

Sparhawk shook his head. "No," he said. "I don't think so."

"What about that Styric who set the church soldiers on us?" Kalten asked.

Sparhawk grunted. "I'd almost forgotten that," he admitted. "It was at about the time that I heard Krager and Harparin talking. Kalten and I were wearing disguises, but there was a Styric who saw through them. Not long after that, we were attacked by some of Annias's people."

"You think there's a connection?" Komier asked.

Sparhawk nodded. "The Styric had been following me around for several days, and I'm fairly sure he was the one who pointed Kalten and me out to the soldiers. That would connect him to Annias."

"It's pretty thin, Sparhawk. Annias has some fairly well known prejudices where Styrics are concerned."

"Not so many that he wouldn't seek out their help if he thought he needed it. On two occasions I've caught him using magic."

"A churchman?" Dolmant's expression was startled. "That's strictly forbidden."

"So was plotting the murder of Count Radun, your Grace. I don't think Annias pays too much attention to the rules. He's not much of a magician, but the fact that he knows how it's done indicates that he's had instruction, and that means a Styric."

Darellon interlaced his slender fingers on the table in front of him. "There are Styrics and then there are Styrics," he noted. "As Abriel pointed out, there's been a great deal of Styric activity in the central kingdoms of late—much of it coming out of Zemoch. If Annias sought out a Styric to instruct him in the secrets, he might possibly have contacted the wrong one."

"I think you're overcomplicating things, Darellon," Dolmant said. "Not even Annias would have dealings with Otha."

"That's presuming that he *knows* he's dealing with Otha."

"My Lords," Sephrenia said very quietly, "consider what happened this morning." Her eyes were very intent. "Would any of you—or the kings you serve—have been deceived by the transparent accusations of the Primate Annias? They were crude, obvious, even childish. You Elenes are a subtle, sophisticated people. If your minds had been alert, you'd have laughed at Annias's clumsy attempts to discredit the Pandions. But you didn't. Neither did your kings. And Annias, who's as subtle as a serpent, presented his case as if he believed it was a stroke of genius."

"Exactly what are you getting at, Sephrenia?" Vanion asked.

"I think we should give some consideration to Lord Darellon's line of thought. The presentation this morning would have overwhelmed a Styric. We are a simple people, and our magicians do not have to work very hard to persuade us to their way of thinking. You Elenes are more skeptical, more logical. You are not so easily deceived—unless you've been tampered with."

Dolmant leaned forward, his eyes betraying his eagerness for a contest at logic. "But Annias is also an Elene, with a mind trained in theological disputation. Why would he have been so clumsy?"

"You're assuming that Annias was speaking in his own voice this morning, Dolmant. A Styric sorcerer—or some creature subject to one—would present his case in terms that would be understood by a simple Styric and then rely upon magic to induce belief."

"Was someone using that kind of magic in that room this morning?" Darellon asked, his face troubled.

"Yes," she replied simply.

"I think we're getting a bit far afield," Komier said. "What we need to do right now is get Sparhawk on his way to Borrata. The quicker we find a cure for Queen Ehlana's illness, the quicker we can eliminate the threat of Annias altogether. Once we cut off his supply of ready cash, he can consort with anybody—or anything—he wants to, for all I care."

"You'd better get ready to ride, Sparhawk," Vanion said. "I'll write down the queen's symptoms for you."

"I don't think that's necessary, Vanion," Sephrenia told him. "I know her condition in much greater detail than you do."

"But you can't write, Sephrenia," he reminded her.

"I won't have to, Vanion," she said sweetly. "I'll tell the physicians in Borrata about the symptoms personally."

"You're going with Sparhawk?" Vanion looked surprised.

"Of course. There are things afoot that seem to be focusing on him. He might need my help when he gets to Cammoria."

"I'll go along, too," Kalten said. "If Sparhawk catches up with Martel in Cammoria, I want to be there to see what happens." He grinned at his friend. "I'll let you have Martel," he offered, "if you'll give me Adus."

"Sounds fair," Sparhawk agreed.

"You'll be passing through Chyrellos on your way to Borrata," Dolmant said. "I'll ride along with you as far as that."

"We'll be honored to have you, your Grace." Sparhawk looked at Count Radun. "Might you want to join us as well, my Lord?" he asked.

"No. Thanks all the same, Sir Sparhawk," the count replied. "I'll return to Arcium with my nephew and Lord Abriel."

Komier was frowning slightly. "I don't want to delay you, Sparhawk," he said, "but Darellon is right. Annias is sure to guess what our next step is likely to be. There are only so many centers of medical learning in Eosia; if this Martel fellow is already in Cammoria and still taking orders from Annias, he's almost certain to try to keep you from reaching Borrata. I think it might be best if you waited in Chyrellos until the knights from our other orders catch up with you. A show of force can sometimes avoid difficulties."

"That's a good idea," Vanion agreed. "The others can join him at the Pandion chapterhouse in Chyrellos and ride out together from there."

Sparhawk rose to his feet. "That's it, then," he said. He glanced at Sephrenia. "Are you going to leave Flute here?"

"No. She goes with me."

"It's going to be dangerous," he warned.

"I can protect her if she needs protection. Besides, the decision is not mine to make."

"Don't you love talking with her?" Kalten said. "All the mental stimulation of trying to puzzle out the meaning of what she's saying."

Sparhawk ignored that.

LATER IN THE courtyard where Sparhawk and the others were preparing to mount for the ride to Chyrellos, the novice, Berit, approached. "There's a lame beggar boy at the gate, my Lord," he said to Sparhawk. "He says he has something urgent to tell you."

"Let him through the gates," Sparhawk said.

Berit looked a bit shocked.

"I know the boy," Sparhawk said. "He works for me."

"As you wish, my Lord," Berit said, bowing. He turned back toward the gate.

"Oh, by the way, Berit," Sparhawk said.

"My Lord?"

"Don't walk too close to the boy. He's a thief and he can steal everything you own before you go ten paces."

"I'll keep that in mind, my Lord."

A few minutes later, Berit came back escorting Talen.

"I've got a problem, Sparhawk," the boy said.

"Oh?"

"Some of the primate's men found out that I've been helping you. They're looking for me all over Cimmura."

"I told you that you were going to get in trouble," Kurik growled at him. Then the squire looked at Sparhawk. "What do we do now?" he asked. "I don't want him locked up in the cathedral dungeon."

Sparhawk scratched his chin. "I guess he'll have to go with us," he said, "at least as far as Demos." He grinned suddenly. "We can leave him with Aslade and the boys."

"Are you insane, Sparhawk?"

"I thought you'd be delighted at the notion, Kurik."

"That's the most ridiculous thing I've ever heard in my life."

"Don't you want him to get to know his brothers?" Sparhawk looked at the boy. "How much did you steal from Berit here?" he bluntly asked the young thief.

"Not very much, really."

"Give it all back."

"I'm very disappointed in you, Sparhawk."

"Life is filled with disappointments. Now give it back."

CHAPTER
ELEVEN

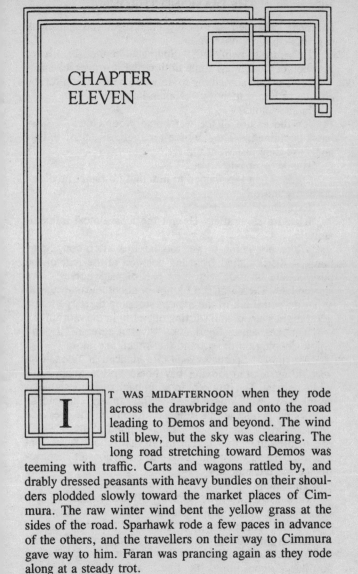

I
T WAS MIDAFTERNOON when they rode
across the drawbridge and onto the road
leading to Demos and beyond. The wind
still blew, but the sky was clearing. The
long road stretching toward Demos was
teeming with traffic. Carts and wagons rattled by, and
drably dressed peasants with heavy bundles on their shoulders plodded slowly toward the market places of Cimmura. The raw winter wind bent the yellow grass at the
sides of the road. Sparhawk rode a few paces in advance
of the others, and the travellers on their way to Cimmura
gave way to him. Faran was prancing again as they rode
along at a steady trot.

"Your horse seems restive, Sparhawk," the Patriarch

Dolmant, wrapped in a heavy black ecclesiastical cloak over his cassock, observed.

"He's just showing off," Sparhawk replied back over his shoulder. "He has some notion that it impresses me."

"It gives him something to do while he's waiting for the chance to bite somebody." Kalten laughed.

"Is he vicious?"

"It's the nature of the war horse, your Grace," Sparhawk explained. "They're bred for aggressiveness. In Faran's case they just went too far."

"Has he ever bitten you?"

"Once. Then I explained to him that I'd rather he didn't do it any more."

"Explained?"

"I used a stout stick. He got the idea almost immediately."

"We're not going to get too far this afternoon, Sparhawk," Kurik called from his position at the rear of the party where he rode with their pair of pack horses. "We started late. There's an inn I know of about a league ahead. What do you think of the idea of stopping there, getting a good night's sleep, and starting out early in the morning?"

"It makes sense, Sparhawk," Kalten agreed. "I don't enjoy sleeping on the ground that much any more."

"All right," Sparhawk said. He glanced at Talen, who was riding a tired-looking bay horse beside Sephrenia's white palfrey. The boy kept looking back over his shoulder apprehensively. "You're being awfully quiet," he said.

"Young people aren't supposed to talk in the presence of their elders, Sparhawk," Talen replied glibly. "That's one of the things they taught me in that school Kurik sent me to. I try to obey the rules—when it doesn't inconvenience me too much."

"The young man is pert," Dolmant observed.

"He's also a thief, your Grace," Kalten warned. "Don't get too close to him if you have any valuables about you."

Dolmant looked sternly at the boy. "Aren't you aware of the fact that thievery is frowned upon by the Church?"

"Yes," Talen sighed, "I know. The Church is very straitlaced about things like that."

"Watch your mouth, Talen," Kurik snapped.

"I can't, Kurik. My nose gets in the way."

"The lad's depravity is perhaps understandable," Dolmant said tolerantly. "I doubt that he's received much instruction in doctrine or morality." He sighed. "In many ways, the poor children of the streets are as pagan as the Styrics." He smiled slyly at Sephrenia, who rode with Flute bundled up in an old cloak in front of her saddle.

"Actually, your Grace," Talen disagreed, "I attend Church services regularly and I always pay close attention to the sermons."

"That's surprising," the patriarch said.

"Not really, your Grace," Talen said. "Most thieves go to church. The offertory provides all sorts of splendid opportunities."

Dolmant looked suddenly aghast.

"Look at it this way, your Grace," Talen explained with mock seriousness. "The Church distributes money to the poor, doesn't she?"

"Of course."

"Well, I'm one of the poor, so I take my share when the plate goes by. It saves the Church all the time and trouble of looking me up to give me the money. I like to be helpful when I can."

Dolmant stared at him, then suddenly burst out laughing.

Some few miles farther along, they encountered a small band of people dressed in the crude, homespun tunics that identified them as Styric. They were on foot and, as soon as they saw Sparhawk and the others, they ran fearfully out into a nearby field.

"Why are they so frightened?" Talen asked, puzzled.

"News travels very rapidly in Styricum," Sephrenia replied, "and there have been incidents lately."

"Incidents?"

Briefly, Sparhawk told him what had happened in the Styric village in Arcium. Talen's face went very pale. "That's awful!" he exclaimed.

"The Church has tried for hundreds of years to stamp out that sort of thing," Dolmant said sadly.

"I think we stamped it out fairly completely in that part

of Arcium," Sparhawk assured him. "I sent some men out to deal with the peasants who were responsible."

"Did you hang them?" Talen asked fiercely.

"Sephrenia wouldn't let us, so my men gave them a switching instead."

"That's all?"

"They used thorn bushes for switches. Thorns grow very long down in Arcium, and I instructed my men to be thorough about it."

"A bit extreme, perhaps," Dolmant said.

"It seemed fitting at the time, your Grace. The Church Knights have close ties with the Styrics and we don't like people who mistreat our friends."

The pale winter sun was sliding into a bank of chill purple cloud behind them when they arrived at a run-down wayside inn. They ate a barely adequate meal of thin soup and greasy mutton and retired early.

It was clear and cold the following morning. The road was frozen iron-hard, and the bracken lining its sides was white with frost. The sun was very bright, but there was little warmth to it. They rode briskly, wrapped tightly in their cloaks to ward off the biting chill.

The road undulated across the hills and valleys of central Elenia, passing through fields lying fallow under the winter sky. Sparhawk looked about as he rode. This was the region where he and Kalten had grown up, and he felt that peculiar sense of homecoming all men feel when returning after many years to the scenes of their childhood. The self-discipline which was so much a part of Pandion training usually made Sparhawk suppress any form of emotionalism, but, despite his best efforts, certain things sometimes touched him deeply.

About midmorning, Kurik called ahead. "There's a rider coming up behind us," he reported. "He's pushing his horse hard."

Sparhawk reined in and wheeled Faran around. "Kalten," he said sharply.

"Right," the big blond man replied, thrusting his cloak aside so that his sword hilt was clear.

Sparhawk also cleared his sword, and the two of them

rode several hundred yards back along the road to intercept the oncoming horseman.

Their precautions, however, proved unnecessary. The
rider was the young novice, Berit. He was wrapped in a
plain cloak, and his hands and wrists were chapped by the
morning chill. His horse, however, was lathered and
steaming. He reined in and approached them at a walk.
"I have a message for you from Lord Vanion, Sir Sparhawk," he said.

"What is it?" Sparhawk asked him.

"The Royal Council has legitimized Prince Lycheas."

"They did *what*?"

"When the kings of Thalesia, Deira, and Arcium insisted that a bastard could not serve as prince regent, the
Primate Annias called the council into session, and they
declared the prince to be legitimate. The primate produced
a document that stated that Princess Arissa had been married to Duke Osten of Vardenais."

"That's absurd," Sparhawk fumed.

"That's what Lord Vanion thought. The document appeared to be quite genuine, though, and Duke Osten died
years ago, so there wasn't any way to refute the claim.
The Earl of Lenda examined the parchment very closely
and finally even he had to vote to legitimize Lycheas."

Sparhawk swore.

"I knew Duke Osten," Kalten said. "He was a confirmed bachelor. There's no way he'd have married. He
despised women."

"Is there some problem?" Patriarch Dolmant asked,
riding back down the road to join them with Sephrenia,
Kurik, and Talen close behind him.

"The royal council has voted to legitimize Lycheas,"
Kalten told him. "Annias produced a paper that says that
Princess Arissa was married."

"How strange," Dolmant said.

"And how convenient," Sephrenia added.

"Could the document have been falsified?" Dolmant
asked.

"Easily, your Grace," Talen told him. "I know a man
in Cimmura who could provide irrefutable proof that

Archprelate Cluvonus has nine wives—including a lady Troll and an Ogress.''

"Well, it's done now," Sparhawk said. "It puts Lycheas one step closer to the throne, I'm afraid."

"When did this happen, Berit?" Kurik asked the novice.

"Late last night."

Kurik scratched at his beard. "Princess Arissa's cloistered at Demos," he said. "If Annias came up with this scheme just recently, she may not know she's a wife."

"Widow," Berit corrected.

"All right—widow, then. Arissa's always been rather proud of the fact that she lay down with just about every man in Cimmura—begging your pardon, your Grace—and that she did it on her own terms without ever having been to the altar. If someone approached her right, it shouldn't be too hard to get her to sign a statement that she's never been married. Wouldn't that sort of muddy up the waters a little?"

"Where did you find this man, Sparhawk?" Kalten asked admiringly. "He's a treasure."

Sparhawk was thinking very fast now. "Legitimacy—or illegitimacy—is a civil matter," he noted, "since it has to do with inheritance rights and things such as that, but the wedding ceremony is always a religious one, isn't it, your Grace?"

"Yes," Dolmant agreed.

"If you and I were to get the kind of statement from Arissa that Kurik just mentioned, could the Church issue a declaration of her spinsterhood?"

Dolmant considered it. "It's highly irregular," he said dubiously.

"But it *is* possible?"

"I suppose so, yes."

"Then Annias could be ordered by the Church to withdraw his spurious document, couldn't he?"

"Of course."

Sparhawk turned to Kalten. "Who inherited Duke Osten's lands and titles?" he asked.

"His nephew—a complete ass. He's very impressed with

his dukedom and he spends money faster than he earns it.''

''How would he react if he were suddenly disinherited and the lands and title were passed to Lycheas instead?''

''You'd be able to hear the screams in Thalesia.''

A slow smile crossed Sparhawk's face. ''I know an honest magistrate in Vardenais, and the affair would be in his jurisdiction. If the current duke were to take the matter into litigation, and if he presented the Church declaration to support his position, the magistrate would rule in his favor, wouldn't he?''

Kalten grinned broadly. ''He wouldn't have any choice.''

''Wouldn't that sort of de-legitimize Lycheas again?''

Dolmant was smiling. Then he assumed a pious expression. ''Let us press on to Demos, dear friends,'' he suggested. ''I feel a sudden yearning to hear the confession of a certain sinner.''

''Do you know something?'' Talen said. ''I always thought that thieves were the most devious people in the world, but nobles and churchmen make us look like amateurs.''

''How would Platime handle the situation?'' Kalten asked as they set off again.

''He'd stick a knife in Lycheas.'' Talen shrugged. ''Dead bastards can't inherit thrones, can they?''

Kalten laughed. ''It has a certain direct charm, I'll admit.''

''You cannot solve the world's problems by murder, Kalten,'' Dolmant said disapprovingly.

''Why, your Grace, I wasn't talking about murder. The Church Knights are the Soldiers of God. If God tells us to kill somebody, it's an act of faith, not murder. Do you suppose the Church could see its way clear to instruct Sparhawk and me to dispatch Lycheas—and Annias—and Otha too, as long as we're at it?''

''Absolutely not!''

Kalten sighed. ''It was only a thought.''

''Who's Otha?'' Talen asked curiously.

''Where did you grow up, boy?'' Berit asked him.

''In the streets.''

"Even in the streets you must have heard of the emperor of Zemoch."

"Where's Zemoch?"

"If you'd stayed in that school I put you in, you'd know," Kurik growled.

"Schools bore me, Kurik," the boy responded. "They spent months trying to teach me my letters. Once I learned how to write my own name, I didn't think I needed any of the rest of it."

"That's why you don't know where Zemoch is—or why Otha may be the one who kills you."

"Why would somebody I don't even know want to kill me?"

"Because you're an Elene."

"Everybody's an Elene—except for the Styrics, of course."

"This boy has a long way to go," Kalten observed. "Somebody ought to take him in hand."

"If it please you, my Lords," Berit said, choosing his words carefully, largely, Sparhawk guessed, because of the presence of the revered patriarch of Demos. "I know that you have pressing matters on your minds. I was never more than a passing fair scholar of history, but I will undertake the instruction of this urchin in the rudiments of the subject."

"I love to listen to this young man talk," Kalten said. "The formality almost makes me swoon with delight."

"Urchin?" Talen objected loudly.

Berit's expression did not change. With an almost casual backhanded swipe he knocked Talen out of his saddle. "Your first lesson, young man, is respect for your teacher," he said. "Never question his words."

Talen came up sputtering and with a small dagger in his fist. Berit leaned back in his saddle and kicked him solidly in the chest, knocking the wind out of him.

"Don't you just adore the learning process?" Kalten asked Sparhawk.

"Now, get back on your horse," Berit said firmly, "and pay attention. I will test you from time to time, and your answers had better be correct."

"Are you going to let him do this?" Talen appealed to his father.

Kurik grinned at him.

"This isn't fair," Talen complained, climbing back into his saddle. He wiped at his bleeding nose. "You see what you did?" he accused Berit.

"Press your finger against your upper lip," Berit suggested, "and don't speak without permission."

"What was that?" Talen demanded incredulously.

Berit raised his fist.

"All right. All right," Talen said, cringing away from the offered blow. "Go ahead. I'll listen."

"I always enjoy seeing a hunger for knowledge in the young," Dolmant observed blandly.

And so Talen's education began as they rode on to Demos. At first he was quite sullen about it, but after a few hours of listening to Berit, he began to be caught up in the story. "Can I ask questions?" he said finally.

"Of course," Berit replied.

"You said that there weren't any kingdoms in those days—just a lot of duchies and the like?"

Berit nodded.

"Then how did this Abrech of Deira gain control of the whole country in the fifteenth century? Didn't the other nobles fight him?"

"Abrech had control of the iron mines in central Deira. His warriors had steel weapons and armor. The people facing him were armed with bronze—or even flint."

"That would make a difference, I guess."

"After he had consolidated his hold on Deira, he turned south into what's now Elenia. It didn't take him very long to conquer the entire region. Then he moved down into Arcium and repeated the process there. After that, he turned toward central Eosia, Cammoria, Lamorkand, and Pelosia."

"Did he conquer all of Eosia?"

"No. It was about that time that the Eshandist Heresy arose in Rendor, and Abrech was persuaded by the Church to give himself over to its suppression."

"I've heard about the Eshandists," Talen said, "but I could never get the straight of what they really believe."

"Eshand was antihierarchical."

"What does that mean?"

"The Hierarchy is composed of higher church officials—primates, patriarchs and the archprelate. Eshand believed that individual priests should decide matters of theology for their congregations and that the Hierocracy of the Church should be disbanded."

"I can see why high churchmen disliked him then."

"At any rate, Abrech gathered a huge army from western and central Eosia to move against Rendor. His eyes were fixed on heaven and so when the earls and dukes of the lands he had conquered asked for steel weapons—the better to fight the heretics, they said—he gave his consent without considering the implications. There were a few battles, but then Abrech's empire suddenly disintegrated. Now that they had the advanced technology that the Deirans had kept secret before, the nobles of west and central Eosia no longer felt obliged to pay homage to Abrech. Elenia and Arcium declared their independence, and Cammoria, Lamorkand, and Pelosia all coalesced into strong kingdoms. Abrech himself was killed in a battle with the Eshandists in southern Cammoria."

"What's all this got to do with Zemoch?"

"I'll get to that in due time."

Talen looked over at Kurik. "You know," he said, "this is a good story. Why didn't they tell it in that school you put me in?"

"Probably because you didn't stay long enough to give them the chance."

"That's possible, I suppose."

"How much farther is it to Demos?" Kalten asked, squinting at the late afternoon sun to gauge the time.

"About twelve leagues," Kurik replied.

"We'll never make that before nightfall. Is there an inn or a tavern hereabouts?"

"There's a village a ways up ahead. They have an inn."

"What do you think, Sparhawk?" Kalten asked.

"I suppose we might as well," the big man agreed. "We wouldn't do the horses any good by riding them all night in the cold."

The sun was going down as they rode up a long hill

toward the village. Since it was behind them, it projected their shadows far out to the front. The village was small, with thatched-roofed stone houses clustered together on either side of the road. The inn at the far end was hardly more than a taproom with a sleeping loft on the second floor. The supper they were provided, however, was far better than the poor fare they had been offered the previous night.

"Are we going to the motherhouse when we get to Demos?" Kalten asked Sparhawk after they had eaten in the low, torchlit common room.

Sparhawk considered it. "It's probably being watched," he said. "Escorting the patriarch back to Chyrellos gives us an excuse to be passing through Demos, but I'd rather not have anyone see his Grace and me go into the cloister to talk with Arissa. If Annias gets any clues about what we've got planned, he'll try to counter us. Kurik, have you got any spare room at your house?"

"There's an attic—and a hay loft."

"Good. We'll be visiting you."

"Aslade will be delighted." Kurik's eyes grew troubled. "Can I talk with you for a moment, Sparhawk?"

Sparhawk pushed back his stool and followed his squire to the far side of the flagstone-floored room.

"You weren't really serious about leaving Talen with Aslade, were you?" Kurik asked quietly.

"No," Sparhawk replied, "probably not. You were right when you said that she might be very unhappy if she finds out about your indiscretion, and Talen has a busy mouth. He could let things slip."

"What are we going to do with him, then?"

"I haven't decided yet. Berit's looking after him and keeping him out of trouble."

Kurik smiled. "I expect it's the first time in his life that Talen's come up against somebody who won't tolerate his clever mouth. That lesson may be more important than all the history he's picking up."

"The same thought had occurred to me." Sparhawk glanced over at the novice, who was talking respectfully with Sephrenia. "I've got a feeling that Berit's going to make a very good Pandion," he said. "He's got character and intelligence, and he was very good in that fight down in Arcium.''

"He was fighting on foot," Kurik said. "We'll know better when we see how he handles a lance."

"Kurik, you've got the soul of a drill sergeant."

"Somebody's got to do it, Sparhawk."

It was cold again the following morning, and the horses' breath steamed in the frosty air as they set out. After they had gone about a mile, Berit resumed his instruction. "All right," he said to Talen, "tell me what you learned yesterday."

Talen was tightly wrapped in a patched old gray cloak that had once belonged to Kurik and he was shivering, but he glibly recited back what Berit had told him the day before. So far as Sparhawk could tell, the boy repeated Berit's words verbatim.

"You have a very good memory, Talen," Berit congratulated him.

"It's a trick," Talen replied with uncharacteristic modesty. "Sometimes I carry messages for Platime, so I've learned how to memorize things."

"Who's Platime?"

"The best thief in Cimmura—at least he was before he got so fat."

"Do you consort with thieves?"

"I'm a thief myself, Berit. It's an ancient and honorable profession."

"Hardly honorable."

"That depends on your point of view. All right, what happened after King Abrech got killed?"

"The war with the Eshandists settled down into a stalemate," Berit took up the account. "There were raids back and forth across the Inner Sea and the Arcian Straits, but the nobles on both sides had other things on their minds. Eshand had died, and his successors were not nearly as zealous as he'd been. The Hierocracy of the Church in Chyrellos kept trying to prod the nobility into pressing the war, but the nobles were far more interested in politics than in theology."

"How long did it go on like that?"

"For nearly three centuries."

"They took their wars seriously in those days, didn't they? Wait a minute. Where were the Church Knights during all of this?"

"I'm just coming to that. When it became obvious that the nobility had lost its enthusiasm for the war, the Hierocracy gathered in Chyrellos to consider alternatives. What finally emerged was the idea of founding the militant orders to continue the struggle. The knights of the four orders all received training far beyond that given ordinary warriors; in addition, they were given instruction in the secrets of Styricum."

"What are those?"

"Magic."

"Oh. Why didn't you say so?"

"I did. Pay attention, Talen."

"Did the Church Knights win the war then?"

"They conquered all of Rendor, and the Eshandists finally capitulated. During their early years the militant orders were ambitious, and they began to carve Rendor up into four huge duchies. But then a far worse danger came out of the east."

"Zemoch?" Talen guessed.

"Exactly. The invasion of Lamorkand came without any—"

"Sparhawk!" Kalten said sharply. "Up there!" He pointed at a nearby hilltop. A dozen armed men had suddenly come riding over the crest and were crashing down through the bracken at a gallop.

Sparhawk and Kalten drew their swords and spurred forward to meet the charge. Kurik ranged out to one side shaking a spiked chain mace free from his saddle. Berit took the other side wielding his heavy-bladed battle-axe.

The two armored knights crashed into the center of the charge. Sparhawk felled two of the attackers in quick succession as Kalten chopped another out of his saddle with a rapid series of savage sword strokes. One man tried to flank them, but fell twitching as Kurik's mace crushed in the side of his head. Sparhawk and Kalten were in the very center of the attackers now, swinging their heavy broadswords in vast overhand strokes. Then Berit charged in from the flank, his axe crunching into the bodies of the riders on that side. After a few moments of concerted violence, the survivors broke and fled.

"What was that all about?" Kalten demanded. The blond man was red-faced and panting from his exertions.

"I'll chase one of them down and ask him, my Lord," Berit offered eagerly.

"No," Sparhawk told him.

Berit's face fell.

"A novice must not volunteer, Berit," Kurik told the young man sternly, "at least, not until he's proficient with his weapons."

"I did all right, Kurik," Berit protested.

"Only because these people weren't very good," Kurik said. "Your swings are too wide, Berit. You leave yourself open for counterstrokes. When we get to my farm in Demos, I'll give you some more instruction."

"Sparhawk!" Sephrenia cried from the bottom of the hill.

Sparhawk spun Faran quickly around and saw five men on foot wearing the rough smocks of Styrics running out of the bushes beside the road toward Sephrenia, Dolmant, and Talen. He swore and drove his spurs into Faran's flanks.

It quickly became obvious that the Styrics were trying to reach Sephrenia and Flute. Sephrenia, however, was not utterly defenseless. One of the Styrics fell squealing to the ground, clutching at his belly. Another dropped to his knees, clawing at his eyes. The other three faltered, fatally as it turned out, because by then Sparhawk was there. He sent one man's head flying with a single swipe of his sword, then drove his blade into the chest of another. The last Styric tried to flee, but Faran took the bit between his teeth and ran him down with three quick bounds and trampled him into the earth with his steel-shod forehooves.

"There!" Sephrenia said sharply, pointing at the hilltop. A robed and hooded figure sat astride a pale horse, watching. Even as the small Styric woman began her incantation, the figure turned and rode back over the hill and out of sight.

"Who were they?" Kalten asked as he joined them on the road.

"Mercenaries," Sparhawk replied. "You could tell by their armor."

"Was that one up on the hill the leader?" Dolmant asked.

Sephrenia nodded.

"He was a Styric, wasn't he?"

"Perhaps, but perhaps something else. I sensed something familiar about him. Once before something tried to attack the little girl. Whatever it was, it was driven off. This time it tried more direct means." Her face grew dreadfully serious. "Sparhawk," she said, "I think we should ride on to Demos as quickly as we can. It's very dangerous out here in the open."

"We could question the wounded," he suggested. "Maybe they could tell us something about this mysterious Styric who seems so interested in you and Flute."

"They won't be able to tell you anything, Sparhawk," she disagreed. "If what was up there on that hill was what I think it was, they won't even have any memory of it."

"All right," he decided, "let's ride then."

It was midafternoon when they reached Kurik's substantial farmstead just outside Demos. The farm showed Kurik's careful attention to detail. The logs forming the walls of his large house had been adzed square and they fit tightly together with no need for chinking. The roof was constructed of overlapping split shakes. There were several outbuildings and storage sheds all built back into the side of the hill just behind the house, and the two-storey barn was of substantial size. The carefully tended kitchen garden was surrounded by a sturdy rail fence. A single brown and white calf stood at the fence looking wistfully at the wilted carrot tops and frost-browned cabbages inside the garden.

Two tall young men about the same age as Berit were splitting firewood in the yard, and two others, slightly older, were repairing the barn roof. They all wore rough canvas smocks.

Kurik swung down from his saddle and approached the

two in the yard. "How long has it been since you sharpened those axes?" he demanded gruffly.

"Father!" one of the young men exclaimed. He dropped
his axe and roughly embraced Kurik. He was, Sparhawk
noticed, at least a head taller than his sire.

The other lad shouted to his brothers on the roof of the
barn, and they came sliding down to leap from the edge
with no apparent concern for life or limb.

Then Aslade came bustling out of the house. She was a
plump woman wearing a gray homespun dress and a white
apron. Her hair was touched at the temples with silver,
but the dimples in her cheeks made her look girlish. She
caught Kurik in a warm embrace, and for several moments
Sparhawk's squire was surrounded by his family. Sparhawk watched almost wistfully.

"Regrets, Sparhawk?" Sephrenia asked him gently.

"A few, I suppose," he admitted.

"You should have listened to me when you were
younger, dear one. That could be you, you know."

"My profession's a little too dangerous for me to in-
clude a wife and children in my life, Sephrenia." He
sighed.

"When the time comes, dear Sparhawk, you won't even
consider that."

"The time, I think, has long since passed."

"We'll see," she replied mysteriously.

"We have guests, Aslade," Kurik told his wife.

Aslade dabbed at her misty eyes with one corner of her
apron and crossed to where Sparhawk and the others sat,
still mounted. "Welcome to our home," she greeted them
simply. She curtsied to Sparhawk and Kalten, both of
whom she had known since they were boys. "My Lords,"
she said formally. Then she laughed. "Come down here,
you two," she said, "and give me a kiss."

Like two clumsy boys, they slid from their saddles and
embraced her. "You're looking well, Aslade," Sparhawk
said, trying to recover some degree of dignity in the presence of Patriarch Dolmant.

"Thank you, my Lord," she said with a mocking little
curtsey. Aslade had known them far too long to pay much
attention to customary usages. Then she smiled broadly.

She patted her ample hips. "I'm getting stouter, Sparhawk," she said. "It comes from all the tasting when I cook, I think." She shrugged goodhumoredly. "But you can't tell if it's right unless you taste it." Then she turned to Sephrenia. "Dear, dear Sephrenia," she said, "it's been *so* long."

"Too long, Aslade," Sephrenia replied, sliding down from the back of her white palfry and taking Aslade in her arms. Then she said something in Styric to Flute, and the little girl came shyly forward and kissed Aslade's palms.

"What a beautiful child," Aslade said. She looked a bit slyly at Sephrenia. "You should have told me, my dear," she said. "I'm a very good midwife, you know, and I'm just a little hurt that you didn't invite me to officiate."

Sephrenia looked startled at that, then suddenly burst out laughing. "It's not like that at all, Aslade," she said. "There's a kinship between the child and me, but not the one you suggested."

Aslade smiled at Dolmant. "Come down from your horse, your Grace," she invited the patriarch. "Would the Church permit us an embrace—a chaste one, of course? Then you'll get your reward. I've just taken five loaves from the oven, and they're still nice and hot."

Dolmant's eyes brightened, and he quickly dismounted. Aslade threw her arms about his neck and kissed him noisily on the cheek. "He married Kurik and me, you know," she said to Sephrenia.

"Yes, dear. I was there, remember?"

Aslade blushed. "I remember very little about the ceremony," she confessed. "I had my mind on other things that day." She gave Kurik a wicked little smile.

Sparhawk carefully concealed a grin when he saw his squire's face redden noticeably.

Aslade looked inquiringly at Berit and Talen.

"The husky lad is Berit," Kurik introduced them. "He's a Pandion novice."

"You're welcome here, Berit," she told him.

"And the boy is my—uh—apprentice," Kurik fumbled. "I'm training him up to be a squire."

Aslade looked appraisingly at the young thief. "His

clothes are a disgrace, Kurik,'' she said critically.
''Couldn't you have found him something better to wear?''

''He's only recently joined us, Aslade,'' Kurik explained a little too quickly.

She looked even more sharply at Talen. ''Do you know
something, Kurik?'' she said. ''He looks almost exactly
the way you looked when you were his age.''

Kurik coughed nervously. ''Coincidence,'' he muttered.

Aslade smiled at Sephrenia. ''Would you believe that I
was after Kurik from the time I was six years old? It took
me ten years, but I got him in the end. Come down from
your horse, Talen. I have a trunk full of clothes my sons
have outgrown. We'll find something suitable for you to
wear.''

Talen's face had a strange, almost wistful expression as
he dismounted, and Sparhawk felt a sharp pang of sympathy as he realized what the usually impudent boy must
be feeling. He sighed and turned to Dolmant. ''Do you
want to go to the cloister now, your Grace?'' he asked.

''And leave Aslade's freshly baked bread to get cold?''
Dolmant protested. ''Be reasonable, Sparhawk.''

Sparhawk laughed as Dolmant turned to Kurik's wife.
''You have fresh butter, I hope?'' he asked.

''Churned yesterday morning, your Grace,'' she replied, ''and I just opened a pot of that plum jam you're
so fond of. Shall we step into the kitchen?''

''Why don't we?''

Almost absently, Aslade picked up Flute in one arm and
wrapped the other about Talen's shoulders. And then, with
the children close to her, she led the way into the house.

THE WALLED CLOISTER in which Princess Arissa was confined stood in a wooded glen on the far side of the city.
Men were seldom admitted into this strict community of
women, but Dolmant's rank and authority in the Church
gained them immediate entry. A submissive little sister
with doelike eyes and a bad complexion led them to a
small garden near the south wall where they found the
princess, sister of the late King Aldreas, sitting on a stone

bench in the wan winter sunlight with a large book in her lap.

The years had touched Arissa only lightly. Her long, dark blonde hair was lustrous, and her eyes a pale blue, so pale as to closely resemble the gray eyes of her niece, Queen Ehlana, although the dark circles beneath them spoke of long, sleepless nights filled with bitterness and a towering resentment. Her mouth was thin-lipped rather than sensual, and there were two hard lines of discontent at its corners. Although Sparhawk knew that she was approaching forty, her features were those of a much younger woman. She did not wear the habit of the sisters of the nunnery, but was wrapped instead in a soft red woolen robe open at the throat, and her head was crowned with an intricately folded wimple. "I'm honored by your visit, gentlemen," she said in a husky voice, not bothering to rise. "I have so few visitors."

"Your Highness," Sparhawk greeted her formally. "I trust you've been well?"

"Well, but bored, Sparhawk." Then she looked at Dolmant. "You've aged, your Grace," she observed spitefully, closing her book.

"But you have not," he replied. "Will you accept my blessing, Princess?"

"I think not, your Grace. The Church has done quite enough for me already." She looked meaningfully around at the walls enclosing the garden, and her refusal of the customary blessing seemed to give her some pleasure.

He sighed. "I see," he said. "What is the book you read?" he asked her.

She held it up for him to see.

"The Sermons of the Primate Subata," he noted, "a most instructional work."

She smiled maliciously. "This particular edition is even more so," she told him. "I had it made especially for me, your Grace. Within this innocent-looking cover, which deceives the mother superior who is my jailer, there lurks a volume of salacious erotic poetry from Cammoria. Would you care to have me read you a few verses?"

His eyes hardened. "No, thank you, Princess," he replied coldly. "You have not changed, I see."

She laughed mockingly. "I see no reason to change, Dolmant. I have merely altered my circumstances."

"Our visit here is not social, Princess," he said. "A rumor has surfaced in Cimmura that prior to your being cloistered here, you were secretly married to Duke Osten of Vardenais. Would you care to confirm—or deny—that rumor?"

"Osten?" She laughed. "That dried up old stick? Who in her right mind would marry a man like that? I like my men younger, more ardent."

"You deny the rumor, then?"

"Of course I deny it. I'm like the Church, Dolmant. I offer my bounty to *all* men—as everyone in Cimmura knows."

"Would you sign a document declaring the rumor to be false?"

"I'll think about it." She looked at Sparhawk. "What are you doing back in Elenia, Sir Knight? I thought my brother exiled you."

"I was summoned back, Arissa."

"How very interesting."

Sparhawk thought of something. "Did you receive a dispensation to attend your brother's funeral, Princess?" he asked her.

"Why, yes, Sparhawk. The Church generously granted me three whole days of mourning. My poor, stupid brother looked very regal as he lay on his bier in his state robes." She critically examined her long, pointed fingernails. "Death improves some people," she added.

"You hated him, didn't you?"

"I held him in contempt, Sparhawk. There's a difference. I always used to bathe whenever I left him."

Sparhawk held out his hand, showing her the blood-red ring on his finger. "Did you happen to notice if he had the mate to this on his finger?" he asked her.

She frowned slightly. "No," she said. "As a matter of fact, he didn't. Perhaps the brat stole it after he died."

Sparhawk clenched his teeth.

"Poor, poor Sparhawk," she said mockingly. "You cannot bear to hear the truth about your precious Ehlana, can you? We used to laugh about your attachment to her when she was a child. Did you have hopes, great champion? I saw her at my brother's funeral. She's not a child anymore, Sparhawk. She has the hips and breasts of a woman now. But she's sealed up in a diamond, isn't she, so you can't even touch her? All that soft, warm skin, and you can't even put so much as a finger on it."

"I don't think we need to pursue this, Arissa." He narrowed his eyes. "Who is your son's father?" he asked her suddenly, hoping to startle the truth out of her.

She laughed. "How could I possibly know that?" she asked. "After my brother's wedding, I amused myself in a certain establishment in Cimmura." She rolled her eyes. "It was both enjoyable and profitable. I made a very great deal of money. Most of the girls there overpriced themselves, but I learned as a child that the secret of great wealth is to sell cheaply to many." She looked maliciously at Dolmant. "Besides," she added, "it's a renewable resource."

Dolmant's face grew stiff, and Arissa laughed coarsely.

"That's enough, Princess," Sparhawk told her. "You would not care then to hazard a guess as to the identity of your bastard's father?" He said it quite deliberately, hoping to sting her into some inadvertent revelation.

Her eyes flashed with momentary anger, then she leaned back on the stone bench with a heavy-lidded look of voluptuous amusement. She put her hands to the front of her scarlet robe. "I'm a bit out of practice, but I suppose I could improvise. Would you like to try me, Sparhawk?"

"I don't think so, Arissa." Sparhawk's voice was flat.

"Ah, the well-known prudery of your family. What a shame, Sparhawk. You interested me when you were a young knight. Now you've lost your queen, and there's not even that pair of rings to prove the connection between the two of you. Wouldn't that mean that you're no longer her champion? Perhaps—if she recovers—you might be able to establish a closer bond with her. She shares my blood, you know, and it might flow as hotly through her veins as it does through mine. If you were to try me, you could compare and find out."

He turned away in disgust, and she laughed again.

"Shall I send for parchment and ink, Princess?" Dolmant asked, "so that we may compose your denial of the rumor concerning your marriage?"

"No, Dolmant," she replied, "I don't think so. This request of yours hints at the interest of the Church in this matter. The Church has done me few favors of late, so why should I exert myself in her behalf? If the people in Cimmura want to amuse themselves with rumors about me, let them. They licked their lips over the truth, now let them enjoy a lie."

"That's your final word then?"

"I might change my mind. Sparhawk's a Church Knight, your Grace, and you're a patriarch. Why don't you order him to see if he can persuade me? Sometimes I persuade easily—sometimes not. It all depends on the persuader."

"I think we've concluded our business here," Dolmant said. "Good day, Princess." He turned on his heel and started across the winter-brown lawn of the garden.

"Come back some time when you can leave your stuffy friend behind, Sparhawk," Arissa said. "We could amuse ourselves."

He turned without answering and followed the patriarch out of the garden. "I think we've wasted our time," he muttered, his face dark and angry.

"Ah, no, my boy," Dolmant said serenely. "In her haste to be offensive, the princess overlooked an important point in canon law. She has just made a free admission in the presence of two ecclesiastical witnesses—you and me. That has all the validity of a signed statement. All it takes is our oaths as to what she said."

Sparhawk blinked. "Dolmant," he said, "you're the most devious man I've ever known."

"I'm glad you approve, my son." The patriarch smiled.

CHAPTER
TWELVE

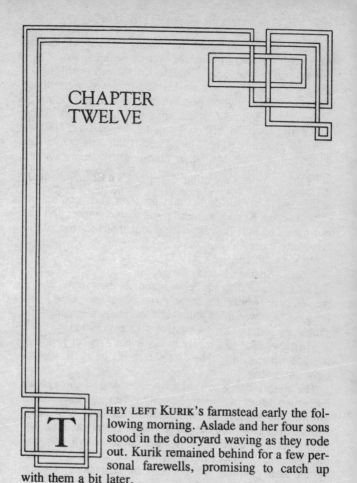

T HEY LEFT KURIK'S farmstead early the following morning. Aslade and her four sons stood in the dooryard waving as they rode out. Kurik remained behind for a few personal farewells, promising to catch up with them a bit later.

"Are we going through the city?" Kalten asked Sparhawk.

"I don't think so," Sparhawk replied. "We can take the road that goes around the north side. I'm fairly sure that we'll be seen, but let's not make it easy for them."

"Would you mind a personal observation?"

"Probably not."

"You really ought to give some thought to letting Kurik retire, you know. He's getting older and he should be spending more time with his family instead of trailing along behind you all over the world. Besides, so far as I know, you're the only Church Knight who still has a squire. The rest of us have learned to get along without them. Give him a good pension and let him stay home.''

Sparhawk squinted at the sun which was just rising above the wooded hilltop lying to the east of Demos. ''You're probably right,'' he agreed, ''but how would I go about telling him? My father placed Kurik in my service before I completed my novitiate. It has to do with being hereditary champion of the royal house of Elenia.'' He smiled wryly. ''It's an archaic position that requires archaic usages. Kurik's a friend more than a squire, and I'm not going to hurt him by telling him that he's too old to serve any more.''

''It's a problem, isn't it?''

''Yes,'' Sparhawk said, ''it is.''

Kurik came riding up behind them as they were passing the cloister where Princess Arissa was confined. His bearded face was a bit glum, but then he straightened his shoulders and assumed a businesslike expression.

Sparhawk looked gravely at his friend, trying to imagine life without him. Then he shook his head. It was totally impossible.

The road leading toward Chyrellos passed through an evergreen forest where the morning sun streamed down through the boughs to spatter the forest floor with gold. The air was crisp and bright, although there was no frost. After they had gone about a mile farther, Berit resumed his narrative. ''The Knights of the Church were consolidating their position in Rendor,'' he told Talen, ''when word reached Chyrellos that Emperor Otha of Zemoch had massed a huge army and was marching into Lamorkand.''

''Wait a minute,'' Talen interrupted him. ''When did all this happen?''

''About five hundred years ago.''

''It wasn't the same Otha Kalten was talking about the other day then, was it?''

''So far as we know, it was.''

''That's impossible, Berit.''

"Otha is perhaps nineteen hundred years old," Sephrenia told the boy.

"I thought this was a history," Talen accused, "not a fairy tale."

"When Otha was a boy, he encountered the Elder God Azash," she explained. "The Elder Gods of Styricum have great powers and are not controlled by any form of morality. One of the gifts they can bestow upon their followers is the gift of a greatly expanded lifetime. That is why some men are willing to follow them."

"Immortality?" he asked her skeptically.

"No," she corrected, "not that. No God can bestow that."

"The Elene God can," Dolmant said, "in a spiritual sense, anyway."

"That's an interesting theological point, your Grace." She smiled. "Some day we'll have to discuss it. Anyway," she continued, "when Otha agreed to worship Azash, the God granted him enormous power, and Otha eventually became emperor of Zemoch. The Styrics and the Elenes in Zemoch have intermarried, and so a Zemoch is not truly a member of either race."

"An abomination in the eyes of God," Dolmant added.

"The Styric Gods feel much the same way," Sephrenia agreed. She looked at Talen again. "To understand Otha—and Zemoch—one needs to understand Azash. He is the most totally evil force on earth. The rites of the worship of him are obscene. He delights in perversion and in blood and in the agonies of sacrificial victims. In their worship of him, the Zemochs have become much less than human and their incursion into Lamorkand was accompanied by unspeakable horrors. Had the invading armies been only Zemochs, however, they might have been met and turned back by conventional forces. But Azash had reinforced them with creatures from the underworld."

"Goblins?" Talen asked disbelievingly.

"Not exactly; but the word will serve, I suppose. It would take most of the morning for me to describe the twenty or so varieties of inhuman creatures Azash has at his command, and you wouldn't like the descriptions."

"This story is getting less believable by the minute,"

Talen noted. "I like the battles and all, but when you start telling me about goblins and fairies, I begin to lose interest. I'm not a child any more, after all."

"In time you may come to understand—and to believe," she said. "Go on with the story, Berit."

"Yes, ma'am," he said. "When the Church realized the nature of the forces that were invading Lamorkand, they summoned the Church Knights back from Rendor. They reinforced the ranks of the four orders with other knights and with common soldiers until the forces of the west were nearly as numerous as those of the Zemoch horde of Otha."

"Was there a battle then?" Talen asked eagerly.

"The greatest battle in the history of mankind," Berit replied. "The two armies met on the plains of Lamorkand near Lake Randera. The physical battle was gigantic, but the supernatural battle on that plain was even more stupendous. Waves of darkness and sheets of flame swept the field. Fire and lightning rained from the sky. Whole battalions were swallowed up by the earth or burned to ashes in sudden flame. The crash of thunder rolled perpetually from horizon to horizon, and the ground itself was torn by earthquakes and the eruption of searing liquid rock. The magic of the Zemoch priests was countered each time by the concerted magic of the Knights of the Church. For three days, the armies were locked in battle before the Zemochs were pushed back. Their retreat became more rapid, eventually turning into a rout. Otha's horde finally broke and ran toward the safety of the border."

"Terrific!" Talen exclaimed excitedly. "And then did our army invade Zemoch?"

"They were too exhausted," Berit told him. "They had won the battle, but not without great cost. Fully half of the Church Knights lay slain upon the battlefield, and the armies of the Elene kings numbered their dead by the scores of thousands."

"They could have done *something*, couldn't they?"

Berit nodded sadly. "They cared for their wounded and buried their dead. Then they went home."

"That's all?" Talen asked incredulously. "This isn't much of a story if that's all they did, Berit."

"They had no choice. They'd stripped the western kingdoms of every able-bodied man to fight the war and had left the crops untended. Winter was coming, and there was no food. They managed to eke their way through that winter, but so many men had been killed or maimed in the battle that when spring came, there weren't enough people—in the west or in Zemoch—to plant new crops. The result was famine. For a century, the only concern in all of Eosia was food. The swords and lances were put aside, and the war horses were hitched to plows.''

"They never talk about that sort of thing in other stories I've heard.'' Talen sniffed.

"That's because those are only stories,'' Berit told him. "This really happened. Anyway,'' he went on, "the war and the famine which followed caused great changes. The militant orders were forced to labor in the fields beside the common people and they gradually began to distance themselves from the Church. Pardon me, your Grace,'' he said to Dolmant, ''but at that time, the Hierocracy was too far removed from the concerns of the commons fully to understand their suffering.''

"There's no need to apologize, Berit,'' Dolmant replied sadly. "The Church has freely admitted her blunders during that era.''

Berit nodded. "The Church Knights became increasingly secularized. The original intent of the Hierocracy had been that the knights should be armed monks who would live in their chapterhouses when they weren't fighting. That concept began to fade. The dreadful casualties in their ranks made it necessary for them to seek a source for new recruits. The preceptors of the orders journeyed to Chyrellos and laid the problem before the Hierocracy in the strongest of terms. The main stumbling block to recruitment had always been the vow of celibacy. At the insistence of the preceptors, the Hierocracy relaxed that rule, and Church Knights were permitted to take wives and father children.''

"Are you married, Sparhawk?'' Talen suddenly asked.

"No,'' the knight replied.

"Why not?''

"He hasn't found any woman silly enough to have him.''

Kalten laughed. "He's not very pretty to begin with and he's got a foul temper."

Talen looked at Berit. "That's the end of the story, then?" he asked critically. "A good story needs an end, you know—something like, 'and they all lived happily ever after.' Yours just sort of dribbles off without going any place."

"History just keeps going, Talen. There aren't any ends. The militant orders are now as much involved in political affairs as they are in the affairs of the Church, and no one can say what lies in store for them in the future."

Dolmant sighed. "All too true," he agreed. "I wish it might have been otherwise, but perhaps God had His reasons for ordaining things this way."

"Wait a minute," Talen objected. "This all started when you were going to tell me about Otha and Zemoch. He sort of fell out of the story a ways back. Why are we so worried about him now?"

"Otha is mobilizing his armies again," Sparhawk told him.

"Are we doing anything about it?"

"We're watching him. If he comes again, we'll meet him the same way we did last time." Sparhawk looked around at the yellow grass gleaming in the bright morning sunlight. "If we want to get to Chyrellos before the month's out, we're going to have to move a little faster," he said, touching his spurs to Faran's flanks.

They rode east for three days, stopping each night in wayside inns. Sparhawk concealed a certain tolerant amusement as Talen, inspired by Berit's recounting of the age-old story, fiercely beheaded thistles with a stick as they rode along. It was midafternoon of the third day when they crested a long hill to look down upon the vast sprawl of Chyrellos, the seat of the Elene Church. The city lay within no specific kingdom, but sat instead at the place where Elenia, Arcium, Cammoria, Lamorkand, and Pelosia touched. It was by far the largest city in all of Eosia. Since it was a Church city, it was dotted with spires and domes; at certain times of the day, the air above it shimmered with the sound of bells, calling the faithful to prayer. No city so large, however, could be given over entirely to

churches. Commerce, almost as much as religion, dominated the society of the holy city, and the palaces of
wealthy merchants vied with those of the patriarchs of the
Church for splendor and opulence. The center and focus
of the city, however, was the Basilica of Chyrellos, a vast,
domed cathedral of gleaming marble erected to the glory
of God. The power emanating from the Basilica was enormous, and it touched the lives of all Elenes from the snowy
wastes of northern Thalesia to the deserts of Rendor.

Talen, who until now had never been out of Cimmura,
gaped in astonishment at the enormous city spread before
them, gleaming in the winter sunlight. "Good God!" he
breathed almost reverently.

"Yes," Dolmant agreed. "He is good, and this is one
of His most splendid works."

Flute, however, seemed unimpressed. She drew out her
pipes and played a mocking little melody on them as if to
dismiss all the splendors of Chyrellos as unimportant.

"Will you go directly to the Basilica, your Grace?"
Sparhawk asked.

"No," Dolmant replied. "It's been a tiring journey,
and I'll need my wits about me when I present this matter
to the Hierocracy. Annias has many friends in the highest
councils of the Church, and they won't like what I'm going
to say to them."

"They can't possibly doubt your words, your Grace."

"Perhaps not, but they can try to twist them around."
Dolmant tugged thoughtfully at one earlobe. "I think my
report might have more impact if I have corroboration.
Are you any good at public appearances?"

"Only if he can use his sword," Kalten said.

Dolmant smiled faintly. "Come to my house tomorrow,
Sparhawk. We'll go over your testimony together."

"Is that altogether legal, your Grace?" Sparhawk asked.

"I won't ask you to lie under oath, Sparhawk. All I
want to do is suggest to you how you should phrase your
answers to certain questions." He smiled again. "I don't
want you to surprise me when we're before the Hierocracy. I hate surprises."

"All right then, your Grace," Sparhawk agreed.

They rode on down the hill to the great bronze gates of

the holy city. The guards there saluted Dolmant and let them all pass without question. Beyond the gate lay a broad street that could only be called a boulevard. Huge houses stood on either side, seeming almost to shoulder at each other in their eagerness to command the undivided attention of passersby. The street teemed with people. Although many of them wore the drab smocks of workmen, the vast majority were garbed in somber, ecclesiastical black.

"Is everybody here a churchman?" Talen asked. The boy's eyes were wide as the sights of Chyrellos overwhelmed him. The cynical young thief from the back alleys of Cimmura had finally seen something he could not shrug off.

"Hardly," Kalten replied, "but in Chyrellos, one commands a bit more respect if he's thought to be affiliated with the Church, so everybody wears black."

"Frankly, I wouldn't mind seeing a bit more color in the streets of Chyrellos," Dolmant said. "All this unrelieved black depresses me."

"Why not start a new trend then, your Grace?" Kalten suggested. "The next time you present yourself at the Basilica, wear a pink cassock—or maybe emerald green. You'd look very nice in green."

"The dome would collapse if I did," Dolmant said wryly.

The patriarch's house, unlike the palaces of most other high churchmen, was simple and unadorned. It was set slightly back from the street and was surrounded by well-trimmed shrubs and an iron fence.

"We'll go on to the chapterhouse then, your Grace," Sparhawk said as they stopped at Dolmant's gate.

The patriarch nodded. "And I'll see you tomorrow."

Sparhawk saluted and then led the others on down the street.

"He's a good man, isn't he?" Kalten said.

"One of the best," Sparhawk replied. "The church is lucky to have him."

The chapterhouse of the Pandion Knights in Chyrellos was a bleak-looking stone building on a little-travelled side street. Although it was not moated as was the one in Cimmura, it was nonetheless surrounded by a high wall and blocked off from the street by a formidable gate. Sparhawk went through the ritual which gained them entry, and they dismounted in the courtyard. The governor of the chapterhouse, a stout man named Nashan came bustling down the stairs to greet them. "Our house is honored, Sir Sparhawk," he said, clasping the big knight's hand. "How did things turn out in Cimmura?"

"We managed to pull Annias's teeth," Sparhawk replied.

"How did he take it?"

"He looked a little sick."

"Good." Nashan turned to Sephrenia. "Welcome, little mother," he greeted her, kissing both her palms.

"Nashan," she replied gravely. "I see that you're not missing too many meals."

He laughed and slapped at his paunch. "Every man needs a vice or two," he said. "Come inside, all of you. I've smuggled a skin of Arcian red into the house—for my stomach's sake, of course—and we can all have a goblet or two."

"You see how it works, Sparhawk?" Kalten said. "Rules can be bent if you know the right people."

Nashan's study was draped and carpeted in red, and the ornate table which served as his desk was inlaid with gold and mother of pearl. "A gesture," he said apologetically as he led them into the room and looked about. "In Chyrellos, we must make these little genuflections in the direction of opulence if we are to be taken seriously."

"It's all right, Nashan," Sephrenia told him. "You weren't selected as governor of this chapterhouse because of your humility."

"One must keep up appearances, Sephrenia," he said. He sighed. "I was never that good a knight," he admitted. "I'm at best only mediocre with the lance, and most of my spells tend to crumble on me about halfway through." He drew in a deep breath and looked around. "I'm a good administrator, though. I know the Church and her politics and I can serve the order and Lord Vanion in that arena probably far better than I could on the field."

"We all do what we can," Sparhawk told him. "I'm told that God appreciates our best efforts."

"Sometimes I feel that I've disappointed Him," Nashan said. "Somewhere deep inside me I think I might have done better."

"Don't flagellate yourself, Nashan," Sephrenia advised. "The Elene God is reputed to be most forgiving. You've done what you could."

They took seats around Nashan's ornate table, and the governor summoned an acolyte who brought goblets and the skin of the deep red Arcian wine. At Sephrenia's request, he also sent for tea for her and milk for Flute and Talen.

"We don't necessarily need to mention this to Lord Vanion, do we?" Nashan said to Sparhawk as he lifted the wineskin.

"Wild horses couldn't drag it out of me, my Lord," Sparhawk told him, holding out his goblet.

"So," Kalten said, "what's happening here in Chyrellos?"

"Troubled times, Kalten," Nashan replied. "Troubled times. The archprelate ages, and the entire city is holding its breath in anticipation of his death."

"Who will be the new archprelate?" Sparhawk asked.

"At the moment there's no way to know. Cluvonus is in no condition to name a successor, and Annias of Cimmura is spending money like water to gain the throne."

"What about Dolmant?" Kalten asked.

"He's too self-effacing, I'm afraid," Nashan replied. "He's so dedicated to the Church that he doesn't have the sense of self that one needs to have to aspire to the golden throne in the Basilica. Not only that, he's made enemies."

"I like enemies." Kalten grinned. "They give you a reason to keep your sword sharp."

Nashan looked at Sephrenia. "Is there something afoot in Styricum?" he asked her.

"What exactly do you mean?"

"The city is suddenly awash with Styrics," he replied. "They say that they're here to seek instruction in the Elene faith."

"That's absurd."

"I thought so myself. The Church has been trying to convert the Styrics for three thousand years without much success, and now they come flocking to Chyrellos on their own accord, begging to be converted."

"No sane Styric would do that," she insisted. "Our Gods are jealous, and they punish apostasy severely." Her eyes narrowed. "Have any of these pilgrims identified their place of origin?" she asked.

"Not that I've heard. They all look like common rural Styrics."

"Perhaps they've made a longer journey than they're willing to reveal."

"You think they might be Zemochs?" Sparhawk asked her.

"Otha's already infested eastern Lamorkand with his agents," she replied. "Chyrellos is the center of the Elene world. It's a logical place for espionage and disruption." She considered it. "We're likely to be here for a while," she observed. "We have to wait for the arrival of the knights from the other orders. I think that perhaps we might spend the time investigating these unusual postulants."

"I can't really get too much involved in that," Sparhawk disagreed. "I have things far more important on my mind just now. We'll deal with Otha and his Zemochs when the time comes. Right now I have to concentrate on restoring Ehlana to her throne and preventing the deaths of certain friends." He spoke obliquely, since he had kept to himself the details of what she had told him had taken place in the throne room in Cimmura.

"It's all right, Sparhawk," she assured him. "I understand your concern. I'll take Kalten with me, and we'll see what we can turn up."

They spent the remainder of the day in quiet conversation in Nashan's ornate study, and the following morning Sparhawk dressed in a mail coat and a simple hooded robe and rode across town to Dolmant's house, where the two of them carefully went over what had happened in Cimmura and Arcium. "It would be futile to level any direct charges at Annias," Dolmant said, "so it's probably best to omit any references to him—or to Harparin. Let's just present the affair as a plot to discredit the Pandion Order and leave it at that. The Hierocracy will draw its own conclusions." He smiled faintly. "The least damaging of those conclusions will be that Annias made a fool of himself in public. If nothing else, that might help to stiffen the resolve of the neutral patriarchs when the time comes to select a new archprelate."

"That's something, anyway," Sparhawk said. "Are we going to present the matter of Arissa's so-called marriage at the same time?"

"I don't think so," Dolmant replied. "It's really not a significant enough thing to require the consideration of the entire Hierocracy. The declarations of Arissa's spinsterhood can come from the patriarch of Vardenais. The alleged wedding took place in his district, and he would be the logical one to draw up the denial that it took place." A smile touched his ascetic face. "Besides," he added, "he's a friend of mine."

"Clever," Sparhawk said admiringly.

"I rather liked it," Dolmant said modestly.

"When are we going before the Hierocracy?"

"Tomorrow morning. There's no point in waiting. All that would do is give Annias time to alert his friends in the Basilica."

"Do you want me to come by here and ride to the Basilica with you?"

"No. Let's go in separately. Let's not give them the slightest hint of what we're up to."

"You're very good at political chicanery, your Grace." Sparhawk grinned.

"Of course I am. How do you think I got to be a patriarch? Come to the Basilica during the third hour after sunrise. That should give me time to present my report first—and to answer all the questions and objections that Annias's supporters are likely to raise."

"Very well, your Grace," Sparhawk said, rising to his feet.

"Be careful tomorrow, Sparhawk. They'll try to trip you up. And for God's sake, don't lose your temper."

"I'll try to remember that."

The following morning Sparhawk dressed carefully. His

black armor gleamed, and his cape and silver surcoat had been freshly pressed. Faran had been groomed until his roan coat shone, and his hooves had been oiled to make them glossy.

"Don't let them back you into a corner, Sparhawk," Kalten warned as he and Kurik boosted the big man into his saddle. "Churchmen can be very devious."

"I'll watch myself." Sparhawk gathered his reins and nudged Faran with his heels. The big roan pranced out through the chapterhouse gate and into the teeming streets of the holy city.

The domed Basilica of Chyrellos dominated the entire city. It was built on a low hill, and it soared toward heaven, gleaming in the wintery sun. The guards at the bronze portal admitted Sparhawk respectfully, and he dismounted before the marble stairs that led up to the great doors. He handed Faran's reins to a monk, adjusted the strap on his shield, and then mounted the steps, his spurs ringing on the marble. At the top of the stairs, an officious young churchman in a black cassock blocked his path. "Sir Knight," the young man protested, "you may not enter while under arms."

"You're wrong, your Reverence," Sparhawk told him. "Those rules don't apply to the militant orders."

"I've never heard of any such exception."

"You have now. I don't want any trouble with you, friend, but I've been summoned by Patriarch Dolmant and I'm going inside."

"But—"

"There's an extensive library here, neighbor. Why don't you go look up the rules again? I'm sure you'll find that you've missed a few. Now stand aside." He brushed past the man in the black cassock and went on into the cool incense-smelling cathedral. He made the customary bow toward the jewel-encrusted altar and moved on down the broad central aisle in the multicolored light streaming through tall, stained-glass windows. A sacristan stood by the altar vigorously polishing a silver chalice.

"Good morning, friend," Sparhawk said to him in his quiet voice.

The sacristan almost dropped the chalice. "You startled

me, Sir Knight,'' he said, laughing nervously. "I didn't hear you come up behind me.''

"It's the carpeting,'' Sparhawk said. "It muffles the sound of footsteps. I understand that the members of the Hierocracy are in session.''

The sacristan nodded.

"Patriarch Dolmant summoned me to testify in a matter he's presenting this morning. Could you tell me where they're meeting?''

"In the archprelate's audience chamber, I believe. Do you want me to show you the way, Sir Knight?''

"I know where it is. Thanks, neighbor.'' Sparhawk went across the front of the nave and out through a side door into an echoing marble corridor. He removed his helm and tucked it under his arm and proceeded along the corridor until he reached a large room where a dozen churchmen sat at tables sorting through stacks of documents. One of the black-robed men looked up, saw Sparhawk in the doorway, and rose. "May I help you, Sir Knight?'' he asked. The top of his head was bald, and wispy tufts of gray hair stuck out over his ears like wings.

"The name is Sparhawk, your Reverence. The Patriarch Dolmant summoned me.''

"Ah, yes,'' the bald churchman said. "The patriarch advised me that he was expecting you. I'll go tell him that you've arrived. Would you care to sit down while you're waiting?''

"No thanks, your Reverence. I'll stand. It's a little awkward to sit down when you're wearing a sword.''

The churchman smiled a bit wistfully. "I wouldn't know about that,'' he said. "What's it like?''

"It's overrated,'' Sparhawk told him. "Would you tell the patriarch that I'm here?''

"At once, Sir Sparhawk.'' The churchman turned and crossed the room to the far door with his sandals slapping on the marble floor. After a few moments he came back. "Dolmant says that you're to go right on in. The archprelate's with them.''

"That's a surprise. I've heard that he's been ill.''

"This is one of his better days, I think.'' The churchman led the way across the room and opened the door for Sparhawk.

The audience chamber was flanked on either side by tier upon tier of high-backed benches. The benches were filled with elderly churchmen in sober black, the Hierocracy of the Elene Church. At the front of the room on a raised dais sat a large golden throne, and seated upon that throne in a white satin robe and golden miter was the Archprelate Cluvonus. The old man was dozing. In the center of the room stood an ornate lectern. Dolmant was there with a sheaf of parchment on the slanted shelf before him. "Ah," he said, "Sir Sparhawk. So good of you to come."

"My pleasure, your Grace," Sparhawk replied.

"Brothers," Dolmant said to the other members of the Hierocracy, "I have the honor to present the Pandion Knight, Sir Sparhawk."

"We have heard of Sir Sparhawk," a lean-faced patriarch seated in the front tier on the left said coldly. "Why is he here, Dolmant?"

"To present evidence in the matter we were just discussing, Makova," Dolmant replied distantly.

"I have heard quite enough already."

"Speak for yourself, Makova," a jovial-looking fat man said from the right tier. "The militant orders are the arm of the Church, and their members are always welcome at our deliberations."

The two men glared at each other.

"Since Sir Sparhawk was instrumental in uncovering and thwarting this plot," Dolmant said smoothly, "I thought that his testimony might prove enlightening."

"Oh, get on with it, Dolmant," the lean-faced patriarch on the left said irritably. "We have matters of much greater importance to take up this morning."

"It shall be as the esteemed patriarch of Coombe wishes." Dolmant bowed. "Sir Sparhawk," he said then, "do you give your oath as a Knight of the Church that your testimony shall be the truth?"

"I do, your Grace," Sparhawk affirmed.

"Please tell the assembly how you uncovered this plot."

"Of course, your Grace." Sparhawk then recounted most of the conversation between Harparin and Krager, omitting their names, the name of the Primate Annias, and all references to Ehlana.

"Is it your custom to eavesdrop on private conversations, Sir Sparhawk?" Makova asked a bit spitefully.

"When it involves the security of the Church or the State, yes, your Grace. I'm sworn to defend both."

"Ah, yes. I'd forgotten that you are also the champion of the queen of Elenia. Does that sometimes not divide your loyalties, Sir Sparhawk?"

"It hasn't so far, your Grace. The interests of the Church and the State are seldom in conflict with each other in Elenia."

"Well said, Sir Sparhawk," the fat churchman on the right approved.

The patriarch of Coombe leaned over and whispered something to the sallow man sitting beside him.

"What did you do after you learned of this conspiracy, Sir Sparhawk?" Dolmant asked then.

"We gathered our forces and rode down into Arcium to intercept the men who were to carry out the attack."

"And why did you not advise the primate of Cimmura of this so-called conspiracy?" Makova asked.

"The scheme involved an attack on a house in Arcium, your Grace," Sparhawk replied. "The primate of Cimmura has no authority there, so the matter didn't concern him."

"Nor the Pandions either, I should say. Why did you not just alert the Cyrinic Knights and let them deal with things?" Makova looked around smugly at those seated near him as if he had just made a killing point.

"The plot was designed to discredit *our* order, your Grace. We felt that gave us sufficient reason to attend to the matter ourselves. Besides, the Cyrinics have their own concerns, and we didn't want to trouble them with so minor an affair."

Makova grunted sourly.

"What happened then, Sir Sparhawk?" Dolmant asked.

"Things went more or less as expected, your Grace. We alerted Count Radun; then, when the mercenaries arrived, we fell on them from behind. Not very many of them escaped.''

"You attacked them from behind without warning?'' Patriarch Makova looked outraged. ''Is this the vaunted heroism of the Pandion Knights?''

"You're nit-picking, Makova,'' the jovial-looking man on the other side of the aisle snorted. ''Your precious Primate Annias made a fool of himself. Quit trying to smooth it over by attacking this knight or trying to impugn his testimony.'' He looked shrewdly at Sparhawk. ''Would you care to hazard a guess as to the source of this conspiracy, Sir Sparhawk?'' he asked.

"We are not here to listen to speculation, Emban,'' Makova snapped quickly. ''The witness can testify only to what he knows, not what he guesses.''

"The patriarch of Coombe is right, your Grace,'' Sparhawk said to Patriarch Emban. ''I swore to speak only the truth, and guesses usually fly wide of that mark. The Pandion Order has offended many people in the past century or so. We are sometimes an acerbic group of men, stiffnecked and unforgiving. Many find that quality in us unpleasant, and old hatreds die hard.''

"True,'' Emban conceded. ''If it came to the defense of the faith, however, I would prefer to place my trust in you stiff-necked and unforgiving Pandions rather than some others I could name. Old hatreds, as you say, die hard, but so do new ones. I've heard about what's going on in Elenia, and it's not too hard to pick out somebody who might profit from the Pandions' disgrace.''

"Do you dare to accuse the Primate Annias?'' Makova cried, jumping to his feet with his eyes bulging.

"Oh, sit down, Makova,'' Emban said in disgust. ''You contaminate us by your very presence. Everybody in this chamber knows who owns you.''

"You accuse *me*?''

"Who paid for that new palace of yours, Makova? Six months ago you tried to borrow money from me, but now you seem to have all you need. Isn't that curious? Who's subsidizing you, Makova?''

"What's all the shouting about?'' a feeble voice asked. Sparhawk looked sharply at the golden throne at the front of the chamber. The Archprelate Cluvonus had come awake and was blinking in confusion as he looked around. The old man's head was wobbling on his stringy neck, and his eyes were bleary.

"A spirited discussion, Most Holy," Dolmant said mildly.

"Now you went and woke me up," the archprelate said petulantly, "and I was having such a nice dream." He reached up, pulled off his miter, and threw it on the floor. Then he sank back on his throne, pouting.

"Would the Archprelate care to hear of the matter under discussion?" Dolmant asked.

"No, I wouldn't," Cluvonus snapped. "So there." Then he cackled as if his infantile outburst had been some enormous joke. The laughter trailed off and he scowled at them. "I want to go back to my room," he declared. "Get out of here, all of you."

The Hierocracy rose to its feet and began to file out.

"You, too, Dolmant," the archprelate insisted in a shrill voice. "And send Sister Clentis to me. She's the only one who really cares about me."

"As you wish, Most Holy," Dolmant said, bowing.

When they were outside, Sparhawk walked beside the patriarch of Demos. "How long has he been like this?" he asked.

Dolmant sighed. "For a year now at least," he replied. "His mind has been failing for quite some time, but it's only in the past year that his senility has reached this level."

"Who is Sister Clentis?"

"His keeper—his nursemaid, actually."

"Is his condition widely known?"

"There are rumors, of course, but we've managed to keep his true state a secret." Dolmant sighed again. "Don't judge him by the way he is now, Sparhawk. When he was younger, he honored the throne of the archprelacy."

Sparhawk nodded. "I know," he agreed. "How is his health otherwise?"

"Not good. He's very frail. It cannot be much longer."

"Perhaps that's why Annias is beginning to move so

quickly." Sparhawk shifted his silver-embossed shield. "Time's on his side, you know."

Dolmant made a sour face. "Yes," he agreed. "That's what makes your mission so vital."

Another churchman came up to join them. "Well, Dolmant," he said, "a very interesting morning. Just how deeply was Annias involved in the scheme?"

"I didn't say anything about the primate of Cimmura, Yarris," Dolmant protested with mock innocence.

"You didn't have to. It all fits together a bit too neatly. I don't think anybody on the council missed your point."

"Do you know the patriarch of Vardenais, Sparhawk?" Dolmant asked.

"We've met a few times." Sparhawk bowed slightly to the other churchman, his armor creaking. "Your Grace," he said.

"It's good to see you again, Sir Sparhawk," Yarris replied. "How are things in Cimmura?"

"Tense," Sparhawk said.

Patriarch Yarris looked at Dolmant. "You know that Makova's going to report everything that happened this morning to Annias, don't you?"

"I wasn't trying to keep it a secret. Annias made an ass of himself. Considering his aspirations, that element of his personality is highly relevant."

"It is indeed, Dolmant. You've made another enemy this morning."

"Makova's never been that fond of me anyway. Incidentally, Yarris, Sparhawk and I would like to present a certain matter to you for your consideration."

"Oh?"

"It involves another ploy by the primate of Cimmura."

"Then let's thwart him, by all means."

"I was hoping you might feel that way about it."

"What's he up to this time?"

"He presented a spurious marriage certificate to the Royal Council in Cimmura."

"Who got married?"

"Princess Arissa and Duke Osten."

"That's ridiculous."

"Princess Arissa said almost the same thing."

"You'll swear to that?"

Dolmant nodded. "So will Sparhawk," he added.

"I assume that the point of the whole thing was to legitimize Lycheas?"

Dolmant nodded again.

"Well, then. Why don't we see if we can disrupt that? Let's go speak with my secretary. He can draw up the necessary document." The patriarch of Vardenais chuckled. "Annias is having a bad month, I'd say. This will make two plots in a row that have failed—and Sparhawk's been involved both times." He looked at the big Pandion. "Keep your armor on, my boy," he suggested. "Annias might decide to have the area between your shoulder blades decorated with a dagger hilt."

After Dolmant and Sparhawk had given their depositions concerning the statements of Princess Arissa, they left the patriarch of Vardenais and continued along the corridor to the nave of the Basilica.

"Dolmant," Sparhawk said, "do you have any idea about why so many Styrics are here in Chyrellos?"

"I've heard about it. The story is that they're seeking instruction in our faith."

"Sephrenia says that's an absurdity."

Dolmant made a wry face. "She's probably right. I've labored for a lifetime and I haven't as yet managed to convert a single Styric."

"They're very attached to their Gods," Sparhawk said. "I'm not trying to be offensive, Dolmant, but there seems to be a very close personal relationship between the Styrics and their Gods. Our God is perhaps a bit remote."

"I'll mention that the next time I talk to Him." Dolmant smiled. "I'm sure He values your opinion."

Sparhawk laughed. "It *was* a bit presumptuous, wasn't it?"

"Yes, as a matter of fact, it was. How long do you think it's going to be until you can leave for Borrata?"

"Several days, anyway. I hate to lose the time, but the knights from the other orders have long journeys to make to reach Chyrellos, and I'm more or less obliged to wait for them. All this waiting is making me very impatient, but there's no help for it, I'm afraid." He pursed his lips.

"I think I'll spend the time nosing around a bit. It'll give me something to do, and all these Styrics are making me curious."

"Be careful in the streets of Chyrellos, Sparhawk," Dolmant advised seriously. "They can be very dangerous."

"The whole world is dangerous lately, Dolmant. I'll keep you posted on what I find out." Then Sparhawk turned and went down the corridor with his spurs clinking on the marble floor.

CHAPTER
THIRTEEN

T WAS NEARLY noon when Sparhawk returned to the chapterhouse. He had ridden slowly through the busy streets of the holy city, paying scant attention to the crowds around him. The deterioration of the Archprelate Cluvonus had saddened him. Despite the rumors that had been circulating of late, actually to see the revered old man's condition had come as a profound personal shock.

He stopped at the heavy gate and perfunctorily went through the ritual that admitted him. Kalten was waiting in the courtyard. "Well?" the blond man asked. "How did it go?"

Sparhawk dismounted heavily and pulled off his helmet. "I don't know if we changed any minds," he replied.

"The patriarchs who support Annias still support him; the ones who oppose him are still on our side; and those who are neutral are still sitting on the fence."

"It was a waste of time, then?"

"Not entirely, I guess. After this, it might be a little harder for Annias to win over any more uncommitted votes."

"I wish you'd make up your mind, Sparhawk." Kalten looked closely at his friend. "You're in a sour mood. What really happened?"

"Cluvonus was there."

"That's a surprise. How did he look?"

"Awful."

"He *is* eighty-five, Sparhawk. You couldn't expect him to look very impressive. People wear out, you know."

"His mind has gone, Kalten," Sparhawk said sadly. "He's childish now. Dolmant doesn't think he's going to last much longer."

"That bad?"

Sparhawk nodded.

"That makes it fairly important for us to get to Borrata and back in a hurry then, doesn't it?"

"Urgent," Sparhawk agreed.

"Do you think we should ride on ahead and let the knights from the other orders catch up with us later?"

"I wish we could. I hate the idea of Ehlana sitting alone in that throne room, but I don't think we dare. Komier was right about a show of unity, and the other orders are sometimes a little touchy. Let's not start off by offending them."

"Did you and Dolmant talk to somebody about Arissa?"

Sparhawk nodded. "The patriarch of Vardenais is handling it."

"The day wasn't an absolute waste, then."

Sparhawk grunted. "I want to change out of this." He rapped on the breastplate of his armor with his knuckles.

"You want me to unsaddle Faran for you?"

"No, I'll be going back out. Where's Sephrenia?"

"In her room, I think."

"Have somebody saddle her horse."

"Is she going somewhere?"

"Probably." Sparhawk went on up the stairs and entered the chapterhouse.

It was about a quarter hour later when he tapped on Sephrenia's door. He had removed his armor and now wore a mail coat beneath a nondescript gray cloak that bore no insignia of his rank or his order. "It's me, Sephrenia," he said through the panels of the door.

"Come in, Sparhawk," she said.

He opened the door and stepped in quietly.

She was sitting in a large chair with Flute in her lap. The child was sleeping with a contented little smile on her face. "Did things go well at the Basilica?" Sephrenia asked.

"It's a little hard to say," he replied. "Churchmen are very good at hiding their emotions. Did you and Kalten find out anything yesterday about all the Styrics here in Chyrellos?"

She nodded. "They're concentrated in the quarter near the east gate. They have a house there somewhere that seems to be a headquarters of some sort. We weren't able to locate it exactly, though."

"Why don't we go see if we can find it?" he suggested. "I need something to do. I'm feeling a bit restless."

"Restless? You, Sparhawk? The man of stone?"

"Impatience, I suppose. I want to get started for Borrata."

She nodded. Then she rose, lifting Flute easily, and laid the child on the bed. Gently she covered the little girl with a gray wool blanket. Flute briefly opened her dark eyes, then smiled and went back to sleep. Sephrenia kissed the small face, then turned to Sparhawk. "Shall we go then?" she said.

"You're very fond of her, aren't you?" Sparhawk asked as the two of them walked along the corridor leading toward the courtyard.

"It goes a bit deeper than that. Someday perhaps you'll understand."

"Have you any idea where this Styric house might be?"

"There's a shopkeeper in the market near the east gate.

He sold some Styrics a number of sides of meat. The porter who delivered them knows where the house is.''

"Why didn't you question the porter?''

"He wasn't there yesterday.''

"Maybe he'll make it to work today.''

"It's worth a try.''

He stopped and gave her a direct look. "I'm not trying to pry into the secrets you've chosen not to reveal, Sephrenia, but could you distinguish between ordinary rural Styrics and Zemochs?''

"It's possible,'' she admitted, "unless they're taking steps to conceal their true identity.''

They went down into the courtyard where Kalten waited with Faran and Sephrenia's white palfrey. The blond knight had an angry expression on his face. "Your horse bit me, Sparhawk,'' he said accusingly.

"You know him well enough not to turn your back on him. Did he draw blood?''

"No,'' Kalten admitted.

"Then he was only being playful. It shows that he likes you.''

"Thanks,'' Kalten said flatly. "Do you want me to come along?''

"No. I think we want to be more or less inconspicuous, and on occasion you have trouble managing that.''

"Sometimes your charm overwhelms me, Sparhawk.''

"We're sworn to speak the truth.'' Sparhawk helped Sephrenia into her saddle, then mounted Faran. "We should be back before dark,'' he told his friend.

"Don't hurry on my account.''

Sparhawk led the small Styric woman out through the gate and into the side street beyond.

"He turns everything into a joke, doesn't he?'' Sephrenia observed.

"Most things, yes. He's been laughing at the world since he was a boy. I think that's why I like him so much. My view of things tends to be a little more bleak, and he helps me keep my perspective.''

They rode on through the now-teeming streets of Chyrellos. Although many local merchants affected the somber black of churchmen, visitors usually did not, and their bright clothing stood out by contrast. Travellers from Cammoria in particular were highly colorful, since their customary silk garments did not fade with the passage of time and remained brightly red or green or blue.

The market place to which Sephrenia led him was some distance from the chapterhouse, and it was perhaps three-quarters of an hour before they reached it.

"How did you find this shopkeeper?" Sparhawk asked.

"There are certain staples in the Styric diet," she replied. "Elenes don't eat those things very often."

"I thought you said that this porter delivered some sides of meat."

"Goat, Sparhawk. Elenes don't care much for goat."

He shuddered.

"How provincial you are," she said lightly. "If it doesn't come from a cow, you won't eat it."

"I suppose it's what you're used to."

"I'd better go to the shop alone," she said. "Sometimes you're a bit intimidating, dear one. We want answers from the porter, and we might not get them if you frighten him. Watch my horse." She handed him her reins and then moved off through the market. Sparhawk watched as she went across the bustling square to speak with a shabby-looking fellow in a blood-smeared canvas smock. After a short time she returned. He got down and helped her back onto her horse.

"Did he tell you where the house is?" he asked.

She nodded. "It's not far—near the east gate."

"Let's go have a look."

As they started out, Sparhawk did something uncharacteristically impulsive. He reached out and took the small woman's hand. "I love you, little mother," he told her.

"Yes," she said calmly, "I know. It's nice of you to say it, though." Then she smiled. It was an impish little smile that somehow reminded him of Flute. "Another lesson for you, Sparhawk," she said. "When you're having dealings with a woman, you cannot say *I love you* too often."

"I'll remember that. Does the same thing apply to Elene women?"

"It applies to all women, Sparhawk. Gender is a far more important distinction than race."

"I shall be guided by you, Sephrenia."

"Have you been reading medieval poetry again?"

"Me?"

They rode through the market place and on into the run-down quarter near the east gate of Chyrellos. While not perhaps the same as the slums of Cimmura, this part of the holy city was far less opulent than the area around the Basilica. There was less color here, for one thing. The tunics of the men in the street were uniformly drab, and the few merchants there were in the crowd wore garments which were faded and threadbare. They did, however, have the self-important expressions which all merchants, successful or not, automatically assume. Then, at the far end of the street, Sparhawk saw a short man in a lumpy, unbleached smock of homespun wool. "Styric," he said shortly.

Sephrenia nodded and drew up the hood of her white robe so that it covered her face. Sparhawk straightened in his saddle and carefully assumed an arrogant, condescending expression such as the servant of some important personage might wear. They passed the Styric, who stepped cautiously aside without paying them any particular heed. Like all members of his race, the Styric had dark, almost black, hair and a pale skin. He was shorter than the Elenes who passed him in this narrow street, and the bones in his face were prominent, as if he had somehow not quite been completed.

"Zemoch?" Sparhawk asked after they had passed the man.

"It's impossible to say," Sephrenia replied.

"Is he concealing his identity with a spell?"

She spread her hands helplessly. "There's no way to tell, Sparhawk. Either he's just an ordinary backwoods Styric with nothing on his mind but his next meal, or he's a very subtle magician who's playing the bumpkin to block out attempts to probe him."

Sparhawk swore under his breath. "This might not be as easy as I thought," he said. "Let's go on then and see what we can find out."

The house to which Sephrenia had been directed sat at the end of a cul-de-sac, a short street that went nowhere.

"That's going to be difficult to watch without being obvious," Sparhawk said as they rode slowly past the mouth of the narrow street.

"Not really," Sephrenia disagreed. She reined in her palfrey. "We need to talk with the shopkeeper there on the corner."

"Did you want to buy something?"

"Not exactly buy, Sparhawk. Come along. You'll see." She slid down out of her saddle and tied the reins of her delicate white horse to a post outside the shop she had indicated. She looked around briefly. "Will your great war horse discourage anyone who might want to steal my gentle little Ch'iel?" she asked. She laid her hand affectionately on the white horse's neck.

"I'll talk to him about it."

"Would you?"

"Faran," Sparhawk said to the ugly roan, "stay here and protect Sephrenia's mare."

Faran nickered, his ears pricked eagerly forward.

"You big old fool," Sparhawk laughed.

Faran snapped at him, his teeth clacking together at the empty air inches from Sparhawk's ear.

"Be nice," Sparhawk murmured.

Inside the shop, a room devoted to the display of cheap furniture, Sephrenia's attitude became ingratiating, even oddly submissive. "Good master merchant," she said with an uncharacteristic tone in her voice, "we serve a great Pelosian noble who has come to Chyrellos to seek solace for his soul in the holy city."

"I don't deal with Styrics," the merchant said rudely, glowering at Sephrenia. "There are too many of you filthy heathens in Chyrellos already." He assumed an expression of extreme distaste, all the while making what Sparhawk knew to be totally ineffective gestures to ward off magic.

"Look, huckster," the big knight said, affecting an insulting Pelosian-accented manner, "do not rise above yourself. My master's chatelaine and I will be treated with respect, regardless of your feeble-minded bigotry."

The shopkeeper bristled at that. "Why—" he began to bluster.

Sparhawk smashed the top of a cheap table into splinters with a single blow of his fist. Then he seized the shop-man's collar and pulled him forward so that they were eye to eye. "Do we understand each other?" he said in a dreadful voice that hovered just this side of a whisper.

"What we require, good master merchant," Sephrenia said smoothly, "is a goodly set of chambers facing the street. Our master has been ever fond of watching the ebb and flow of humanity." She lowered her eyelashes modestly. "Have you such a place above-stairs?"

The shopkeeper's face was a study in conflicting emotions as he turned to mount the stairs toward the upper floor.

The chambers above were shabby—one might even go so far as to say ratty. They had at some time in the past been painted, but the pea-soup green paint had peeled and now hung in long strips from the walls. Sparhawk and Sephrenia were not interested in paint, however. It was to the dirty window at the front of the main chamber that their eyes went.

"There's more, little lady," the shopkeeper said, more respectfully than before.

"We can conduct our own inspection, good master merchant." She cocked her head slightly. "Was that the step of a customer I heard from below?"

The shopkeeper blinked and then he bolted downstairs.

"Can you see the house up the street from the window?" Sephrenia asked.

"The panes are dirty." Sparhawk lifted the hem of his gray cloak to wipe away the dust and grime.

"Don't," she said sharply. "Styric eyes are very sharp."

"All right," he said. "I'll look through the dust. Elene eyes are just as sharp." He looked at her. "Does that happen every time you go out?" he asked.

"Yes. Common Elenes are not much smarter than common Styrics. Frankly I'd rather have a conversation with a toad than with either breed."

"Toads can talk?" He was a little surprised at that.

"If you know what you're listening for, yes. They're not very stimulating conversationalists, though."

The house at the end of the street was not impressive. The lower floor was constructed of field stone, crudely mortared together, and the second story was of roughly squared-off timbers. It seemed somehow set off from the houses around it, as if drawing in a kind of isolated separateness. As they watched, a Styric wearing the poorly woven wool smock which was the characteristic garb of his race moved up the street toward the house. He looked around furtively before he entered.

"Well?" Sparhawk asked.

"It's hard to say," Sephrenia replied. "It's the same as with that one we saw in the street. He's either simple or very skilled."

"This could take a while."

"Only until dark, if I'm right," she said as she drew a chair up to the window.

In the next several hours, a fair number of Styrics entered the house, and, as the sun sank into a dense, dirty-looking cloud bank on the western horizon, others began to arrive. A Cammorian in a bright yellow silk robe went furtively up the cul-de-sac and was immediately admitted. A booted Lamork in a polished steel cuirass and accompanied by two crossbow-bearing men-at-arms marched arrogantly up to the doors of the house and gained entry just as quickly. Then, as the chill winter twilight began to settle over Chyrellos, a lady in a deep purple robe and attended by a huge manservant in bullhide armor such as that commonly worn by Pelosians went up the center of the short street, moving with a stiff-legged, abstracted pace. Her eyes seemed vacant and her movements jerky. Her face, however, bore an expression of ineffable ecstasy.

"Strange visitors to a Styric house," Sephrenia commented.

Sparhawk nodded and looked around the darkening room. "Do you want some light?" he asked her.

"No. Let's not be seen to be here. I'm certain that the street is being watched from the upper floor of the house." Then she leaned against him, filling his nostrils with the woody fragrance of her hair. "You can hold my hand, though," she offered. "For some reason, I've always been a little afraid of the dark."

"Of course," he said, taking her small hand in his big one. They sat together for perhaps another quarter hour as the street outside grew darker.

Suddenly Sephrenia gave an agonized little gasp.

"What's the matter?" he asked in alarm.

She did not immediately reply but rose to her feet instead, raising her hands, palms up, above her. A dim figure seemed to stand before her, a figure that was more shadow than substance, and a faint glow seemed to stretch between its widespread, gauntleted hands. Slowly it held forth that silvery nimbus. The glow grew momentarily brighter, then coalesced into solidity as the shadow before her vanished. She sank back into her chair, holding the long, slender object with a curious kind of sorrowful reverence.

"What was that, Sephrenia?" Sparhawk demanded.

"Another of the twelve knights has fallen," she said in a voice that was almost a moan. "This is his sword, a part of my burden."

"Vanion?" he asked, almost choking with a dreadful sense of fear.

Her fingers sought the crest on the pommel of the sword she held, feeling the design in the darkness. "No," she said. "It was Lakus."

Sparhawk felt a wrench of grief. Lakus was an elderly Pandion, a man with snowy hair and a grim visage whom all the knights of Sparhawk's generation had revered as a teacher and a friend.

Sephrenia buried her face in Sparhawk's armored shoulder and began to weep. "I knew him as a boy, Sparhawk," she lamented.

"Let's go back to the chapterhouse," he suggested gently. "We can do this another day."

She lifted her head and wiped at her eyes with her hand. "No, Sparhawk," she said firmly. "Something's happening in that house tonight—something that may not happen again for a while."

He started to say something, but then he felt an oppressive weight that seemed to be located just behind his ears. It was as if someone had just placed the heels of his hands at the back of his skull and pushed inward. Sephrenia leaned intently forward. "Azash!" she hissed.

"What?"

"They're summoning the spirit of Azash," she said with a terrible note of urgency in her voice.

"That nails it down, then, doesn't it?" he said, rising to his feet.

"Sit down, Sparhawk. This isn't played out yet."

"There can't be that many."

"And what will you learn if you go up the street and chop the house and everyone in it to pieces? Sit down. Watch and learn."

"I'm obliged, Sephrenia. It's part of the oath. It has been for five centuries."

"Bother the oath," she snapped. "This is more important."

He sank back into his chair, troubled and uncertain. "What are they doing?" he asked.

"I told you. They're raising the spirit of Azash. That can only mean that they're Zemochs."

"What are the Elenes doing in there, then? The Cammorian, the Lamork, and that Pelosian woman?"

"Receiving instruction, I think. The Zemochs didn't come here to learn, but to teach. This is serious, Sparhawk—more deadly serious than you could ever imagine."

"What do we do?"

"For the moment, nothing. We sit here and watch."

Again Sparhawk felt that oppressive weight at the base of his skull, and then a fiery tingling that seemed to run through all his veins.

"Azash has answered the summons," Sephrenia said quietly. "It's very important to sit quietly now and for both of us to keep our thoughts neutral. Azash can sense hostility directed at him."

"Why would Elenes participate in the rites of Azash?"

"Probably for the rewards he will give them for worshiping him. The Elder Gods have always been most lavish with their rewards—when it suits them to be."

"What kind of reward could possibly pay for the loss of one's soul?"

She shrugged, a barely perceptible motion in the growing darkness. "Longevity, perhaps. Wealth, power—and in the case of the woman, beauty. It could even be other things—things I don't care to think about. Azash is twisted and he soon twists those who worship him."

In the street below, a workman with a handcart and a torch clattered along over the cobblestones. He took an unlighted torch from the cart, set it in an iron ring protruding from the shop front below, and ignited it. Then he rattled on.

"Good," Sephrenia murmured. "Now we'll be able to see them when they come out."

"We've already seen them."

"They'll be different, I'm afraid."

The door to the Styric house opened, and the silk-robed Cammorian emerged. As he passed through the circle of torchlight below, Sparhawk saw that his face was very pale, and his eyes were wide with horror.

"That one will not return," Sephrenia said quietly. "Most likely he'll spend the rest of his life trying to atone for his venture into the darkness."

A few minutes later, the booted Lamork came out into the street. His eyes burned, and his face was twisted into an expression of savage cruelty. His impassive crossbowmen marched along behind him.

"Lost," Sephrenia sighed.

"What?"

"The Lamork is lost. Azash has him."

Then the Pelosian lady emerged from the house. Her purple robe was carelessly open at the front, and beneath it she was naked. As she came into the torchlight, Sparhawk could see that her eyes were glazed and that her nude body was splattered with blood. Her hulking attendant made some effort to close the front of her robe, but she hissed at him, thrusting his hand away, and went off down the street shamelessly flaunting her body.

"And that one is more than lost," Sephrenia said. "She will be dangerous now. Azash rewarded her with powers.'' She frowned. ''I'm tempted to suggest that we follow her and kill her.''

''I'm not sure that I could kill a woman, Sephrenia.''

''She's not even a woman anymore, but we'd have to behead her, and that could cause some outrage in Chyrellos.''

''Do *what*?''

''Behead her. It's the only way to be certain that she's really dead. I think we've seen enough here, Sparhawk. Let's go back to the chapterhouse and talk with Nashan. Tomorrow I think we should report this to Dolmant. The Church has ways to deal with this sort of thing.'' She rose to her feet.

''Let me carry the sword for you.''

''No, Sparhawk. It's *my* burden. I must carry it.'' She tucked Lakus's sword inside her robe and led the way toward the door.

They went downstairs again, and the shopkeeper came out of the back of his establishment rubbing his hands together. ''Well?'' he said eagerly, ''will you be taking the rooms?''

''Totally unsuitable,'' Sephrenia sniffed. ''I wouldn't keep my master's dog in a place like that.'' Her face was very pale, and she was visibly trembling.

''But—''

''Just unlock the door, neighbor,'' Sparhawk said, ''and we'll be on our way.''

''What took you so long, then?''

Sparhawk gave him a flat, cold stare, and the shopkeeper swallowed hard and went to the door, fishing in his tunic pocket for the key.

Outside, Faran was standing protectively beside Sephrenia's palfrey. There was a torn scrap of rough cloth on the cobblestones under his hooves.

''Trouble?'' Sparhawk asked him.

Faran snorted derisively.

''I see,'' Sparhawk said.

''What was that about?'' Sephrenia asked wearily as Sparhawk helped her to mount.

''Someone tried to steal your horse,'' he shrugged. ''Faran persuaded him not to.''

"Can you really communicate with him?"

"I more or less know what he's thinking. We've been together for a long time." He hauled himself up into his saddle, and the two of them rode off down the street in the direction of the Pandion chapterhouse.

They had gone perhaps a half mile when Sparhawk had a momentary premonition. He reacted instantly, driving Faran's shoulder against the white palfrey. The smaller horse lurched to one side, even as a crossbow bolt buzzed spitefully through the space where Sephrenia had been an instant before. "Ride, Sephrenia!" he barked as the bolt clashed against the stones of a house fronting the street. He looked back, drawing his sword. But Sephrenia had already thumped her heels to the white horse's flanks and plunged off down the street at a clattering gallop with Sparhawk closely behind her, shielding her body with his own.

After they had crossed several streets, Sephrenia slowed her pace. "Did you see him?" she asked. She had Lakus's sword in her hand now.

"I didn't have to see him. A crossbow means a Lamork. Nobody else uses them."

"The one who was in the house with the Styrics?"

"Probably—unless you've gone out of your way to offend other Lamorks of late. Could Azash or one of his Zemochs have sensed your presence back there?"

"It's possible," she conceded. "No one can be absolutely certain just how far the power of the Elder Gods goes. How did you know that we were about to be attacked?"

"Training, I suppose. I've learned to know when someone's pointing a weapon at me."

"I thought it was pointed at me."

"It amounts to the same thing, Sephrenia."

"Well, he missed."

"*This* time. I think I'll talk to Nashan about getting you a mail shirt."

"Are you mad, Sparhawk?" she protested. "The weight alone would put me on my knees—not to mention the awful smell."

''Better the weight and the smell than an arrow between the shoulder blades.''

''Totally out of the question.''

''We'll see. Put the sword away and let's move on. You need rest, and I want to get you inside the chapterhouse where it's safe before someone else takes a shot at you.''

CHAPTER
FOURTEEN

T HE FOLLOWING DAY, about midmorning, Sir Bevier arrived at the gates of the Pandion chapterhouse in Chyrellos. Sir Bevier was a Cyrinic Knight from Arcium. His formal armor was burnished to a silvery sheen, and his surcoat was white. His helmet had no visor, but rather bore heavy cheekpieces and a formidable nose guard. He dismounted in the courtyard, hung his shield and his Lochaber axe on his saddlebow, and removed his helmet. Bevier was young and somewhat slender. His complexion was olive and his hair curly and blue-black.

With some show of ceremony, Nashan descended the steps of the chapterhouse with Sparhawk and Kalten to greet him. "Our house is honored, Sir Bevier," he said.

Bevier inclined his head stiffly. "My Lord," he responded, "I am commanded by the preceptor of my order to convey to you his greetings."

"Thank you, Sir Bevier," Nashan said, somewhat taken aback by the young knight's stiff formality.

"Sir Sparhawk," Bevier said then, again inclining his head.

"Do we know each other, Bevier?"

"Our preceptor described you to me, my Lord Sparhawk—you and your companion, Sir Kalten. Have the others arrived yet?"

Sparhawk shook his head, "No. You're the first."

"Come inside, Sir Bevier," Nashan said then. "We'll assign you a cell so that you can get out of your armor, and I'll speak to the kitchen about a hot meal."

"And it please you, my Lord, might I first visit your chapel? I have been some days on the road and I feel sorely the need for prayer in a consecrated place."

"Of course," Nashan said to him.

"We'll see to your horse," Sparhawk told the young man.

"Thank you, Lord Sparhawk." Bevier bent his head again and followed Nashan up the steps.

"Oh, he's going to be a jolly travelling companion," Kalten said ironically.

"He'll loosen up once he gets to know us," Sparhawk said.

"I hope you're right. I'd heard that the Cyrinics are a shade formal, but I think our young friend there might be carrying it to extremes." Curiously, he unhooked the Lochaber from the saddlebow. "Can you imagine using this thing on somebody?" He shuddered. The Lochaber axe had a heavy, two-foot blade surmounted at its forward end with a razor-sharp, hawklike bill. Its heavy handle was about four feet long. "You could shuck a man out of his armor like an oyster out of its shell with this."

"I think that's the idea. It *is* sort of intimidating, isn't it? Put it away, Kalten. Don't play with another man's toys."

After Sir Bevier had completed his prayers and changed out of his armor, he joined them in Nashan's ornate study.

"Did they give you something to eat?" Nashan asked.

"It isn't necessary, my Lord," Bevier replied. "If I may be permitted, I'll join you and your knights in refectory for the noon meal."

"Of course," Nashan replied. "You're more than welcome to join us, Bevier."

Sparhawk then introduced Bevier to Sephrenia. The young man bowed deeply to her. "I have heard much of you, Lady," he said. "Our instructors in the Styric secrets hold you in great esteem."

"You're kind to say so, Sir Knight. My skills are the result of age and practice, however, and do not result from any particular virtue."

"Age, Lady? Surely not. You can scarce be much older than I, and I will not see my thirtieth year for some months yet. The bloom of youth has not yet left your cheeks, and your eyes quite overwhelm me."

Sephrenia smiled warmly at him, then looked critically at Kalten and Sparhawk. "I hope you two are paying attention," she said. "A little polish wouldn't hurt either of you."

"I was never much good at formality, little mother," Kalten confessed.

"I've noticed," she said. "Flute," she said a bit wearily then, "please put the book down. I've asked you again and again not to touch one."

Several days later, Sir Tynian and Sir Ulath arrived, riding together. Tynian was a good-humored Alcione Knight from Deira, the kingdom lying to the north of Elenia. His broad, round face was open and friendly. His shoulders and chest were powerfully muscled as the result of years of bearing Deiran armor, the heaviest in the world. Over his massive armor he wore a sky-blue surcoat. Ulath was a hulking Genidian Knight, fully a head taller than Sparhawk. He did not wear armor, but rather a plain mail shirt and a simple conical helmet. Covering his shirt, he wore a green surcoat. He carried a large round shield and a heavy war axe. Ulath was a silent, withdrawn man who seldom spoke. His blond hair hung in two braids down his back.

"Good morning, gentlemen," Tynian said to Sparhawk

and Kalten as he dismounted in the courtyard of the chapterhouse. He looked at them closely. "You would be Sir Sparhawk," he said. "Our preceptor said that you'd broken your nose sometime." He grinned then. "It's all right, Sparhawk. It doesn't interfere with your kind of beauty."

"I'm going to like this man," Kalten said.

"And you must be Kalten," Tynian said. He thrust out his hand, and Kalten took it before he realized that the Alcione was holding a dead mouse concealed in his palm. With a startled oath, he jerked his hand back. Tynian howled with laughter.

"I think I could get to like him as well," Sparhawk noted.

"My name is Tynian," the Alcione Knight introduced himself. "My silent friend there is Ulath from Thalesia. He caught up with me a few days ago. Hasn't spoken ten words since then."

"You talk enough for both of us," Ulath grunted, sliding out of his saddle.

"That's God's own truth," Tynian admitted. "I have this overwhelming fondness for the sound of my own voice."

Ulath thrust out his huge hand. "Sparhawk," he said.

"No mice?" Sparhawk asked.

A faint smile touched Ulath's face as they clasped hands. Then he shook hands with Kalten, and the four of them went up the steps into the chapterhouse.

"Has Bevier arrived yet?" Tynian asked Kalten.

"A few days back. Have you ever met him?"

"Once. Our preceptor and I made a formal visit to Larium, and we were introduced to the Cyrinics in their motherhouse there. I found him to be a bit stiff-necked and formal."

"That hasn't changed much."

"Didn't think it had. Exactly what are we going to do down in Cammoria? Preceptor Darellon can be infuriatingly closemouthed on occasion."

"Let's wait until Bevier joins us," Sparhawk suggested. "I get the feeling that he might be a little touchy, so let's not offend him by talking business out of his presence."

"Good thinking, Sparhawk. This show of unity could

fall apart on us if Bevier starts sulking. I'll have to admit that he can be a good man in a fight, though. Is he still carrying that Lochaber?''

''Oh, yes,'' Kalten said.

''Gruesome thing, isn't it? I saw him practicing with it at Larium. He cut the top off a post as thick as my leg with one swipe at a full gallop. I get the feeling that he could ride through a platoon of foot troops and leave a trail of loose heads behind him ten yards wide.''

''Let's hope it doesn't come to that,'' Sparhawk said.

''If that's your attitude, Sparhawk, you're going to take all the fun out of this excursion.''

''I *am* going to like him,'' Kalten said.

Sir Bevier joined them in Nashan's study after the completion of noon services in the chapel. As closely as Sparhawk could determine, Bevier had not missed services once since his arrival.

''All right then,'' Sparhawk said, rising to his feet when they were all assembled, ''this is sort of where we stand. Annias, the primate of Cimmura, has his eyes on the archprelate's throne here in Chyrellos. He controls the Elenian royal council, and they're giving him money out of the royal treasury. He's trying to use that money to buy enough votes in the Hierocracy to win election after Cluvonus dies. The preceptors of the four orders want to block him.''

''No decent churchman would accept money for his vote,'' Bevier said, his voice verging on outrage.

''I'll grant that,'' Sparhawk agreed. ''Unfortunately, many churchmen are far from decent. Let's be honest about it, gentlemen. There's a wide streak of corruption in the Elene Church. We might wish it were different, but we have to face the facts. Many of those votes *are* for sale. Now—and this is important—Queen Ehlana is unwell; otherwise, she wouldn't allow Annias to have access to the treasury. The preceptors agree that the best way to stop Annias is to find some way to cure the queen and put her back in power. That's why we're going to Borrata. There are physicians at the university there who might be able to determine the nature of her illness and find a cure for it.''

''Are we taking your queen with us?'' Tynian asked.

"No. That's quite impossible."

"It's going to be a little hard for the physicians to find out much then, isn't it?"

Sparhawk shook his head. "Sephrenia, the Pandion instructor in the secrets, will be going with us. She can describe Queen Ehlana's symptoms in great detail and she can raise an image of the queen if the physicians need a closer look."

"Seems a bit roundabout," Tynian noted, "but if that's the way we have to do it, then that's the way we'll do it."

"There's a great deal of unrest in Cammoria right now," Sparhawk went on. "The central kingdoms are all infested with Zemoch agents, and they're trying to stir up as much trouble as they can. Not only that, Annias is fairly certain to guess at what we're trying to do, so he'll try to interfere."

"Borrata's a long way from Cimmura, isn't it?" Tynian asked. "Does Primate Annias have so long an arm?"

"Yes," Sparhawk said, "he does. There's a renegade Pandion in Cammoria who sometimes works for Annias. His name is Martel, and he's likely to try to stop us."

"Only once," Ulath grunted.

"Let's not go out of our way looking for a fight, though," Sparhawk cautioned. "Our main task is to get Sephrenia safely to Borrata and back. There's been at least one attempt on her life already."

"We'll want to discourage that," Tynian said. "Are we taking anybody else with us?"

"My squire, Kurik," Sparhawk replied, "and probably a young Pandion novice named Berit. He shows some promise, and Kurik's going to need somebody along to help him care for the horses." He thought a moment. "I think we'll take a boy along as well," he said.

"Talen?" Kalten sounded surprised at that. "Is that really a good idea, Sparhawk?"

"Chyrellos is corrupt enough already. I don't think it's a good idea to turn that little thief loose in the streets. Besides, I think we may find uses for his specialized talents. The only other person going with us will be a little girl named Flute."

Kalten stared at him in astonishment.

"Sephrenia won't leave her behind," Sparhawk explained, "and I'm not sure she *can* be left behind. You remember how easily she got out of that nunnery in Arcium?"

"You've got a point there, I guess," Kalten conceded.

"A very straightforward presentation, Sir Sparhawk," Bevier said approvingly. "When will we leave?"

"First thing in the morning," Sparhawk replied. "It's a long way to Borrata, and the archprelate isn't getting younger. Patriarch Dolmant says that he could die at any time, and that's when Annias will start to move."

"We must make our preparations then," Bevier said, rising to his feet. "Will you gentlemen be joining me in the chapel for evening services?" he asked.

Kalten sighed. "I suppose we should," he said. "We *are* Church Knights, after all."

"And a bit of God's help wouldn't hurt, would it?" Tynian added.

Late that afternoon, however, a company of church soldiers arrived at the gates of the chapterhouse. "I have a summons from the Patriarch Makova for you and your companions, Sir Sparhawk," the captain in charge of the soldiers said when Sparhawk and the others came down into the courtyard. "He would speak with you in the Basilica at once."

"We'll get our horses," Sparhawk said. He led the rest of the knights into the stables. Once inside, he swore irritably.

"Trouble?" Tynian asked him.

"Makova's a supporter of Primate Annias," Sparhawk replied, leading Faran out of his stall. "I've got a strong suspicion that he's going to try to hinder us."

"We must respond to his summons, however," Bevier said, swinging his saddle up onto his horse's back. "We are Church Knights and must obey the commands of a member of the Hierocracy, no matter what his affiliation."

"And there's that company of soldiers out there, too," Kalten added. "I'd say that Makova doesn't take too many chances."

"Surely he doesn't think we'd refuse?" Bevier said.

"You don't know Sparhawk that well yet," Kalten told him. "He can be contrary at times."

"Well, we don't have any choice in the matter," Sparhawk said. "Let's go to the Basilica and see what the patriarch has to say to us."

They led their horses out into the courtyard and mounted. At a crisp command from the captain, the soldiers formed up around them.

The square in front of the Basilica was strangely deserted as Sparhawk and his friends dismounted.

"Looks to me as if they're expecting trouble," Kalten noted as they started up the broad marble stairs.

When they entered the vast nave of the church, Bevier went down on his knees and clasped his hands in front of him.

The captain and a squad of his soldiers entered behind them. "We must not keep the patriarch waiting," he said. There was a certain arrogant tone in his voice that irritated Sparhawk for some reason. He muffled that feeling, however, and piously dropped to his knees beside Bevier. Kalten grinned and also knelt. Tynian nudged Ulath, and they, too, went down on their knees.

"I said—" the captain began, his voice rising slightly.

"We heard you, neighbor," Sparhawk said to him. "We'll be with you presently."

"But—"

"You can wait over there. We won't be too long."

The captain turned and stalked off.

"Nice touch, Sparhawk," Tynian murmured.

"We *are* Church Knights, after all," Sparhawk replied. "It won't hurt Makova to wait awhile. I'm sure he'll enjoy the anticipation."

"I'm sure," Tynian agreed.

The five knights remained kneeling for perhaps ten minutes while the captain stalked about impatiently.

"Have you finished, Bevier?" Sparhawk asked politely when the Cyrinic unclasped his hands.

"Yes," Bevier answered, his face alight with devotion. "I feel cleansed now and at peace with the world."

"Try to hang on to that feeling. The patriarch of Coombe

is likely to irritate us all.'' Sparhawk rose to his feet.
''Shall we go, then?''

''Well, *finally*,'' the captain snapped as they joined him
and his men.

Bevier looked at him coldly. ''Have you any rank, Captain?'' he asked, ''aside from your military one, I mean?''

''I am a marquis, Sir Bevier.''

''Excellent. If our devotions offend you, I will be more
than happy to give you satisfaction. You may have your
seconds call upon me at any time. I will be at your complete disposal.''

The captain paled visibly and shrank back. ''I am merely
following my orders, my Lord. I would not dream of giving offense to a Knight of the Church.''

''Ah,'' Bevier said distantly. ''Let us proceed, then. As
you stated so excellently earlier, we must not keep the
patriarch of Coombe waiting.''

The captain led them to a hallway branching out from
the nave.

''Nicely done, Bevier,'' Tynian whispered.

The Cyrinic smiled briefly.

''There's nothing like the offer of a yard or so of steel
in his belly to remind a man of his manners,'' Kalten
added.

The chamber to which the captain led them was grandiose with deep maroon carpeting and drapes and polished
marble walls. The lean-faced patriarch of Coombe sat at
a long table reading a parchment. He looked up as they
were admitted, his face angry. ''What took so long?'' he
snapped at the captain.

''The Knights of the Church felt obliged to spend a few
moments in devotions before the main altar, your Grace.''

''Oh. Of course.''

''May I withdraw, your Grace?''

''No. Stay. It shall fall to you to enforce the dictates I
will issue here.''

''As it please your Grace.''

Makova then looked sternly at the knights. ''I am told
that you gentlemen are planning a foray into Cammoria,''
he said.

"We haven't made any secret of it, your Grace," Sparhawk replied.

"I forbid it."

"Might one ask why, your Grace?" Tynian asked mildly.

"No. One may not. The Church Knights are subject to the authority of the Hierocracy. Explanations are not required. You are all to return to the Pandion chapterhouse and you will remain there until it pleases me to send you further instructions." He smiled a chill smile. "I believe you will all be returning home very shortly." Then he drew himself up. "That will be all. You have my permission to withdraw. Captain, you will see to it that these knights do not leave the Pandion chapterhouse."

"Yes, your Grace."

They all bowed and silently filed out the door.

"That was short, wasn't it?" Kalten said as they went back down the corridor with the captain some distance in the lead.

"There wasn't much point in fogging the issue with lame excuses," Sparhawk replied.

Kalten leaned toward his friend. "Are we going to obey his orders?" he whispered.

"No."

"Sir Sparhawk," Bevier gasped, "surely you would not disregard the commands of a patriarch of the Church?"

"No, not really. All I need is a different set of orders."

"Dolmant?" Kalten guessed.

"His name does sort of leap to mind, doesn't it?"

They had, however, no opportunity for side trips. The officious captain insisted upon escorting them directly back to the chapterhouse. "Sir Sparhawk," he said as they reached the narrow street where the house stood, "you will be so good as to advise the governor of your establishment that this gate is to remain closed. No one is to enter or leave."

"I'll tell him," Sparhawk replied. Then he nudged Faran and rode on into the courtyard.

"I didn't think he'd actually seal the gate," Kalten muttered. "How are we going to get word to Dolmant?"

"I'll think of something," Sparhawk said.

Later, as twilight crept in over the city, Sparhawk paced along the parapet surmounting the wall of the chapterhouse, glancing from time to time down into the street outside.

"Sparhawk," Kurik's gruff voice came from the yard below, "are you up there?"

"Yes. Come on up."

There was the sound of footsteps on the stone stairs leading up to the parapet. "You wanted to see us?" Kurik asked as he, Berit, and Talen came up out of the shadows clotting the stairway.

"Yes. There's a company of church soldiers outside. They're blocking the gate, and I need to get a message to Dolmant. Any ideas?"

Kurik scratched his head as he mulled it over.

"Give me a fast horse and I can ride through them," Berit offered.

"He'll make a good knight," Talen said. "Knights love to charge, I'm told."

Berit looked sharply at the boy.

"No hitting," Talen said, shrinking back. "We agreed that there wasn't going to be any more hitting. I pay attention to the lessons, and you don't hit me any more."

"Have you got a better idea?" Berit asked.

"Several." Talen looked over the wall. "Are the soldiers patrolling the streets outside the walls?" he asked.

"Yes," Sparhawk said.

"That's not really a problem, but it might have been easier if they weren't." Talen pursed his lips as he thought it over. "Berit," he said, "are you any good with a bow?"

"I've been trained," the novice said a bit stiffly.

"That's not what I asked. I said are you any good?"

"I can hit a mark at a hundred paces."

Talen looked at Sparhawk. "Don't you people have anything better to do?" he asked. Then he looked at Berit again. "You see that stable over there?" he asked, pointing across the street, "the one with the thatched roof?"

"Yes."

"Could you get an arrow into the thatch?"

"Easily."

"Maybe training pays off after all."

"How many months did you practice cutting purses?" Kurik asked pointedly.

"That's different, father. There's a profit involved in that."

"Father?" Berit sounded astonished.

"It's a long story," Kurik told him.

"Any man in the world listens to a bell that rings for any reason whatsoever," Talen said, affecting a school-teacherish tone, "and no man can possibly avoid gawking at a fire. Can you lay your hands on a length of rope, Sparhawk?"

"How long a length?"

"Long enough to reach the street. Here's how it goes. Berit wraps his arrow with tinder and sets fire to it. Then he takes a shot at that thatched roof. The soldiers will all run to this street to watch the fun. That's when I go down the rope on the far side of the building. I can be out on the street in less than a minute with no one the wiser."

"You can't set fire to a man's stable," Kurik objected, sounding horrified.

"They'll put it out, Kurik," Talen said in a patient tone. "They'll have lots of warning, because we'll all stand up here shouting 'Fire!' at the top of our lungs. Then I'll skin down the rope on the far wall and be five streets away before the excitement dies down. I know where Dolmant's house is and I can tell him whatever you want him to know."

"All right," Sparhawk approved.

"Sparhawk!" Kurik exclaimed. "You're not going to let him do this, are you?"

"It's tactically sound, Kurik. Diversion and subterfuge are part of any good plan."

"Do you have any idea of how much thatch—and wood—there is in this part of town?"

"It might give the church soldiers something useful to do," Sparhawk shrugged.

"That's hard, Sparhawk."

"Not nearly as hard as the notion of Annias sitting on the archprelate's throne. Let's get what we need. I want to be out of Chyrellos before the sun comes up tomorrow and I can't do that with all those soldiers camped outside the gate.''

They went down the stairs to fetch rope, a bow, and a quiver of arrows.

"What's afoot?" Tynian asked as he, Kalten, Bevier, and Ulath met them in the courtyard.

"We're going to get word to Dolmant," Sparhawk told him.

Tynian looked at the bow Berit was carrying. "With that?" he asked. "Isn't that rather a long shot?"

"There's a little more to it than that," Sparhawk told him. He quickly sketched in the plan. Then, as they started up the steps, he put his hand on Talen's shoulder. "This isn't going to be the safest thing in the world," he told the boy. "I want you to be careful out there."

"You worry too much, Sparhawk," Talen replied. "I could do this in my sleep."

"You might need some kind of note to give to Dolmant," Sparhawk said.

"You're not serious? If I get stopped, I can lie my way out of trouble, but not if I've got a note in my pocket. Dolmant knows me, and he'll know that the message is from you. Just leave everything to me, Sparhawk."

"Don't stop to pick any pockets along the way."

"Of course not," Talen replied, just a little too glibly.

Sparhawk sighed. Then he quickly told the boy what to say to the patriarch of Demos.

The plan went more or less as Talen had outlined it. As soon as the patrol had passed in the narrow street, Berit's arrow arched out like a falling star and sank into the thatched stable roof. It sputtered there for a moment or two, and then bluish-colored flame ran quickly up to the ridgepole, turning sooty orange first, then bright yellow as the flames began to spread.

"Fire!" Talen yelled.

"Fire!" the rest echoed.

In the street below, the church soldiers came pounding around the corner to be met by the nearly hysterical owner of the stables. "Good masters!" the poor man cried, wringing his hands. "My stable! My horses! My house! My God!"

The officious captain hesitated, looking first at the fire then back at the looming wall of the chapterhouse in an agony of indecision.

"We'll help you, Captain," Tynian called down from the wall. "Open the gate!"

"No!" the captain shouted back. "Stay inside."

"You could lose half of the holy city, you blockhead!" Kalten roared at him. "That fire will spread if you don't do something immediately."

"You!" the captain snapped at the commoner who owned the stable. "Fetch buckets and show me the nearest well." He turned quickly to his men. "Form up a line," he commanded. "Go to the front gate of the Pandion house and bring back every man we can spare." He sounded decisive now. Then he squinted up at the knights on the parapet. "But leave a detachment on guard there," he ordered.

"We can still help, Captain," Tynian offered. "There's a deep well here. We can turn out our men and pass buckets to your men outside the gate. Our major concern here must be the saving of Chyrellos. Everything else must be secondary to that."

The captain hesitated.

"Please, Captain!" Tynian's voice throbbed with sincerity. "I beg of you. Let us help."

"Very well," the captain snapped. "Open your gate. But no one is to leave the chapterhouse grounds."

"Of course not," Tynian replied.

"Nicely done," Ulath grunted, tapping Tynian on the shoulder with his fist.

Tynian grinned at him. "Talking *does* pay off now and then, my silent friend. You should try it sometime."

"I'd rather use an axe."

"Well, I guess I'll be leaving now, my lords." Talen said. "Was there anything you'd like to have me pick up for you—since I'll be out and about anyway?"

"Keep your mind on what you're supposed to do," Sparhawk told him. "Just go talk to Dolmant."

"And be careful," Kurik growled. "You're a disappointing son sometimes, but I don't want to lose you."

"Sentimentality, father?" Talen said, affecting surprise.

"Not really," Kurik replied. "Just a certain sense of responsibility to your mother."

"I'll go with him," Berit said.

Talen looked critically at the rangy novice. "Forget it," he said shortly. "You'd just be in my way. Forgive me, revered teacher, but your feet are too big and your elbows stick out too far to move around quietly, and I don't have time to teach you how to sneak right now." The boy disappeared into the shadows along the parapet.

"Where did you find that rare youth?" Bevier asked.

"You wouldn't believe it, Bevier," Kalten replied. "You absolutely wouldn't believe it."

"Our Pandion brothers are perhaps a bit more worldly than the rest of us, Bevier," Tynian said sententiously. "We who fix our eyes firmly on heaven are not so versed in the seamier side of life as they are." He looked piously at Kalten. "We all serve, however, and I'm sure that God appreciates your efforts, no matter how dishonest or depraved."

"Well put," Ulath said with an absolutely straight face.

The fire in the thatched roof continued to smoke and steam as the church soldiers threw bucket after bucket of water onto it during the next quarter hour. Gradually, by sheer dint of numbers and the volume of water poured on it, the fire was quenched, leaving the owner of the stable bemoaning the saturation of his store of fodder, but preventing any spread of the flames.

"Bravo, Captain, bravo!" Tynian cheered from atop the wall.

"Don't overdo it," Ulath muttered to him.

"It's the first time I've ever seen any of those fellows do anything useful," Tynian protested. "That sort of thing ought to be encouraged."

"We could set some more fires, if you'd like," the huge Genidian offered. "We could keep them hauling water all week."

Tynian tugged at one earlobe. "No," he said after a moment's thought. "They might get bored with the novelty and decide to let the city burn." He glanced at Kurik. "Did the boy get away?" he asked.

"As slick as a snake going down a rat hole," Sparhawk's squire replied, trying to conceal the note of pride in his voice.

"Someday you'll have to tell us about why the lad keeps calling you father."

"We might get to that one day, my Lord Tynian," Kurik muttered.

As the first light of dawn crept up the eastern sky, there came the measured tread of hundreds of feet some distance up the narrow street outside the front gate of the chapterhouse. Then the Patriarch Dolmant, astride a white mule, came into view at the head of a battalion or more of red-liveried soldiers.

"Your Grace," the soot-smeared captain who had been blocking the gate of the chapterhouse exclaimed, rushing forward with a salute.

"You are relieved, Captain," Dolmant told him. "You may return with your men to your barracks." He sniffed a bit disapprovingly. "Tell them to clean up," he suggested. "They look like chimney sweeps."

"Your Grace," the captain faltered, "I was commanded by the patriarch of Coombe to secure this house. May I send to him for confirmation of your Grace's counterorder?"

Dolmant considered it. "No, Captain," he said. "I don't think so. Retire at once."

"But, your Grace!"

Dolmant slapped his hands sharply together, and the troops massed at his back moved into position, their pikes advanced. "Colonel," Dolmant said in the mildest of tones to the commander of his troops, "would you be so good as to escort the captain and his men back to their barracks?"

"At once, your Grace," the officer replied with a sharp salute.

"And I think they should be confined there until they are presentable."

"Of course, your Grace," the colonel said soberly. "I myself shall conduct the inspection."

"Meticulously, Colonel—most meticulously. The honor of the Church is reflected in the appearance of her soldiers."

"Your Grace may rely upon my attention to the most minute detail," the colonel assured him. "The honor of our service is also reflected by the appearance of our lowliest soldier."

"God appreciates your devotion, Colonel."

"I live but to serve Him, your Grace," the colonel bowed deeply.

Neither man smiled, nor winked.

"Oh," Dolmant said then, "before you leave, Colonel, bring me that ragged little beggar boy. I think I'll leave him with the good brothers of this order—as an act of charity, of course."

"Of course, your Grace." The colonel snapped his fingers, and a burly sergeant dragged Talen by the scruff of the neck to the patriarch. Then Dolmant's battalion advanced on the captain and his men, effectively pinning them against the high wall of the chapterhouse with their pikes. The sooty soldiers of the patriarch of Coombe were quickly disarmed and then marched off under close guard.

Dolmant affectionately reached down and patted the slender neck of his white mule; then he looked critically up at the parapet. "Haven't you left yet, Sparhawk?" he asked.

"We were just making our preparations, your Grace."

"The day wears on, my son," Dolmant told him. "God's work cannot be accomplished by sloth."

"I'll keep that in mind, your Grace," Sparhawk said. Then his eyes narrowed, and he stared hard down at Talen. "Give it back," he commanded.

"What?" Talen answered with a note of anguish in his voice.

"All of it. Every last bit."

"But, Sparhawk—"

"*Now*, Talen."

Grumbling, the boy began to remove all manner of small, valuable objects from inside his clothes, depositing them in the hands of the startled patriarch of Demos. "Are you satisfied now, Sparhawk?" he demanded a bit sullenly, glaring up at the parapet.

"Not entirely, but it's a start. I'll know better after I search you once you're inside the gate."

Talen sighed and dug into several more hidden pockets, adding more items to Dolmant's already overflowing hands.

"I assume you're taking this boy with you, Sparhawk?" Dolmant asked, tucking his valuables inside his cassock.

"Yes, your Grace," Sparhawk replied.

"Good. I'll sleep better knowing that he's not roaming the streets. Make haste, my son, and God speed." Then the patriarch turned his mule and rode on back up the street.

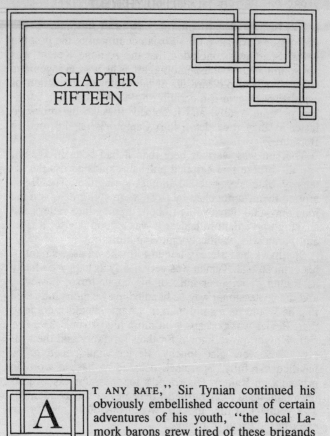

CHAPTER FIFTEEN

A T ANY RATE," Sir Tynian continued his obviously embellished account of certain adventures of his youth, "the local Lamork barons grew tired of these brigands and came to our chapterhouse to enlist our aid in exterminating them. We had all grown rather bored with patrolling the Zemoch border, so we agreed. To be honest about the whole thing, we looked upon the affair as something in the nature of a sporting event—a few days of hard riding and a nice brisk fight at the end."

Sparhawk let his attention wander. Tynian's compulsive talking had been virtually uninterrupted since they had left Chyrellos and crossed the border into the southern kingdom of Cammoria. Although the stories were at first amusing, they eventually grew repetitious. To hear Tynian

tell it, he had figured prominently in every major battle
and minor skirmish on the Eosian continent in the past ten
years. Sparhawk concluded that the Alcione Knight was
not so much an unabashed braggart as he was an ingenious
storyteller who put himself in the center of the action of
each story to give it a certain immediacy. It was a harm-
less pastime, really, and it helped to make the miles go
faster as they rode down into Cammoria on the road to
Borrata.

The sun was warmer here than it had been in Elenia,
and the breeze that skipped puffball clouds across the in-
tensely blue sky smelled almost springlike. The fields
around them, untouched by frost, were still green, and the
road unwound like a white ribbon, dipping into valleys and
snaking up verdant hillsides. It was a good day for a ride,
and Faran was obviously enjoying himself.

Sparhawk had already begun to make an assessment of
his companions. Tynian was very nearly as happy-go-lucky
as Kalten. The sheer bulk of his upper torso, however,
and the professional way he handled his weapons indicated
that he would be a solid man in a fight, should it come to
that. Bevier was perhaps a bit more high-strung. The Cyrinic Knights were known for their formality and their piety. They were also touchy. Bevier would need to be
handled carefully. Sparhawk decided to have a word in
private with Kalten. His friend's fondness for casual jest-
ing might need to be curbed where Bevier was concerned.
The young Cyrinic, though, would obviously also be an
asset in the event of trouble.

Ulath was an enigma. He had a towering reputation, but
Sparhawk had not had many dealings with the Genidian
Knights of far northern Thalesia. They were reputed to be
fearsome warriors, but the fact that they wore chain mail
instead of steel-plate armor concerned him a bit. He decided to feel out the huge Thalesian on that score. He
reined Faran in slightly to allow Ulath to catch up with
him.

"Nice morning," he said pleasantly.

Ulath grunted. Getting him to talk might prove difficult.
Then, surprisingly, he actually volunteered something. "In

Thalesia, there's still two feet of snow on the ground,'' he said.

"That must be miserable."

Ulath shrugged. "You get used to it, and snow makes for good hunting—boars, stags, Trolls, that sort of thing."

"Do you actually hunt Trolls?"

"Sometimes. Every so often a Troll goes crazy. If he comes down into the valleys where Elenes live and starts killing cows—or people—we have to hunt him down."

"I've heard that they're fairly large."

"Yes. Fairly."

"Isn't it a bit dangerous to fight one with only chain-mail armor?"

"It's not too bad, really. They only use clubs. A man might get his ribs broken sometimes, but that's about all."

"Wouldn't full armor be an advantage?"

"Not if you have to cross any rivers—and we have a lot of rivers in Thalesia. A man can peel off a mail shirt even if he's sitting on the bottom of a river. It might be a little hard to hold your breath long enough to get rid of a full suit of armor, though."

"That makes sense."

"We thought so ourselves. We had a preceptor a while back who thought that we should wear full armor like the other orders—for the sake of appearances. We threw one of our brothers dressed in a mail shirt into the harbor at Emsat. He got out of his shirt and came to the surface in about a minute. The preceptor was wearing full armor. When we threw him in, he didn't come back up. Maybe he found something more interesting to do down there."

"You drowned your preceptor?" Sparhawk asked in astonishment.

"No," Ulath corrected. "His armor drowned him. Then we elected Komier as preceptor. He's got better sense than to make foolish suggestions like that."

"You Genidians appear to be an independent sort of order. You actually elect your own preceptors?"

"Don't you?"

"Not really, no. We send a panel of names to the Hierocracy and let them do the choosing."

"We make it easier for them. We only send them one name."

Kalten came back down the road at a canter. The big blond man had been riding about a quarter of a mile in the lead to scout out possible danger. "There's something strange up ahead, Sparhawk," he said tensely.

"How do you mean strange?"

"There's a pair of Pandions at the top of the next hill." There was a slightly strained note in Kalten's voice, and he was visibly sweating.

"Who are they?"

"I didn't go up there to ask."

Sparhawk looked sharply at his friend. "What's the matter?" he asked.

"I'm not sure," Kalten replied. "I just had a strong feeling that I shouldn't go near them, for some reason. I think they want to talk with you. Don't ask me where I got that idea either."

"All right," Sparhawk said. "I'll go see what they want." He spurred Faran into a gallop and thudded up the long slope of the road toward the hilltop. The two mounted men wore black Pandion armor, but they gave none of the customary signs of greeting as Sparhawk approached, and neither of them raised his visor. Their horses were peculiarly gaunt, almost skeletal.

"What is it, brothers?" Sparhawk asked, reining Faran in a few yards from the pair. He caught a momentary whiff of an unpleasant smell, and a chill ran through him.

One of the armored figures turned slightly and pointed a steel-clad arm down into the next valley. He did not speak, but appeared to be pointing at a winter-denuded elm grove at one side of the road about a half mile farther on.

"I don't quite—" Sparhawk started; then he caught the sudden glint of sunlight on polished steel among the spidery branches of the grove. He shaded his eyes with one hand and peered intently at the cluster of trees. He saw a hint of movement and another flash of reflected light. "I see," he said gravely. "Thank you, my brothers. Would you care to join us in routing the ambushers waiting below?"

For a long moment, neither black-armored figure responded, then one of them inclined his head in assent. They both moved then, one to either side of the road, and sat their horses, waiting.

Puzzled by their strange behavior, Sparhawk rode back down the road to rejoin the others. "We've got some trouble up ahead," he reported. "There's a group of armed men hiding in a grove of trees in the next valley."

"An ambush?" Tynian asked.

"People don't usually hide unless they've got some mischief in mind."

"Could you tell how many there are?" Bevier asked, loosening his Lochaber from its sling on his saddlebow.

"Not really."

"One way to find out," Ulath said, reaching for his axe.

"Who are the two Pandions?" Kalten asked nervously.

"They didn't say."

"Did they give you the same kind of feeling they gave me?"

"What kind of feeling?"

"As if my blood had just frozen."

Sparhawk nodded. "Something like that," he admitted. "Kurik," he said then, "you and Berit take Sephrenia, Flute, and Talen to some place out of sight."

The squire nodded curtly.

"All right then, gentlemen," Sparhawk said to the other knights, "let's go have a look."

They started out at a rolling trot, five armored knights mounted on war horses and wielding a variety of unpleasant-looking weapons. At the top of the hill they were joined by the two silent men in black armor. Once again Sparhawk caught that unpleasant smell, and once again his blood ran strangely cold.

"Has anybody got a horn?" Tynian asked. "We should let them know we're coming."

Ulath unbuckled one of his saddlebags and took out the curled and twisted horn of some animal. It was quite large and had a brass mouthpiece at its tip.

"What kind of an animal has horns like that?" Kalten asked him.

"Ogre," Ulath replied. Then he set the mouthpiece to his lips and blew a shattering blast.

"For the glory of God and the honor of the Church!" Bevier exclaimed, rising in his stirrups and flourishing his Lochaber.

Sparhawk drew his sword and drove his spurs into Faran's flanks. The big horse plunged eagerly ahead, his ears laid back and his teeth bared.

There were shouts of chagrin from the elm grove as the Church Knights plunged down the hill at a gallop with the grass whipping at the legs of their chargers. Then perhaps eighteen armored men on horseback broke out of their concealment and rode out into the open to meet the charge.

"They want a fight!" Tynian shouted jubilantly.

"Watch yourselves when we mix with them!" Sparhawk warned. "There may be more hiding in the grove!"

Ulath continued to sound his horn until the last moment. Then he quickly stuffed it back into his saddlebag and began to whirl his great war axe about his head.

Three of the ambushers had held back; just before the two parties crashed together, they turned tail and rode off at a dead run, flogging their horses in sheer panic.

The initial impact might easily have been heard a mile away. Sparhawk and Faran were slightly in the lead, with the others fanned out and back in a kind of wedge formation. Sparhawk stood up in his stirrups to deliver broad overhand strokes to the right and the left as he crashed into the strangers. He split open a helmet and saw blood and brains come gushing out as the man fell stiffly out of his saddle. On his next stroke his sword sheared through an upraised shield, and he heard a scream as his blade bit into the arm to which the shield was strapped. Behind him he could hear the sounds of other blows and shrieks as his friends followed him through the mêlée.

Their rush through the center of the ambushers left ten down, killed or maimed, but, as they whirled to attack again, a half-dozen more came crashing out of the grove to attack them from the rear.

"Go ahead!" Bevier shouted as he wheeled his horse. "I'll hold these off while you finish the rest!" He raised his Lochaber and charged.

"Help him, Kalten!" Sparhawk called to his friend, then led Tynian, Ulath, and the two strangers against the dazed survivors of their first attack. Tynian's broadsword had a much wider blade than those of the Pandions and thus a great deal more weight. That weight made the weapon savagely efficient, and Tynian cut through flesh or armor with equal ease. Ulath's axe, of course, had no finesse or subtlety. He hewed at men as a woodsman might hew at trees.

Sparhawk briefly saw one of the two strange Pandions rise in his stirrups to deliver a vast overhand blow. What the knight held in its gauntleted fist, however, was not a sword, but rather that same kind of glowing nimbus that had been given to Sephrenia in the shabby upstairs apartment in Chyrellos by the insubstantial ghost of Sir Lakus. The nimbus appeared to pass completely through the body of the awkward mercenary the Pandion faced. The man's face went absolutely white, and he stared down at his chest in horror, but there was no blood, and his rust-splotched armor remained intact. With a shriek of terror, he threw his sword away and fled. Then Sparhawk's attention was diverted by another enemy.

When the last of the ambushers had fallen, Sparhawk wheeled Faran to go to the aid of Bevier and Kalten, but saw that it was largely unnecessary. Three of the men who had come charging out of the elm grove were already down. Another was doubled over in his saddle with both hands pressed to his belly. The other two were trying desperately to parry the blows of Kalten's sword and Bevier's Lochaber axe. Kalten feinted with his sword, then smoothly slapped his opponent's weapon out of his hand, even as Bevier lopped the head off his man with an almost casual backhand swipe.

"Don't kill him!" Sparhawk shouted to Kalten as the blond man raised his sword.

"But—" Kalten protested.

"I want to question him."

Kalten's face grew bleak with disappointment as Sparhawk rode back across the littered turf toward him and Bevier.

Sparhawk reined Faran in. "Get off your horse," he told the frightened and exhausted captive.

The man slid down. Like that worn by his fallen companions, his armor was a mishmash of unmatched pieces. It was rusty and dented in places, but the sword Kalten had knocked from his hand was polished and sharp.

"You're a mercenary, I take it," Sparhawk said to him.

"Yes, my Lord," the fellow faltered in a Pelosian accent.

"This didn't turn out too well, did it?" Sparhawk asked in an almost comradely fashion.

The fellow laughed nervously, looking at the carnage around him. "No, my Lord, not at all the way we expected."

"You did your best," Sparhawk said to him. "Now, we'll need the name of the man who hired you."

"I didn't ask his name, my Lord."

"Describe him then."

"I—I cannot, my Lord."

"This interview is going to get a lot less pleasant, I think," Kalten said.

"Stand him in a fire," Ulath suggested.

"I've always liked pouring boiling pitch inside their armor—slowly," Tynian said.

"Thumbscrews," Bevier said firmly.

"You see how it is, neighbor," Sparhawk said to the now ashen-faced prisoner. "You *are* going to talk. We're here, and the man who hired you isn't. He might have threatened you with unpleasant things, but we're going to do them to you. Save yourself a great deal of discomfort and answer my questions."

"My Lord," the man blubbered, "I *can't*—even if you torture me to death."

Ulath slid down from his saddle and approached the cringing captive. "Oh, stop that," the Genidian said. He raised a hand, palm outstretched, over the prisoner's head and spoke in a harsh, grating language Sparhawk did not understand but uneasily suspected was not a human tongue. The captured mercenary's eyes went blank, and he fell to his knees. Falteringly and with absolutely no expression in his voice, he began to speak in the same language as Ulath had.

"He's been bound in a spell," the Genidian Knight reported. "Nothing we could have done to him would have made him talk."

The mercenary went on in that dreadful language, speaking more rapidly now.

"There were two who hired him," Ulath translated, "a hooded Styric and a man with white hair."

"Martel!" Kalten exclaimed.

"Very likely," Sparhawk agreed.

The prisoner spoke again.

"It was the Styric who put the spell on him," Ulath said. "It's one I'm not familiar with."

"I don't think I am either," Sparhawk admitted. "We'll see if Sephrenia knows it."

"Oh," Ulath added, "that's one other thing. This attack was directed at her."

"What?"

"The orders these men had were to kill the Styric woman."

"Kalten!" Sparhawk barked, but the blond man was already spurring his horse.

"What about him?" Tynian pointed at the prisoner.

"Let him go," Sparhawk shouted as he galloped off after Kalten. "Come on!"

As they rode over the hilltop, Sparhawk looked back. The two strange Pandions were nowhere in sight. Then, up ahead, he saw them. A group of men had surrounded the rocky knoll where Kurik had hidden Sephrenia and the others. The two black-armored knights were sitting their horses coolly between the attackers and the knoll. They were making no effort to fight, but merely stood their ground. As Sparhawk watched, one of the attackers launched a javelin which appeared to pass directly through the body of one of the black-armored Pandions with no visible effect.

"Faran!" Sparhawk barked, "run!" It was something he seldom did. He called upon Faran's loyalty instead of his training. The big horse shuddered slightly, then stretched himself out in a run that quickly outdistanced the others.

The attackers numbered perhaps ten men. They were recoiling visibly from the two shadowy Pandions blocking their path. Then one of them looked around and saw Sparhawk descending upon them with the others rushing along behind him, and he shouted a warning. After a moment of stunned paralysis, the shabby attackers bolted, fleeing across the meadow, fleeing in a kind of panic Sparhawk had seldom seen in professionals. He charged up the side of the outcrop with Faran's steel-shod hooves striking sparks from the stones. Just below the crest, he reined in. "Is everybody all right?" he called to Kurik.

"We're fine," Kurik replied, looking over the hasty breastwork of stone he and Berit had erected. "It was touch and go until those two knights got here, though." Kurik's eyes looked a bit wild as he stared at the pair who had warded off the assailants. Sephrenia came up to the breastwork beside him, and her face was deathly pale.

Sparhawk turned to the two strange Pandions. "I think it's time for introductions, brothers," he said, "and some explanations."

The two made no reply. He looked at them a bit more closely. The horses upon which they sat now appeared even more skeletal, and Sparhawk shuddered as he saw that the animals had no eyes, but only vacant eye sockets, and that their bones protruded through their tattered coats. Then the two knights removed their helmets. Their faces seemed somehow filmy and indistinct, almost transparent, and they, too, were eyeless. One of them appeared very young and he had butter-colored hair. The other was old, and his hair was white. Sparhawk recoiled slightly. He knew both of them; he knew that they both were dead.

"Sir Sparhawk," the ghost of Parasim said, his voice hollow and emotionless, "pursue thy quest with diligence. Time will not stay for thee."

"Why have you returned from the house of the dead?" Sephrenia asked the two in a profoundly formal tone. Her voice was trembling.

"Our oath hath the power to bring us out of the shadows if need be, little mother," the form of Lakus replied, his voice also hollow and void of all emotion. "Others will also fall, and our company will increase ere the queen returns to health." The hollow-eyed shade turned then to Sparhawk. "Guard well our beloved mother, Sparhawk, for she is in grave peril. Should she fall, our deaths are without purpose, and the queen will die."

"I will, Lakus," Sparhawk promised.

"Know also one last thing. In Ehlana's death, thou shalt lose more than a queen. The darkness hovers at the gate, and Ehlana is our only hope of light." Then the two of them shimmered and vanished.

The four other knights came charging up the rocky slope and reined in. Kalten's face was pallid and he was visibly trembling. "Who were they?" he asked.

"Parasim and Lakus," Sparhawk replied quietly.

"Parasim? He's dead."

"So's Lakus."

"Ghosts?"

"So it would seem."

Tynian dismounted and pulled off his massive helmet. He was also pale and sweating. "I've dabbled at times in necromancy," he said, "though not usually by choice. Usually a spirit has to be summoned, but sometimes they'll appear on their own—particularly if they left something important unfinished."

"This was important," Sparhawk said bleakly.

"Was there something else you wanted to tell us, Sparhawk?" Ulath asked then. "You seem to have left a few things out."

Sparhawk looked at Sephrenia. Her face was still deathly pale, but she straightened and nodded to him.

Sparhawk took a deep breath. "Ehlana would be dead, but is being preserved by a spell that keeps her sealed within a crystal. The spell was the result of the combined efforts of Sephrenia and twelve Pandions," he explained.

"I'd been sort of wondering about that," Tynian said.

"There's only one problem with it," Sparhawk continued. "The knights will die one by one until only Sephrenia is left."

"And then?" Bevier asked, his voice shaking.

"Then I will also depart," Sephrenia replied simply.

A stifled sob escaped the young Cyrinic. "Not while I have breath," he said in a choked voice.

"Someone, however, is trying to speed things up," Sparhawk went on. "This is the third attempt on Sephrenia's life since we left Cimmura."

"But I have survived them," she said as if they were of no moment. "Were you able in any way to identify the people behind this attack?"

"Martel and some Styric," Kalten told her. "The Styric had put a spell on the mercenaries to keep them from talking, but Ulath broke it somehow. He spoke with a prisoner in a language I didn't understand. The man answered in the same tongue."

She looked inquiringly at the Thalesian knight.

"We spoke in the language of the Trolls," Ulath shrugged. "It's a nonhuman tongue, so it circumvented the spell."

She stared at him in horror. "You called upon the Troll-Gods?" she gasped.

"Sometimes it's necessary, Lady," he replied. "It's not too dangerous if you're careful."

Bevier's face was tear-streaked. "And it please you, my Lord Sparhawk," he said, "I shall personally undertake the protection of the Lady Sephrenia. I shall remain constantly at this valiant lady's side, and should there be further encounters, I pledge you my life that she shall not be harmed."

A brief expression of consternation crossed Sephrenia's face, and she looked appealingly at Sparhawk.

"Probably not a bad idea," he said, ignoring her unspoken objection. "All right then, Bevier. Stay with her."

Sephrenia gave him a withering look.

"Are we going to get the dead under the ground?" Tynian asked.

Sparhawk shook his head. "We don't have time to be gravediggers. My brothers are dying one by one, and Sephrenia's at the end of the list. If we see some peasants, we'll tell them where the bodies are. The loot they'll get will more than pay for the digging. Let's move along."

* * *

BORRATA WAS A university town that had grown up around the stately buildings of the oldest center of higher learning in Eosia. On occasion in the past, the Church had strongly urged that the institution be moved to Chyrellos, but the faculty had always resisted that notion, obviously desiring to maintain their independence and the absence of Church supervision.

Sparhawk and his companions took rooms in one of the local inns late in the afternoon on the day they arrived. The inn was more comfortable and certainly cleaner than the roadside ones in which they had stayed in Elenia and here in Cammoria.

The following morning, Sparhawk put on his mail coat and his heavy wool cloak.

"Do you want us to go with you?" Kalten asked as his friend came down into the common room on the main floor of the inn.

"No," Sparhawk replied. "Let's not turn it into a parade. The university isn't very far from here, and I can protect Sephrenia along the way."

Sir Bevier looked as if he were about to protest. He had taken his self-appointed role as Sephrenia's protector very seriously, seldom moving more than a few feet from her side during the journey to Borrata. Sparhawk looked at the earnest young Cyrinic. "I know you've been keeping watch outside her door every night, Bevier," he said. "Why don't you get some sleep? You won't be much good to her—or the rest of us—if you fall out of your saddle."

Bevier's face stiffened.

"He didn't mean it personally, Bevier," Kalten said. "Sparhawk just hasn't quite figured out the meaning of the word *diplomatic* yet. We're all hoping that someday it might come to him."

Bevier smiled faintly, then he laughed. "I think it might take me some time to adjust to you Pandions," he said.

"Look upon it as educational," Kalten suggested.

"You know that if you and the lady are successful in finding that cure, we're likely to encounter all kinds of trouble on the way back to Cimmura," Tynian said to Sparhawk. "We'll probably run into whole armies trying to stop us."

"Madel," Ulath suggested cryptically, "or Sarri-nium."

"I don't quite follow," Tynian admitted.

"Those armies you mentioned will try to block the road to Chyrellos to keep us from getting there—and then on into Elenia. If we ride south to either of those seaports, we can hire a ship and sail around to Vardenais on the west coast of Elenia. It's faster to travel by sea anyway."

"Let's decide that after we find the cure," Sparhawk said.

Sephrenia came down the stairs with Flute. "Are we ready then?" she asked.

Sparhawk nodded.

She spoke briefly to Flute. The little girl nodded and crossed the room to where Talen sat. "You've been selected, Talen," Sephrenia told the boy. "Watch over her while I'm gone."

"But—" he started to object.

"Just do as she says, Talen," Kurik told him wearily.

"I was going to go out and have a look around."

"No," his father said, "as a matter of fact, you weren't."

Talen's expression grew sulky. "All right," he said as Flute climbed up into his lap.

Since the university grounds were so close, Sparhawk decided against taking their horses, and he and Sephrenia walked through the narrow streets of Borrata. The small woman looked around. "I haven't been here in a long time," she murmured.

"I can't imagine what interest a university could hold for you," Sparhawk smiled, "considering your views on reading."

"I wasn't studying, Sparhawk. I was teaching."

"I should have guessed, I suppose. How are you getting on with Bevier?"

"Fine, except that he won't let me do anything for myself—and that he keeps trying to convert me to the Elene faith." Her tone was slightly tart.

"He's just trying to protect you—your soul as well as your person."

"Are you trying to be funny?"

He decided not to answer that.

The grounds of the University of Borrata were parklike, and students and members of the faculty strolled contemplatively across the well-kept lawns.

Sparhawk stopped a young man in a lime-green doublet. "Excuse me, neighbor," he said, "but could you direct me to the medical college?"

"Are you ill?"

"No. A friend of mine is, though."

"Ah. The physicians occupy that building over there." The student pointed at a squat-looking structure made of gray stone.

"Thank you, neighbor."

"I hope your friend gets better soon."

"So do we."

When they entered the building, they encountered a rotund man in a black robe.

"Excuse me, sir," Sephrenia said to him. "Are you a physician?"

"I am."

"Splendid. Have you a few moments?"

The rotund man had been looking closely at Sparhawk. "Sorry," he said curtly. "I'm busy."

"Could you direct us to one of your colleagues, then?"

"Try any door," he said, waving his hand and walking quickly away from them.

"That's an odd attitude for a healer," Sparhawk said.

"Every profession attracts its share of louts," she replied.

They crossed the antechamber and Sparhawk rapped on a dark-painted door.

"What is it?" a weary voice said.

"We need to consult a physician."

There was a long pause. "Oh, all right," the weary voice replied, "come in."

Sparhawk opened the door and held it for Sephrenia.

The man seated behind the cluttered desk in the cubicle had deep circles beneath his eyes, and it appeared that he had foregone shaving some weeks ago. "What is the nature of your illness?" he asked Sephrenia in a voice hovering on exhaustion.

"I'm not the one who's ill," she replied.

"Him, then?" the doctor pointed at Sparhawk. "He looks robust enough to me."

"No," she said. "He's not ill either. We're here on behalf of a friend."

"I don't go to people's houses."

"We weren't asking you to do that," Sparhawk said.

"Our friend lives some distance away," Sephrenia said. "We thought that if we described her symptoms to you, you might be able to hazard a guess as to the cause of her malady."

"I don't make guesses," he told her shortly. "What are the symptoms?"

"Much like those of the falling-sickness," Sephrenia told him.

"That's it, then. You've already made the diagnosis yourself."

"There are certain differences, however."

"All right. Describe the differences."

"There's a fever involved—quite a high one—and profuse sweating."

"The two don't match, little lady. With a fever, the skin is dry."

"Yes, I know."

"Have you a medical background?"

"I'm familiar with certain folk remedies."

He snorted. "My experience tells me that folk remedies kill more than they cure. What other symptoms did you notice?"

Sephrenia meticulously described the illness that had rendered Ehlana comatose.

The physician, however, seemed not to be listening, but was staring instead at Sparhawk. His face became suddenly alert, his eyes narrowed and his expression sly. "I'm sorry," he said when Sephrenia had finished. "I think you'd better go back and take another look at your friend. What you just described matches no known illness." His tone was abrupt, even curt.

Sparhawk straightened, clenching his fist, but Sephrenia laid her hand on his arm. "Thank you for your time,

learned sir," she said smoothly. "Come along then," she
told Sparhawk.

The two of them went back out into the corridor.

"Two in a row," Sparhawk muttered.

"Two what?"

"People with bad manners."

"It stands to reason, perhaps."

"I don't follow you."

"There's a certain natural arrogance in those who
teach."

"*You've* never displayed it."

"I keep it under control. Try another door, Sparhawk."

In the next two hours, they spoke with seven physicians.
Each of them, after a searching look at Sparhawk's face,
pretended ignorance.

"I'm starting to get a peculiar feeling about this," he
growled as they emerged from yet another office. "They
take one look at me, and they suddenly become stupid—
or is that just my imagination?"

"I've noticed that, too," she replied thoughtfully.

"My face isn't that exciting, I know, but it's never struck
anyone dumb before."

"It's a perfectly good face, Sparhawk."

"It covers the front of my head. What else can you
expect from a face?"

"The physicians of Borrata seem less skilled than we'd
been led to believe."

"We've wasted more time, then?"

"We haven't finished yet. Don't give up hope."

They came finally to a small, unpainted door set back
in a shabby alcove. Sparhawk rapped, and a slurred voice
responded, "Go away."

"We need your help, learned sir," Sephrenia said.

"Go bother somebody else. I'm busy getting drunk right
now."

"That does it!" Sparhawk snapped. He grasped the door
handle and pushed, but the door was locked from the inside. Irritably, he kicked it open, splintering the frame.

The man inside the tiny cubicle blinked. He was a
shabby little man with a crooked back and bleary eyes.
"You knock very loudly, friend," he observed. Then he

belched. "Well, don't just stand there. Come in." His head weaved back and forth. He was shabbily dressed, and his wispy gray hair stuck out in all directions.

"Is there something in the water around here that makes everybody so churlish?" Sparhawk asked acidly.

"I wouldn't know," the shabby man replied. "I never drink water." He drank noisily from a battered tankard.

"Obviously."

"Shall we spend the rest of the day exchanging insults, or would you rather tell me about your problem?" The physician squinted myopically at Sparhawk's face. "So you're the one," he said.

"The one what?"

"The one we aren't supposed to talk to."

"Would you like to explain that?"

"A man came here a few days ago. He said that it would be worth a hundred gold pieces to every physician in the building if you left empty-handed."

"What did he look like?"

"He had a military bearing and white hair."

"Martel," Sparhawk said to Sephrenia.

"We should have guessed almost immediately," she replied.

"Take heart, friends," the messy little man told them expansively. "You've found your way to the finest physician in Borrata." He grinned then. "My colleagues all fly south with the ducks in the fall going, 'Quack, quack, quack.' You couldn't get a sound medical opinion out of any one of them. The white-haired man said that you'd describe some symptoms. Some lady someplace is very ill, I understand, and your friend—this Martel you mentioned—would prefer that she didn't recover. Why don't we disappoint him?" He drank deeply from his tankard.

"You're a credit to your profession, good doctor," Sephrenia said.

"No. I'm a vicious-minded old drunkard. Do you really want to know why I'm willing to help you? It's because I'll enjoy the screams of anguish from my colleagues when all that money slips through their fingers."

"That's as good a reason as any, I suppose," Sparhawk said.

"Exactly." The slightly tipsy physician peered at Sparhawk's nose. "Why didn't you have that set when it got broken?" he asked.

Sparhawk touched his nose. "I was busy with other things."

"I can fix it for you if you'd like. All I have to do is take a hammer and break it again. Then I can set it for you."

"Thanks all the same, but I'm used to it now."

"Suit yourself. All right, what are these symptoms you came here to describe?"

Once again Sephrenia ran down the list for him.

He sat scratching at his ear with his eyes narrowed. Then he rummaged through the litter piled high on his desk and pulled out a thick book with a torn leather cover. He leafed through it for several moments, then slammed it shut. "Just as I thought," he said triumphantly. He belched again.

"Well?" Sparhawk said.

"Your friend was poisoned. Has she died yet?"

A chill caught at Sparhawk's stomach. "No," he replied.

"It's only a matter of time." The physician shrugged. "It's a rare poison from Rendor. It's invariably fatal."

Sparhawk clenched his teeth. "I'm going to go back to Cimmura and disembowel Annias," he grated, "with a dull knife."

The disreputable little physician suddenly looked interested. "You do it this way," he suggested. "Make a lateral incision just below the navel. Then kick him over backward. Everything ought to fall out at that point."

"Thank you."

"No charge. If you're going to do something, do it right. I take it that this Annias person is the one you think was responsible?"

"Undoubtedly."

"Go ahead and kill him then. I despise a poisoner."

"Is there an antidote for this poison?" Sephrenia asked.

"None that I know of. I'd suggest talking with several physicians I know in Cippria, but your friend will be dead before you could get back."

"No," Sephrenia disagreed. "She's being sustained."

"I'd like to know how you managed that."

"The lady is Styric," Sparhawk told him. "She has access to certain unusual things."

"Magic? Does that really work?"

"At times, yes."

"All right, then. Maybe you do have time." The seedy-looking doctor ripped a corner off one of the papers on his desk and dipped a quill into a nearly dry inkpot. "The first two names here are those of a couple of fairly adept physicians in Cippria," he said as he scrawled on the paper. "This last one is the name of the poison." He handed the paper to Sparhawk. "Good luck," he said. "Now get out of here so I can continue what I was doing before you kicked in my door."

CHAPTER
SIXTEEN

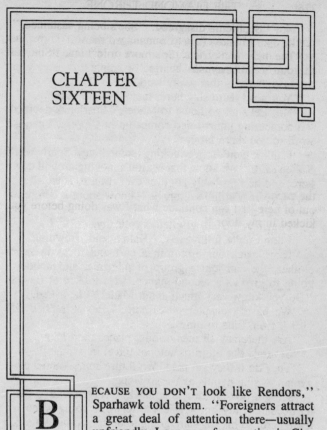

ECAUSE YOU DON'T look like Rendors,"
Sparhawk told them. "Foreigners attract
a great deal of attention there—usually
unfriendly. I can pass for a native in Cippria. So can Kurik. Rendorish women
wear veils, so Sephrenia's appearance won't be a problem.
The rest of you are going to have to stay behind."

They were gathered in a large room on the upper floor
of the inn near the university. The room was bare with
only a few benches along the walls and no curtains at the
narrow window. Sparhawk had reported what the tipsy
physician had said and the fact that Martel had attempted
subterfuge this time rather than a physical confrontation.

"We could put something on our hair to change the
color," Kalten protested. "Wouldn't that get us by?"

"It's the manner, Kalten," Sparhawk explained. "I could dye you green, and people would still know that you're an Elenian. The same's more or less true of the rest of you. You all have the bearing of knights. It takes years to erase that."

"You want us to stay here, then?" Ulath asked.

"No. Let's all go down to Madel," Sparhawk decided. "If something unexpected comes up in Cippria, I can get word to you there faster."

"I think you're overlooking something, Sparhawk," Kalten said. "We know that Martel's moving around down here, and he's probably got eyes everywhere. If we all ride out of Borrata in full armor, he'll know about it before we cover half a league."

"Pilgrims," Ulath grunted cryptically.

"I don't quite follow you," Kalten said, frowning.

"If we pack our armor in a cart and dress in sober clothes, we can join a group of pilgrims, and nobody's going to give us a second glance." He looked at Bevier. "Do you know very much about Madel?" he asked.

"We have a chapterhouse there," Bevier replied. "I visit it from time to time."

"Are there any shrines or holy places there?"

"Several. But pilgrims seldom travel in winter."

"They do if they get paid. We'll hire some—and a clergyman to sing hymns as we go along."

"It's got possibilities, Sparhawk," Kalten said. "Martel doesn't really know *which* way we're going when we leave here, so his spies are going to be spread fairly thin."

"How will we know this Martel person?" Bevier asked. "Should we encounter him while you're in Cippria, I mean?"

"Kalten knows him," Sparhawk replied, "and Talen has seen him once." Then he remembered something. He looked over at the boy, who was making a cat's cradle to entertain Flute. "Talen," he said, "could you draw pictures of Martel and Krager?"

"Of course."

"And we can conjure up the image of Adus as well," Sephrenia added.

"Adus is easy," Kalten said. "Just put armor on a gorilla and you've got him."

"All right, we'll do it that way, then," Sparhawk said. "Berit."

"Yes, Lord Sparhawk?"

"Go find a church somewhere—a poor one. Talk with the vicar. Tell him that we'll finance a pilgrimage to the shrines in Madel. Ask him to pick a dozen or so of his neediest parishioners and to bring them here tomorrow morning. We'll want him to come with us as well—to be the caretaker of our souls. And tell him that we'll make a sizable contribution to his church if he agrees."

"Won't he ask about our motives, my Lord?"

"Tell him that we've committed a dreadful sin and want to atone for it," Kalten shrugged. "Just don't be too specific about the sin."

"Sir Kalten!" Bevier gasped. "You would lie to a churchman?"

"It's not exactly a lie, Bevier. We've all committed sins. I've sinned at least a half-dozen times this week already. Besides, the vicar of a poor church isn't going to ask too many questions when there's a contribution involved."

Sparhawk took a leather pouch from inside his tunic. He shook it a few times, and a distinctive jingling sound came from it. "All right, gentlemen," he said, untying the top of the pouch, "we've reached the part of this service you all enjoy the most—the offertory. God appreciates a generous giver, so don't be shy. The vicar will need cash to hire pilgrims." He passed the pouch around.

"Do you think God might accept a promissory note?" Kalten asked.

"God might. I won't. Put something in the pouch, Kalten."

The group that gathered in the innyard the following morning was uniformly shabby—widows in patched mourning, out-of-work artisans and several hungry beggars. They were all mounted on weary nags or sleepy-looking mules. Sparhawk looked at them from the window. "Tell the innkeeper to feed them," he said to Kalten.

"There's quite a number of them, Sparhawk."

"I don't want them fainting from hunger a mile out of town. You take care of that while I go talk with the vicar."

"Anything you say." Kalten shrugged. "Should I bathe them, too? Some of them look a bit unwashed."

"That won't be necessary. Feed their horses and mules as well."

"Aren't we being a little overgenerous?"

"You get to carry any horse that collapses."

"Oh. I'll see to it right away, then."

The vicar of the poor church was a thin, anxious-looking man in his sixties. His silvery hair was curly, and his face was drawn and deeply lined with care. "My Lord," he said, bowing deeply to Sparhawk.

"Please, good vicar," Sparhawk said to him, "just 'pilgrim' is adequate. We are all equal in the service of God. My companions and I wish simply to join with your good, pious folk and to journey to Madel that we may worship at the holy shrines there for the solace of our souls and in the certain knowledge of the infinite mercy of God."

"Well said—uh—pilgrim."

"Would you join us at table, good vicar?" Sparhawk asked him. "We will go many miles before we sleep tonight."

The vicar's eyes grew suddenly bright. "I would be delighted, my Lord—uh, pilgrim, that is."

The feeding of the Cammorian pilgrims and their mounts took quite some time and stretched the capacity of the kitchen and the stable grain bins to a considerable degree.

"I've never seen people eat so much," Kalten grumbled. Clad in a sturdy, unmarked cloak, he swung up into his saddle just outside the inn.

"They were hungry," Sparhawk told him. "At least we can see to it that they get a few good meals before they have to return to Borrata."

"Charity, Sir Sparhawk?" Bevier asked. "Isn't that a bit out of character? The grim-faced Pandions are not noted for their tender sensibilities."

"How little you know them, Sir Bevier," Sephrenia murmured. She mounted her white palfrey, then held down her hands to Flute, but the little girl shook her head, walked over to Faran, and reached out her tiny hand. The big roan lowered his head, and she caressed his velvety nose. Sparhawk felt an odd quiver run through his mount's body. Then Flute insistently raised her hands to the big Pandion. Gravely, Sparhawk leaned over and lifted her into her accustomed place in front of the saddle and enfolded her in his cloak. She nestled against him, took out her pipes, and began to play that same minor melody she had been playing when they had first found her.

The vicar at the head of their column intoned a brief prayer, invoking the protection of the God of the Elenes during their journey, an invocation punctuated by questioning—even skeptical—trills from Flute's pipes.

"Behave yourself," Sparhawk whispered to her. "He's a good man and he's doing what he thinks is right."

She rolled her eyes roguishly. Then she yawned, snuggled closer to him, and promptly went to sleep.

They rode south out of Borrata under a clear morning sky with Kurik and the two-wheeled cart containing their armor and equipment clattering along behind them. The breeze was gusty and it tugged at the ragged clothing of the pilgrims patiently plodding along behind their vicar. A line of low mountains lay to the west, touched with snow on their peaks, and the sunlight glistened on those white fields. Their pace as they rode seemed to Sparhawk leisurely—even lackadaisical—though the panting and wheezing of the poor mounts of the pilgrims was a fair indication that the beasts were being pressed as hard as was possible.

It was about noon when Kalten rode forward from his station at the rear of the column. "There are riders coming up behind us," he reported quietly to avoid alarming nearby pilgrims. "They're pushing hard."

"Any idea of who they are?"

"They're wearing red."

"Church soldiers, then."

"Notice how quick he is?" Kalten observed to the others.

"How many?" Tynian asked.

"It looks to be a reinforced platoon."

Bevier loosened his Lochaber axe in its sling.

"Keep that under cover," Sparhawk told him. "The rest of you hide your weapons as well." Then he raised his voice. "Good vicar," he called ahead. "How about a hymn? The miles go easier with sacred music for company."

The vicar cleared his throat and began to sing in a rusty, off-key voice. Wearily, but responding automatically to their pastor's lead, the other pilgrims joined in.

"Sing!" Sparhawk commanded his companions, and they all raised their voices in the familiar hymn. As they bawled their song, Flute lifted her pipes and played a mocking little counterpoint.

"Stop that," Sparhawk murmured to her. "And if there's trouble, slide down and run out into that field."

She rolled her eyes at him.

"Do as you're told, young lady. I don't want you getting trampled if there's a fight."

The church soldiers, however, pounded past the column of hymn-singing pilgrims with hardly a glance and were soon lost in the distance ahead.

"Tense," Ulath commented.

"Truly," Tynian agreed. "Trying to fight in the middle of a crowd of terrified pilgrims might have been interesting."

"Do you think they were searching for us?" Berit asked.

"It's hard to say," Sparhawk replied. "I wasn't going to stop them to ask, though."

They moved southward toward Madel in easy stages to conserve the sorry mounts of the vicar's parishioners, and they arrived on the outskirts of the port city about noon on the fourth day out of Borrata. When the town came into view, Sparhawk rode forward to join the vicar at the head of the column. He handed the good man a pouch full of coins. "We'll be leaving you here," he said. "A matter has come up that needs our attention."

The vicar gave him a speculative look. "This was all subterfuge, wasn't it, my Lord?" he asked gravely. "I may be only the poor pastor of a poverty-stricken chapel, but I recognize the manner and bearing of Church Knights when I see them."

"Forgive us, good vicar," Sparhawk replied. "Take

your people to the holy places here in Madel. Lead them in prayer and then see to it that they're well-fed. Then return to Borrata and use whatever money is left as you see fit.''

"And may I do this with a clear conscience, my son?''

"The clearest, good pastor. My friends and I serve the Church in a matter of gravest urgency, and your aid will be appreciated by the members of the Hierocracy in Chyrellos—most of them, at any rate.'' Then Sparhawk turned Faran around and rode back to his companions. "All right, Bevier,'' he said. "Take us to your chapterhouse.''

"I have been considering that, Sir Sparhawk,'' Bevier replied. "Our chapterhouse here is closely watched by local authorities and all manner of other folk. Even garbed as we are, we would surely be recognized.''

Sparhawk grunted. "You're probably right. Can you think of any alternatives?''

"Perhaps so. As it happens, I have a kinsman—a marquis from eastern Arcium—who has a villa on the outskirts of the city. I have not seen him for some years—our family disapproves of him because he's in trade—but perhaps he will remember me. He's a good-natured fellow, and if I approach him right, he might extend his hospitality.''

"It's worth a try, I guess. All right. Lead the way.''

They rode around the western outskirts of Madel to an opulent house surrounded by a low wall built of the local sandstone. The house was set back some distance from the road and was surrounded by tall evergreens and well-groomed lawns. There was a graveled court directly in front of the house, and they dismounted there. A servant in sober livery emerged from the house and approached inquiringly.

"Would you be so good as to advise the marquis that his second cousin, Sir Bevier, and several friends would like to have a word with him?'' the Cyrinic inquired politely.

"At once, my Lord.'' The servant turned and reentered the house.

The man who emerged from the house a few moments later was stout and had a florid face. He wore one of the colorful silk robes common in southern Cammoria rather than Arcian doublet and hose, and his welcoming grin was broad. "Bevier," he greeted his distant cousin with a warm handclasp. "What are you doing in Cammoria?"

"Seeking refuge, Lycien," Bevier replied. His open young face clouded momentarily. "The family has not treated you well, Lycien," he admitted. "I could not blame you if you turned me and my friends away."

"Nonsense, Bevier. The decision to take up trading was mine. I knew how the rest of the family would feel about it. I'm delighted to see you. You mentioned refuge?"

Bevier nodded. "We're here on Church business of some delicacy," he said, "and there are a few too many eyes watching the Cyrinic chapterhouse in the city. I know it's a great deal to ask, but might we impose on your hospitality?"

"By all means, my boy, by all means." Marquis Lycien clapped his hands sharply, and several grooms came out of the stables. "See to the mounts of these visitors and their cart," the marquis ordered. Then he laid his hand on Bevier's shoulder. "Come in," he invited them all. "My house is yours." He turned and led the way through the low, arched doorway and on into the house. Once they were inside, they followed him to a pleasant room with low, cushioned furniture and a fireplace where several logs crackled and snapped. "Please, friends, sit," Lycien said. Then he looked speculatively at them. "This Church business of yours must be very important, Bevier," he guessed. "Gathering from their features, I'd say that your friends represent all four of the militant orders."

"Your eyes are sharp, Marquis," Sparhawk told him.

"Am I going to get in trouble over this?" Lycien asked. Then he grinned. "Not that I care, mind you. It's just that I like to be prepared."

"It's not too likely," Sparhawk assured him. "Particularly if we're successful in our mission. Tell me, my Lord, do you have contacts in the harbor?"

"Extensive ones, Sir . . . "

"Sparhawk," the Pandion supplied.

"Champion of the queen of Elenia?" Lycien looked surprised. "I heard that you'd returned from your exile in Rendor; but aren't you a bit far afield? Shouldn't you be in Cimmura trying to circumvent the attempts of the Primate Annias to depose your lady?''

"You're well-informed, my Lord," Sparhawk said.

"I have widespread commercial contacts." Lycien shrugged. He winked at Bevier. "That's what disgraced me in the eyes of the family. My agents and the masters of my ships gather much information in the course of their dealings.''

"I gather, my Lord, that you're not overly fond of the primate of Cimmura?''

"The man's a scoundrel.''

"Our sentiments exactly," Kalten agreed.

"Very well, then, my Lord," Sparhawk said. "What we're involved with is an attempt to counter the growing power of the primate. If we're successful, we can stop him in his tracks. I'd tell you more, but it might be dangerous for you if you knew too many of the details.''

"I can appreciate that, Sir Sparhawk," Lycien said. "Tell me, in what way can I help?''

"Three of us need to go to Cippria," Sparhawk replied. "For the sake of your own safety, it might be better if we were to take the ship of an independent sea captain rather than one of your own vessels. If you could direct us to such a captain and perhaps give us a discreetly worded letter of introduction to him, we can take care of the rest.''

"Sparhawk," Kurik said sharply, looking around the room, "what happened to Talen?''

Sparhawk turned quickly. "I thought he was bringing up the rear when we came in.''

"So did I.''

"Berit," Sparhawk said, "go find him.''

"At once, my Lord." The novice hurried from the room.

"Some problem?" Lycien asked.

"A wayward boy, cousin," Bevier told him. "From what I gather, he needs to be watched rather closely.''

"Berit will find him." Kalten laughed. "I have a great deal of confidence in that young man. Talen may come back with a few bumps and contusions, but I'm sure they'll be very educational for him.''

"Well, if it's all under control, then," Lycien said,

"why don't I send word to the kitchen? I'm sure you're all hungry. And in the meantime, perhaps some wine?" He assumed a pious expression that was obviously feigned. "I know that the Knights of the Church are abstemious, but a touch or so of wine is good for the digestion, or so I've heard."

"I've heard that, too," Kalten agreed.

"Could I prevail upon you for a cup of tea, my Lord?" Sephrenia asked, "and some milk for the little girl? I'm not sure that wine would be good for either of us."

"Of course, madame," Lycien replied jovially. "I should have thought of that myself."

It was midafternoon when Berit returned with Talen in tow. "He was down near the harbor," the novice reported, still firmly holding the boy by the neck of his tunic. "I searched him thoroughly. He hadn't had time to steal anything yet."

"I just wanted to look at the sea," the boy protested. "I've never seen the sea before."

Kurik was grimly removing his wide leather belt.

"Now, wait a minute, Kurik," Talen said, struggling to free himself from Berit's grasp. "You wouldn't really do that, would you?"

"Watch me."

"I picked up some information," Talen said quickly. "If you thrash me, I'll keep it to myself." He looked appealingly at Sparhawk. "It's important," he said. "Tell him to put his belt back on, and I'll let you know what I found out."

"All right, Kurik," Sparhawk said. "Let it pass—for the moment anyway." Then he looked sternly at the boy. "This had better be good, Talen," he threatened.

"It is, Sparhawk. Believe me."

"Let's have it."

"Well, I was going down this street. As I said, I wanted to see the harbor and all the ships and things. Anyway, I was passing a wine shop and I saw a man coming out."

"Amazing," Kalten said. "Do people in Madel actually frequent wine shops?"

"You both know this man. It was Krager, the one you had me watching in Cimmura. I followed him. He went into a shabby-looking inn down by the waterfront. I can take you there if you want.''

"Put your belt back on, Kurik," Sparhawk said.

"Do we have time for this?" Kalten asked.

"I think we should take time. Martel's already tried to interfere with us a couple times. If it *was* Annias who poisoned Ehlana, he'll definitely want to keep us from finding any kind of antidote. That means that Martel will try to get to Cippria before I do. We can wring that information out of Krager if we can catch him."

"We'll go with you," Tynian said eagerly. "This whole thing will be easier if we can cut Annias's hands off here in Madel."

Sparhawk considered it, then shook his head. "I don't think so," he said. "Martel and his hirelings know Kalten and me. He doesn't know the rest of you. If the two of us can't catch up with Krager, you'll all be looking around Madel for him. That's going to be easier if he doesn't know what you look like."

"Makes sense," Ulath agreed.

Tynian looked profoundly disappointed. "Sometimes you think too much, Sparhawk," he said.

"It's a trait of his," Kalten told him.

"Will these cloaks of ours attract any attention in the streets of Madel, my Lord?" Sparhawk asked the marquis.

Lycien shook his head. "It's a port city," he said. "There are people here from all over the world, so two more strangers won't attract that much notice."

"Good," Sparhawk said. He started toward the door with Kalten and Talen at his heels. "We should be back before long," he said.

They left their horses behind and went into the city on foot. Madel was situated on an estuary, and the smell of the sea was very strong, carried inland by a stiff onshore breeze. The streets were narrow and crooked and grew increasingly run-down as the two knights and the boy approached the harbor.

"How far is this inn?" Kalten asked.

"Not too much farther," Talen assured him.

Sparhawk stopped. "Did you get the chance to look around a bit after Krager went inside?" he asked the boy.

"No. I was going to, but Berit caught me before I had time."

"Why don't you do it now? If Kalten and I go marching up to the front door and Krager happens to be watching, he'll be out the back door before we get inside. See if you can find that back door for us."

"Right," Talen said, his eyes sparkling with excitement. He scurried off down the street.

"Good lad there," Kalten said, "in spite of his bad habits." He frowned. "How do you know this inn has a back door?" he asked.

"Every inn has a back door, Kalten—in case of fire, if nothing else."

"I guess I hadn't thought of that."

When Talen returned, he was running as hard as he could. There were about ten men chasing him; in the lead, roaring unintelligibly, was Adus.

"Look out!" Talen shouted as he ran past.

Sparhawk and Kalten whipped their swords out from under their cloaks and stepped slightly apart to meet the charge. The men following Adus were shabbily dressed and carried a variety of weapons, rusty swords, axes, and spiked maces. "Kill them!" Adus bellowed, slowing slightly and waving his men on.

The fight was short. The men rushing up the narrow street appeared to be common waterfront roughnecks, and they were no match for the two trained knights. Four of them were down before the others realized that they had made a tactical blunder. Two more collapsed onto the bloody stones before the rest could turn to flee. Then Sparhawk leaped over the sprawled bodies and rushed at Adus. The brute parried the knight's first stroke, then seized his sword hilt in both hands and flailed at Sparhawk with it. Sparhawk easily deflected those blows and countered deftly, inflicting painful cuts and bruises on his opponent's mailed ribs and shoulders. After a moment, Adus fled, running hard and clutching at his side with a bloody hand.

"Why didn't you chase him?" Kalten demanded, coming up puffing and with his blood-smeared sword still in his hand.

"Because Adus can run faster than I can," Sparhawk shrugged. "I've known that for years."

Talen came back down the street, breathing hard. He looked admiringly at the hacked and bleeding bodies sprawled on the cobblestones. "Well done, my Lords," he congratulated them.

"What happened?" Sparhawk asked.

"I went on past the inn." Talen shrugged. "Then I went around back. That big one who just got away was hiding in the alley with these others. He made a grab for me, but I dodged. Then I ran."

"Good thinking," Kalten said.

Sparhawk sheathed his sword. "Let's get away from here," he said.

"Why not follow Adus?" Kalten asked.

"Because they're setting traps for us. Martel's using Krager as bait to lead us around by the nose. That's probably why we keep finding him so easily."

"Would that mean that they can recognize me as well?" Talen sounded shocked.

"Probably," Sparhawk said. "They found out that you were working for me in Cimmura, remember? Krager probably knew that you were following him around and gave your description to Adus. Adus may not have a brain, but his eyes are sharp." He muttered an oath. "Martel's even more clever than I thought, and he's starting to irritate me."

"It's about time," Kalten murmured as they started back up the crooked street.

PART THREE

DABOUR

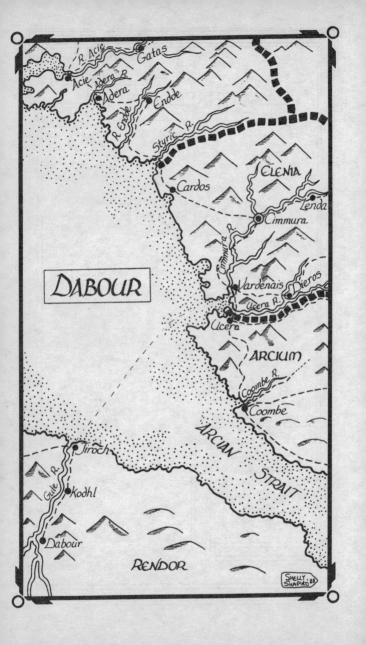

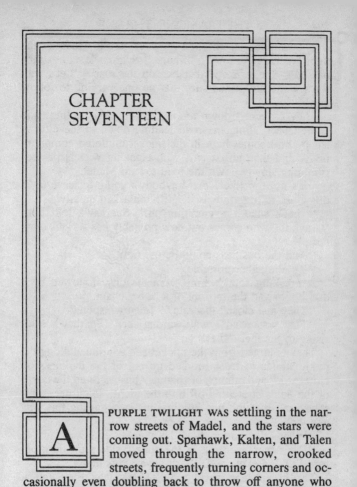

CHAPTER
SEVENTEEN

A PURPLE TWILIGHT WAS settling in the narrow streets of Madel, and the stars were coming out. Sparhawk, Kalten, and Talen moved through the narrow, crooked streets, frequently turning corners and occasionally even doubling back to throw off anyone who might possibly be following them.

"Aren't we being just a little overcautious?" Kalten said after about a half hour.

"Let's not take any chances with Martel," Sparhawk replied. "He's entirely capable of throwing a few people away just for the chance to hunt us down. I'd rather not wake up in the middle of the night to find Lycien's house surrounded by mercenaries."

"You've got a point there, I suppose."

293

They slipped out through the west gate of Madel as the light faded even more. "In here," Sparhawk said as they passed a thicket some distance up the road. "Let's wait for a while and make sure that no one's trying to follow us."

They crouched down among the rustling saplings and peered back along the road leading down to the city. A sleepy bird somewhere in the thicket muttered complainingly, and then an ox cart with creaking wheels passed, rumbling slowly down the road toward Madel.

"It's not too likely that anybody's going to leave town this close to nightfall, is it?" Kalten asked quietly.

"That's what I'm counting on," Sparhawk told him. "Anybody who comes out now probably has serious business."

"And the business could be us, right?"

"It's altogether possible."

A creaking sound came from the city, followed by a dull boom and the rattling of a heavy chain.

"They just closed the gate," Talen whispered.

"That was what I was waiting for," Sparhawk said, rising to his feet. "Let's go."

They emerged from the thicket and continued along the road. Stands of trees loomed up out of the darkness on either side, and clumps of shadowy bushes lined the edges of the fields stretching off into the night. Talen nervously stayed close to the two knights, his eyes darting this way and that.

"What's the matter, boy?" Kalten asked him.

"I've never been out in the countryside after dark before," Talen explained. "Is it always this black?"

The blond man shrugged. "That's why they call it night."

"Why doesn't somebody put up some torches?" Talen complained.

"What for? So the rabbits can see where they're going?"

Lycien's house stood in the deep shadows of the surrounding evergreens with only a single torch at the gate. Talen was visibly relieved when they walked into the graveled yard in front of the entrance.

"Any luck?" Tynian asked, emerging from the main entrance.

"We ran into some trouble," Sparhawk replied. "Let's go inside."

"I told you that you should have let the rest of us come along," the bulky-shouldered Alcione said accusingly as they entered the building.

"It wasn't *that* much trouble," Kalten assured him.

The others were waiting in the large room to which Lycien had first led them. Sephrenia rose to her feet, looking closely at the blood spatters on the two Pandions' cloaks. "Are you all right?" she asked, her voice mirroring her concern.

"We ran into a group of sportive fellows," Kalten replied lightly. He looked down at his cloak. "The blood is all theirs."

"What happened?" she asked Sparhawk.

"Adus tried to ambush us when we got to the inn," he told her. "He had a group of waterfront toughs with him." He paused reflectively. "You know, we've been running across Krager just about every time we turn around. Once—or even twice—might have been sheer coincidence, but it's starting to happen just a little too frequently, and every time we try to follow him, there's some kind of ambush."

"You think it's deliberate?" Tynian asked.

"It's beginning to look that way, isn't it?"

"Would this Martel put a friend in such danger?" Bevier sounded surprised.

"Martel doesn't have any friends," Sparhawk told him. "Adus and Krager are hirelings, nothing more. They're useful, but he feels no particular attachment for them. I don't think he'd shed many tears if something happened to Krager." He began to pace up and down, staring thoughtfully at the floor. "Maybe we can turn the tables on him." He looked at Kalten. "Why don't you let yourself be seen in the streets of Madel?" he suggested. "Don't take too many chances, but let people know you're in town."

"Why not?" Kalten shrugged.

Tynian grinned. "Martel and his hirelings don't know

the rest of us, so we can sort of loiter along behind Kalten without attracting attention. Is that the idea?''

Sparhawk nodded. ''If they think Kalten's alone, it might bring them out into the open. I'm getting a little tired of Martel's games, so maybe it's time for us to play a few of our own.'' He looked at Bevier's cousin. ''How excited do the local authorities get about street brawls, my Lord?'' he asked.

Lycien laughed. ''Madel is a seaport, Sir Sparhawk. Brawling is second nature to sailors. The authorities don't pay much attention to their little scuffles—except to remove the bodies, of course. Public sanitation, you understand.''

''Good.'' Sparhawk looked at his friends. ''You may not get a chance at Krager or Adus, but you might be able to divide Martel's attention. That could be what it takes to get Kurik and Sephrenia and me aboard a ship unnoticed. I'd rather not have to keep looking over my shoulder when we get to Cippria.''

''About the only tricky part is going to be getting you to the harbor without being seen,'' Kalten said.

''It won't be necessary to go to the harbor,'' Lycien said. ''I have some warehouses on the river about five miles from here. A fair number of independent sea captains deliver cargoes to me there, and I'm sure arrangements for your passage can be made without any need for going into the city.''

''Thank you, my Lord,'' Sparhawk said. ''That solves a problem.''

''When do you plan to leave?'' Tynian asked.

''I don't see much point in delaying.''

''Tomorrow, then?''

Sparhawk nodded.

''I need to talk with you, Sparhawk,'' Sephrenia said. ''Would you mind coming to my room?''

He followed her out the door, slightly puzzled. ''Is it something we can't discuss in front of the others?'' he asked her.

''It might be better if they don't hear us arguing.''

''Are we going to argue?''

''Probably.'' She opened the door to her room and led

him inside. Flute sat cross-legged on the bed, her dark eyebrows knit in concentration as she wove the intricate mesh of a cat's cradle out of a strand of wool yarn. It was far more complex than the one Talen had made when he had demonstrated it to her. She looked up, smiled at them, and proudly extended her little hands to show them her handiwork.

"She'll be going with us," Sephrenia said.

"Absolutely not!" Sparhawk said sharply.

"I told you we'd argue about this."

"It's an absurd idea, Sephrenia."

"We all do many absurd things, dear one." She smiled affectionately at him.

"Don't do that," he said. "You're not going to win me over that way."

"Don't be tiresome, Sparhawk. You've been around her long enough to know that she always does what she decides to do, and she's decided that she's going with us to Rendor."

"She won't if I have anything to say about it."

"That's the whole point, Sparhawk. You don't. You're dealing with something you can't understand. She's going to come with us in the end anyway, so why not just give in gracefully?"

"Gracefulness is not one of my strong points."

"I've noticed."

"All right, Sephrenia," he said flatly, "just who is she, anyway? You recognized her the first moment we saw her, didn't you?"

"Of course."

"Why of course? She's only about six years old, and you haven't left the Pandions for generations. How could you possibly know her?"

She sighed. "Elene logic always clouds an issue with facts. The child and I are kindred in a rather peculiar sense of the word. We know each other in a way you couldn't begin to comprehend."

"Thanks," he said drily.

"I'm not belittling your intelligence, dear one," she told him, "but there's a part of Styric life you're not prepared to accept—either intellectually or philosophically."

He frowned slightly, his eyes narrowed in thought. "All right, Sephrenia," he said, "let me have a try at the Elene logic you're so fond of dismissing. Flute is a child, hardly more than a baby."

The little girl made a face at him.

He ignored that and went on. "She suddenly appeared in an uninhabited region near the Arcian border far from any kind of human habitation. We tried to leave her at that nunnery south of Darra, and she not only managed to escape but also got a goodly distance ahead of us even though we were travelling at a gallop. Then she somehow managed to persuade Faran to let her on his back, and Faran won't let anybody near him except me unless I tell him to. When she met Dolmant, you could tell by his face that he sensed something very unusual about her. Not only that, you bully full-grown knights like a drill sergeant, but anytime Flute decides to do something or go someplace, you give in without a fight. Wouldn't you say that all of that suggests that she's not an ordinary child?"

"You're the one who's exercising his logic. I wouldn't dream of interfering."

"All right then. Let's see where logic takes us. I've seen a fair number of Styrics. With the exception of you and the other magicians, they're all fairly primitive and not very bright—no offense intended, of course."

"Of course." Her expression was amused.

"Since we've already established the fact that Flute is not an ordinary child, what does that leave us?"

"What would be your guess, Sparhawk?"

"Since she's not ordinary, she must be special. In Styricum, that can only mean one thing. She's a magician. Nothing else could explain her."

She applauded ironically. "Excellent, Sparhawk," she congratulated him.

"But that's impossible, Sephrenia. She's only a child. She hasn't had time to learn the secrets."

"Some few are born with that knowledge. Besides, she's older than she looks."

"How old?"

"You know that I won't tell you that. The knowledge

of the exact moment of one's birth can be a powerful weapon in the hands of an enemy.''

A disturbing thought came to him. "You're preparing for your own death, aren't you, Sephrenia? If we fail, the twelve Pandions who were in the throne room with you will die one by one, and then you'll die, too. You're preparing Flute to be your successor."

She laughed. "Now *that*, dear Sparhawk, is a very interesting idea. I'm surprised you came up with it, considering the fact that you're an Elene."

"That's a very irritating habit you've picked up lately, you know? Don't try to be mysterious with me, Sephrenia, and don't treat me like a child just because I'm an Elene."

"I'll try to remember that. You'll agree to let her come with us, then?"

"Do I have any choice?"

"No. As a matter of fact, you don't."

THEY ROSE EARLY the next morning and gathered in the dew-drenched yard in front of Marquis Lycien's house. The newly risen sun was very bright and it slanted down through the trees, casting the peculiarly bluish-colored shadows of early morning.

"I'll get word to you from time to time," Sparhawk told those who were remaining behind.

"Be careful down there, Sparhawk," Kalten said.

"I'm always careful." Sparhawk swung himself up onto Faran's back.

"God speed, Sir Sparhawk," Bevier said.

"Thank you, Bevier." Sparhawk looked around at the other knights. "Don't be so glum, gentlemen," he told them. "If we're lucky, this won't take very long." He looked at Kalten again. "If you run into Martel, give him my regards."

Kalten nodded. "With an axe in the face, I think."

Marquis Lycien mounted a fat bay horse and led the way out onto the road which passed his house. The morning was crisp, though not actually cold. Spring, Sparhawk decided, was not very far off. He shifted his shoulders slightly. The sober businessman's doublet Lycien had lent him did not really fit very well. It bound in some places and was uncomfortably loose in others.

"We'll turn off just up ahead," Lycien told them. "There's a track through the woods that leads down to my wharves and the little settlement that's grown up around them. Will you want me to bring your horses back after you go on board ship?"

"No, my Lord," Sparhawk replied. "I think we'll take them with us. We don't know exactly what's going to happen in Rendor. We might need dependable mounts, and I've seen what passes for a horse in Cippria."

What Lycien had modestly called a "little settlement" turned out to be a fair-sized village complete with shipyards, houses, inns, and taverns. A dozen vessels were moored at the wharves with longshoremen swarming over them.

"Quite an operation, my Lord," Sparhawk said as they rode down the muddy street toward the river.

"One has had a certain success," Lycien said self-deprecatingly. He smiled. "Besides, I save enough in moorage fees to offset more than the cost of keeping the place up." He looked around. "Why don't you and I step into that tavern over there, Sir Sparhawk?" he suggested. "The independent sea captains favor that one."

"All right," Sparhawk agreed.

"I'll introduce you as Master Cluff," Lycien said as he swung down from his bay. "It's not much of a name, I'll admit, but it's fairly nondescript, and I've discovered that seafaring men love to talk, but they're not always very selective in their choice of listeners. I've gathered that you might prefer to keep this business of yours more or less confidential."

"You're perceptive, my Lord," Sparhawk replied, also dismounting. "This shouldn't take too long," he said to Kurik and Sephrenia.

"Isn't that what you said the last time you went to Rendor?" Kurik asked him.

"We can all hope that this time might be different."

Lycien led the way into a rather sedate wharfside tavern. The ceiling was low, with dark, heavy beams decorated here and there with ships' lanterns. There was a broad window near the front, and golden morning sunlight streamed in through it, setting the fresh straw on the floor to gleaming. Several substantial-looking men of middle years sat at a table by the window, talking over brimming tankards. They looked up as the marquis led Sparhawk to their table. "My Lord," one of them respectfully greeted Lycien.

"Gentlemen," Lycien said, "this is Master Cluff, an acquaintance of mine. He's asked me to introduce him."

They all looked at Sparhawk inquiringly.

"I have a bit of a problem, gentlemen," Sparhawk told them. "May I join you?"

"Have a seat," one of the sea captains, a solid-looking man with silver-shot curly hair, invited.

"I'll leave you gentlemen, then," Lycien said. "There's something that needs my attention." He inclined his head slightly, turned, and went back out of the tavern.

"He probably wants to see if there's some way he can raise the mooring fees," one of the captains said wryly.

"My name's Sorgi," the captain with the curly hair introduced himself to Sparhawk. "What's this problem you mentioned, Master Cluff?"

Sparhawk coughed slightly as if a little embarrassed. "Well," he said, "it all started a few months ago. I happened to hear about a lady who lives not far from here," he began, embellishing as he went along. "Her father is old and very wealthy, so the lady stands to inherit a sizable estate. One of my problems has always been the fact that I have some expensive tastes and very little in my purse to support them. It occurred to me that a rich wife might solve that problem."

"That makes sense," Captain Sorgi said. "That's about the only reason I can think of for getting married at all."

"I couldn't agree more," Sparhawk replied. "Anyway, I wrote her a letter pretending that we had some mutual friends and I was a little surprised when she answered my letter with a great deal of warmth. Our letters grew more and more friendly, and she finally invited me to call on her. I went even deeper in debt to my tailor and set out for her father's house in high spirits and splendid new clothes."

"Sounds to me as if everything was going according to your plan, Master Cluff," Sorgi said. "What's this problem of yours?"

"I'm just getting to that, Captain. The lady is of middle years and very wealthy. If she were even remotely presentable, someone would have snapped her up years ago, so I didn't have my hopes too high on that score. I assumed that she was plain—perhaps even homely. I had not, however, expected a horror." He feigned a shudder. "Gentlemen, I cannot even describe her to you. No matter how rich she was, it wouldn't have been worth waking up to *that* every morning. We spoke together briefly—about the weather, I think—and then I made my apologies and left. She has no brothers, so I wasn't worried about the possibility of someone looking me up to object to my bad manners. What I didn't count on, though, was all her cousins. She's got a whole platoon of them, and they've been following me for weeks now."

"They don't want to kill you, do they?" Sorgi asked.

"No," Sparhawk replied in an anguished tone. "They want to drag me back and force me to marry her."

The captains all roared with laughter, pounding on the table in glee. "I think you've outsmarted yourself, Master Cluff," one of them said, wiping the tears of mirth from his eyes.

Sparhawk nodded glumly. "You're probably right," he admitted.

"You should have found some way to get a look at her before you sent the first letter," Sorgi grinned.

"I know that now," Sparhawk agreed. "Anyhow, I think it's time I left the country for a while until the cousins stop looking for me. I've got a nephew living in Cippria in Rendor who's been doing fairly well of late. I'm sure I can impose on him until I can get my feet on the ground again. Is it possible that one of you gentlemen might be sailing there soon? I'd like to book passage for myself and a couple of family retainers. I'd go to the main docks in Madel, but I've got a strong feeling that the cousins are watching them."

"What say you, gentlemen?" Captain Sorgi said expansively. "Shall we help this good fellow out of his predicament?"

"I'm going to Rendor, right enough," one of the others replied, "but I'm committed to Jiroch."

Sorgi thought about it. "I was going to Jiroch myself," he mused, "and then on to Cippria, but I might be able to rearrange my schedule just a bit."

"I won't be able to help," a rough-voiced sea captain growled. "My ship's having her bottom scraped. I can give you some advice, though. If these cousins are watching the main wharves in Madel, they're probably watching these as well. Everybody in town knows about Lycien's docks here." He tugged at one earlobe. "I've smuggled a few people out of a few places in my time—when the price was right." He looked at the captain who was bound for Jiroch. "When do you sail, Captain Mabin?"

"With the noon tide."

"And you?" the helpful captain asked Sorgi.

"The same."

"Good. If the cousins are watching the docks here, they may try to hire a ship and follow our bachelor friend. Have him openly board Mabin's ship. Then, when you're downriver a ways and out of sight, transfer him to Sorgi's ship. If the cousins decide to follow, Mabin can lead them off toward Jiroch, and Master Cluff will be safe on his way to Cippria. That's the way I'd do it."

"You've got a very ingenious mind, my friend." Sorgi laughed. "Are you sure that people are the only things you've smuggled in the past?"

"We've all avoided customs officers from time to time, haven't we, Sorgi?" the rough-voiced captain said. "We live at sea. Why should we pay taxes to support the kingdoms of the landsmen? I'd gladly pay taxes to the King of the Ocean, but I can't seem to find his palace."

"Well said, my friend," Sorgi applauded.

"Gentlemen," Sparhawk said. "I'm eternally in your debt."

"Not exactly eternally, Master Cluff," Sorgi said. "A man who admits to having financial difficulties pays for his passage *before* he boards. He does on my ship, at least."

"Would you accept half here and half when we reach Cippria?" Sparhawk countered.

"I'm afraid not, my friend. I like you well enough, but I'm sure you can see my position in the matter."

Sparhawk sighed. "We have horses," he added. "I suppose you'll charge extra to carry them as well?"

"Naturally."

"I was afraid of that."

The loading of Faran, Sephrenia's palfrey, and Kurik's stout gelding took place behind a screen of sailcloth Sorgi's sailors were ostensibly mending. Shortly before noon, Sparhawk and Kurik boarded the ship bound for Jiroch. They moved openly up the gangway, followed by Sephrenia, who carried Flute in her arms.

Captain Mabin greeted them on the quarterdeck. "Ah," he grinned, "here's our reluctant bridegroom. Why don't you and your friends walk around the deck until we sail? Give all the cousins plenty of chances to see you."

"I've had a few second thoughts about this, Captain Mabin," Sparhawk said. "If the cousins hire a ship and follow you—and if they catch up with you—it's going to be fairly obvious that I'm not on board."

"Nobody's going to catch up with me, Master Cluff." The captain laughed. "I've got the fastest ship on the Inner Sea. Besides, it's obvious that you don't know very much about seafaring etiquette. Nobody boards another man's ship at sea unless he's prepared for a fight. It's just not done."

"Oh," Sparhawk said. "I didn't know that. We'll stroll around the deck, then."

"Bridegroom?" Sephrenia murmured as they moved away from the captain.

"It's a long story," Sparhawk told her.

"There seem to be a fair number of these long stories cropping up lately. Someday we'll have to sit down so that you can tell them to me."

"Someday perhaps."

"Flute," Sephrenia said quite firmly, "come down from there."

Sparhawk looked up. The little girl was halfway up a rope ladder stretching from the rail to the yardarm. She pouted just a bit, then did as she was told. "You always know exactly where she is, don't you?" he asked Sephrenia.

"Always," she replied.

The transfer from one ship to the other took place in midriver some distance downstream from Lycien's wharves and was concealed by a great deal of activity on both ships. Captain Sorgi quickly bustled his passengers belowdecks to get them out of sight, and then the two ships proceeded sedately downriver, bobbing side by side like two matrons returning home from church.

"We're passing the wharves of Madel," Sorgi called down the companionway to them some short time later. "Keep your face out of sight, Master Cluff, or I may have a deck full of your betrothed's cousins on my hands."

"This is *really* making me curious, Sparhawk," Sephrenia said. "Couldn't you give me just the tiniest clue?"

"I made up a story," he shrugged. "It was lurid enough to seize the attention of a group of sailors."

"Sparhawk's always been very good at making up stories," Kurik observed. "He used to lie himself in and out of trouble regularly when he was a novice." The grizzled squire was seated on a bunk with the drowsing Flute nestled in his lap. "You know," he said quietly, "I never had a daughter. They smell better than little boys, don't they?"

Sephrenia burst out laughing. "Don't tell Aslade," she cautioned. "She may decide to try for one."

Kurik rolled his eyes upward in dismay. "Not again," he said. "I don't mind babies around the house, but I couldn't bear the morning sickness again."

About an hour later, Sorgi came down the companionway. "We're clearing the mouth of the estuary now," he reported, "and there's not a single vessel to the rear. I'd say that you've made good your escape, Master Cluff."

"Thank God," Sparhawk replied fervently.

"Tell me, my friend," Sorgi said thoughtfully, "is the lady really as ugly as you say?"

"Captain Sorgi, you wouldn't believe how ugly."

"Maybe you're a bit too delicate, Master Cluff. The sea's getting colder, my ship's getting old and tired, and the winter storms are making my bones ache. I could stand a fair amount of ugliness if the lady's estate happened to be as large as you say. I might even consider returning some of your passage money in exchange for a letter of introduction. Maybe you overlooked some of her good qualities.''

"We could talk about that, I suppose," Sparhawk conceded.

"I need to go topside," Sorgi said. "We're far enough past the city that it's safe for you and your friends to come on deck now." He turned and went back up the companionway.

"I think I can save you all the trouble of telling me that long story you mentioned earlier," Sephrenia told Sparhawk. "You didn't actually use that tired old fable about the ugly heiress, did you?"

He shrugged. "As Vanion says, the old ones are the best."

"Oh, Sparhawk, I'm disappointed in you. How are you going to avoid giving that poor captain the imaginary lady's name?"

"I'll think of something. Why don't we go up on deck before the sun sets?"

Kurik spoke in a whisper. "I think the child's asleep," he said. "I don't want to wake her. You two go on ahead."

Sparhawk nodded and led Sephrenia out of the cramped cabin.

"I always forget how gentle he is," Sephrenia said softly.

Sparhawk nodded. "He's the best and kindest man I know," he said simply. "If it weren't for class distinctions, he'd have made an almost perfect knight."

"Is class really all that important?"

"Not to me, it isn't, but I didn't make the rules."

They emerged on deck in the slanting, late-afternoon sunlight. The breeze blowing offshore was brisk, catching the tops of the waves and turning them into sun-splashed froth. Captain Mabin's vessel, bound for Jiroch, was heeling over in that breeze on a course almost due west through the broad channel of the Arcian Strait. Her sails bellied out, snowy white in the afternoon sun, and she ran before the wind like a skimming sea bird.

"How far do you make it to Cippria, Captain Sorgi?" Sparhawk asked as he and Sephrenia stepped up onto the quarterdeck.

"A hundred and fifty leagues, Master Cluff," Sorgi replied. "Three days, if this wind holds."

"That's good time, isn't it?"

Sorgi grunted. "We could make better if this poor old tub didn't leak so much."

"Sparhawk!" Sephrenia gasped, taking him urgently by the arm.

"What is it?" He looked at her in concern. Her face had gone deathly pale.

"Look!" She pointed.

Some distance from where Captain Mabin's graceful ship was running through the Arcian Strait, a single, densely black cloud had appeared in an otherwise unblemished sky. It seemed somehow to be moving against the wind, growing larger and more ominously black by the moment. Then it began to swirl, ponderously at first, but then faster and faster. As it spun, a long, dark finger twitched and jerked down from its center, reaching down and down until its inky tip touched the roiling surface of the strait. Tons of water were suddenly drawn up into the swirling maw as the vast funnel moved erratically across the heaving sea.

"Waterspout!" the lookout shouted down from the mast. The sailors rushed to the rail to gape in horror at the swirling spout.

Inexorably the vast thing bore down on Mabin's helpless ship, and then the vessel, which suddenly appeared very tiny, vanished in the seething funnel. Chunks and pieces of her timbers spun out of the great waterspout hundreds of feet in the air to settle with agonizing slowness to the surface again. A single piece of sail fluttered down like a stricken white bird.

Then, as suddenly as they had come, the black cloud and its deadly waterspout were gone.

So was Mabin's ship.

The surface of the sea was littered with debris, and a vast cloud of white gulls appeared, swooping and diving over the wreckage as if to mark the vessel's passing.

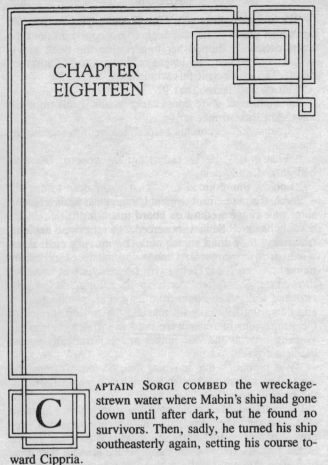

CHAPTER
EIGHTEEN

C APTAIN SORGI COMBED the wreckage-
strewn water where Mabin's ship had gone
down until after dark, but he found no
survivors. Then, sadly, he turned his ship
southeasterly again, setting his course toward Cippria.

Sephrenia sighed and turned from the rail. "Let's go
below, Sparhawk."

He nodded and followed her down the companionway.

Kurik had lighted a single oil lamp, and it swung from
a low overhead beam, filling the small, dark-paneled com-
partment with swaying shadows. Flute had awakened and
she sat at the bolted-down table in the center of the cabin,
looking suspiciously at the bowl sitting in front of her.

308

"It's just stew, little girl," Kurik was saying to her. "It won't hurt you."

She delicately dipped her fingers into the thick gravy and lifted out a dripping chunk of meat. She sniffed at it, then looked questioningly at the squire.

"Salt pork," he told her.

She shuddered and dropped the chunk back into the gravy. Then she firmly pushed the bowl away.

"Styrics don't eat pork, Kurik," Sephrenia told him.

"The ship's cook said that this is what the sailors eat," he said defensively. He looked at Sparhawk. "Was the captain able to find any survivors from the other ship?"

Sparhawk shook his head. "That waterspout tore it all to pieces. The same thing probably happened on board that one."

"It's lucky we weren't on board that one."

"Very lucky," Sephrenia agreed. "Waterspouts are like tornadoes. They don't appear out of completely clear skies and they don't move against the wind or change direction the way that one did. It was being consciously directed."

"Magic?" Kurik said. "Is that really possible—to call up weather like that, I mean?"

"I don't think *I* could do it."

"Who did then?"

"I don't know for certain." Her eyes, however, showed a certain suspicion.

"Let's get it out into the open, Sephrenia," Sparhawk said. "You've guessed something, haven't you?"

Her expression grew a bit more certain. "In the past few months we've had several encounters with a hooded figure in a Styric robe. You saw it several times in Cimmura, and it tried to have us ambushed on our way to Borrata. Styrics seldom cover their faces. Have you ever noticed that?"

"Yes, but I don't quite make the connection."

"This thing had to cover its face, Sparhawk. It's not human."

He stared at her. "Are you sure?"

"I can't be absolutely positive until I see its face, but the evidence is beginning to pile up, wouldn't you say?"

"Could Annias actually do something like that?"

"It's not Annias. He might know a little rudimentary

magic, but he couldn't begin to raise a thing like that. Only Azash could have done it. He's the only one who dares to summon such beings. The Younger Gods will not, and even the other Elder Gods have forsworn the practice."

"Why would Azash want to kill Captain Mabin and his crew?"

"The ship was destroyed because the creature thought that we were on board."

"That goes a little far, Sephrenia," Kurik objected skeptically. "If it's so powerful, why did it sink the wrong boat?"

"The creatures of the underworld are not very sophisticated, Kurik," she replied. "Our simple ruse may have deceived it. Power and wisdom don't always go hand in hand. Many of the greatest magicians of Styricum were as stupid as stumps."

"I don't quite follow this," Sparhawk admitted with a puzzled frown. "What we're doing has nothing to do with Zemoch. Why would Azash go out of his way to help Annias?"

"It may be that there isn't any connection. Azash always has his own motives. It's quite possible that what he's doing has nothing to do with Annias at all."

"It doesn't wash, Sephrenia. If you're right about this thing, it's been working for Martel, and Martel works for Annias."

"Are you so sure that the creature is working for Martel and not the other way around? Azash can see the shadows of the future. One of us might be a danger to him. The seeming alliance between Martel and the creature may be no more than a matter of convenience."

He began to gnaw worriedly at a fingernail. "That's all I need," he said, "something else to worry about." Then a thought struck him. "Wait a minute. Do you remember what the ghost of Lakus said—that darkness was at the gate and that Ehlana was our only hope of light? Could Azash be that darkness?"

She nodded. "It's possible."

"If that's the case, then wouldn't it be Ehlana he's trying to destroy? She's totally protected by that crystal that encases her, but if something happens to us before we can find a way to heal her, she'll die, too. Maybe that's why Azash has joined forces with the primate.''

''Aren't you both stretching things a bit?'' Kurik asked. ''You're basing a great deal of speculation on a single incident.''

''It doesn't hurt to be ready for eventualities, Kurik,'' Sparhawk replied. ''I hate surprises.''

The squire grunted and rose to his feet. ''You two must be hungry,'' he said. ''I'll go down to the galley and get you some supper. We can talk some more while you're eating.''

''No pork,'' Sephrenia told him firmly.

''Bread and cheese, then?'' he suggested. ''And maybe some fruit?''

''That would be fine, Kurik. You'd probably better bring enough for Flute as well. I know she's not going to eat that stew.''

''That's all right,'' he said. ''I'll eat it for her. I don't have the same kind of prejudices that you Styrics do.''

IT WAS OVERCAST when they reached the port city of Cippria three days later. The cloud cover was high and thin, and there was no trace of moisture in it. The city was low, with squat white buildings thickly walled to ward off the heat of the southern sun. The wharves jutting out into the harbor were constructed of stone, since Rendor was a kingdom largely devoid of trees.

Sparhawk and the others came up on deck, wearing hooded black robes, just as the sailors were mooring Captain Sorgi's ship to one of the wharves. They went up the three steps to the quarterdeck to join the curly-haired seaman.

''Get some fenders between our side and that wharf!'' Sorgi roared at the seamen who were snubbing off the mooring lines. He shook his head in disgust. ''I have to tell them that every single time we dock,'' he muttered. ''All they can think about when we make port is the nearest alehouse.'' He looked at Sparhawk. ''Well, Master Cluff,'' he said. ''Have you changed your mind?''

''I'm afraid not, Captain,'' Sparhawk replied, setting

down the bundle containing his spare clothing. "I'd like to oblige you, but the lady I mentioned seems to have all her hopes pinned on me. It's for your own good, actually. If you show up at her house with an introduction from me, her cousins might decide to wring my location out of you— and being wrung is not anybody's idea of a good time. Besides, I don't want to take any chances."

Sorgi grunted. Then he looked at them all curiously. "Where did you come by the Rendorish clothing?"

"I did some bargaining in your forecastle yesterday." Sparhawk shrugged, plucking at the front of the hooded black robe he wore. "Some of your sailors like to be unobtrusive when they make port here in Rendor."

"How well I know," Sorgi said wryly. "I spent three days looking for the ship's cook the last time I was in Jiroch." He looked at Sephrenia, who was also robed in black and wore a heavy veil across her face. "Where did you find anything to fit her?" he asked. "None of my sailors are that small."

"She's very adept with her needle." Sparhawk did not think it necessary to explain exactly how Sephrenia had changed the color of her white robe.

Sorgi scratched at his curly hair. "I can't for the life of me understand why most Rendors wear black," he said. "Don't they know that it's twice as hot?"

"Maybe they haven't realized that yet," Sparhawk replied. "Rendors are none too bright in the first place, and they've only been here for five thousand years."

Sorgi laughed. "Maybe that's it," he said. "Good fortune here in Cippria, Master Cluff," he said. "If I happen to run across any cousins, I'll tell them that I've never heard of you."

"Thank you, Captain," Sparhawk said, clasping Sorgi's hand. "You have no idea how much I appreciate that."

They led their horses down the slanting gangway to the wharf. At Kurik's suggestion, they covered their saddles with blankets to conceal the fact that they were not of Rendorish construction. Then they all tied their bundles to their saddles, mounted, and moved away from the harbor at an unobtrusive walk. The streets were teeming with Rendors. The city dwellers sometimes wore lighter-colored clothing, but the desert people were all dressed in unrelieved black and had their hoods up. There were few women in the street, and they were all veiled. Sephrenia rode subserviently behind Sparhawk and Kurik with her hood pulled far forward and her veil drawn tightly across her nose and mouth.

"You know the customs here, I see," Sparhawk said back over his shoulder.

"I was here many years ago," she replied, drawing her robe around Flute's knees.

"How many years?"

"Would you like to have me tell you that Cippria was only a fishing village then?" she asked archly. "Twenty or so mud huts?"

He looked back at her sharply. "Sephrenia, Cippria's been a major seaport for fifteen hundred years."

"My," she said, "has it really been that long? It seems like only yesterday. Where *does* the time go?"

"That's impossible!"

She laughed gaily. "How gullible you can be sometimes, Sparhawk," she said. "You know I'm not going to answer that kind of question, so why keep trying?"

He suddenly felt more than a little sheepish. "I suppose I asked for that, didn't I?" he admitted.

"Yes, you did."

Kurik was grinning broadly.

"Go ahead and say it," Sparhawk told him sourly.

"Say what, my Lord?" Kurik's eyes were wide and innocent.

They rode up from the harbor, mingling with robed Rendors in the narrow, twisting streets. Although the overcast veiled the sun, Sparhawk could still feel the heat radiating out from the white-plastered walls of the houses and shops. He could also catch the familiar scents of Rendor. The air was close and dusty, and there was the pervading odor of mutton simmering in olive oil and pungent spices. There was the cloying fragrance of heavy perfumes, and overlaying it all was the persistent reek of the stockyards.

Near the center of town, they passed the mouth of a narrow alley. A chill touched Sparhawk, and suddenly, as clearly as if they were actually ringing out their call, he seemed once again to hear the sound of the bells.

"Something wrong?" Kurik asked as he saw his lord shudder.

"That's the alley where I saw Martel last time."

Kurik peered up the alley. "Tight quarters in there," he noted.

"That's all that kept me alive," Sparhawk replied. "They couldn't come at me all at once."

"Where are we going, Sparhawk?" Sephrenia asked from the rear.

"To the monastery where I stayed after I was wounded," he replied. "I don't think we want to be seen in the streets. The abbot and most of the monks out there are Arcian and they know how to keep secrets."

"Will I be welcome there?" she asked dubiously. "Arcian monks are conservative and they have certain prejudices where Styrics are concerned."

"This particular abbot is a bit more cosmopolitan," Sparhawk assured her, "and I have a few suspicions about his monastery, anyway."

"Oh?"

"I don't think these monks are entirely what they seem and I wouldn't be at all surprised to find a secret armory inside the monastery, complete with burnished armor, blue surcoats, and a variety of weapons."

"Cyrinics?" she asked, a bit surprised.

"The Pandions aren't the only ones who want to keep an eye on Rendor," he replied.

"What's that smell?" Kurik asked as they approached the western outskirts of town.

"The stockyards," Sparhawk told him. "A great deal of beef is shipped out of Cippria."

"Do we have to go through any kind of a gate to get out?"

Sparhawk shook his head. "The city walls were pulled down during the suppression of the Eshandist Heresy. The local people didn't bother to rebuild them."

They emerged from the narrow street they were following into acre upon acre of stock pens filled with bawling, scrubby-looking cows. It was late afternoon by now, and the overcast had begun to take on a silvery sheen.

"How much farther to the monastery?" Kurik asked.

"A mile or so."

"It's quite a distance from that alley back there, isn't it?"

"I noticed that myself about ten years ago."

"Why didn't you take shelter someplace closer?"

"There wasn't anyplace safe. I could hear the bells from the monastery, so I just kept following the sound. It gave me something to think about."

"You could have bled to death."

"That same thought crossed my mind a few times that night."

"Gentlemen," Sephrenia said, "do you suppose we could move along? The night comes on very quickly here in Rendor, and it gets cold in the desert after the sun goes down."

The monastery lay beyond the stockyards on a high, rocky hill. It was surrounded by a thick wall, and the gate was closed. Sparhawk dismounted before the gate and tugged on a stout cord hanging beside it. A small bell tinkled inside. After a moment, the shutter of a narrow, barred window cut into the stones beside the gate opened. The brown-bearded face of a monk peered out warily.

"Good evening, brother," Sparhawk said. "Do you suppose I might have a word with your abbot?"

"Can I give him your name?"

"Sparhawk. He might remember me. I stayed here for a time a few years back."

"Wait," the monk said brusquely, closing the shutter again.

"Not very cordial, is he?" Kurik said.

"Churchmen aren't really welcome in Rendor," Sparhawk replied. "A bit of caution is probably only natural."

They waited as the twilight faded.

Then the shutter opened again. "Sir Sparhawk!" a voice more suited to a parade ground than a religious community boomed.

"My Lord Abbot," Sparhawk replied.

"Wait there a moment. We'll open the gate."

There was a rattling of chains and the grating sound of a heavy bar sliding through thick iron rings. Then the gate ponderously swung open, and the abbot came out to greet them. He was a bluff, hearty-looking man with a ruddy face and an imposing black beard. He was quite tall, and his shoulders were massive. "It's good to see you again, my friend," he said, clasping Sparhawk's hand in a crushing grip. "You're looking well. You seemed a bit pale and wan when you left the last time you were here."

"It's been ten years, my Lord," Sparhawk pointed out. "In that length of time a man either heals or dies."

"So he does, Sir Sparhawk. So he does. Come inside and bring your friends."

Sparhawk led Faran through the gate with Sephrenia and Kurik close behind. There was a court inside, and the walls surrounding it were as bleak as those surrounding the monastery. They were unadorned by the white mortar customary on the walls of Rendorish buildings, and the windows which pierced them were perhaps a trifle narrower than monastic architecture would have dictated. They would, Sparhawk noted professionally, make excellent vantage points for archers.

"How can I help you, Sparhawk?" the abbot asked.

"I need refuge again, my Lord Abbot," Sparhawk replied. "That's getting to be sort of a habit, isn't it?"

The abbot grinned at him. "Who's after you this time?" he asked.

"No one that I know of, my Lord, and I think I'd like to keep it that way. Is there someplace we can talk privately?"

"Of course." The abbot turned to the brown-bearded monk who had first opened the shutter. "See to their horses, brother." It was not a request, but had all the crispness of a military command. The monk straightened noticeably, though he did not quite salute.

"Come along then, Sparhawk," the abbot boomed, clapping the big knight on the shoulder with one meaty hand.

Kurik dismounted and went to help Sephrenia. She handed Flute down to him and slipped from her saddle.

The abbot led them through the main door and into a

vaulted stone corridor dimly lighted at intervals by small oil lamps. Perhaps it was the scent of the oil, but the place had a peculiar odor of sanctity—and of safety—about it. That smell sharply reminded Sparhawk of the night ten years before. "The place hasn't changed much," he noted, looking around.

"The Church is timeless, Sir Sparhawk," the abbot replied sententiously, "and her institutions try to match that quality."

At the far end of the corridor, the abbot opened a severely simple door, and they followed him into a book-lined room with a high ceiling and an unlighted charcoal brazier in the corner. The room was quite comfortable-looking—far more so than the studies of abbots in the monasteries of the north. The windows were made of thick triangular pieces of glass joined with strips of lead and they were draped in pale blue. The floor was strewn with white sheepskin rugs, and the unmade bed in the far corner was quite a bit wider than the standard monastic cot. The jammed bookcases reached from floor to ceiling.

"Please, sit down," the abbot said, pointing at several chairs standing in front of a table piled high with documents.

"Still trying to catch up, my Lord?" Sparhawk smiled, pointing at the documents and taking one of the chairs.

The abbot made a wry face. "I give it a try every month or so," he replied. "Some men just aren't made for paperwork." He looked sourly at the litter on his table. "Sometimes I think a fire in here might solve the problem. I'm sure the clerks in Chyrellos wouldn't even miss all my reports." He looked curiously at Sparhawk's companions.

"My man Kurik," Sparhawk introduced his squire.

"Kurik," the abbot nodded.

"And the lady is Sephrenia, the Pandion instructor in the secrets."

"Sephrenia herself?" The abbot's eyes widened and he rose to his feet respectfully. "I've been hearing stories about you for years, madame. Your reputation is quite exalted." He smiled broadly at her in welcome.

She removed her veil and returned his smile. "You're very kind to say so, my Lord." She sat and gathered Flute up into her lap. The little girl nestled down and regarded the abbot with her large dark eyes.

"A beautiful child, Lady Sephrenia," the abbot said. "Your daughter by any chance?"

She laughed. "Oh, no, my Lord Abbot," she said. "The child's a Styric foundling. We call her Flute."

"What an odd name," he murmured. Then he returned his gaze to Sparhawk. "You hinted at a matter you wanted to keep private," he said curiously. "Why don't you tell me about it."

"Do you get much news about what's happening on the continent, my Lord?"

"I'm kept informed, yes." The bearded abbot said it rather cautiously as he sat down again.

"Then you know about the situation in Elenia?"

"The queen's illness, you mean? And the ambitions of Primate Annias?"

"Right. Anyway, a while back, Annias came up with a very complicated scheme to discredit the Pandion Order. We were able to thwart it. After the general meeting in the palace, the preceptors of the four orders gathered in a private session. Annias hungers for the archprelate's throne and he knows that the militant orders will oppose him."

"With swords if necessary," the abbot agreed fervently. "I'd like to cut him down myself," he added. Then he realized that he had perhaps gone too far. "If I weren't a member of a cloistered order, of course," he concluded lamely.

"I understand perfectly, my Lord," Sparhawk assured him. "The preceptors discussed the matter and they concluded that all of the primate's power—and any hope he has of extending it to Chyrellos—is based on his position in Elenia, and he'll keep that authority only for so long as Queen Ehlana's indisposed." He grimaced. "That's a silly word, isn't it? She's barely clinging to her life, and I called it *indisposed*. Oh, well, you know what I'm talking about."

"We all flounder from time to time, Sparhawk," the abbot forgave him. "I know most of the details already. Last week I got word from Patriarch Dolmant about what was afoot. What did you find out in Borrata?"

"We talked with a physician there, and he told us that Queen Ehlana has been poisoned."

The abbot came to his feet swearing like a pirate. "You're her champion, Sparhawk! Why didn't you go back to Cimmura and run your sword through Annias?"

"I was tempted," Sparhawk admitted, "but I decided that it's more important right now to see if we can find an antidote. There'll be plenty of time later to deal with Annias, and I'd rather not be rushed when it gets down to that. Anyway, the physician in Borrata told us that he thinks the poison is of Rendorish origin and he directed us to a couple of his colleagues here in Cippria."

The abbot began to pace up and down, his face still dark with rage. When he began to speak, all traces of monkly humility were gone from his voice. "If I know Annias, he's probably been trying to stop you every step of the way. Am I right?"

"Fairly close, yes."

"And the streets of Cippria aren't the safest places in the world—as you found out that night ten years ago. All right, then," he said decisively, "this is the way we're going to do it. Annias knows that you're looking for medical advice, right?"

"If he doesn't, then he's been asleep."

"Exactly. If you go near a physician, you'll probably need him for yourself, so I won't let you do that."

"Won't let, my Lord?" Sephrenia asked mildly.

"Sorry," the abbot mumbled. "Maybe I got a little carried away there. What I meant to say is that I advise against it in the strongest possible terms. What I'll do instead is send some monks out to bring the physicians here. That way you'll be able to talk with them without chancing the streets of Cippria. We'll work out a way afterward to slip you out of town."

"Would an Elenian physician actually agree to call on a patient at home?" Sephrenia asked him.

"He will if his own health is of any concern to him," the abbot replied darkly. He suddenly looked a bit sheepish. "That didn't sound very monkly, did it?" he apologized.

"Oh, I don't know," Sparhawk said blandly. "There are monks, and then there are monks."

"I'll send some of the brothers into the city to fetch them right now. What are the names of these physicians?"

Sparhawk fished the scrap of parchment the tipsy doctor in Borrata had given him out of an inside pocket and handed it to the abbot.

The bluff man glanced at it. "You know this first one already, Sparhawk," he said. "He's the one who treated you the last time you were here."

"Oh? I didn't really catch his name."

"I'm not surprised. You were delirious most of the time." The abbot squinted at the parchment. "This other one died about a month ago," he said, "but Doctor Voldi here can probably answer just about any question you might have. He's a little impressed with himself, but he's the best physician in Cippria." He rose, went to the door, and opened it. A pair of youthful monks stood outside. They were, Sparhawk noted, quite similar to the two young Pandions who normally stood guard outside Vanion's door in the chapterhouse in Cimmura. "You," the abbot sharply ordered one of them, "go into the city and bring Doctor Voldi to me. Don't take no for an answer."

"At once, my Lord," the young monk replied. With a certain amusement, Sparhawk noted that the monk's feet twitched slightly as if he were about to snap his heels together.

The abbot closed the door and returned to his seat. "It should be about an hour, I expect." He looked at Sparhawk's grin. "Something funny, my friend?" he asked.

"Not at all, my Lord. It's just that your young monks have a very crisp manner about them."

"Does it really show that much?" the abbot asked, looking a little abashed.

"Yes, my Lord. If you know what you're looking for, it does."

The abbot made a wry face. "Fortunately, the local people aren't very familiar with that sort of thing. You'll be discreet about this discovery, won't you, Sparhawk?"

"Of course, my Lord. I was fairly sure about the nature

of your order when I left here ten years ago and I haven't told anyone yet.''

"I should have guessed, I suppose. You Pandions tend to have very sharp eyes." He rose to his feet. "I'll have some supper sent up. There's a fairly large partridge that grows hereabouts, and I have an absolutely splendid falcon." He laughed. "That's what I do instead of making out the reports I'm supposed to send to Chyrellos. What do you say to a bit of roast fowl?''

"I think we could manage that," Sparhawk replied.

"And in the meantime, could I offer you and your friends some wine? It's not Arcian red, but it's not too bad. We make it here on the grounds. The soil hereabouts isn't much good for anything but raising grapes.''

"Thank you, my Lord Abbot," Sephrenia replied, "but might the child and I have milk instead?''

"I'm afraid that all we have is goat's milk, Lady Sephrenia," he apologized.

Her eyes brightened. "Goat's milk would be just fine, my Lord. Cow's milk is so bland, and we Styrics prefer something a bit more robust.''

Sparhawk shuddered.

The abbot sent the other young monk to the kitchen for milk and supper, then poured red wine for Sparhawk, Kurik, and himself. He leaned back in his chair then, idly toying with the stem of his goblet. "Can we be frank with each other, Sparhawk?" he asked.

"Of course.''

"Did any word get to you in Jiroch about what happened here in Cippria after you left?''

"Not really," Sparhawk replied. "I was a bit submerged at that time.''

"You know how Rendors feel about the use of magic?''

Sparhawk nodded. "They call it witchcraft, as I recall.''

"They do indeed, and they look on it as a worse crime than murder. Anyway, just after you left, we had an outbreak of that sort of thing. I got involved in the investigation since I'm the ranking churchman in the area." He smiled ironically. "Most of the time Rendors spit as I go by, but the minute somebody whispers 'witchcraft,' they come running to me with their faces white and their eyes bulging out. Usually the accusations are completely false. The average Rendor couldn't remember the Styric words of the simplest spell if his life depended on it, but charges crop up from time to time—usually based on spite, jealousy, and petty hatreds. This time, though, the affair was quite different. There was actual evidence that somebody in Cippria was using magic of a fair degree of sophistication." He looked at Sparhawk. "Were any of the men who attacked you that night at all adept in the secrets?"

"One of them is, yes."

"Perhaps that answers the question then. The magic seems to have been a part of an attempt to locate something—or someone. Maybe you were the object of that search."

"You mentioned sophistication, my Lord Abbot," Sephrenia said intently. "Could you be a bit more specific?"

"There was a glowing apparition stalking the streets of Cippria," he replied. "It seemed to be sheathed in lightning of some kind."

She drew in her breath sharply. "And what exactly did this apparition do?"

"It questioned people. None of them could remember the questions afterward, but the questioning appears to have been quite severe. I saw a number of the burns with my own eyes."

"Burns?"

"The apparition would seize whomever it wanted to question. Wherever it touched them, it left a burned place. One poor woman had a burn that encircled her entire forearm. I'd almost say that it was in the shape of a hand—except that it had far too many fingers."

"How many fingers?"

"Nine, and two thumbs."

She hissed. "A Damork," she said.

"I thought you said that the Younger Gods had stripped Martel of the power to summon those things," Sparhawk said to her.

"Martel didn't summon it," she replied. "It was sent to do his bidding by someone else."

"It amounts to almost the same thing, then, doesn't it?"

"Not exactly. The Damork is only marginally under Martel's control."

"But all this happened ten years ago," Kurik shrugged. "What difference does it make now?"

"You're missing the point, Kurik," she replied gravely. "We thought that the Damork had appeared only recently, but it was here in Cippria ten years ago, before anything we're involved with now even began."

"I don't quite follow you," he admitted.

Sephrenia looked at Sparhawk. "It's you, dear one," she said in a deadly quiet voice. "It's not me or Kurik or Ehlana or even Flute. The Damork's attacks have all been directed at you. Be very, very careful, Sparhawk. Azash is trying to kill you."

CHAPTER NINETEEN

DOCTOR VOLDI WAS a fussy little man in his sixties. His hair was thinning on top, and he had carefully combed it forward to conceal the fact. It was also quite obvious that he dyed it to hide the encroaching gray. He removed his dark cloak, and Sparhawk saw that he wore a white linen smock. He smelled of chemicals and he had an enormous opinion of himself.

It was quite late when the little physician was ushered into the abbot's littered study, and he was struggling without much success to cover his irritation at having been called out at that hour. "My Lord Abbot," he stiffly greeted the black-bearded churchman with a jerky little bow.

324

"Ah, Voldi," the abbot said, rising to his feet, "so good of you to come."

"Your monk said that the matter was urgent, my Lord. May I see the patient?"

"Not unless you're prepared to make a very long journey, Doctor Voldi," Sephrenia murmured.

Voldi gave her a long, appraising look. "You appear not to be a Rendor, madame," he noted. "Styric, I should say, judging from your features."

"Your eyes are keen, Doctor."

"I'm sure you remember this fellow," the abbot said, pointing at Sparhawk.

The doctor looked blankly at the big Pandion. "No," he said, "I can't say that—" Then he frowned. "Don't tell me," he added, absently brushing his hair forward with the palm of his hand. "It was about ten years ago, wasn't it? Weren't you the one who'd been knifed?"

"You have a good memory, Doctor Voldi," Sparhawk said. "We don't want to keep you out too late, so why don't we get down to cases? We were referred to you by a physician in Borrata. He greatly respects your opinion in certain areas." Sparhawk quickly appraised the little fellow and decided to apply a bit of judicious flattery. "Of course, we'd have probably come to you anyway," he added. "Your reputation has spread far beyond the borders of Rendor."

"Well," Voldi said, preening himself slightly. Then he assumed a piously modest expression. "It's gratifying to know that my efforts on behalf of the sick have received some small recognition."

"What we need, good Doctor," Sephrenia injected, "is your advice in treating a friend of ours who has recently been poisoned."

"Poisoned?" Voldi said sharply. "Are you sure?"

"The physician in Borrata was quite certain," she replied. "We described our friend's symptoms in great detail, and he diagnosed the condition as being the effects of a rather rare Rendorish poison called—"

"Please, madame," he said, holding up one hand. "I prefer to make my own diagnoses. Describe the symptoms for me."

"Of course." Patiently she repeated what she had told the physicians at the University of Borrata.

The little doctor paced up and down as she talked, his hands clasped behind him and his eyes on the floor. "I think we can rule out the falling-sickness right at the outset," he mused when she had finished. "Some other diseases, however, do result in convulsions." He affected a wise expression. "It's the combination of the fever and sweating that's the crucial clue," he lectured. "Your friend's illness is not a natural disease. My colleague in Borrata was quite correct in his diagnosis. Your friend has indeed been poisoned, and I would surmise that the poison involved was darestim. The desert nomads here in Rendor call it deathweed. It kills sheep in the same way that it kills people. The poison is very rare, since the nomads uproot every bush they come across. Does my diagnosis agree with that of my Cammorian colleague?"

"Exactly, Doctor Voldi," she said admiringly.

"Well, that's it, then." He reached for his cloak. "I'm glad to have been of help."

"All right," Sparhawk said. "Now what do we do?"

"Make arrangements for a funeral," Voldi shrugged.

"What about an antidote?"

"There isn't any. I'm afraid your friend is doomed." There was an irritating smugness about the way he said it. "Unlike most poisons, darestim attacks the brain instead of the blood. Once it's ingested—poof." He snapped his fingers. "Tell me, does your friend have rich and powerful enemies? Darestim is fearfully expensive."

"The poisoning was politically motivated," Sparhawk said bleakly.

"Ah, politics." Voldi laughed. "Those fellows have all the money, don't they?" He frowned then. "It does seem to me—" He broke off, palming at his hair again. "Where *did* I hear that?" He scratched at his head, disturbing the carefully slicked-down hair. Then he snapped his fingers again. "Ah yes," he said triumphantly, "I have it now. I've heard some rumors—only rumors, mind you—that a physician in Dabour has effected a few cures among members of the king's family in Zand. Normally that information would have been immediately disseminated to all other physicians, but I have some suspicions about the matter. I know the fellow, and there have been some ugly stories about him circulating in medical circles for years now. There are some who maintain that his miraculous-appearing cures are the result of certain forbidden practices.''

"Which practices?" Sephrenia asked intently.

"Magic, madame. What else? My friend in Dabour would immediately lose his head if word got out that he was practicing witchcraft."

"I see," she said. "Did this rumor about a cure come to you from one single source?"

"Oh, no," he replied. "Any number of people have told me about it. The king's brother and several nephews fell ill. The physician from Dabour—Tanjin his name is—was summoned to the palace. He confirmed that they had all been poisoned with darestim, then he cured them. Out of gratitude, the king suppressed the information of exactly how the cures were effected, and he issued Tanjin a full pardon just to make sure." He smirked. "Not that the pardon is much good, mind you, since the king's authority doesn't go much beyond the walls of his own palace in Zand. Anyway, anyone with the slightest bit of medical knowledge knows how it was done." He assumed a lofty expression. "I wouldn't stoop to that myself," he declared, "but Doctor Tanjin is notoriously greedy, and I imagine that the king paid him handsomely."

"Thank you for your assistance, Doctor Voldi," Sparhawk said then.

"I'm sorry about your friend," Voldi said. "By the time you get to Dabour and back, he'll be long since dead, I'm afraid. Darestim works rather slowly, but it's always fatal."

"So's a sword through the belly," Sparhawk said grimly. "At the very least, we'll be able to avenge our friend."

"What a dreadful thought," Voldi shuddered. "Are you at all acquainted with the kind of damage a sword does to someone?"

"Intimately," Sparhawk replied.

"Oh, that's right. You would be, wouldn't you? Would

you like to have me take a look at those old wounds of yours?''

"Thanks all the same, Doctor. They're quite healed now.''

"Splendid. I'm rather proud of the way I cured those, you know. A lesser physician would have lost you. Well, I must be off now. I have a full day ahead of me tomorrow.'' He wrapped his cloak about him.

"Thank you, Doctor Voldi,'' the abbot said. "The brother at the door will escort you home again.''

"My pleasure, my Lord Abbot. It's been a stimulating discussion.'' Voldi bowed and left the room.

"Pompous little ass, isn't he?'' Kurik muttered.

"Yes, he is,'' the abbot agreed. "He's very good, though.''

"It's thin, Sparhawk,'' Sephrenia sighed, "very, very thin. All we have are rumors, and we don't have time for wild-goose chases.''

"I don't see that we have any choice, do you? We have to go to Dabour. We can't ignore the slightest chance.''

"It may not be quite as thin as you think, Lady Sephrenia,'' the abbot said. "I know Voldi very well. He wouldn't confirm anything he hasn't seen with his own eyes, but I've heard a few rumors myself to the effect that some members of the family of the king of Rendor fell ill and then recovered.''

"It's all we've got,'' Sparhawk said. "We've got to follow through on it.''

"The fastest way to Dabour is by sea along the coast and then up the Gule River,'' the abbot suggested.

"No,'' Sephrenia said firmly. "The creature that's been trying to kill Sparhawk has probably realized by now that it failed last time. I don't think we want to be looking over our shoulders for waterspouts every foot of the way.''

"You'll have to go to Dabour by way of Jiroch anyway,'' the abbot told them. "You can't go overland. No one crosses the desert between here and Dabour, even at this time of year. It's totally impassable.''

"If that's the way we have to do it, then that's the way we'll do it,'' Sparhawk said.

"Be careful out there," the abbot cautioned seriously. "The Rendors are in a state of turmoil right now."

"They're always in a state of turmoil, my Lord."

"This is a bit different. Arasham's at Dabour preaching up a new holy war."

"He's been doing that for over twenty years now, hasn't he? He stirs up the desert people all winter, and then in the summer they go back to their flocks."

"That's what's different about this time, Sparhawk. Nobody pays much attention to the nomads, but somehow the old lunatic's beginning to sway the people who live in the cities, and that makes it a little more serious. Arasham's elated, of course, and he's holding his desert nomads firmly at Dabour. He's got quite an army."

"The city people in Rendor aren't all *that* stupid. What's impressing them so much?"

"I've heard that there are some people spreading rumors. They're telling the townsfolk that there's a great deal of sympathy for the resurgence of the Eshandist movement in the northern kingdoms."

"That's absurd," Sparhawk scoffed.

"Of course it is, but they've managed to persuade a fair number of people here in Cippria that for the first time in centuries a rebellion against the Church might have some chance of success. Not only that, there have been fairly large shipments of arms filtering into the country."

A suspicion began to grow in Sparhawk's mind. "Have you any idea who's been circulating these rumors?" he asked.

The abbot shrugged. "Merchants, travellers from the north, and the like. They're all foreigners. They usually stay in that quarter near the Elenian consulate."

"Isn't *that* curious?" Sparhawk mused. "I'd been summoned to the Elenian consulate that night when I was attacked in the street. Is Elius still the consul?"

"Why, yes, as a matter of fact, he is. What are you getting at, Sparhawk?"

"One more question, my Lord. Have your people by any chance seen a white-haired man going in and out of the consulate?"

"I couldn't really say. I didn't tell them to look for that

sort of thing. You have someone particular in mind, I gather?''

"Oh, I do indeed, my Lord Abbot." Sparhawk rose and began to pace up and down. "Why don't I have another try at Elene logic, Sephrenia," he said. He began to tick items off on his fingers. "One: The Primate Annias aspires to the archprelate's throne. Two: All four militant orders oppose him, and their opposition could block his ambitions. Three: In order to get that throne, he must discredit or divert the Church Knights. Four: The Elenian consul here in Cippria is his cousin. Five: The consul and Martel have had dealings with each other before. I got some personal evidence of that ten years ago.''

"I didn't know that Elius was related to the primate," the abbot said, looking a bit surprised.

"They don't make an issue of it," Sparhawk told him. "Now then," he continued, "Annias wants the Church Knights out of Chyrellos when the time comes to elect a new archprelate. What would the Church Knights do if there were an uprising here in Rendor?''

"We'd descend on the kingdom in full battle array," the abbot declared, forgetting that his choice of words clearly confirmed Sparhawk's suspicions about the nature of his order.

"And that would effectively remove the militant orders from the debate over the election in Chyrellos, wouldn't it?''

Sephrenia looked at Sparhawk speculatively. "What kind of man is this Elius?''

"He's a petty time server with little intelligence and less imagination.''

"He doesn't sound very impressive.''

"He isn't.''

"Then someone else would have to be giving him instructions, wouldn't they?''

"Precisely." Sparhawk turned once more to the abbot. "My Lord," he said, "do you have any way to get messages to Preceptor Abriel at your motherhouse in Larium? Messages that can't be intercepted?''

The abbot gave him a frosty stare.

"We agreed to be frank with each other, my Lord,''

Sparhawk reminded him. "I'm not trying to embarrass you, but this is a matter of the greatest urgency."

"All right, Sparhawk," the abbot replied a bit stiffly. "Yes, I can get a message to Lord Abriel."

"Good. Sephrenia knows all the details and she can fill you in. Kurik and I have something to attend to."

"Just what are you planning?" the abbot demanded.

"I'm going to pay a call on Elius. He knows what's been going on, and I think I can persuade him to share the information. We need confirmation of all this before you send the message to Larium."

"It's too dangerous."

"Not as dangerous as having Annias in the archprelacy, is it?" Sparhawk considered it. "Do you happen to have a secure cell someplace?" he asked.

"We have a penitent's cell down in the cellar. The door can be locked, I suppose."

"Good. I think we'll bring Elius back here to question him. Then you can lock him up. I can't let him go, once he knows I'm here, and Sephrenia disapproves of random murders. If he just disappears, there'll be some uncertainty about what happened to him."

"Won't he make an outcry when you take him captive?"

"Not very likely, my Lord," Kurik assured him, drawing his heavy dagger. He slapped the hilt solidly against his palm. "I can practically guarantee that he'll be asleep."

The streets were quiet. The overcast which had obscured the sky that afternoon had cleared, and the stars were very bright overhead.

"No moon," Kurik said quietly as he and Sparhawk crept through the deserted streets. "That's a help."

"It's been rising late the past three nights," Sparhawk said.

"How late?"

"We've got a couple more hours."

"Can we make it back to the monastery by then?"

"We have to." Sparhawk stopped just before they reached an intersection and peered around the corner of a house. A man wearing a short cape and carrying a spear and a small lantern was shuffling sleepily along the street.

"Watchman," Sparhawk breathed, and he and Kurik stepped into the shadows of a deeply recessed doorway.

The watchman plodded on past, the lantern swinging from his hand casting looming shadows against the walls of the buildings.

"He should be more alert," Kurik growled disapprovingly.

"Under the circumstances your sense of what's proper might be a little misplaced."

"Right is right, Sparhawk," Kurik replied stubbornly.

After the watchman was out of sight, they crept on up the street.

"Are we just going to walk up to the gate of the consulate?" Kurik asked.

"No. When we get close to it, we'll go in over the roof-tops."

"I'm not a cat, Sparhawk. Leaping from roof to roof isn't my idea of entertainment."

"The houses are all built up against each other in that part of town. The roof tops are just like a highway."

"Oh," Kurik grunted. "That's different, then."

The consulate of the kingdom of Elenia was a fairly large building surrounded by a high, white-mortared wall. There were torches set on long poles at each corner, and a narrow lane running alongside the wall.

"Does that lane run all the way around it?" Kurik asked.

"It did the last time I was here."

"There's a significant hole in your plan then, Sparhawk. I can't jump all the way from one of these rooftops to the top of that wall."

"I don't think I could either." Sparhawk frowned. "Let's go around and look at the other side."

They crept through a series of narrow streets and alleys that wound along the back sides of the houses facing the consulate wall. A dog came out and barked at them until Kurik shied a rock at him. The dog yelped and ran off on three legs.

"Now I know how a burglar feels," Kurik muttered.

"There," Sparhawk said.

"There where?"

"Right over there. Some helpful fellow is doing some repairs on his roof. See that pile of beams stacked up against the side of that wall? Let's go see how long they are."

They crossed the alley to the stack of building material. Kurik studiously measured the beams off with his feet. "Marginal," he observed.

"We'll never know until we try," Sparhawk told him.

"All right. How do we get up on the roof?"

"We'll lean the beams against the wall. If we slant them up right, we should be able to scramble up and then pull them up after us."

"I'm glad you don't have to construct your own siege engines, Sparhawk," Kurik observed sourly. "All right. Let's try it."

They leaned several beams against the wall, and Kurik, grunting and sweating, hauled himself up to the roof. "All right," he whispered down over the edge, "come on up."

Sparhawk climbed up the beam, picking up a large splinter in his hand in the process. Then he and Kurik laboriously hauled the beams up after them and carried them one by one across the roof to the side facing the consulate wall. The flickering torches atop the wall cast a faint glow across the rooftops. As they were carrying the last beam, Kurik stopped suddenly. "Sparhawk," he called softly.

"What?"

"Two roofs over. There's a woman lying there."

"How do you know it's a woman?"

"Because she's stark naked, that's how."

"Oh," Sparhawk said, "that. It's a Rendorish custom. She's waiting for the moon to rise. They have a superstition here that the first rays of the moon on a woman's belly increases her fertility."

"Won't she see us?"

"She won't say anything if she does. She's too busy waiting for the moon. Press on, Kurik. Don't stand there gawking at her."

They struggled manfully to push a beam out over the narrow lane, a task made more difficult by the fact that their leverage diminished as they shoved the beam out farther and farther. Finally the stubborn beam clunked down on top of the consulate wall. They slid several more beams across along its top, then rolled them to one side to form a narrow bridge. As they were shoving the last one across, Kurik suddenly stopped with a muttered oath.

"What's wrong?" Sparhawk asked him.

"How did we get up on this roof, Sparhawk?" Kurik asked acidly.

"We climbed up a slanted beam."

"Where did we want to go?"

"To the top of the wall of the consulate over there."

"Then why are we building bridges?"

"Because—" Sparhawk stopped, feeling suddenly very foolish. "We could have just leaned a beam against the wall of the consulate, couldn't we?"

"Congratulations, my Lord," Kurik said sarcastically.

"The bridge was such a perfect solution to the problem," Sparhawk said defensively.

"But totally unnecessary."

"That doesn't really invalidate the solution, does it?"

"Of course not."

"Why don't we just go on across?"

"You go ahead. I think I'll go talk with the naked lady for a while."

"Never mind, Kurik. She has her mind on other things."

"I'm sort of an expert on fertility, if that's what's really bothering her."

"Let's go, Kurik."

They crossed their makeshift bridge to the top of the consulate wall and then crept along it until they reached a place where the branches of a well-watered fig tree reached up out of the shadows below. They climbed down the tree and stood for a moment or two beside it while Sparhawk got his bearings.

"You wouldn't happen to know where the consul's bed-chamber is, would you?" Kurik whispered.

"No," Sparhawk replied softly, "but I can guess. It's the Elenian consulate, and all official Elenian buildings are more or less the same. The private quarters will be up-stairs in the back."

"Very good, Sparhawk," Kurik said drily. "That narrows things down considerably. Now we only have to search about a quarter of the building."

They crept through a shadowy garden and entered by way of an unlocked back door. They passed through a darkened kitchen and into the dimly lit central hall. Kurik suddenly jerked Sparhawk back into the kitchen.

"What—" Sparhawk started to object in a hoarse whisper.

"Shhh!"

Out in the hall there was the bobbing glow of a candle. A matronly woman, a housekeeper or perhaps a cook, walked toward the kitchen door. Sparhawk shrank back as she stood framed in the doorway. Then she took hold of the handle and firmly closed the door.

"How did you know she was coming?" Sparhawk whispered.

"I don't know," Kurik whispered back. "I just did." He put his ear to the door. "She's moving on," he reported softly.

"What's she doing up at this time of the night?"

"Who knows? Maybe she's just making sure all the doors are locked. Aslade does that every night." He listened again. "There," he said, "she just closed another door, and I can't hear her out there any more. I think she went to bed."

"The staircase should be just opposite the main entryway," Sparhawk whispered. "Let's get up on the second floor before somebody else comes wandering by."

They darted out into the hallway and up a broad flight of stairs to the upper floor.

"Look for an ornate door," Sparhawk whispered. "The consul's the master of the house, so he's likely to have the most luxurious room. You go that way, and I'll go this."

They separated and went in opposite directions on tiptoe. At the end of the hallway, Sparhawk found an elaborately carved door decorated with gilt paint. He opened it carefully and looked inside. By the light of a single dimly glowing oil lamp he saw a stout, florid-faced man of fifty or so lying on his back in the bed. The man was snoring loudly. Sparhawk recognized him. He softly closed the

door and went looking for Kurik. His squire met him at
the head of the stairs.

"How old a man is the consul?" Kurik whispered.

"About fifty."

"The one I saw wasn't him, then. There's a carved door
at the far end. There's a young fellow about twenty in bed
with an older woman."

"Did they see you?"

"No. They were busy."

"Oh. The consul's sleeping alone. He's down at this
end of the hall."

"Do you suppose the woman at the other end could be
his wife?"

"That's their business, isn't it?"

Together they tiptoed back down to the gilt-painted door.
Sparhawk eased it open, and they went inside and crossed
the floor to the bed. Sparhawk reached out and took the
consul's shoulder. "Your Excellency," he said quietly,
shaking the man.

The consul's eyes flew open, then glazed and went blank
as Kurik rapped him sharply behind the ear with the hilt
of his dagger. They trussed the unconscious man up in a
dark blanket, and Kurik unceremoniously slung the limp
form over his shoulder. "Is that everything we need here?"
he asked.

"That's it," Sparhawk said. "Let's go."

They crept back down the stairs and into the kitchen
again. Sparhawk carefully closed the door leading into the
main part of the house. "Wait here," he breathed to Kurik. "Let me check the garden. I'll whistle if it's clear."
He slipped out into the shadowed garden and carefully
moved from tree to tree, his eyes alert. He suddenly realized that he was enjoying himself immensely. He hadn't
had so much pure fun since he and Kalten had been boys
and had regularly slipped out of his father's house in the
middle of the night bent on mischief.

He whistled a very poor imitation of a nightingale.

After a moment, he heard Kurik's hoarse whisper coming from the kitchen door. "Is that you?"

For an instant, he was tempted to whisper back, "No,"
but then he got himself under control again.

They had some difficulty getting the inert body of the consul up the fig tree, but finally managed by main strength. Then they crossed their makeshift bridge and pulled the beams back onto the roof.

"She's still there," Kurik whispered.

"Who is?"

"The naked lady."

"It's her roof."

They dragged the beams back to the far side of the roof and lowered them again. Then Sparhawk climbed down and caught the consul's body when Kurik lowered it to him. Kurik joined him a moment later, and they restacked the beams against the wall.

"All nice and neat," Sparhawk said with satisfaction, brushing his hands together.

Kurik hefted the body up onto his shoulder again. "Won't his wife miss him?" he asked.

"Not very much, I wouldn't think—if that was her in the bedroom at the other end of the hall. Why don't we go back to the monastery?"

They traded off carrying the body and reached the outskirts of town in about half an hour, dodging several watchmen along the way. The consul, draped over Sparhawk's shoulder, groaned and stirred weakly.

Kurik rapped him on the head again.

When they entered the abbot's study, Kurik unceremoniously dumped the unconscious man on the floor. He and Sparhawk looked at each other for a moment, then they both burst into uncontrollable laughter.

"What's so funny?" the abbot demanded.

"You should have come along, my Lord," Kurik gasped. "I haven't had so much fun in years." He began laughing again. "The bridge was the best, I think."

"I sort of liked the naked lady," Sparhawk disagreed.

"Have you two been drinking?" the abbot asked suspiciously.

"Not a drop, my Lord," Sparhawk replied. "It's a thought, though, if you've got anything handy. Where's Sephrenia?"

"I persuaded her that she and the child should get some

sleep.'' The abbot paused. ''*What* naked lady?'' he demanded, his eyes afire with curiosity.

''There was a woman up on a roof going through that fertility ritual,'' Sparhawk told him, still laughing. ''She sort of distracted Kurik for a moment or two.''

''Was she pretty?'' The abbot grinned at Kurik.

''I couldn't really say, my Lord. I wasn't looking at her face.''

''My Lord Abbot,'' Sparhawk said then, a bit more seriously, though he still felt enormously exuberant, ''we're going to question Elius as soon as he wakes up. Please don't be alarmed by some of the things we say to him.''

''I quite understand, Sparhawk,'' the abbot replied.

''Good. All right, Kurik, let's wake up his Excellency here and see what he has to say for himself.''

Kurik stripped the blanket off the consul's limp body and began pinching the unconscious man's ears and nose. After a moment, the consul's eyelids fluttered. Then he groaned and opened his eyes. He stared blankly at them for a moment, then sat up quickly. ''Who are you? What's the meaning of this?'' he demanded.

Kurik smacked him firmly across the back of the head.

''You see how it is, Elius,'' Sparhawk said blandly. ''You don't mind if I call you Elius, do you? Possibly you may remember me. The name's Sparhawk.''

''Sparhawk?'' the consul gasped. ''I thought you were dead.''

''That's a highly exaggerated rumor, Elius. Now, the fact of the matter is that you've been abducted. We have a number of questions for you. Things will go much more pleasantly for you if you answer them freely. Otherwise, you're in for a very bad night.''

''You wouldn't dare!''

Kurik hit him again.

''I'm the consul of the kingdom of Elenia,'' Elius blustered, trying to cover the back of his head with both hands, ''and the cousin of the primate of Cimmura. You can't do this to me.''

Sparhawk sighed. ''Break a few of his fingers, Kurik,'' he suggested, ''just to show him that we *can* do this to him.''

Kurik set his foot against the consul's chest, pushed him back onto the floor, and seized the weakly struggling captive's right wrist.

"No!" Elius squealed. "Don't! I'll tell you anything you want."

"I told you he'd cooperate, my Lord," Sparhawk said conversationally to the abbot, pulling off his Rendorish robe to stand revealed in his mailcoat and sword belt, "just as soon as he understood the seriousness of the situation."

"Your methods are direct, Sir Sparhawk," the abbot noted.

"I'm a plain man, my Lord," Sparhawk replied, scratching at one mailed armpit. "Subtlety isn't one of my strong points." He nudged the captive with one foot. "All right, then, Elius, I'll make things simple for you. All you have to do at first is confirm a number of statements." He drew up a chair and sat down, crossing his legs. "First of all, your cousin, the primate of Cimmura, has his eyes on the throne of the archprelacy, right?"

"You have no proof of that."

"Break his thumb, Kurik."

Still holding the consul's wrist in his grip, Kurik pried open the man's clenched fist and grasped his thumb. "In how many places, my Lord?" he asked politely.

"Do as many as you can, Kurik. Give him something to think about."

"No! No! It's true!" Elius gasped, his eyes wide with terror.

"We're making real progress here," Sparhawk observed with a relaxed smile. "Now. You've had dealings in the past with a white-haired man named Martel. He works for your cousin from time to time. Am I right?"

"Y—yes," Elius faltered.

"Notice how it gets easier as you go along? In fact it was you who set Martel and his hirelings on me that night about ten years ago, wasn't it?"

"It was his idea," Elius blurted quickly. "I'd received orders from my cousin to co-operate with him. He suggested that I summon you that night. I had no idea that he intended to kill you."

"You're very naïve then, Elius. Lately, a fair number

of travellers from the northern kingdoms have been circulating rumors here in Cippria that there's a ground swell of sympathy for Rendorish aims in those kingdoms. Is Martel in any way connected with that campaign?''

Elius started at him, his lips pressed fearfully shut.

Slowly, Kurik began to bend his thumb back.

''Yes! Yes!'' Elius squeaked, arching back in pain.

''You were almost backsliding there, Elius,'' Sparhawk chided. ''I'd watch that if I were you. The whole purpose of Martel's campaign here is to persuade the city dwellers of Rendor to join with the desert nomads in an Eshandist uprising against the Church. Am I right?''

''Martel doesn't confide in me all that much, but I suppose that's his ultimate goal, yes.''

''And he's supplying weapons, right?''

''I've heard that he is.''

''This next one is tricky, Elius, so listen carefully. The real point here is to stir things up so that the Church Knights will have to come here and quiet them down again. Isn't that so?''

Elius nodded sullenly. ''Martel himself hasn't said so, but my cousin intimated as much to me in his last letter.''

''And the uprising is to be timed to coincide with the election of the new archprelate in the Basilica of Chyrellos?''

''I really don't know that, Sir Sparhawk. Please believe me. You're probably right, but I can't really say for certain.''

''We'll let that one pass for the moment. Now, I have a burning curiosity. Just where is Martel right now?''

''He's gone to Dabour to talk with Arasham. The old man's trying to whip his followers into a frenzy so that they'll start burning churches and expropriating Church lands. Martel was very upset when he heard about it and he hurried to Dabour to try to head it off.''

''Probably because it was premature?''

''I'd imagine as much, yes.''

''I guess that's about all then, Elius,'' Sparhawk said benignly. ''I certainly want to thank you for your cooperation tonight.''

"You're letting me go?" the consul asked incredulously.

"No, I'm afraid not. Martel's an old friend of mine. I want to surprise him when I get to Dabour, so I can't risk having you get word to him that I'm coming. There's a penitent's cell down in the cellar of this monastery. I'm sure you feel very penitent just now and I want to give you some time to reflect on your sins. The cell is quite comfortable, I'm told. It has a door, four walls, a ceiling, and even a floor." He looked at the abbot. "It *does* have a floor, doesn't it, my Lord?"

"Oh, yes," the abbot confirmed, "a nice cold stone one."

"You can't do that!" Elius protested shrilly.

"Sparhawk," Kurik agreed, "you really can't confine a man in a penitent's cell against his will. It's a violation of Church law."

"Oh," Sparhawk said peckishly, "I suppose you're right. I did want to avoid all the mess. Go ahead and do it the other way, then."

"Yes, my Lord," Kurik said respectfully. He drew his dagger. "Tell me, my Lord Abbot," he said, "does your monastery have a graveyard?"

"Yes, rather a nice one, actually."

"Oh, good. I hate just to drag them out into the open countryside and leave them for the jackals." He took hold of the consul's hair and tipped his head back. Then he set the edge of his dagger against the cringing man's throat. "This won't take a moment, your Excellency," he said professionally.

"My Lord Abbot," Elius squealed.

"I'm afraid it's altogether out of my hands, your Excellency," the abbot said with mock piety. "The Church Knights have their own laws. I wouldn't dream of interfering."

"Please, my Lord Abbot," Elius pleaded. "Confine me to the penitent's cell."

"Do you sincerely repent your sins?" the abbot asked.

"Yes! Yes! I am heartily ashamed!"

"I am afraid, Sir Sparhawk, that I must intercede on

this penitent's behalf,'' the abbot said. ''I cannot permit you to kill him until he has made his peace with God.''

''That's your final decision, my Lord Abbot?'' Sparhawk asked.

''I'm afraid it is, Sir Sparhawk.''

''Oh, all right. Let us know as soon as he's completed his penance. Then we'll kill him.''

''Of course, Sir Sparhawk.''

After the violently trembling Elius had been taken away by a pair of burly monks, the three men in the room began to laugh.

''That was rare, my Lord,'' Sparhawk congratulated the abbot. ''It was exactly the right tone.''

''I'm not a complete novice at this sort of thing, Sparhawk,'' the abbot said. He looked at the big Pandion shrewdly. ''You Pandions have a reputation for brutality—particularly where questioning captives is concerned.''

''It seems to me I've heard some rumors to that effect, yes,'' Sparhawk admitted.

''But you don't really do anything to people, do you?''

''Not usually, no. It's the reputation that persuades people to co-operate. Do you have any idea how hard—and messy—it is actually to torture people? We planted those rumors about our order ourselves. After all, why work if you don't have to?''

''My feelings exactly, Sparhawk. Now,'' the abbot said eagerly, ''why don't you tell me about the naked lady and the bridge—and anything else you might have run across? Don't leave anything out. I'm only a poor cloistered monk and I don't really get much fun out of life.''

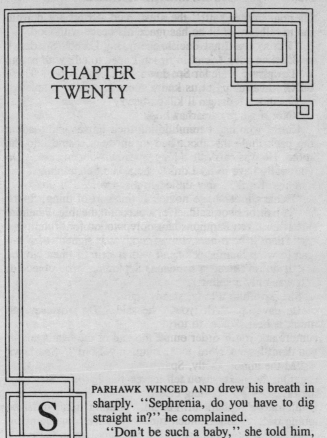

CHAPTER
TWENTY

S PARHAWK WINCED AND drew his breath in sharply. "Sephrenia, do you have to dig straight in?" he complained.

"Don't be such a baby," she told him, continuing to pick at the sliver in his hand with her needle. "If I don't get it all out, it's going to fester."

He sighed and gritted his teeth together as she continued to probe. He looked at Flute, who had both hands across her mouth as if to stifle a giggle.

"You think it's funny?" he asked her crossly.

She lifted her pipes and blew a derisive little trill.

"I've been thinking, Sparhawk," the abbot said. "If Annias has people in Jiroch the same as he has here in

Cippria, wouldn't it be safer just to go around it and avoid the possibility of being recognized?''

"I think we'll have to chance it, my Lord," Sparhawk said. "I've got a friend in Jiroch I need to talk with before we go upriver." He looked down at his black robe. "These ought to get us past a casual glance."

"I think it's dangerous, Sparhawk."

"Not if we're careful, I hope."

Kurik, who had been saddling their horses and loading the pack mule the abbot had given them, came into the room. He was carrying a long, narrow wooden case. "Do you really have to take this?" he asked Sephrenia.

' Yes, Kurik," she replied in a sad voice. "I do."

"What's in it?"

A pair of swords. They're a part of the burden I bear.''

"It's a pretty large box for only two swords."

"There'll be others, I'm afraid," she sighed, then began to wrap Sparhawk's hand with a strip of linen cloth.

"It doesn't need a bandage, Sephrenia," he objected. "It was only a splinter."

She gave him a long, steady stare.

He gave up. "All right," he said. "Do whatever you think is best."

"Thank you." She tied off the end of the bandage.

"You'll send word to Larium, my Lord?" Sparhawk asked the abbot.

"On the next ship that leaves the harbor, Sir Sparhawk."

Sparhawk thought a moment. "I don't think we'll be going back to Madel," he said. "We have some companions staying at the house of the Marquis Lycien there."

The abbot nodded. "I know him," he said.

"Could you get word to them as well? Tell them that if everything works out at Dabour, we'll be going home from there. I think they might as well go on back to Cimmura."

"I'll see to it, Sparhawk."

Sparhawk tugged thoughtfully at the knot on his bandage.

"Leave it alone," Sephrenia told him.

He took his hand away. "I'm not trying to tell the preceptors what to do," he said to the abbot, "but you might

suggest in your message that a few small contingents of
Church Knights in the streets of Rendorish cities right now
might remind the local population of just how unpleasant
things can get if they pay too much attention to all these
rumors.''

"And head off the need for whole armies later on," the
abbot agreed. "I'll definitely mention it in my report."

Sparhawk rose to his feet. "I'm in your debt again, my
Lord Abbot," he said. "You always seem to be here when
I need you."

"We serve the same master, Sparhawk," the abbot replied. He grinned then. "Besides," he added, "I sort of
like you. You Pandions don't always do things the way we
would, but you get results, and that's what counts, isn't
it?"

"We can hope."

"Be careful in the desert, my friend, and good luck."

"Thank you, my Lord."

They went down to the central court of the monastery
as the bells began to chime their call to morning prayers.
Kurik tied Sephrenia's sword case to the pack mule's saddle, and they all mounted. Then they rode out through the
front gate with the sound of the bells hovering in the air
above them.

Sparhawk's mood was pensive as they reached the dusty
coast road and turned west toward Jiroch.

"What is it, Sparhawk?" Sephrenia asked him.

"Those bells have been calling me for ten years now,"
he replied. "Somehow I've always known that someday
I'd come back to this monastery." He straightened in his
saddle. "It's a good place," he said. "I'm a little sorry
to leave it, but . . ." He shrugged and rode on.

The morning sun was very bright and it reflected back
blindingly from the wasteland of rock, sand, and gravel
lying on the left side of the road. On the right side was a
steep bank leading down to a gleaming white beach, and
beyond that lay the deep blue waters of the Inner Sea.
Within an hour it was quite warm. A half hour later it was
hot.

"Don't they ever get a winter down here?" Kurik asked,
mopping at his streaming face.

"This *is* winter, Kurik," Sparhawk told him.

"What's it like in the summer?"

"Unpleasant. In the summer you have to travel at night."

"How far is it to Jiroch?"

"About five hundred leagues."

"Three weeks at least."

"I'm afraid so."

"We should have gone by ship—waterspouts or no."

"No, Kurik," Sephrenia disagreed. "None of us could be of any help to Ehlana if we're all lying on the bottom of the sea."

"Won't that thing that's after us just use magic to locate us anyway?"

"It seems that it can't do that," she replied. "When it was looking for Sparhawk ten years ago, it had to question people. It couldn't just sniff him out."

"I'd forgotten that," he admitted.

They rose early each day, even before the stars faded, and pushed their horses hard during the early morning hours before the sun became a bludgeon at midday. Then they rested in the scant shade of the tent the abbot had pressed on them, while their mounts grazed listlessly on scrubby forage in the blistering sun. As the sun lowered toward the west, they rode on, usually until well after dark. Occasionally, they reached some desert spring, inevitably surrounded by lush vegetation and shade. At times, they lingered for a day to rest their horses and to gather the strength to face the savage sun again.

It was at such a spring, where crystal water came purling out of a rocky slope to gather in an azure pool surrounded by palm trees, that the shade of a black-armored Pandion Knight visited them. Sparhawk, clad in only a loincloth, had just emerged dripping from the pool when he saw the mounted figure approaching from the west. Although the sun stood at the figure's back, it cast no shadow, and he could clearly see the sun-blasted hillsides through both horse and man. Once again he caught that charnelhouse reek; as the figure approached, he saw that its horse was little more than a vacant-eyed skeleton. He made no attempt to reach a weapon, but stood shivering

despite the furnacelike heat as the mounted specter bore
down on them. Some few yards away, the shade reined in
its skeletal mount and, with a deadly slow motion, drew
its sword. "Little mother," it intoned hollowly to Sephrenia, "I have done all that I could." It raised the hilt
of its weapon to its visor in a salute, then reversed the
blade and offered the hilt across its insubstantial forearm.

Sephrenia, pale and faltering, crossed the hot gravel to
the specter and took the sword hilt in both hands. "Thy
sacrifice shall be remembered, Sir Knight," she said in a
trembling voice.

"What is remembrance in the House of the Dead, Sephrenia? I did what duty commanded of me. That alone
is my solace in the eternal silence." Then it turned its
visored countenance toward Sparhawk. "Hail, brother,"
it said in that same empty voice. "Know that thy course
is aright. At Dabour shalt thou find that answer which we
have sought. Shouldst thou succeed in thy quest, we shall
salute thee with our hollow cheers in the House of the
Dead."

"Hail, brother," Sparhawk replied in a choked voice,
"and farewell."

Then the specter vanished.

With a long, shuddering moan, Sephrenia collapsed. It
was as if the weight of the suddenly materialized sword
had crushed her to earth.

Kurik rushed forward, scooped her slight form up in his
arms, and carried her back into the shade beside the pool.

Sparhawk, however, moved at a resolute pace toward
the spot where she had fallen, heedless of the blistering
gravel under his naked feet, and retrieved his fallen brother's sword.

Behind him, he heard the sound of Flute's pipes. The
melody was one that he had not heard before. It was questioning and filled with a deep sadness and an aching kind
of longing. He turned around with the sword in his hand.
Sephrenia lay on a blanket in the shade of the palms. Her
face seemed drawn, and quite suddenly dark circles had
appeared beneath her now-closed eyes. Kurik knelt anx-
iously beside her, and Flute sat cross-legged not far away

with her pipes to her lips, sending her strange, hymnlike song soaring into the air.

Sparhawk crossed the gravel and stopped in the shade. Kurik rose and joined him. "She won't be able to go on today," the squire said quietly, "perhaps not even tomorrow."

Sparhawk nodded.

"This is weakening her terribly, Sparhawk," Kurik continued gravely. "Each time one of those twelve knights dies, she seems to wilt a little more. Wouldn't it be better to send her back to Cimmura when we get to Jiroch?"

"Perhaps so, but she wouldn't go."

"You're probably right," Kurik agreed glumly. "You *do* know that you and I could move faster if we didn't have her and the little girl along, though, don't you?"

"Yes, but what would we do without her when we got to where we're going?"

"You've got a point there, I guess. Did you happen to recognize that ghost?"

Sparhawk nodded. "Sir Kerris," he said shortly.

"I never got to know him very well," Kurik admitted. "He always seemed a little stiff and formal."

"He was a good man, though."

"What did he say to you? I was too far away to hear him."

"He said that we're on the right course and that we'll find the answer we need at Dabour."

"Well, now," Kurik said. "That helps, doesn't it? I was about half-afraid that we were chasing shadows."

"So was I," Sparhawk admitted.

Flute had laid aside her pipes and now sat beside Sephrenia. She reached out and took the stricken woman's hand and held it. Her small face was grave, but betrayed no other emotion.

An idea came to Sparhawk. He went to where Sephrenia lay. "Flute," he said quietly.

The little girl looked up at him.

"Can you do something to help Sephrenia?"

Flute shook her head a bit sadly.

"It is forbidden." Sephrenia's voice was hardly more than a whisper, and her eyes were still closed. "Only those of us who were present can bear this burden.'' She drew in a deep breath. ''Go put some clothes on, Sparhawk,'' she said then. ''Don't walk around like that in front of the child.''

They remained in the shade beside the pool for the remainder of that day and all of the next. On the morning of the third day, Sephrenia rose and resolutely began to gather up her things. ''Time is moving along, gentlemen,'' she said crisply, ''and we still have a long way to go.''

Sparhawk looked closely at her. Her face was still haggard, and the deep circles beneath her eyes had not lessened. As she bent to pick up her veil, he saw several silvery strands in her glistening black hair. ''Wouldn't you be stronger if we stayed here another day?'' he asked her.

''Not appreciably, Sparhawk,'' she replied in a weary voice. ''My condition can't be improved by resting. Let's move on. It's a long way to Jiroch.''

They rode at an easy pace at first, but after a few miles, Sephrenia spoke rather sharply. ''Sparhawk,'' she said, ''it's going to take all winter if we keep sauntering along like this.''

''All right, Sephrenia, whatever you say.''

It was perhaps ten days later when they arrived in Jiroch. Like Cippria, the port city in western Rendor was a low, flat town with thick-walled, flat-roofed houses thickly plastered with white mortar. Sparhawk led them through a series of twisting alleys to a section of town not far from the river. It was a quarter where foreigners were, if not actually encouraged, at least tolerated. While most of the people in the streets were still Rendors, there was a fair spattering of brightly robed Cammorians, a number of Lamorks, and even a few Elenians in the crowd. Sparhawk and the others kept their hoods up and rode slowly to avoid attracting attention.

It was late morning when they reached a modest house set some distance back from the street. The man who owned the house was Sir Voren, a Pandion Knight, although few in Jiroch were aware of that fact. Most people in the port city thought of him as a moderately prosperous Elenian merchant. He did, in fact, engage in trade. Some

years, he even made a profit. Sir Voren's real purpose for
being in Jiroch was not commercial, however. There were
a goodly number of Pandion Knights submerged in the
general population of Rendor, and Voren was their only
contact with the motherhouse at Demos. All their com-
munications and dispatches passed through his hands to
be concealed in the boxes and bales of goods he shipped
from the harbor.

A slack-lipped servant with dull, uncurious eyes led
Sparhawk and the others through the house and on into a
walled garden filled with the shade of fig trees and the
musical trickle of a marble fountain in the center. Neatly
tended flowerbeds lined the walls, and the nodding blos-
soms were a riot of colors. Voren was seated on a bench
beside the fountain. He was a tall, thin man with a sardonic sense of humor. His years in this southern kingdom
had browned his skin until it was the color of an old saddle. Though he was of late middle age, his hair was untouched by gray, but his tanned face was a tracery of
wrinkles. He wore no doublet, but rather a plain linen shirt
open at the neck. He rose as they entered the garden.

"Ah, Mahkra," he greeted Sparhawk with a brief, sidelong glance at the servant, "so good to see you again, old
boy."

"Voren," Sparhawk responded with a Rendorish bow,
a sinuous movement that was half genuflection.

"Jintal," Voren said to the servant then, "be a good
fellow and take this to my factor down at the docks." He
folded a sheet of parchment in half and handed it to the
swarthy-faced Rendor.

"As you command, Master," the servant replied, bowing.

They waited until the sound of the front door of the
house closing announced that the servant had departed.

"Nice enough fellow there," Voren observed. "Of
course he's fearfully stupid. I'm always careful to hire servants who aren't too bright. An intelligent servant is usually a spy." Then his eyes narrowed. "Wait here a
moment," he said. "I want to be sure he really left the
house." He crossed the garden and went back inside.

"I don't remember his being that nervous," Kurik said.

"This is a nervous part of the world," Sparhawk replied.

After a few moments, Voren returned. "Little mother," he greeted Sephrenia warmly, kissing her palms. "Will you give me your blessing?"

She smiled, touched his forehead, and spoke in Styric.

"I've missed that," he confessed, "even though I haven't done much lately that deserves blessing." Then he looked at her more closely. "Aren't you well, Sephrenia?" he asked her. "Your face seems very drawn."

"The heat, perhaps," she said, passing a slow hand across her eyes.

"Sit here," he said, pointing at his marble bench. "It's the coolest place in all of Jiroch." He smiled sardonically. "Which isn't saying all that much, I'll grant you."

She sat on the bench, and Flute clambered up beside her.

"Well, Sparhawk," Voren said, clasping his friend's hand, "what brings you back to Jiroch so soon? Did you leave something behind, perhaps?"

"Nothing I can't live without," Sparhawk replied drily.

Voren laughed. "Just to show you how good a friend I am, I won't tell Lillias that you said that. Hello, Kurik. How's Aslade?"

"She's well, my Lord Voren."

"And your sons? You have three, don't you?"

"Four, my Lord. The last one was born after you left Demos."

"Congratulations," Voren said, "a little late, maybe, but congratulations all the same."

"Thank you, my Lord."

"I need to talk with you, Voren," Sparhawk said, cutting across the pleasantries, "and we don't have much time."

"And here I thought this was a social visit." Voren sighed.

Sparhawk let that pass. "Has Vanion managed to get word to you about what's been going on in Cimmura?"

The lightly ironic smile faded from Voren's face, and he nodded seriously. "That's one of the reasons I was surprised to see you," he said. "I thought you were going to Borrata. Did you have any luck there?"

"I don't know how lucky it was, but we found out something we're trying to track down." He clenched his teeth together. "Voren," he said darkly, "Ehlana was poisoned."

Voren stared at him for a moment, then swore. "I wonder how long it'd take me to get back to Cimmura," he said in an icy voice. "I think I'd like to rearrange Annias just a bit. He'd look much better without his head, don't you think?"

"You'd have to stand in line, my Lord Voren," Kurik assured him. "I know at least a dozen other people with the same idea."

"Anyway," Sparhawk went on, "we found out that it was a Rendorish poison and we've heard of a physician in Dabour who might know of an antidote. That's where we're going now."

"Where are Kalten and the others?" Voren asked. "Vanion wrote that you had him and some knights from the other orders with you."

"We left them in Madel," Sparhawk replied. "They didn't look—or act—very Rendorish. Have you heard of a Doctor Tanjin in Dabour?"

"The one who's reputed to have cured the king's brother of some mysterious ailment? Of course. He might not want to talk about it, though. There are some shrewd guesses going around about how he managed those cures, and you know how Rendors feel about magic."

"I'll persuade him to talk about it," Sparhawk told him.

"You might wish that you hadn't left Kalten and the others behind," Voren told him. "Dabour's a very unfriendly place right now."

"I'll have to manage alone. I sent word to them from Cippria to go back home and wait for me there."

"Whom did you find in Cippria that you could really trust enough to carry messages for you?"

"I went to the abbot of that Arcian monastery on the east side of town. I've known him for a long time."

Voren laughed. "Is he still trying to conceal the fact that he's a Cyrinic?"

"Do you know *everything*, Voren?"

"That's what I'm here for. He's a good man, though. His methods are a little pedestrian, but he gets things done."

"What's happening in Dabour right now?" Sparhawk asked. "I don't want to walk in there with my eyes closed."

Voren sprawled on the grass near Sephrenia's feet and hooked his hands about one knee. "Dabour's always been a strange place," he replied. "It was Eshand's home, and the desert nomads think of it as a holy city. At any given time there are usually a dozen or so religious factions all fighting with each other for control of the holy places there." He smiled wryly. "Would you believe that there are twenty-three tombs there, all purporting to be the final resting place of Eshand? I strongly suspect that at least some of them are spurious—unless they dismembered the holy man after his death and buried him piecemeal."

Sparhawk sank to the grass beside his friend. "This is just a thought," he said, "but could we throw some clandestine support to one of the other factions and undermine Arasham's position?"

"It's a nice idea, Sparhawk, but at the moment there *aren't* any other factions. After Arasham received his epiphany, he spent forty years exterminating all possible rivals. There was a blood bath in central Rendor of colossal proportions. Pyramids of skulls dot the desert out there. Finally, he gained control of Dabour and he rules there with an authority so total that he makes Otha of Zemoch look like a liberal. He has thousands of rabid followers who blindly follow his every lunatic whim. They roam the streets with sun-baked brains and burning eyes, searching for any infraction of obscure religious laws. Hordes of the unwashed and lice-ridden and only marginally human rage through the streets in search of the opportunity to burn their neighbors at the stake."

"That's direct enough," Sparhawk said. He glanced at Sephrenia. Flute had dipped a handkerchief into the fountain and was gently bathing the small woman's face with it. Peculiarly, Sephrenia had her head laid against the little girl's shoulder as if *she* were the child. "Arasham has gathered an army, then?" he asked Voren.

Voren snorted. "Only an idiot would call it an army. They can't march anywhere because they have to pray every half-hour, and they blindly obey even the obvious misstatements of that senile old man." He laughed harshly. "Arasham sometimes stumbles over the language—which isn't surprising, since he's probably at least half baboon—and once, during his campaigns back in the hinterlands, he gave an order. He meant to say, 'Fall upon your foes,' but it came out wrong. Instead, he said, 'Fall upon your swords,' and three whole regiments did exactly that. Arasham rode home alone that day, trying to figure out what had gone wrong."

"You've been here too long, Voren." Sparhawk laughed. "Rendor's starting to sour your disposition."

"I can't abide stupidity and filth, Sparhawk, and Arasham's followers believe devoutly in the sanctity of ignorance and dirt."

"You're starting to develop a fine flair for rhetoric, though."

"Contempt is a powerful seasoning for one's words," Voren admitted. "I can't say what I think openly here in Rendor, so I have plenty of time to polish my phrases in private." His face grew serious. "Be very careful in Dabour, Sparhawk," he advised. "Arasham has a couple dozen disciples—some of whom he even knows. They're the ones who really control the city and they're all as crazy as he is."

"That bad?"

"Worse, probably."

"You've always been such a cheerful fellow, Voren," Sparhawk said drily.

"It's a failing of mine. I try to look on the bright side of things. Is anything happening in Cippria I ought to know about?"

"You might want to look into this," Sparhawk said, plucking at the grass beside him. "There are some foreigners going about there trying to encourage the belief that the peasantry in the Elene kingdoms in the north is on the verge of open rebellion against the Church because they support the goals of the Eshandist movement.''

"I've heard some rumors about that," Voren said. "It hasn't gone very far here in Jiroch yet."

"It's just a question of time until it does, I think. It's fairly well organized."

"Any idea of who's behind it?"

"Martel, and we all know for whom he works. The whole idea is to stir up the city dwellers to join with Arasham in an uprising against the Church here in Rendor at the same time that the Hierocracy is gathering in Chyrellos to elect a new archprelate. The Church Knights would have to come here to put the fire out, and that would give Annias and his supporters a free hand in the election. We've passed the word to the militant orders, so they should be able to take steps." Sparhawk rose from the grass. "How long is your servant likely to take to run his errand?" he asked. "It might be better if we were gone when he came back. He may not be too bright, but I know Rendors, and they like to gossip."

"I think you've got a little time left. Jintal's fastest pace is a leisurely saunter. You'll have time to eat something, and I'll give you some fresh supplies."

"Is there any safe place to stay in Dabour?" Sephrenia asked the sardonic man.

"No place in Dabour is really safe, Sephrenia," Voren replied. He looked at Sparhawk. "Do you remember Perraine?" he asked.

"Lean fellow? Almost never talks?"

"That's him. He's in Dabour posing as a cattle buyer. He goes by the name Mirrelek, and he's got a place near the stockyards. The desert people need him—unless they want to eat all their own cows—so he has more or less the free run of the city. He'll put you up and keep you out of trouble." Voren grinned a bit slyly. "Speaking of trouble, Sparhawk," he said, "I'd strongly advise you to get out of Jiroch before Lillias finds out that you're back."

"Is she still unhappy?" Sparhawk said. "I thought that she'd have found someone to comfort her by now."

"I'm sure she has—several, probably—but you know Lillias. She holds grudges."

"I left her full title to the shop," Sparhawk said a bit defensively. "She should be doing very well by now if she pays attention to business."

"The last I heard, she was, but that's not the point. The whole thing is that you said your farewells—and left your bequest—in a note. You didn't give her the chance to scream, weep, and threaten to kill herself."

"That was sort of the idea."

"You were terribly unkind to her, my friend. Lillias thrives on high drama; when you slipped out in the middle of the night the way you did, you robbed her of a wonderful opportunity for histrionics." Voren was grinning openly.

"Do you really have to pursue this?"

"I'm just trying to give you a friendly warning, Sparhawk. All you'll have to face at Dabour are several thousand howling fanatics. Here in Jiroch, you'll have to face Lillias, and she's much, much more dangerous."

CHAPTER
TWENTY-ONE

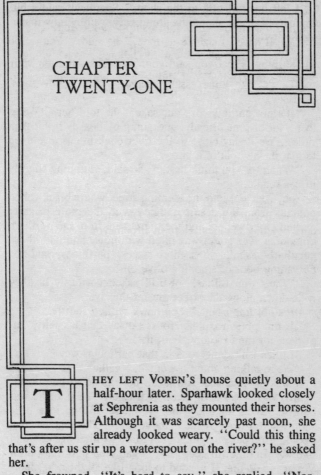

HEY LEFT VOREN'S house quietly about a half-hour later. Sparhawk looked closely at Sephrenia as they mounted their horses. Although it was scarcely past noon, she already looked weary. "Could this thing that's after us stir up a waterspout on the river?" he asked her.

She frowned. "It's hard to say," she replied. "Normally, I'd say no, there's not enough open water. But the creatures of the underworld can overcome some natural laws if they choose." She thought a moment. "How wide is the river here?" she asked.

"Not very," he replied. "There's not enough water in the whole of Rendor to make a wide river."

"The river banks would make it very hard to direct a

357

spout," she said thoughtfully. "You saw how erratically the one that destroyed Mabin's ship was moving."

"We'll have to chance it, then," he said. "You're too exhausted to ride all the way to Dabour, and it's going to get hotter as we ride south."

"Don't take unnecessary chances just for my sake, Sparhawk."

"It's not entirely for your sake," he told her. "We've lost a lot of time already, and going by boat is faster than riding. We'll stay close to the river bank in case we need to get off the boat in a hurry."

"Whatever you think best," she said, slumping slightly in her saddle.

They rode out into the teeming street where black-robed nomads from the desert mingled with the more brightly garbed city dwellers and the merchants from the northern kingdoms. The street was filled with noise and with those peculiarly Rendorish scents—spices, perfumes, and the pervading odor of smoking olive oil.

"Who's this Lillias?" Kurik asked curiously as they rode down along the street toward the river.

"It's not important," Sparhawk replied shortly.

"If this person is dangerous, I'd say that it's fairly important for me to know about it."

"Lillias isn't dangerous in that particular way."

"We're talking about a woman, I gather."

It was obvious that Kurik did not intend to be put off. Sparhawk made a sour face. "All right," he said. "I was here in Jiroch for ten years. Voren set me up in a little shop where I went by the name Mahkra. The idea was that I could drop out of sight so that Martel's hirelings couldn't find me. In order to keep busy, I gathered information for Voren. To do that, I needed to look like all the other merchants on that street. They all had mistresses, so I needed one, too. Her name was Lillias. Satisfied?"

"That was quick. The lady has a short temper, I take it?"

"No, Kurik. She has a very long one. Lillias is the kind of woman who nurses grudges."

"Oh, that kind. I'd like to meet her."

"No, you wouldn't. I don't think you'd care for all the screaming and dramatics."

"That bad?"

"Why do you think I slipped out of town in the middle of the night? Do you suppose we could drop this?"

Kurik started to chuckle. "Excuse me for laughing, my Lord," he said, "but as I recall, you weren't exactly brimming with sympathy when I told you about *my* indiscretion with Talen's mother."

"All right. We're even, then." Sparhawk clamped his lips shut and rode on, ignoring Kurik's laughter.

The docks that jutted out into the muddy flow of the Gule River were rickety affairs and they were draped with smelly fishnets. Dozens of the wide-beamed river boats that plied the stream between Jiroch and Dabour were moored to them. Dark-skinned sailors clad in loincloths and with cloths wound about their heads lounged on their decks. Sparhawk dismounted and approached an evil-looking one-eyed man in a loose-fitting striped robe. The one-eyed man stood on the dock bawling orders at a lazy-looking trio of sailors aboard a mud-smeared scow.

"Your boat?" the knight asked.

"What of it?"

"Is it for hire?"

"That depends on the price."

"We can work that out. How many days to Dabour?"

"Three, maybe four days, depending on the wind." The captain was assessing Sparhawk and the others with his good eye. His surly expression changed, and he smiled an oily smile. "Why don't we talk about the price, noble sir?" he suggested.

Sparhawk made some pretense at haggling, then dipped into the pouch of coins Voren had given him and counted silver into the riverman's grimy hand. The man's single eye came alight when he saw the pouch.

They boarded the boat and tethered their horses amidships as the three sailors slipped the hawsers, pushed the boat out into the current, and raised the single, slanted sail. The river was sluggish, and the stiff onshore breeze blowing in off the Arcian Strait pushed them upstream against the current at a goodly speed.

"Watch yourselves," Sparhawk muttered to his companions as they unsaddled their mounts. "Our captain appears to be an independent businessman with his eye open for opportunities." He walked aft to where the one-eyed man stood at the tiller. "I want you to keep as close to shore as you can," he said.

"What for?" The captain's lone eye became suddenly wary.

"My sister's afraid of water," Sparhawk improvised. "If I give you the word, put your boat up against the bank so that she can get off."

"You're paying." The captain shrugged. "We'll do it any way you like."

"Do you run at night?" Sparhawk asked him.

The captain shook his head. "Some do, but I don't. There are too many snags and hidden rocks for my taste. We moor up against the bank when it gets dark."

"Good. I like prudence in a sailor. It makes for safer journeys—which brings up a point." He opened the front of his robe to reveal his mail coat and the heavy broadsword belted at his side. "Do you get my meaning?" he asked.

The captain's face clouded with chagrin. "You have no right to threaten me on my own boat," he blustered.

"As you said before, I'm paying. Your crew looks a little undependable to me, Captain, and your own face isn't one to inspire trust."

The captain's face grew sullen. "You don't have to be insulting," he said.

"If I've misjudged you, I'll apologize later. We have certain valuables with us and we'd prefer to keep them. My friends and I will sleep on the foredeck. You and your men can sleep aft. I trust that won't inconvenience you too much?"

"Aren't you being a little overcautious?"

"Nervous times, neighbor. Nervous times. Remember, when we tie up to the bank for the night, keep your men on the aft deck—and warn them against sleepwalking. A boat can be a very dangerous place for that sort of thing, and I'm a light sleeper." He turned and walked back forward.

The river banks on either side were covered with thick, rank vegetation, though the hills rising behind those narrow strips of green were barren and rock-strewn. Sparhawk and his friends sat on the foredeck, keeping a careful eye on the captain and his sailors and watching for any signs of unusual-looking weather. Flute sat astride the bowsprit playing her pipes while Sparhawk spoke quietly with Sephrenia and Kurik. Sephrenia already knew the customs of the country, so Sparhawk's instruction was directed primarily at his squire. He cautioned him about the many minor things that could be taken as personal insults, and about other things that were considered sacrilegious.

"Who made up all these stupid rules?" Kurik demanded.

"Eshand," Sparhawk replied. "He was crazy, and crazy people take great comfort in rituals."

"Anything else?"

"One other thing. If you should happen to encounter any sheep, you have to step aside for them."

"Say that again?" Kurik's tone was incredulous.

"It's very important, Kurik."

"You're not serious!"

"Deadly serious. Eshand was a shepherd when he was a boy and he used to go absolutely wild when someone rode through his flock. When he came to power, he announced that God had revealed to him that sheep were holy animals and that everyone had to give way to them."

"That's crazy, Sparhawk," Kurik protested.

"Of course it is. It's the law here, though."

"Isn't it strange how the Elene God's revelations always seem to coincide exactly with the prejudices of His prophets?" Sephrenia murmured.

"Do they do anything at all like normal people?" Kurik asked.

"Not many things, no."

As the sun went down, the captain moored his boat against the river bank, and he and his sailors spread pallets on the aft deck. Sparhawk rose and went amidships. He laid his hand on Faran's neck. "Stay awake," he told the big roan. "If someone starts creeping around in the middle of the night, let me know about it."

Faran bared his teeth and shifted around until he was resolutely facing aft. Sparhawk patted his rump familiarly and went back forward.

They took a cold supper of bread and cheese, then spread their blankets on the deck.

"Sparhawk," Kurik said after they had settled down for the night.

"Yes, Kurik?"

"I just had a thought. Are there many people riding in and out of Dabour?"

"Usually, yes. Arasham's presence there tends to attract large crowds."

"I sort of thought so. Wouldn't we be a little less conspicuous if we got off this boat a league or so this side of Dabour and joined one of the groups of pilgrims riding into the city?"

"You think of everything, don't you, Kurik?"

"That's what you pay me for, Sparhawk. Sometimes you knights aren't too practical. It's a squire's job to keep you out of trouble."

"I appreciate that, Kurik."

"No extra charge," Kurik said.

The night passed uneventfully, and at dawn the sailors cast off their moorings and raised the sail again. They passed the town of Kodhl about midmorning of the following day and sailed on up river toward the holy city of Dabour. The river between the two towns was heavily travelled. There seemed to be no organized pattern to the traffic, and the boats occasionally bumped into each other. Such incidents were usually accompanied by an exchange of curses and insults.

It was about noon on the fourth day when Sparhawk went aft to have a word with the one-eyed captain. "We're getting fairly close, aren't we?" he asked.

"About five more leagues," the captain replied, moving his tiller slightly to avoid an oncoming boat. "Mangy son of a three-legged donkey!" he bellowed at the steersman of the other vessel.

"May your mother break out in warts!" the steersman replied pleasantly.

"I think my friends and I might want to go ashore before we actually reach the city," Sparhawk said to the captain. "We want to look around a bit before we meet any of Arasham's followers, and the docks are likely to be watched rather closely."

"That might be a wise move," the captain agreed. "Besides, I get a feeling that you might be up to no good and I'd rather not get involved."

"It works out for both of us, then, doesn't it?"

It was early afternoon when the captain put his tiller over and drove the prow of his boat up onto a narrow strip of sandy beach. "This is about as close as I can get you," he told Sparhawk. "The bank gets marshy just up ahead."

"How far is Dabour from here?" Sparhawk asked him.

"Four, maybe five miles."

"Close enough, then."

The sailors ran the gangway out to the sand from amidships, and Sparhawk and his friends led their horses and their pack mule down to the beach. They had no sooner disembarked than the sailors pulled in the gangway and pushed the boat out into the river with long poles. Then the captain maneuvered his craft out into the current and moved back down river. There was no exchange of farewells.

"Are you going to be all right?" Sparhawk asked Sephrenia. Her face was still drawn, although the dark circles under her eyes had begun to fade.

"I'll be fine, Sparhawk," she assured him.

"If we lose too many more of those knights, though, you won't be, will you?"

"I don't really know," she replied. "I've never been in this exact position before. Let's go on to Dabour and talk with Doctor Tanjin."

They rode up off the beach through the scrubby bushes that bordered it and soon reached the dusty road that led to Dabour. There were other travellers on that road, black-robed nomads for the most part, with their dark eyes afire with religious fervor. Once they were forced to the side of the road by a herd of sheep. The herders, mounted on mules, rode arrogantly and deliberately blocked the road as much as possible with their animals. Their expressions clearly dared anyone to object.

"I never liked sheep very much," Kurik muttered, "and I like sheepherders even less."

"Don't let it show," Sparhawk advised him.

"They eat a lot of mutton down here, don't they?"

Sparhawk nodded.

"Isn't it sort of inconsistent to butcher and eat a sacred animal?"

"Consistency is not one of the more notable characteristics of the Rendorish mind."

As the sheep passed, Flute raised her pipes and played a peculiarly discordant little melody. The sheep suddenly grew wild-eyed, milled for a moment, then stampeded across the desert with the sheepherders in frantic pursuit. Flute covered her mouth with a soundless giggle.

"Stop that," Sephrenia chided.

"Did what I think happened just happen?" Kurik said in amazement.

"I wouldn't be at all surprised," Sparhawk said.

"I really like that little girl, you know?" Kurik was grinning broadly.

They rode on at the tail end of a crowd of pilgrims. After a time they crested a low hill and saw the city of Dabour spread out below them. There were the usual white-plastered houses clustered near the river, but beyond them, stretching in all directions, were hundreds of large black tents. Sparhawk shaded his eyes with one hand and scanned the city. "The cattle pens are over there," he said, pointing to the eastern edge of town. "We should be able to find Perraine there somewhere."

They angled down the hill, avoiding the buildings and tents in the southern section of Dabour. As they began to ride through a cluster of tents pitched between them and the pens, a bearded nomad with a brass pendant set with a bit of glass hanging on a chain about his neck stepped out from behind a tent to bar their path. "Where do you think you're going?" he demanded. He made a quick, imperious gesture with one hand, and a dozen other black-robed men came out into the open with long pikes in their hands.

"We have business at the cattle pens, noble sir," Sparhawk replied mildly.

"Oh, really?" the bearded man sneered. "I see no cows." He looked around at his followers with a self-congratulatory smirk as if terribly pleased with his own cleverness.

"The cows are coming, noble sir," Sparhawk told him. "We were sent on ahead to make arrangements."

The man with the pendant knit his brows, trying hard to find something wrong with that. "Do you know who I am?" he demanded finally in a pugnacious tone of voice.

"I'm afraid not, noble sir," Sparhawk apologized. "I haven't had the pleasure of making your acquaintance."

"You think you're very clever, don't you?" the officious fellow demanded. "All these soft answers don't deceive me in the least."

"I wasn't trying to be deceptive, neighbor," Sparhawk said with a slight edge coming into his voice, "merely polite."

"I am Ulesim, favored disciple of holy Arasham," the bearded man said, striking his chest with his fist.

"I'm overwhelmed by the honor of meeting you," Sparhawk said, bowing in his saddle.

"That's all you have to say?" Ulesim exclaimed, his eyes bulging at the imagined insult.

"As I said, Lord Ulesim, I'm overwhelmed. I hadn't expected to be greeted by so illustrious a man."

"I'm not here to greet you, cowherd. I'm here to take you into custody. Get down off your horses."

Sparhawk gave him a long look, assessing the situation. Then he swung down from Faran's back and helped Sephrenia to dismount.

"What's this all about, Sparhawk?" she whispered as she lifted Flute down.

"I'd guess that he's a minor bootlicker trying to assert his own importance," Sparhawk whispered back. "We don't want to stir anything up, so let's do as he says."

"Take the prisoners to my tent," Ulesim commanded grandly after a moment's hesitation. The favored disciple didn't seem to know exactly what to do.

The pikemen stepped forward threateningly, and one of them led the way toward a tent surmounted by a dropping pennon made of dirty green cloth.

They were roughly shoved into the tent, and the flap was tied down.

Kurik's expression was filled with contempt. "Amateurs," he muttered. "They hold those pikes like shepherd's crooks and they didn't even search us for weapons."

"They may be amateurs, Kurik," Sephrenia said softly, "but they've managed to take us prisoner."

"Not for long," Kurik growled, reaching under his robe for his dagger. "I'll cut a hole in the back of the tent, and we can be on our way."

"No," Sparhawk said quietly. "We'd have a horde of howling fanatics on our heels in about two minutes if we did that."

"We're not just going to sit here?" Kurik asked incredulously.

"Let me handle it, Kurik."

They sat waiting in the stifling tent as the minutes dragged by.

After a bit, the tent flap opened and Ulesim entered with two of his men close behind him. "I will have your name from you, cowherd," he said arrogantly.

"I am called Mahkra, Lord Ulesim," Sparhawk replied meekly, "and this is my sister, her daughter, and my servant. May I ask why we have been detained?"

Ulesim's eyes narrowed. "There are those who refuse to accept holy Arasham's authority," he declared. "I, Ulesim, his most favored disciple, have taken it upon myself to root out these false prophets and send them to the stake. Holy Arasham relies upon me completely."

"Is that still going on?" Sparhawk asked in mild surprise. "I thought that all opposition to Arasham had been stamped out decades ago."

"Not so! Not so!" Ulesim half shrieked. "There are still plotters and conspirators hiding in the desert and lurking in the cities. I will not rest until I have unearthed every one of these criminals and consigned them to the flames."

"You have nothing to fear from me or my band, Lord Ulesim," Sparhawk assured him. "We revere the holy prophet of God and pay him homage in our prayers."

"So you say, Mahkra, but can you prove your identity and satisfy me that you have legitimate business in the holy city?'' The fanatic smirked at his two cohorts as if he had just scored a tremendous point.

"Why yes, Lord Ulesim,'' Sparhawk replied calmly, "I believe I can. We are here to speak with a cattle buyer named Mirrelek. Do you perhaps know him?''

Ulesim puffed himself up. "What would I, the favored disciple of holy Arasham, have to do with some common cattle buyer?''

One of the disciple's toadies leaned forward and whispered at some length in Ulesim's ear. The disciple's expression grew less and less certain and finally even a bit frightened. "I will send for this cattle buyer you mentioned," he declared grudgingly. "If he confirms your story, well and good; but if not, I will take you to holy Arasham himself for judgment.''

"As the Lord Ulesim wishes,'' Sparhawk bowed. "If you would have your messenger tell Mirrelek that Mahkra is here with greetings from his little mother, I'm sure he'll come here immediately and clear up this whole matter.''

"You'd better hope so, Mahkra,'' the bearded disciple said threateningly. He turned to the toady who had whispered in his ear. "Go fetch this Mirrelek. Repeat the message of this cowherd to him and tell him that I, Ulesim, favored disciple of holy Arasham, command his presence immediately.''

"At once, favored one,'' the fellow replied and scurried from the tent. Ulesim glowered at Sparhawk for a moment, then he and his other sycophant left the tent.

"You've still got your sword, Sparhawk,'' Kurik said. "Why didn't you just let the air out of that windbag? I could have dealt with the other two.''

"It wasn't necessary.'' Sparhawk shrugged. "I know Perraine well enough to know that by now he's managed to make himself indispensable to Arasham. He'll be here shortly and put Ulesim-favored-disciple-of-holy-Arasham in his place.''

"Aren't you gambling, Sparhawk?'' Sephrenia asked. "What if Perraine doesn't recognize the name Mahkra? As I recall, you were in Jiroch, and he's been here in Dabour for years.''

"He may not recognize the name I go by here in Rendor," Sparhawk replied, "but he can't fail to recognize yours, little mother. It's a very old password. The Pandions have been using it for years."

She blinked. "I'm very flattered," she said, "but why didn't someone tell me?"

Sparhawk turned to her in some surprise. "We all thought you knew."

It was perhaps a quarter of an hour later when Ulesim escorted a lean, saturnine man in a striped robe into the tent. Ulesim's manner was obsequious and his expression worried. "This is the fellow I was telling you about, honored Mirrelek," he fawned.

"Ah, Mahkra," the lean man said, coming forward to take Sparhawk's hand warmly in his own. "So good to see you again. What seems to be the trouble here?"

"A slight misunderstanding is all, Mirrelek," Sparhawk replied, bowing slightly to his fellow Pandion.

"Well, that's all straightened out now." Sir Perraine turned to the favored disciple. "Isn't it, Ulesim?"

"O—of course, honored Mirrelek," Ulesim faltered, his face visibly pale now.

"Whatever possessed you to detain my friends?" Perraine's tone was mild, but there was a slight edge to it.

"I—I'm only trying to protect holy Arasham."

"Oh? And did he ask for your protection?"

"Well—not in so many words."

"I see. That was very brave of you, Ulesim. Surely you know how holy Arasham feels about those who act independently of his instructions? Many have lost their heads for taking too much upon themselves."

Ulesim began to tremble violently.

"I'm sure he'll forgive you when I tell him of the incident, however. A lesser man would be sent to the block immediately, but after all, you're his favorite disciple, aren't you? Was there anything else, Ulesim?"

Mutely, his face pasty white, Ulesim shook his head.

"My friends and I will be going, then. Coming, Mahkra?" Sir Perraine led them from the tent.

As they rode through the city of tents that had grown up on the outskirts of Dabour, Perraine talked at length about how depressed the cattle market currently was. The tents they passed had apparently been pitched at random, and there was nothing resembling a street. Hordes of dirty children ran and played in the sand, and dispirited-looking dogs rose from the shady side of each tent they passed to bark indifferently a few times before returning to flop down out of the sun again.

Perraine's house was a square, blocklike structure that stood in the center of a patch of weedy ground just beyond the tents. "Come inside," the knight told them loudly as they reached the door. "I want to hear more about this cattle herd of yours."

They went in, and he closed the door. It was dim and cool inside. The house had but a single room. There were rudimentary cooking facilities on one side and an unmade bed on the other. A number of large, porous jugs hung from the rafters, each seeping moisture which dripped into puddles on the floor. A table and two benches sat in the middle of the room. "It's none too ornate," Perraine apologized.

Sparhawk looked meaningfully at the lone window at the back of the house, a window that seemed only loosely shuttered. "Is it safe to talk?" he asked in a low voice.

Perraine laughed. "Oh, yes, Sparhawk," he replied. "In my spare time I've been nurturing a thorn bush outside that window. You'd be amazed at how much it's grown and how long the thorns are. You're looking well, my friend. I haven't seen you since we were novices." Perraine spoke with the faintest trace of an accent. Unlike most Pandions, he was not an Elenian, but came instead from somewhere in the vast reaches of central Eosia. Sparhawk had always liked him.

"You seem to have learned how to talk, Perraine," Sephrenia said. "You were always so silent before."

He smiled. "It was my accent, little mother," he said. "I didn't want people making fun of me." He took her wrists and kissed her palms in greeting and asked her blessing.

"You remember Kurik?" Sparhawk said.

"Of course," Perraine replied. "He trained me with the lance. Hello, Kurik. How's Aslade?"

"Very well, Sir Perraine," Kurik said. "I'll tell her you

asked. What was that business back there all about—with Ulesim, I mean?''

"He's one of the officious toads who've attached themselves to Arasham.''

"Is he really a disciple?''

Perraine snorted. "I doubt that Arasham even knows his name,'' he said. "Of course there are days when Arasham doesn't even know his own. There are dozens like Ulesim—self-appointed disciples who go around bothering honest people. He's probably five miles out into the desert by now and riding very hard to get away. Arasham is very firm with people who overstep what little authority he gives them. Why don't we all sit down?''

"How did you manage to accumulate so much power, Perraine?'' Sephrenia asked him. "Ulesim behaved as if you were some kind of king.''

"It wasn't really too hard,'' he replied. "Arasham has only two teeth in his head—and they don't meet. I give him a tender, milk-fed veal every other week as a token of my unspeakable regard for him. Old men are very interested in their bellies, so Arasham is profuse in his thanks. The disciples aren't blind, so they defer to me because of Arasham's supposed favor. Now, what brings you to Dabour?''

"Voren suggested that we look you up,'' Sparhawk said. "We need to talk with someone here and we didn't want to attract too much attention.''

"My house is yours,'' Perraine said ironically, "such as it is. Who is it you need to talk with?''

"A physician named Tanjin,'' Sephrenia told him, removing her veil.

Perraine looked at her rather closely. "You *are* looking a bit unwell, Sephrenia,'' he said, "but couldn't you find a physician in Jiroch?''

She smiled briefly. "It's not for me, Perraine,'' she told him. "It has to do with someone else. Do you know this Tanjin?''

"Everybody in Dabour knows him. He keeps quarters in the back of an apothecary shop in the central square. His house is being watched, though. There are rumors going about that he dabbles in magic sometimes, and the zealots have been trying to catch him at it.''

"It might be better to walk to the square, wouldn't you say?'' Sparhawk asked.

Perraine nodded.

"And I think we'll wait until just before the sun goes down. That way we'll have some darkness when we come out—just in case we need it.''

"You want me to go with you?''

"It might be better if Sephrenia and I went alone,'' Sparhawk replied. "You have to stay here, and we don't. If Tanjin's under suspicion, visiting him could jeopardize your position here in Dabour.''

"Stay out of alleys, Sparhawk,'' Kurik growled.

Sparhawk motioned to Flute, and she came to him obediently. He put his hands on her shoulders and looked directly into her face. "I want you to stay here with Kurik,'' he told her.

She looked at him gravely, then impudently crossed her eyes at him.

"Stop that,'' he said. "Listen to me, young lady, I'm serious.''

"Just ask her, Sparhawk,'' Sephrenia advised. "Don't try to order her around.''

"Please, Flute,'' he implored. "Will you *please* stay here?''

She smiled sweetly, put her hands together in front of her, and curtsied.

"You see how easy it is?'' Sephrenia said.

"Since we've got some time, I'll fix you all something to eat,'' Perraine said, rising to his feet.

"Did you know that all your bottles are leaking, Sir Perraine?'' Kurik said, pointing at the dripping vessels hanging from the rafters.

"Yes,'' Perraine replied. "They make a mess on the floor, but they help to keep it cool in here.'' He went to the hearth and fumbled for a few moments with flint, steel, and tinder. He built up a very small fire of twigs and twisted chunks of the branches of desert shrubs. Then he set a kettle on the fire, took a large pan, and poured oil in it. He set the pan on the coals and took several chunks of meat out of a covered bowl. As the oil began to smoke, he dropped the meat into the pan. "I'm afraid its only mutton," he apologized. "I wasn't expecting company." He spiced the sizzling meat liberally to disguise its flavor, then brought heavy plates to the table. He went back to the fire and opened an earthenware jar. He took a pinch of tea from the jar, dropped it into a mug, and poured hot water from the kettle into the mug. "For you, little mother," he said, delivering the mug to her with a flourish.

"How very nice," she said. "You're such a dear, Perraine."

"I live but to serve," he said a bit grandiosely. He brought fresh figs and a slab of cheese to the table, then set the smoking pan in the center of it.

"You've missed your calling, my friend," Sparhawk said.

"I learned to cook for myself a long time ago. I could afford a servant, but I don't trust strangers." He sat down. "Be careful out there, Sparhawk," he cautioned as they began to eat. "Arasham's followers are a bit limp between the ears and they're all obsessed with the idea of catching some neighbor committing a minor transgression. Arasham preaches every evening, after the sun goes down, and he manages to come up with some new prohibition every night."

"What's the latest one?" Sparhawk asked.

"Killing flies. He says that they're the messengers of God."

"You're not serious."

Perraine shrugged. "I think he's running out of things to forbid, and his imagination is severely limited. You want some more of this mutton?"

"Thanks all the same, Perraine," Sparhawk said, taking a fig instead, "but one chunk of mutton is my limit."

"One chunk a day?"

"No. One a year."

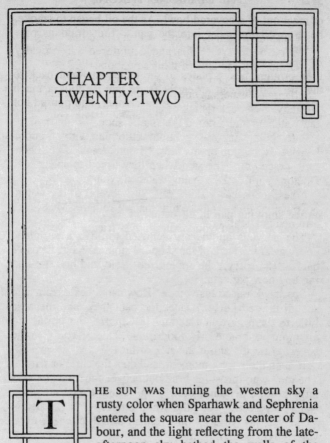

CHAPTER
TWENTY-TWO

T HE SUN WAS turning the western sky a
rusty color when Sparhawk and Sephrenia
entered the square near the center of Dabour, and the light reflecting from the late-
afternoon sky bathed the walls of the
buildings and the faces of the people in the square with a
ruddy glow. Sephrenia had her left arm bound up in a
makeshift sling, and Sparhawk held her other elbow solic-
itously as they walked.

"It's right over there," he said quietly, nodding his head
toward the far side.

Sephrenia drew her veil a bit tighter across her nose and
mouth, and they moved through the crowd milling around
in the middle of the square.

Here and there along the walls of the buildings leaned

hooded nomads in black robes, their eyes alert and filled with suspicion as they peered at every face that passed.

"True believers," Sparhawk muttered sardonically, "ever alert for the sins of their neighbors."

"It's always been that way, Sparhawk," she replied. "Self-righteousness is one of the most common—and least attractive—characteristics of man." They passed one of the watchers and entered the smelly shop.

The apothecary was a chubby little man with an apprehensive expression on his face. "I don't know if he'll consent to see you," he said when they asked to speak with Doctor Tanjin. "He's being watched, you know."

"Yes," Sparhawk said. "We saw several of the watchers outside. Please advise him that we're here. My sister's arm needs attention."

The nervous apothecary scurried through a curtained doorway at the back of the shop. A moment later, he came back. "I'm sorry," he apologized. "He said he's not taking any new patients."

Sparhawk raised his voice. "How can a healer refuse to see an injured person? Does the oath they take mean so little to them here in Dabour? In Cippria, the physicians are more honorable. My good friend, Doctor Voldi, would never refuse his aid to the sick or hurt."

It hung there for a moment, and then the curtains parted. The man who thrust his head out between them had a very large nose, a pendulous lower lip, jutting ears, and weak, watery eyes. He wore the white smock of a physician. "Did you say Voldi?" he asked in a high-pitched, nasal voice. "Do you know him?"

"Of course," Sparhawk replied. "He's a small man who's going bald, and he dyes his hair. He has a very large opinion of himself."

"That's Voldi, all right. Bring your sister back here— and be quick. Don't let anybody outside the shop see you."

Sparhawk took Sephrenia's elbow and escorted her back through the curtains.

"Did anyone see you come in?" the big-nosed man asked nervously.

"Any number of them, I'd imagine." Sparhawk

shrugged. "They line the walls of the square like a flock of vultures, trying to sniff out sin."

"It's not safe to talk that way in Dabour, my friend," Tanjin warned.

"Perhaps." Sparhawk looked around. The room was shabby and was piled high in the corners with open wooden boxes and stacks of books. A persistent bumblebee batted its head against the single dirty window, trying to get out. There was a low couch against one wall and several straight-backed wooden chairs and a table in the center. "Shall we get down to business, Doctor Tanjin?" he suggested.

"All right," the physician said to Sephrenia, "sit here, and I'll have a look at that arm."

"You may if it's going to make you happy, Doctor," she replied, taking the chair and removing her arm from the sling. She pulled back the sleeve of her robe to reveal a surprisingly girlish arm.

The doctor looked a bit hesitantly at Sparhawk. "You understand, of course, that I'm not being forward with your sister's person, but I must examine her."

"I understand the procedure, Doctor."

Tanjin took a deep breath and then bent Sephrenia's wrist back and forth several times. Then he gently ran his fingers up her forearm and bent her elbow. He swallowed hard and probed at her upper arm. Then he moved her arm up and down with his fingers lightly touching her shoulder. His close-set eyes narrowed. "There's nothing wrong with this arm," he accused.

"How kind you are to say so," she murmured, removing her veil.

"Madame!" he said in a shocked voice. "Cover yourself!"

"Oh, do be serious, Doctor," she told him. "We're not here to talk about arms and legs."

"You're spies!" he gasped.

"In a manner of speaking, yes," she replied calmly. "But even spies have reason to consult with physicians once in a while."

"Leave at once," he ordered.

"We just got here," Sparhawk said, pushing back his

hood. "Go ahead, sister dear," he said to Sephrenia. "Tell him why we're here."

"Tell me, Tanjin," she said, "does the word 'darestim' mean anything to you?"

He started guiltily and looked at the curtained doorway, backing away from her.

"Don't be modest, Doctor," Sparhawk told him. "Word's been going about that you cured the king's brother and several of his nephews after they'd been poisoned with darestim."

"There's no proof of that."

"I don't need proof. I need a cure. A friend of ours has the same condition."

"There's no antidote or cure for darestim."

"Then how is it that the king's brother still lives?"

"You're working with them," the doctor accused, pointing vaguely out toward the square. "You're trying to trick me into a confession."

"Them who?" Sparhawk asked.

"The fanatics who follow Arasham. They're trying to prove that I use witchcraft in my practice."

"Do you?"

The doctor shrank back. "Please leave," he begged. "You're putting my life in terrible danger."

"As you've probably noticed, Doctor," Sephrenia said, "we are not Rendorish. We do not share the prejudices of your countrymen, so magic does not offend us. It's quite routine in the place we come from."

He blinked at her uncertainly.

"This friend of ours—the one I mentioned before—is very dear to us," Sparhawk told him, "and we'll go to any lengths to find a cure for this poison." To emphasize his point, he opened his robe. "Any lengths at all."

The doctor gaped at his mail coat and sheathed sword.

"There's no need to threaten the doctor, brother dear," Sephrenia said. "I'm sure he'll be more than happy to describe the cure he's found. He *is* a healer, after all."

"Madame, I don't know what you're talking about," Tanjin said desperately. "There is no cure for darestim. I don't know where you heard all these rumors, but I can assure you that they're absolutely false. I do *not* use witchcraft in my practice." He threw another quick, nervous glance at the curtained doorway.

"But Doctor Voldi in Cipbria told us that you *did*, in fact, cure members of the king's family."

"Well—yes, I suppose I did, but the poison wasn't darestim."

"What was it, then?"

"Un—porgutta—I think." He was obviously lying.

"Then why was it that the king sent for you, Doctor?" she pressed. "A simple purge will cleanse the body of porgutta. Any apprentice physician knows that. Surely it couldn't have been so mild a poison."

"Un—well, maybe it was something else. I forget, exactly."

"I think, dear brother," Sephrenia said then to Sparhawk, "that the good doctor needs some reassurance—some positive proof that he can trust us and that we are what we say we are." She looked at the irritating bumblebee still stubbornly trying to break its way out through the window. "Have you ever wondered why you never see a bumblebee at night, Doctor?" she asked the frightened physician.

"I've never given it any thought."

"Perhaps you should." She began to murmur in Styric as her fingers wove the designs of the spell.

"What are you doing?" Tanjin exclaimed. "Stop that!" He started to move toward her with one hand outstretched, but Sparhawk stopped him.

"Don't interfere," the big knight said.

Then Sephrenia pointed her finger and released the spell.

The buzzing sound of insect wings was suddenly joined by a tiny, piping voice that sang joyously in a tongue unknown to man. Sparhawk looked quickly at the dust-clouded window. The bumblebee was gone, and in its place there hovered a tiny female figure directly out of folklore. Her pale hair cascaded down her back between her rapidly beating gossamer wings. Her little nude body was perfectly formed, and her minuscule face was so lovely as to stop the breath.

"That is how bumblebees think of themselves," Sephrenia said quite calmly, "and perhaps that is what they truly are—by day a common insect, but by night a creature of wonder.''

Tanjin had fallen back on his shabby couch with his eyes wide and his mouth agape.

''Come here, little sister,'' Sephrenia crooned to the fairy, extending one hand.

The fairy swooped about the room, her transparent wings buzzing and her tiny voice soaring. Then she delicately settled on Sephrenia's outstretched palm with her wings still fanning at the air. Sephrenia turned and stretched her hand out to the shaking physician. ''Isn't she beautiful?'' she asked. ''You may hold her if you like—but be wary of her sting.'' She pointed at the tiny rapier in the fairy's hand.

Tanjin shrank away with his hands behind his back. ''How did you do that?'' he asked in a trembling voice.

''Do you mean that you can't? The charges against you *must* be false, then. This is a very simple spell—quite rudimentary, actually.''

''As you can see, Doctor,'' Sparhawk said, ''we have no qualms about magic. You can speak freely to us with no fear of being denounced to Arasham or his fanatic followers.''

Tanjin tightly clamped his lips shut, continuing to stare at the fairy seated sedately on Sephrenia's palm with fluttering wings.

''Don't be tiresome, Doctor,'' Sephrenia said. ''Just tell us how you cured the king's brother, and we'll be on our way.''

Tanjin began to edge away from her.

''I think, dear brother, that we're wasting our time here,'' she said to Sparhawk. ''The good doctor refuses to cooperate.'' She raised her hand. ''Fly, little sister,'' she told the fairy, and the tiny creature soared once again into the air. ''We'll be going now, Tanjin,'' she said.

Sparhawk started to object, but she laid one restraining hand on his arm and started toward the door.

''What are you going to do about that?'' Tanjin cried, pointing at the circling fairy.

''Do?'' Sephrenia said. ''Why nothing, Doctor. She's quite happy here. Feed her sugar from time to time, and put out a small dish of water for her. In return, she'll sing for you. Don't try to catch her, though. That would make her very angry.''

"You can't leave her here!" he exclaimed in anguish. "If anyone sees her here, I'll be burned at the stake for witchcraft.''

"He sees directly to the central point, doesn't he?'' Sephrenia said to Sparhawk.

"The scientific mind is noted for that.'' Sparhawk grinned. "Shall we go, then?''

"Wait!'' Tanjin cried.

"Was there something you wanted to tell us, Doctor?'' Sephrenia asked mildly.

"All right. All right. But you must swear to keep it a secret that I told you this.''

"Of course. Our lips are sealed.''

Tanjin drew in a deep breath and scurried to the curtained doorway to make certain that no one was listening outside. Then he turned and motioned them into a far corner where he spoke in a hoarse whisper. "Darestim is so virulent that there's no natural remedy or antidote,'' he began.

"That's what Voldi told us,'' Sparhawk said.

"You'll note that I said no *natural* remedy or antidote,'' Tanjin continued. "Some years ago in the course of my studies, I came across a very old and curious book. It predated Eshand's time and it had been written before his prohibitions came into effect. It seems that the primitive healers here in Rendor routinely utilized magic in treating their patients. Sometimes it worked, sometimes it didn't— but they effected some astonishing cures. The practice had one common element. There are a number of objects in the world which have enormous power. The physicians of antiquity used that sort of thing to cure their patients.''

"I see,'' Sephrenia said. "Styric healers sometimes resort to the same desperate measure.''

"The practice is quite common in the Tamul Empire on the Daresian continent,'' Tanjin went on, "but it's fallen into disfavor here in Eosia. Eosian physicians prefer scientific techniques. They're more reliable, for one thing, and Elenes have always been suspicious of magic. But dar-

estim is so potent that none of the customary antidotes
have any effect. Magical objects are the only possible
cure."

"And what did you use to cure the king's brother and
nephews?" Sephrenia asked.

"It was an uncut gem of a peculiar color. I think it
originally came from Daresia, though I can't really be sure.
It's my belief that the Tamul Gods infused it with their
power."

"And where is that gem now?" Sparhawk asked intently.

"Gone, I'm afraid. I had to grind it to a powder and
mix it with wine to cure the king's relatives."

"You idiot!" Sephrenia exploded. "That is *not* the way
to use such an object. You need only touch it to the patient's body and call forth its power."

"I'm a trained physician, madame," he replied stiffly.
"I cannot turn insects into fairies, nor levitate myself, nor
cast spells upon my enemies. I can only follow the normal
practices of my profession, and that means that the patient
must ingest the medication."

"You destroyed a stone that might have healed thousands for the sake of just a few!" With some effort she
controlled her anger. "Do you know of any other such
objects?" she asked him.

"A few." He shrugged. "There's a great spear in the
imperial palace in Tamul, several rings in Zemoch, though
I doubt that they'd be much good in healing people. It's
rumored that there's a jeweled bracelet in Pelosia somewhere, but that might be only a myth. The sword of the
king of the island of Mithrium was reputed to have great
power, but Mithrium sank into the sea eons ago. I've also
heard that the Styrics have quite a few magic wands."

"That's also a myth," she told him. "Wood is too frag-
ile for that kind of power. Any others?"

"The only one I know of is the jewel on the royal crown
of Thalesia, but that's been lost since the time of the Zemoch invasion." He frowned. "I don't think this will help
very much," he added, "but Arasham has a talisman that
he claims is the most holy and powerful thing in all the
world. I've never seen it myself, so I can't say for sure,

and Arasham's wits aren't so firmly set in his head that he'd be any kind of an authority. You'd never be able to get it away from him in any case.''

Sephrenia reattached her veil across the lower part of her face. ''Thank you for your candor, Doctor Tanjin,'' she said. ''Be assured that no one will learn of your secret from us.'' She thought a moment. ''I think you should splint this,'' she said, holding out her arm. ''That should prove to the curious that we had a legitimate reason for this visit, and it should protect you as well as us.''

''That's a very good idea, madame.'' Tanjin fetched a couple of slats and a long strip of white cloth.

''Would you take a bit of friendly advice, Tanjin?'' Sparhawk asked him as he began to splint Sephrenia's arm.

''I'll listen.''

''Do that. If it were me, I'd gather up a few things and go to Zand. The king can protect you there. Get out of Dabour while you still can. Fanatics make the jump from suspicion to certainty very easily, and it won't do you much good if you're proved innocent *after* you've been burned at the stake.''

''But everything I own is here.''

''I'm sure that'll be a great comfort to you when your toes are on fire.''

''Do you really think I'm in that much danger?'' Tanjin asked in a weak voice, looking up from his task.

Sparhawk nodded. ''That much and more. I'd estimate that you'll be lucky to live out the week if you stay here in Dabour.''

The doctor began to tremble violently as Sephrenia slipped her splinted arm back into the sling. ''Wait a minute,'' he said as they started toward the door. ''What about that?'' He pointed at the fairy swooping through the air near the window.

''Oh,'' Sephrenia said. ''Sorry. I almost forgot about her.'' She mumbled a few words and made a vague gesture.

The bumblebee went back to batting its head against the window.

It was dark when they emerged from the apothecary's shop into the nearly deserted square.

"It's not very much," Sparhawk said dubiously.

"It's more than we had before. At least we know how to cure Ehlana. All we need to do now is to find one of these objects."

"Would you be able to tell if Arasham's talisman has any real power?"

"I think so."

"Good. Perraine says that Arasham preaches every night. Let's go find him. I'll listen to a dozen sermons if it puts me close to a cure."

"How do you propose to get it away from him?"

"I'll think of something."

A black-robed man suddenly blocked their path. "Stop right there," he commanded.

"What's your problem, neighbor?" Sparhawk asked him.

"Why are you not at the feet of holy Arasham?" the robed man asked accusingly.

"We were just on our way," Sparhawk replied.

"All Dabour knows that holy Arasham speaks to the multitudes at sundown. Why are you deliberately absenting yourselves?"

"We arrived only today," Sparhawk explained, "and I had to seek medical attention for my sister's injured arm."

The fanatic scowled suspiciously at Sephrenia's sling. "Surely you did not consult with the wizard Tanjin?" he said in an outraged tone.

"When one is in pain, one does not ask to see the healer's credentials," Sephrenia told him. "I can assure you, however, that the doctor used no witchcraft. He set the broken bone and splinted it for me in the same way any other physician would have."

"The righteous do not consort with wizards," the zealot declared stubbornly.

"I'll tell you what, neighbor," Sparhawk said pleasantly. "Why don't I break *your* arm? Then you can visit the doctor yourself. If you watch him very closely, you should be able to tell if he's using witchcraft or not."

The fanatic stepped back apprehensively.

"Come now, friend," Sparhawk told him enthusiastically, "be brave. It won't hurt all that much, and think of

how much holy Arasham will appreciate your zeal in root-
ing out the abomination of witchcraft.''

"Could you tell us where we might find the place where
holy Arasham speaks to the multitudes?'' Sephrenia interposed. "Our souls hunger and thirst for his words.''

"Over that way,'' the nervous man said, pointing. "You
can see the light from the torches.''

"Thanks, friend,'' Sparhawk said, bowing slightly. He
frowned. "How is it that you yourself are not at the services this evening?''

"I—uh—I have a sterner duty,'' the fellow declared. "I
must seek out those who are absent without cause and
deliver them up for judgment.''

"Ah,'' Sparhawk said, "I see.'' He turned away, then
turned back. "Are you sure you wouldn't like to have me
break your arm for you? It won't take but a minute.''

The fanatic hurried away from them.

"Must you threaten everyone you meet, Sparhawk?''
Sephrenia asked.

"He irritated me.''

"You irritate very easily, don't you?''

He considered it. "Yes,'' he admitted, "I suppose I do.
Shall we go?''

They went through the dark streets of Dabour until they
reached the tents pitched on the outskirts. Some distance
toward the south a ruddy glow pulsed up toward the glit-
tering stars. They moved quietly past the tents toward the
light.

The flickering torches were set on tall poles surrounding
a kind of natural amphitheater on the southern edge of
town, a sort of depression between two hills. The hollow
was filled with Arasham's followers, and the deranged holy
man himself stood atop a large boulder halfway up the
side of one of the hills. He was tall and gaunt with a long
gray beard and bushy black eyebrows. His voice was strident as he harangued his followers, but his words were
difficult to understand because of his lack of teeth. When
Sparhawk and Sephrenia joined the crowd, the old man
was in the middle of an extended and highly involuted
proof of God's special favor—which had, he declared, been
bestowed upon him in a dream. There were huge logical

gaps in his argument and great leaps of what passed for faith here in Rendor.

"Is he making any sense at all?" Sephrenia whispered to Sparhawk in a puzzled tone as she removed the splints and the sling.

"Not that I can detect," he whispered back.

"I didn't think so. Does the Elene God actually encourage that sort of hysterical gibberish?"

"He never has to me."

"Can we get any closer?"

"I don't think so. The crowd's pretty thick in front of where he's standing."

Arasham then turned to one of his favorite topics, a denunciation of the Church. The organized Elene religion, he maintained, was cursed by God for its failure to recognize his exalted status as the chosen and beloved spokesman of the Most High.

"But the wicked shall be punished!" he lisped in a toothless shriek with spittle flying from his lips. "My followers are invincible! Be patient for but a little more time, and I will raise my holy talisman and lead you into war against them! They will send their accursed Church Knights to do war upon us, but fear them not! The power of this holy relic will sweep them before us like chaff before the wind!" He held something high over his head in his tightly clenched fist. "The spirit of the blessed Eshand himself has confirmed this to me!"

"Well?" Sparhawk whispered to Sephrenia.

"He's too far away," she murmured. "I can't feel anything one way or the other. We're going to have to get closer. I can't even tell what he's holding."

Arasham's voice sank into a harshly conspiratorial tone. "I tell you this, O ye faithful, and my words are true. The voice of God has revealed to me that even now our movement is spreading through the fields and forests of the kingdoms of the north. The ordinary people there—our brothers and sisters—grow weary of the yoke of the Church and they will join our holy cause."

"It was Martel who told him that," Sparhawk muttered, "and if he thinks that Martel is the voice of God, then he's even crazier than I thought." He rose up on his tiptoes and looked over the heads of the crowd. A large pavilion stood some distance down the hill from where Arasham was preaching. It was surrounded by a palisade of stout poles. "Let's work our way around this crowd," he suggested. "I think I've located the old man's tent."

Slowly they moved back until they were at the edge of the crowd. Arasham continued his rambling harangue, but his slurred words were lost in the distance and the murmuring of his followers. Sparhawk and Sephrenia slipped around the crowd toward the palisade and the dark pavilion inside it. When they were perhaps twenty paces away, Sparhawk touched Sephrenia's arm, and they stopped. A number of armed men stood before the opening at the front of the palisade. "We'll have to wait until he finishes preaching," Sparhawk murmured.

"Would you like to tell me what you have in mind?" she said. "I hate surprises."

"I'm going to see if I can get us into his tent. If that talisman of his really has any power, it might be difficult to get it away from him in the middle of this crowd."

"How do you propose to manage that, Sparhawk?"

"I thought I'd try flattery."

"Isn't that a bit dangerous—and very obvious?"

"Of course it's obvious, but you have to be obvious when you're dealing with deranged people. They don't have the concentration to grasp subtlety."

Arasham's voice was rising to a shrill climax, and his followers cheered at the end of each of his mumbled pronouncements. Then he delivered his benediction, and the crowd began to break up. Surrounded by a knot of jealous disciples, the holy man began to walk slowly through the milling throng toward his tent. Sparhawk and Sephrenia moved to place themselves in his path.

"Stand aside!" one of the disciples commanded harshly.

"Forgive me, exalted disciple," Sparhawk said loudly enough for his words to carry to the tottering old man, "but I bear a message from the king of Deira for holy Arasham. His majesty sends greetings to the true head of the Elene Church."

Sephrenia made a slightly strangled noise.

"Holy Arasham takes no note of kings," the disciple sneered arrogantly. "Now stand aside."

"A moment there, Ikkad," Arasham mumbled in a surprisingly weak voice. "We would hear more of this message from our brother of Deira. It may well be that this is the communication mentioned by God when last He spoke with us."

"Most holy Arasham," Sparhawk said with a deep bow, "His majesty, King Obler of Deira, greets you as his brother. Our king is very old, and age always brings wisdom."

"Truly," Arasham agreed, stroking his own long, gray beard.

"His majesty has long contemplated the teachings of the blessed Eshand," Sparhawk continued, "and he has also eagerly followed your own career here in Rendor. He has regarded the activities of the Church with increasing disfavor. He has found churchmen to be hypocritical and self-serving."

"My very words," Arasham said ecstatically. "I have said so myself a hundred times and more."

"His majesty acknowledges that you are the source and wellspring of his thought, holy Arasham."

"Well," Arasham replied, preening himself slightly.

"His majesty believes that the time has come for a purification of the Elene Church and he further believes that you are the one who has been chosen by God to purge the Church of her sins."

"Did you hear my sermon tonight?" the old man asked eagerly. "I preached to that self-same topic."

"Truly," Sparhawk said. "I was amazed at how closely your words coincided with those of his majesty when he charged me with his message to you. Know, however, holy Arasham, that his majesty intends to provide more aid to you than the mere comfort of his greetings and his respectful affection. The details of his further intentions, though, must be for your ears alone." He looked around suspiciously at the crowd pressing in upon them. "In a gathering so large as this, there may be several who are not what they seem, and if what I have to tell you should reach

Chyrellos, the Church would bend all her efforts to hinder his majesty's design.''

Arasham tried without much success to look shrewd. "Your prudence becomes you, young man," he agreed. "Let us go into my pavilion so that you may more fully disclose the mind of my dear brother Obler to me."

Pushing aside the officious disciples, Sparhawk thrust his way through their ranks to offer the support of his arm and shoulder to the elderly zealot. "Holy one," he said in a fawning tone, "fear not to lean upon me, for as the blessed Eshand has commanded, it is the duty of the young and strong to serve the aged and wise."

"How truly you speak, my son."

They passed thus through the gate of the palisade and across a stretch of sand dotted with sheep droppings.

The interior of Arasham's pavilion was far more luxurious than might have been expected from its severe exterior. A single lamp burned expensive oil in the center, and priceless carpets covered the rude sand floor. Silken fabric curtained off the rearward portions of the pavilion, and from behind those curtains came the giggling of adolescent boys.

"Please sit and take your ease," Arasham invited expansively, sinking down upon a cluster of silken cushions. "Let us take some refreshment, and then you may tell me of the intent of my dear brother Obler of Deira." He clapped his hands sharply together, and a doe-eyed boy emerged from behind one of the silken panels.

"Bring us some of the fresh melon, Saboud," Arasham told him.

"As you command, Most Holy." The boy bowed and retired behind the silken screen.

Arasham leaned back on his cushions. "I am not at all surprised at the communication you have brought me concerning the growing sentiment for our cause in Deira," he lisped to Sparhawk. "Word has reached me that such feelings are not uncommon in the kingdoms of the north. Indeed, another such message has but recently arrived." He paused thoughtfully. "It occurs to me—perhaps at the prompting of God Himself, who ever joins His thought with mine—that you and the other messenger may know each other.'' He turned toward a silken panel that concealed a dimly lighted part of the tent. ''Come forth, my friend and advisor. Look upon the face of our noble visitor from Deira and tell me if you know him.''

A shadow moved behind the panel. It seemed to hesitate for a moment, and then a robed and hooded figure emerged into the lamplight. The hooded man was only slightly shorter than Sparhawk and he had the heavy shoulders of a warrior. He reached up and pushed back his hood to reveal his piercing black eyes and his thick mane of snowy white hair.

In a kind of curious detachment, Sparhawk wondered what it was exactly that kept him from instantly drawing his sword.

''Indeed, most holy Arasham,'' Martel said in his deep, resonant voice, ''Sparhawk and I have known each other for a long time.''

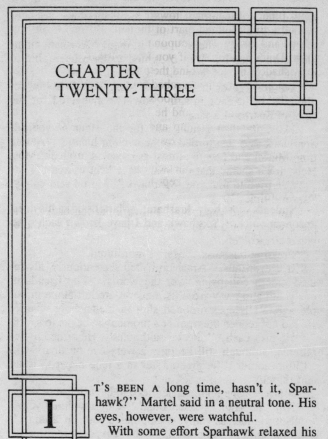

CHAPTER
TWENTY-THREE

I T'S BEEN A long time, hasn't it, Spar-hawk?'' Martel said in a neutral tone. His eyes, however, were watchful.

With some effort Sparhawk relaxed his tightly clenched muscles. "Yes, it has,'' he replied. "It must be ten years now at least. We should try to get together more often.''

"We'll have to make a point of that.''

It hung there. The two continued to look directly into each others' faces. The air seemed to crackle with tension as each waited for the other to make the first move.

"Sparhawk,'' Arasham mused, "a most unusual name. It seems to me that I've heard it somewhere before.''

"It's a very old name,'' Sparhawk told him. "It's been

passed down through my family for generations. Some of my ancestors were men of note.''

''Perhaps that's where I heard it, then,'' Arasham mumbled complacently. ''I'm delighted to have been able to reunite two old and dear friends.''

''We are forever in your debt, Most Holy,'' Martel replied. ''You cannot imagine how I've hungered for the sight of Sparhawk's face.''

''No more than I hungered for the sight of yours,'' Sparhawk said. He turned to the ancient lunatic. ''At one time Martel and I were almost as close as brothers, Most Holy. It's a shame that the years have kept us apart.''

''I've tried to find you, Sparhawk,'' Martel said coolly, ''several times.''

''Yes, I heard about that. I always hurried back to the place where you'd been seen, but by the time I got there, you'd already left.''

''Pressing business,'' Martel murmured.

''It is ever thus,'' Arasham lisped sententiously, his ruined mouth collapsing over the words. ''The friends of our youth slip away from us, and we are left alone in our old age.'' His eyes dropped shut in melancholy reverie. He did not reopen them; after a moment he began to snore.

''He tires easily,'' Martel said quietly. He turned to Sephrenia, although still keeping a wary eye on Sparhawk. ''Little mother,'' he greeted her in a tone between irony and regret.

''Martel.'' She inclined her head in the briefest of nods.

''Ah,'' he said. ''It seems that I've disappointed you.''

''Not so much as you've disappointed yourself, I think.''

''Punishment, Sephrenia?'' he asked sardonically. ''Don't you think I've been punished enough already?''

''It's not in my nature to punish people, Martel. Nature gives neither rewards nor punishment—only consequences.''

''All right, then. I accept the consequences. Will you at least permit me to greet you—and to seek your blessing?'' He took her wrists and turned her palms up.

''No, Martel,'' she replied, closing her hands, ''I don't think so. You're no longer my pupil. You've found another to follow.''

"That wasn't entirely my idea, Sephrenia. You rejected me, you remember." He sighed and released her wrists. Then he looked back at Sparhawk. "I'm really rather surprised to see you, brother mine," he said, "considering all the times I've sent Adus to deal with you. I'll have to speak sharply with him about that—provided you haven't killed him, of course."

"He was bleeding a little the last time I saw him," Sparhawk said, "but not very seriously."

"Adus doesn't pay much attention to blood—not even his own."

"Would you like to step out of the way, Sephrenia?" Sparhawk said, opening the front of his robe and shifting his sword hilt around slightly. "Martel and I were having a little discussion the last time we saw each other. I think it's time we continued it."

Martel's eyes narrowed, and he opened his own robe. Like Sparhawk, he also wore mail and a broadsword. "Excellent notion, Sparhawk," he said, his deep voice dropping to little more than a whisper.

Sephrenia stepped between them. "Stop that, both of you," she commanded. "This isn't the time or the place. We're right in the middle of an army. If you play this game of yours here in Arasham's tent, you'll have half of Rendor in here with you before it's over."

Sparhawk felt a hot surge of disappointment, but he knew that she was right. Regretfully, he took his hand away from his sword hilt. "Sometime soon, however, Martel," he said in a dreadfully quiet voice.

"I'll be happy to oblige you, dear brother," Martel replied with an ironic bow. His eyes narrowed speculatively. "What are you two doing here in Rendor?" he asked. "I thought you were still in Cammoria."

"It's a business trip."

"Ah, you've found out about the darestim, I see. I hate to tell you this, but you're wasting your time. There's no antidote. I checked that very carefully before I recommended it to a certain friend in Cimmura."

"You're pressing your luck, Martel," Sparhawk told him ominously.

"I always have, brother mine. As they say, no risk, no

profit. Ehlana will die, I'm afraid. Lycheas will succeed her, and Annias will become archprelate. I expect to reap quite a handsome profit from that.''

"Is that all you ever think about?"

"What else is there?" Martel shrugged. "Everything else is only an illusion. How's Vanion been lately?"

"He's well," Sparhawk replied. "I'll tell him you asked."

"That's assuming that you live long enough to see him again. Your situation here is precarious, my old friend."

"So's yours, Martel."

"I know, but I'm used to it. You're weighted down with scruples and the like. I left all that behind a long time ago.''

"Where's your tame Damork, Martel?" Sephrenia asked suddenly.

He looked only slightly surprised and he recovered instantly. "I really haven't the slightest idea, little mother," he replied. "It comes to me without being summoned, so I never know when it's going to turn up. Perhaps it returned to the place it came from. It has to do that every so often, you know."

"I've never been that curious about the creatures of the underworld.''

"That could be a serious oversight."

"Perhaps."

Arasham stirred on his cushions and opened his eyes. "Did I doze off?" he asked.

"Only briefly, Most Holy," Martel said. "It gave Sparhawk and me time to renew our friendship. We had much to discuss."

"Very much," Sparhawk agreed. He hesitated slightly, but then decided that Martel was so sure of himself that he'd probably miss the significance of the question. "You mentioned a talisman during your sermon, holy one," he said to Arasham. "Might we be permitted to see it?"

"The holy relic? Of course." The old man fumbled inside his robe and drew out something that appeared to be a twisted lump of bone. He held it out proudly. "Do you know what this is, Sparhawk?" he asked.

"No, Most Holy. I'm afraid not."

"The blessed Eshand began life as a shepherd, you know."

"Yes, I'd heard so."

"One day when he was quite young, a ewe in his flock gave birth to a pure white lamb that was like none other he had ever seen. Unlike all other sheep of that breed, this infant ram bore horns upon its head. It was, of course, a sign from God. The pure lamb, obviously, symbolized the blessed Eshand himself, and the fact that the lamb was horned could only mean one thing—that Eshand had been chosen to chastise the Church for her iniquity."

"How mysterious are the ways of God," Sparhawk marveled.

"Truly, my son. Truly. Eshand cared for the ram most tenderly, and in time it began to speak to him, and its voice was the voice of God himself. And thus God instructed Eshand in that which he must do. This holy relic is a piece of the horn of that very ram. Now you can see why it has such enormous power."

"Clearly, Most Holy," Sparhawk said in a reverent tone of voice. "Come closer, little sister," he said to Sephrenia. "View this miraculous relic."

She stepped forward and looked intently at the twisted bit of horn in Arasham's hand. "Remarkable," she murmured. She glanced at Sparhawk, shaking her head almost imperceptibly.

The bitter taste of disappointment filled his mouth.

"The power of this talisman will overcome all the concerted might of the accursed Church Knights and their foul witchcraft," Arasham declared. "God Himself has told me so." He smiled almost shyly. "I have discovered a truly remarkable thing," he told them confidentially. "When I am alone, I can lift the holy relic to my ear and hear the voice of God. Thus He instructs me even as He instructed the blessed Eshand."

"A miracle!" Martel said in mock amazement.

"Is it not?" Arasham beamed.

"We are quite overcome with gratitude that you have consented to let us view the talisman, Most Holy," Sparhawk said, "and we will spread word of it throughout the kingdoms of the north, won't we, Martel?"

"Oh, of course, of course." Martel's face was slightly puzzled, and he was looking suspiciously at Sparhawk.

"I perceive now that our coming here is a part of God's design," Sparhawk continued. "It is our mission to tell all the kingdoms of the north of this miracle—through every village and at every crossroads. Even now I feel the spirit of God infusing my tongue with eloquence so that I might better describe what I have seen." He reached out and clapped Martel on the left shoulder—quite firmly. "Don't you feel it as well, dear brother?" he asked enthusiastically.

Martel winced slightly, and Sparhawk could feel the shoulder shrinking from under his hand. "Why, yes," Martel admitted in a slightly pained voice, "as a matter of fact, I believe I do."

"Wondrous is the might of God!" Arasham exulted.

"Yes," Martel said, rubbing at his shoulder, "wondrous."

The idea had been slow in coming, in part perhaps because of the surprise of once again seeing Martel, but now it all began to fall into place. Sparhawk was suddenly glad that Martel was here. "And now, Most Holy," he said, "let me give you the remainder of his majesty's message to you."

"Of course. My ears are open to you."

"His majesty commands me to implore you to give him time to marshal his forces before you move against the venal Church here in Rendor. He must move with caution in his mobilization because the Hierocracy in Chyrellos has spies everywhere. He wishes devoutly to aid you, but the Church is powerful, and he must mass sufficient force to overcome her might in Deira at one stroke, lest she recover and crush him. It is his thought that should you mount your campaign here in the south at the same time he mounts his in the north, the Church will be confounded, not knowing which way to turn, and by moving swiftly you may take advantage of her confusion and win victory after victory. The impact of these victories will dishearten and demoralize the forces of the Church, and you may both march triumphant upon Chyrellos."

"Praise God!" Arasham exclaimed, starting to his feet and brandishing his sheep's horn like a weapon.

Sparhawk raised one hand. "*But*," he cautioned, "this grand design, which can only have come from God Himself, has no chance of success unless you and his majesty attack simultaneously."

"I can see that, of course. God's own voice has instructed me in just such strategy."

"I was sure that he had." Sparhawk let his face assume an expression of extreme cunning. "Now," he went on, "the Church is as sly as a serpent, and she has ears everywhere. Despite our best efforts to maintain secrecy, she may uncover our plan. Her first recourse has always been deceit."

"I have seen that in her," Arasham admitted.

"It may well be that once she has uncovered our plan, she will attempt deception, and what better way to deceive you than to send false messengers to you to declare that his majesty is in readiness when indeed he is not? Thus the Church could defeat you and your disciples one by one."

Arasham frowned. "That's true, isn't it?" he said. "But how may we avoid being deceived?"

Sparhawk pretended to think about it. Then he suddenly snapped his fingers. "I have it!" he exclaimed. "What better way to confound the deceitfulness of the Church than by the word—a word known only to you and to me and to King Obler of Deira? Thus may you know that a message is genuine. Should any come to you with the message that the time has come, but who cannot repeat the word to you, that man will be most surely a serpent of the Church sent to deceive you, and you should deal with him accordingly."

Arasham thought about it. "Why, yes," he mumbled finally. "I believe that might indeed confound the Church. But what word can be so locked in our hearts that none may seek it out?"

Sparhawk threw a covert glance at Martel, whose face was suddenly filled with chagrin. "It must be a word of power," he said, squinting at the roof of the tent as if deep in thought. The whole ploy was obvious—even childish—but it was the kind of thing that would appeal to the senile old Arasham, and it provided a marvelous opportunity to settle a few scores with Martel, just for old times' sake.

Sephrenia sighed and lifted her eyes in resignation. Sparhawk felt a little ashamed of himself at that point. He looked at Arasham, who was leaning forward in anticipation, chewing upon emptiness with his toothless mouth and setting his long beard to waggling.

"I will, of course, accept your pledge of secrecy without question, Most Holy," Sparhawk said in feigned humility. "I, however, swear by my life that the word I am about to give you in profoundest secrecy shall never again pass my lips until I divulge it to King Obler in Acie, the capital of his kingdom."

"And I also pledge my oath to you, noble friend Sparhawk," the old man cried in an excess of enthusiasm. "Torture will not drag the word from my lips." He made some attempt to draw himself up regally.

"Your pledge honors me, Most Holy," Sparhawk replied with a deep Rendorish bow. He approached the old man, bent, and whispered, "Ramshorn." Arasham, he noted, didn't smell very good.

"The perfect word!" Arasham cried. He seized Sparhawk's head in a pair of wiry arms and kissed him soundly full on the mouth.

Martel, his face pale with anger, had tried to draw near enough to hear, but Sephrenia stepped in front of him. His eyes flashed angrily, and with obvious effort he restrained his first impulse to thrust her out of his way.

She raised her chin and looked him full in the face. "Well?" she said.

He muttered something, turned, and stalked to the far side of the tent where he stood gnawing at a knuckle in frustration.

Arasham still clung to Sparhawk's neck. "My beloved son and deliverer," he cried with his rheumy eyes filled with tears. "Surely you have been sent to me by God Himself. We cannot fail now. God is on our side. Let the wicked tremble before us."

"Truly," Sparhawk agreed, gently disengaging the old man's arms from about his neck.

"A thought, holy one," Martel said shrewdly, though his face was still white with fury. "Sparhawk is only human and, therefore, mortal. The world is full of mischance. Might it not be wiser to—"

"Mischance?" Sparhawk cut him off quickly. "Where is your faith, Martel? This is God's design, not mine. God will not permit me to die until I have performed this service for Him. Have faith, dear brother. God will sustain and keep me against all perils. It is my destiny to fulfill this task, and God will see to it that I do not fail."

"Praise God!" Arasham exclaimed ecstatically, ending the discussion.

The doe-eyed boy brought in the melons at that point, and the conversation shifted to more general matters. Arasham delivered another rambling diatribe against the Church while Martel sat scowling at Sparhawk. Sparhawk kept his eyes on his melon, which was surprisingly good. It had all been too easy, somehow, and that worried him just a little. Martel was too clever, too devious, to have been so easily circumvented. He looked appraisingly across the tent at the white-haired man he had hated for so long. Martel's expression was baffled, frustrated—and that was also not like him. The Martel he had known as a youth would never have revealed such emotions. Sparhawk began to feel a little less sure of himself.

"A thought has just occurred to me, Most Holy," he said. "Time is crucial in this affair, and it is essential that my sister and I return to Deira at once to advise his majesty that all here in Rendor is ready, and to convey to his ears alone that word which is locked in both our hearts. We have good horses, of course, but a fast boat could take us downriver and deliver us to the seaport at Jiroch days earlier. Perhaps you—or one of your disciples—might know of some dependable boat-owner here in Dabour whom I could hire."

Arasham blinked at him vaguely. "A boat?" he mumbled.

A faint movement caught Sparhawk's eye, and he saw

Sephrenia move her arm as if only shaking back her sleeve. Instantly he knew what she had been doing all along.

"Hire, my son?" Arasham beamed at him. "Let there be no talk of hiring. I have a splendid boat at my disposal. You will take it, and with my blessing. I will send armed men with you and a regiment—no, a legion—to patrol the banks of the river to make sure you reach Jiroch safely."

"It shall be as you command, Most Holy," Sparhawk said. He looked across the tent at Martel with a beatific smile. "Is it not amazing, dear brother," he said. "Truly such wisdom and generosity can only come from God."

"Yes," Martel replied darkly, "I'm sure of it."

"I must make haste, holy Arasham," Sparhawk rushed on, rising to his feet. "We left our horses and belongings in the care of a servant in a house on the outskirts of town. My sister and I will retrieve them at once and return within the hour."

"As you see fit, my son," Arasham said eagerly, "and I will instruct my disciples to have the boat and the soldiers made ready for your journey downriver."

"Let me show you the way out of the compound, dear brother," Martel said from between clenched teeth.

"Gladly, dear brother," Sparhawk said. "Your company, as always, fills my heart with joy."

"Return directly, Martel," Arasham instructed. "We must discuss this wondrous turn of fortune and offer thanks to God for His grace in providing it."

"Yes, Most Holy," Martel said, bowing. "I shall come back immediately."

"Within the hour, Sparhawk," Arasham said.

"Within the hour, Most Holy," Sparhawk agreed with a deep bow. "Come along then, Martel," he said, once again smacking his hand down on the renegade's shoulder.

"Of course." Martel winced, once again shrinking from Sparhawk's comradely blow.

Once they were outside the pavilion, Martel turned on Sparhawk, his face white with fury. "Just what do you think you're doing?" he demanded.

"Testy today, aren't we, old boy?" Sparhawk said mildly.

"What are you up to, Sparhawk?" Martel snarled,

looking around to be sure that no one in the crowd of hovering disciples could hear him.

"I just spiked your wheel, Martel," Sparhawk replied. "Arasham will sit here until he petrifies unless someone brings him that secret word. I can almost guarantee you that the Church Knights will be in Chyrellos when the time comes to elect the new archprelate, because there won't be anything going on in Rendor to drag them away."

"Very clever, Sparhawk."

"I'm glad you liked it."

"This is one more debt you owe me," Martel grated.

"Feel free to call them in at any time, dear brother," Sparhawk said. "I'll be more than happy to accommodate you." He took Sephrenia by the elbow and led her away.

"Are you completely out of your senses, Sparhawk?" she demanded once they were out of earshot of the fuming Martel.

"I don't think so," he replied. "Of course crazy people never really know, do they?"

"What were you *doing* in there? Do you realize how many times I had to step in to keep you out of trouble?"

"I noticed that. I couldn't have pulled it off without you."

"Will you stop smirking and tell me what was behind all that?"

"Martel was getting too close to our real reason for being here," he explained. "I had to throw something else in his path to keep him from realizing that we'd unearthed a possible antidote for the poison. It all worked out rather well, even if I do say so myself."

"If you knew you were going to do that before you went into the tent, why didn't you tell me?"

"How could I have known, Sephrenia? I didn't even know Martel was there until I saw him."

"You mean . . ." Her eyes went suddenly very wide.

He nodded. "I sort of made it up as I went along," he confessed.

"Oh, Sparhawk," she said disgustedly, "you know better than that."

He shrugged. "It was about the best I could do on short notice."

"Why did you keep hitting Martel on the shoulder like that?"

"He broke that shoulder when he was about fifteen. It's always been very sensitive."

"That was cruel," she accused.

"So was what happened in that alley back in Cippria ten years ago. Let's go get Kurik and Flute. I think we've done about all we can here in Dabour."

ARASHAM'S BOAT WAS more like a barge than the scow which had carried them upriver and it was perhaps four times as large. Banks of oarsmen lined each side, and black-robed zealots with swords and javelins clustered in the torchlit bow and stern. Martel had preceded them to the rickety dock and he stood alone there, some distance from the hot-eyed disciples on shore, as Sparhawk, Sephrenia, Kurik, and Flute embarked. The renegade's white hair gleamed in the starlight, and his face was very nearly as pale.

"You're not going to get away with this, Sparhawk," he said in a low voice.

"Oh?" Sparhawk said. "I think you'd better look again, Martel. It seems to me that I already did. You can try to follow me, of course, but all those troops patrolling the river banks are probably going to get in your way. Besides, I think that once you get over your pique, you'll realize that about the only thing you can do is stay here and try to wheedle that magic word out of Arasham. Everything you've set up here in Rendor will be at a standstill until you do."

"You'll pay for this, Sparhawk," Martel promised darkly.

"I thought I already had, old boy," Sparhawk replied, "in Cippria, I believe it was." He reached out, and Martel jerked his shoulder out of range. Instead, however, Sparhawk patted him on the cheek insultingly. "Take care of yourself, Martel," he said. "I want to see you again—soon—and I want you to be well and in full possession of your faculties. Believe me, you're going to need them." Then he turned and went up the gangway to the waiting barge.

The sailors cast off all lines and pushed the barge out into the slowly moving current. Then they ran out their oars and began to row slowly downriver. The dock behind them and the solitary man standing on the end of it shrank out of sight.

"Oh, God!" Sparhawk cried exultantly, "I loved that!"

The run downriver took them a day and a half, and they disembarked a league or so upstream from Jiroch to avoid any watchers Martel might have managed to get to the docks ahead of them. The precaution was probably unnecessary, Sparhawk admitted, but there was no point in taking chances. They entered the city through the west gate and mingled with the crowds as they made their way to Voren's house again. It was late afternoon when they entered.

Voren was a trifle surprised at their reappearance. "That was quick," he said as they entered his garden.

"We were lucky," Sparhawk shrugged.

"More than lucky," Sephrenia said darkly. The small woman's temper had not noticeably improved since they had left Dabour, and she still refused even to talk to Sparhawk.

"Did something go wrong?" Voren asked mildly.

"Not that *I* noticed," Sparhawk replied blithely.

"Stop congratulating yourself, Sparhawk," she snapped. "I'm vexed with you, very vexed."

"I'm sorry about that, Sephrenia, but I did the best I could." He turned to Voren. "We ran into Martel," he explained, "and I managed to stop him in his tracks. His whole scheme just collapsed around his ears."

Voren whistled. " I don't see anything wrong with that, Sephrenia."

"It's not what he did, Voren. It was the way he did it."

"Oh?"

"I don't want to talk about it." She gathered Flute up in her arms, went to the bench by the fountain, and sat muttering darkly to the little girl in Styric.

"We need a way to get aboard a fast ship bound for Vardenais without being seen," Sparhawk told Voren. "Can you come up with something?"

"Quite easily," Voren replied. "Every so often the true

identity of one of our brothers is exposed. We've devised a way to get them out of Rendor safely." He smiled ironically. "It was the first thing I did when I got to Jiroch, actually. I was fairly sure I was going to need it for myself almost immediately. I have a wharf down in the harbor. There's a waterfront inn not far away. It's run by one of our brothers, and it has all the things an inn usually has—taproom, stables, sleeping rooms upstairs, and the like. It's also got a cellar, and there's a passageway running from that one to the cellar of my main warehouse. At low tide you can board a ship directly from that cellar without being seen by anyone on shore."

"Would that fool the Damork, Sephrenia?" Sparhawk asked her.

She glared at him for a moment, then relented. She touched the fingertips of one hand lightly to her temple. Sparhawk noted that there was more silver there now. "I think it would," she replied. "We don't even know that the Damork is here. Martel could actually have been telling us the truth."

"I wouldn't count on it," Kurik grunted.

"Even so," she continued, "the Damork probably couldn't begin to grasp the concept of a cellar—much less underground passageways."

"What's a Damork?" Voren asked.

Sparhawk told him and described what had happened to Captain Mabin's ship in the Arcian Straits just out from Madel.

Voren rose and began to pace up and down. "That's not the sort of thing our escape route was designed to cope with," he admitted. "I think I'd better take some additional precautions. I've got six ships in port just now. Why don't I just send them all out at the same time? If you sail out in the middle of a flotilla, it might add a bit more confusion."

"Isn't that a bit elaborate?" Sparhawk asked him.

"Sparhawk, I know how modest you are, but you're probably the most important man in the world just now—at least you are until you get to Cimmura and make your report to Vanion. I'm not going to take any chances with you if I can help it." He went to the garden wall and squinted at the setting sun. "We're going to have to hurry," he told them. "Low tide this evening comes just after dusk, and I'll want you in the cellar when the ship's rail drops below the edge of the wharf. I'll go with you to make sure you get on board safely."

They all rode out together toward the waterfront. Their route took them through the familiar quarter where Sparhawk had maintained his shop during the years he had been hidden here. The buildings on either side of the streets were almost like old friends, and he thought he recognized a few of the people hurrying home through the narrow streets as the sun sank toward the western horizon.

"Brute!" The voice from behind them probably carried halfway across the Arcian Straits, and it was painfully familiar. "Assassin!"

"Oh, no!" Sparhawk groaned, reining Faran in. "And we were so close." He looked longingly at the waterfront inn to which Voren was leading them and which was but one street away.

"Monster!" the voice went on in a strident tone.

"Uh—Sparhawk," Kurik said mildly, "is it my imagination, or is that lady trying to get your attention?"

"Just let it lie, Kurik."

"Anything you say, my Lord."

"Assassin! Brute! Monster! Deserter!"

There was a brief pause. "Murderer!" the woman added.

"I never did that," Sparhawk murmured. He sighed and turned Faran around. "Hello, Lillias," he said to the robed and veiled woman who had been shouting at him. He spoke in as mild and inoffensive a tone as he could manage.

"Hello, Lillias?" she shrieked. "*Hello, Lillias!* Is that all you have to say for yourself, brigand?"

Sparhawk tried very hard not to smile. In a peculiar way, he loved Lillias and he was pleased to see her enjoying herself so much. "You're looking well, Lillias," he said conversationally, knowing that a comment like that would spur her to new heights.

"Well? *Well?* When you have murdered me? When you have cut my heart out? When you have sunk me in the mire of deepest despair?'' She leaned back in a tragic posture, head up and arms thrown wide. ''Hardly a morsel of food has passed my lips since that hateful day when you abandoned me penniless in the gutter.''

''I left you the shop, Lillias,'' he protested. ''It fed us both before I left. Surely it still feeds you.''

''Shop! What do I care about the shop? It is my heart that you have broken, Mahkra!'' She thrust back her hood and ripped off her veil. ''Assassin!'' she cried. ''Look at your handiwork!'' She began to tear at her long, glossy black hair and to gouge at her dark, full-lipped face with her fingernails.

''Lillias!'' Sparhawk barked in the tone he had only had to use a few times during their years together. ''Stop that! You'll hurt yourself.''

But Lillias was in full voice now, and there was no stopping her. ''Hurt?'' she cried tragically. ''What do I care about hurt? How can you hurt a dead woman? You want to see hurt, Mahkra? Look at my heart!'' She ripped open the front of her robe. It was not her heart, however, that she revealed.

''Oh, my goodness,'' Kurik said in an awed voice, staring at the woman's suddenly revealed attributes. Voren turned his head aside, concealing a smile. Sephrenia, however, looked at Sparhawk with a slightly different expression.

''Oh, God,'' Sparhawk groaned. He swung down from his saddle. ''Lillias!'' he muttered sharply to her, ''cover yourself! Think of the neighbors—and all the children watching.''

''What do I care about the neighbors? Let them look!'' She thrust out her full breasts. ''What does shame mean to a woman whose heart is dead?''

Grimly, Sparhawk advanced on her. When he got close enough, he spoke quietly to her from between clenched teeth. ''They're very nice, Lillias,'' he said, ''but I don't really think they're much of a surprise to any man within six streets in any direction. Do you really want to go on with this?''

She suddenly looked a little less certain, but she did not close the front of her robe.

"Have it your way," he shrugged. Then he, too, raised his voice. "Your heart is not dead, Lillias," he declared to the audience breathlessly clustered on the second floor balconies. "Far from it, I think. What of Georgias the baker? And Nendan the sausage maker?" He was selecting names at random.

Her face blanched, and she shrank back, covering her generous bosom with her robe. "You know?" she faltered.

That hurt him just a little, but he covered it. "Of course," he declared, still playing to the balconies, "but I forgive you. You are much woman, Lillias, and not meant to be alone." He reached out and gently covered her hair with her hood again. "Have you been well?" he asked her very softly.

"I get by," she whispered.

"Good. Are we almost done?"

"I think we need something to round it out, don't you?" Her face looked hopeful.

He tried very hard to keep from laughing.

"This is serious, Mahkra," she hissed. "My position in the community depends on it."

"Trust me," he murmured. "You have betrayed me, Lillias," he said to the balconies, "but I forgive you, for I have not been here to keep you from straying."

She considered that for a moment, then sobbed, fell into his arms, and buried her face in his chest. "It's just that I missed you so much, my Mahkra. I weakened. I am but a poor, ignorant woman—a slave to my passions. Can you ever truly forgive me?"

"What is there to forgive, my Lillias?" he said grandly. "You are like the earth, like the sea. To give is a part of your nature."

She thrust herself back from him. "Beat me!" she demanded. "I deserve to be beaten!" Huge tears, genuine for all he knew, stood in her glowing black eyes.

"Oh, no," he refused, knowing exactly where *that* would lead. "No beatings, Lillias," he said. "Only this," and he gave her a single chaste kiss full on the lips. "Be well, Lillias," he murmured softly. Then he stepped back quickly before she could wrap her arms about his neck.

He knew just how strong her arms were. "And now, though it rends my soul, I must leave you again," he declaimed. He reached out and drew her veil once again across her face. "Think of me from time to time whilst I seek out the fate that destiny has in store for me." He did manage to resist the impulse to lay his hand on his heart.

"I knew it!" she cried, more to the onlookers than to him. "I knew that you were a man of affairs! I shall carry our love in my heart for all eternity, my Mahkra, and I shall remain faithful to you to the grave. And if you live, come back to me." She had both arms spread wide again. "And if you do not, send your ghost to me in my dreams, and I will comfort your pale shade as best I can."

He backed away from her outstretched arms. Then he spun so that his robe would swirl dramatically—he owed her that much—and vaulted into Faran's saddle. "Farewell, my Lillias," he said melodramatically, jerking the reins to make Faran rear and paw the air with his front hooves. "And if we do not meet again in this world, may God grant that we meet once more in the next." And he drove his heels into Faran's flanks and charged past her at a gallop.

"Did you do all that on purpose?" Sephrenia asked as they dismounted in the courtyard of the waterfront inn.

"I might have gotten a little carried away," Sparhawk admitted. "Lillias does that to a man from time to time." He smiled a bit ruefully. "She gets her heart broken on an average of three times a week," he noted clinically. "She was always militantly unfaithful and just a little dishonest where the cashbox was concerned. She's vain and vulgar and self-indulgent. She's deceptive and greedy and grossly overdramatic." He paused then, thinking back over the years. "I liked her, though. She's a good girl, despite her faults, and living with her was never dull. I owed her that performance. She'll be able to walk through the quarter like a queen now, and it didn't really cost me all that much, did it?"

"Sparhawk," she said gravely, "I will never understand you."

"That's what makes it all so much fun, isn't it, little mother?" He grinned at her.

Flute, still sitting on Sephrenia's white horse, blew a mocking little trill on her pipes.

"Talk with her," Sparhawk suggested to Sephrenia. "She understands."

Flute rolled her eyes at him, then generously held out her hands to permit him to help her down.

CHAPTER
TWENTY-FOUR

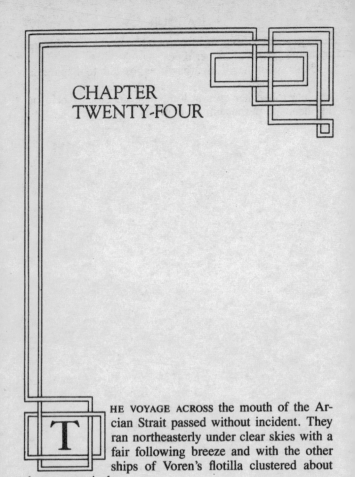

T HE VOYAGE ACROSS the mouth of the Arcian Strait passed without incident. They ran northeasterly under clear skies with a fair following breeze and with the other ships of Voren's flotilla clustered about them protectively.

About noon on the third day out, Sparhawk came up on deck to join Sephrenia in the bow where she and Flute stood looking out over the sparkling waves. "Are you still cross with me?" he asked her.

She sighed. "No. I suppose not."

Sparhawk was not entirely certain how to put his vague sense of unease into words, so he approached it obliquely. "Sephrenia," he said, "did it seem to you that everything in Dabour went just a little too smoothly? I somehow get the feeling that I'm being led around by the nose again.''

"How do you mean, exactly?''

"I know you tampered with Arasham a few times that night, but did you do anything to Martel?''

"No. He'd have felt it if I'd tried and he'd have countered me.''

"That's what I thought. What was wrong with him, then?''

"I'm not sure I follow you.''

"He acted almost like a schoolboy. We both know Martel. He's intelligent and he thinks very fast on his feet. What I did was so obvious that he should have seen through it almost immediately, but he didn't do a thing. He just stood there like an idiot and let me pull his whole scheme down around his ears. It was just too easy, and that worries me.''

"He didn't really expect to see us in Arasham's tent, Sparhawk. Maybe the surprise threw him off balance.''

"Martel doesn't surprise all that easily.''

She frowned. "No,'' she admitted, "he doesn't, does he?'' She thought about it. "Do you remember what Lord Darellon was saying before we left Cimmura?''

"Not exactly, no.''

"He said that Annias behaved like a simpleton when he presented his case to the Elene kings. He announced the death of Count Radun without even verifying the fact that the count had really died.''

"Oh, yes, now I remember. And you said that the whole scheme—the attempt to murder the count and to lay the blame on the Pandions—might have originated with a Styric magician.''

"Perhaps it goes a little farther than that. We know that Martel has had contacts with a Damork, and that means that Azash is involved somehow. Azash has always dealt with Styrics, so he's had very little experience with the subtleties of the Elene mind. The Gods of Styricum are very direct and they seldom prepare for contingencies— probably because of the Styric lack of sophistication. Now, the whole purpose of the plot in Arcium and the one in Rendor has been to keep the Church Knights out of Chyrellos during the election. Annias behaved the way a Styric would have in the palace at Cimmura, and Martel behaved the same way in Arasham's tent.''

"You're a little inconsistent, Sephrenia," he objected. "First you try to tell me that Styrics are unsophisticated, then you come up with an explanation so complicated that I can't even follow it. Why don't you just say what you mean?"

"Azash has always dominated the minds of his followers," she replied, "and for the most part, they've been Styrics. If Annias and Martel both start behaving like Styrics, it raises some very interesting possibilities, wouldn't you say?"

"I'm sorry, Sephrenia, but I can't accept that. Whatever other faults he may have, Martel's still an Elene; and Annias is a churchman. Neither one of them would give his soul to Azash."

"Not consciously, perhaps, but Azash has ways to subvert the minds of people he finds useful."

"Where does all this lead?"

"I'm not entirely sure, but it seems that Azash has some reason to want Annias to be the new archprelate. It's something we might want to keep in mind. If Azash is controlling Annias and Martel, they're both going to be thinking like Styrics, and Styrics don't react very fast when they're surprised. It's a racial trait. Surprise could be our best weapon."

"Was that why you were so angry with me—because I surprised you?"

"Of course. I thought you knew that."

"Next time, I'll try to warn you."

"I'd appreciate that."

Two days later their ship entered the estuary of the River Ucera and sailed up toward the Elenian port city of Vardenais. As they approached the wharves, however, Sparhawk saw trouble. Men in red tunics were patrolling the waterfront.

"Now what?" Kurik asked as the two of them crouched behind a low deckhouse to keep out of sight.

Sparhawk frowned. "I suppose we could sail across the bay and go inland on the Arcian side."

"If they're watching the seaports, they're bound to be patrolling the border as well. Use your head, Sparhawk."

"Maybe we could slip across at night."

"Isn't what we're doing a little too important to hang it all on a *maybe*?" Kurik asked pointedly.

Sparhawk started to swear. "We've *got* to get to Cimmura," he said. "It's getting close to the time when another of the twelve knights is going to die, and I don't know how much more of the weight Sephrenia can carry. Think, Kurik. You're always better at tactics than I am."

"That's because I don't wear armor. The sense of invincibility does funny things to a man's brains."

"Thanks," Sparhawk said drily.

Kurik knit his brows in thought.

"Well?" Sparhawk said impatiently.

"I'm working on it. Don't rush me."

"We're getting closer to that wharf, Kurik."

"I can see that. Can you tell if they're searching any of the ships?"

Sparhawk raised his head and peered over the top of the deckhouse. "They don't seem to be."

"Good. That means we won't have to make any spur-of-the-moment decisions. We can go below and work this out."

"Any ideas at all?"

"You're pushing, Sparhawk," Kurik said disapprovingly. "That's one of your failings, you know. You always want to dash into the middle of things before you've thought your way completely through what you're going to do."

Their ship hove to beside a tar-smeared wharf, and the sailors cast lines to the longshoremen clustered there. Then they ran out the gangway and began to carry boxes and bales down to the wharf.

There was a clattering sound from the hold, and Faran trotted up on deck. Sparhawk stared at his war horse in amazement. Flute sat cross-legged on the big roan's broad back playing her pipes. The melody she played was a peculiarly drowsy one, almost like a lullaby. Before Sparhawk and Kurik could run to intercept her, she tapped

Faran's back with the side of her foot, and he placidly walked down the gangway to the wharf.

"What is she *doing*?" Kurik exclaimed.

"I can't even begin to guess. Go get Sephrenia—fast!"

On the wharf, Flute rode directly toward the squad of church soldiers stationed at the far end. The soldiers had been closely examining every disembarking passenger and sailor, but they paid no attention to Flute and the roan horse. She impudently rode back and forth in front of them several times, then turned. She seemed to be looking directly at Sparhawk and, still playing her pipes, she raised one little hand and motioned to him.

He stared at her.

She made a little face and then quite deliberately rode directly through the soldiers' ranks. They absently stepped aside for her, but not one of them so much as looked at her.

"What's going on down there?" he demanded as Sephrenia and Kurik joined him behind the deckhouse.

"I'm not altogether sure," Sephrenia replied, frowning.

"Why aren't the soldiers paying any attention to her?" Kurik asked as Flute rode through the ranks of red tunics once again.

"I don't think they can see her."

"But she's right there in front of them."

"That doesn't seem to matter." Her face slowly took on an expression of wonder. "I'd heard about this," she murmured. "I thought it was just an old folktale, but perhaps I was wrong." She turned to Sparhawk. "Has she looked back at the ship at all since she rode down onto that wharf?"

"She sort of motioned to me to follow her," he said.

"You're sure?"

"That's the way it looked to me."

She drew in a deep breath. "Well," she said, "there's one way to find out, I suppose." Before Sparhawk could stop her, she rose and walked out from behind the deckhouse.

"Sephrenia!" he called after her, but she continued on across the deck as if she had not heard him. She reached the rail and stood there.

"She's right out in plain sight," Kurik said in a strangled tone.

"I can see that."

"The soldiers are certain to have a description of her. Has she gone out of her mind?"

"I doubt it. Look." Sparhawk pointed toward the soldiers on the wharf. Although Sephrenia was standing in plain view, they did not even appear to look at her.

Flute, however, saw her and made another of those imperious little gestures.

Sephenia sighed and looked at Sparhawk. "Wait here," she said.

"Wait where?"

"Here—on board ship." She turned, walked to the gangway, and went on down to the wharf.

"That rips it," Sparhawk said bleakly, rising to his feet and drawing his sword. Quickly he counted the soldiers on the wharf. "There aren't that many of them," he said to Kurik. "If we can take them by surprise, there might be a chance."

"Not a very good one, Sparhawk. Let's wait a moment and see what happens."

Sephrenia walked up the wharf and stopped directly in front of the soldiers.

They ignored her.

She spoke to them.

They paid no attention.

Then she turned back toward the ship. "It's all right, Sparhawk," she called. "They can't see us—or hear us. Bring the other horses and our things."

"Magic?" Kurik asked in a stunned voice.

"Not any kind that I ever heard about," Sparhawk replied.

"I guess we'd better do what she says, then," Kurik advised, "and sort of immediately. I'd hate to be right in the middle of those soldiers when the spell wears off."

It was eerie to walk down the gangway in plain view of the church soldiers and to saunter casually up the wharf until they were face to face with them. The soldiers' expressions were bored, and they gave no indication that anything at all was amiss. They routinely stopped every sailor and passenger leaving the wharf, but paid no attention whatsoever to Sparhawk, Kurik, and the horses. The soldiers stepped out of the way with no command from their corporal and immediately closed ranks again once Sparhawk and Kurik had led the horses off the wharf and onto the cobblestones of the street.

Without a word, Sparhawk lifted Flute down from Faran's back and saddled the big roan. "All right," he said to Sephrenia when he had finished, "how did she do it?"

"The usual way."

"But she can't talk—or at least she doesn't. How did she cast the spell?"

"With her pipes, Sparhawk. I thought you knew that. She doesn't speak the spell, she plays it on her pipes."

"Is that possible?" His tone was incredulous.

"You just saw her do it."

"Could you do it that way?"

She shook her head. "I'm just a bit tone deaf, Sparhawk," she confessed. "I can't really tell one note from another, except in a general sort of way, and the melody has to be very precise. Shall we go, then?"

They rode up through the streets of Vardenais from the harbor.

"Are we still invisible?" Kurik asked.

"We're not actually invisible, Kurik," Sephrenia replied, wrapping her cloak about Flute, who still played the drowsy tune on her pipes. "If we were, we wouldn't be able to see each other."

"I don't understand at all."

"The soldiers knew we were there, Kurik. They stepped out of the way for us, remember? They just chose not to pay any attention to us."

"Chose?"

"Perhaps that was the wrong word. Let's say they were encouraged not to."

They rode out through the north gate of Vardenais without being stopped by the guards posted there and were soon on the high road to Cimmura. The weather had changed since they had left Elenia many weeks before. The chill of winter had gone now, and the first budding leaves of spring tipped the branches of the trees at the

sides of the road. Peasants plodded across their fields behind their plows, turning over the rich black loam. The
rains had passed, and the sky was bright blue, dotted here
and there with puffy white clouds. The breeze was fresh
and warm, and the earth smelled of growth and renewal.
They had discarded their Rendorish robes before leaving
the ship, but Sparhawk still found his mail coat and padded tunic uncomfortably warm.

Kurik was looking out at the freshly plowed fields they
passed with an appraising eye. "I hope the boys have finished with the plowing at home," he said. "I'd hate to
have that chore in front of me when I get back."

"Aslade will see to it that they get it done," Sparhawk
assured him.

"You're probably right." Kurik made a wry face.
"When you get right down to it, she's a better farmer than
I am."

"Women always are," Sephrenia told him. "They're
more in tune with the moon and the seasons. In Styricum,
women always manage the fields."

"What do the men do?"

"As little as possible."

It took them nearly five days to reach Cimmura, and
they arrived on an early spring afternoon. Sparhawk reined
in atop a hill a mile or so west of town. "Can she do it
again?" he asked Sephrenia.

"Can who do what again?"

"Flute. Can she make people ignore us again?"

"I don't know. Why don't you ask her?"

"Why don't *you* ask her? I don't think she likes me."

"Whatever gave you that idea? She adores you." Sephrenia leaned forward slightly and spoke in Styric to the
little girl who rested against her.

Flute nodded and made an obscure kind of circling gesture with one hand.

"What did she say?" Sparhawk asked.

"Approximately that the chapterhouse is on the other
side of Cimmura. She suggests that we circle the city rather
than ride through the streets."

"Approximately?"

"It loses a great deal in translation."

"All right. We'll do it her way, then. I definitely don't want Annias to find out that we're back in Cimmura."

They rode on around the city, passing through open fields and sparse woodlands and keeping about a mile back from the city wall. Cimmura was not an attractive city, Sparhawk decided. The peculiar combination of its location and the prevailing weather seemed to capture the smoke from its thousands of chimneys and to hold it in a continual pall just above the rooftops. That lowering cloud of smoke made the place look perpetually grimy.

They finally reached a thicket about a half mile from the walls of the chapterhouse. Once again the land was dotted with peasants at work, and the road leading out from the east gate was alive with brightly dressed travellers.

"Tell her it's time," Sparhawk said to Sephrenia. "I'd imagine that a fair number of those people out there are working for Annias."

"She knows, Sparhawk. She's not stupid."

"No. Only a little flighty."

Flute made a face at him and began to play her pipes. It was that same lethargic, almost drowsy tune she had played in Vardenais.

They started across the field toward the few houses clustered outside the chapterhouse. Though he was certain that the people they passed would pay no attention to them, Sparhawk instinctively tensed at each encounter.

"Relax, Sparhawk," Sephrenia ordered him crisply. "You're making it harder for her."

"Sorry," he mumbled. "Habit, I guess." With some effort he pulled a kind of calm about himself.

A number of workmen were repairing the road that led up to the gates of the fortress.

"Spies," Kurik grunted.

"How do you know that?" Sparhawk asked.

"Look at the way they're laying the cobblestones, Sparhawk. They haven't got the faintest idea of what they're doing."

"It does look a bit slipshod, doesn't it?" Sparhawk agreed, looking critically at the section of newly laid stone as they rode past the unseeing road gang.

"Annias must be getting old," Kurik said. "He never used to be this obvious."

"He's got a lot on his mind, I guess."

They clattered up the road to the drawbridge and then on across it and into the courtyard, passing the indifferent quartet of armored knights on guard at the gate.

A young novice was drawing water from the well in the center of the courtyard, laboriously winding the creaking windlass mounted at the well mouth. With a final little flourish, Flute took her pipes from her lips.

The novice choked out a startled oath and reached for his sword. The windlass squealed as the bucket plummeted down again.

"Easy, brother," Sparhawk told him, dismounting.

"How did you get past the gate?" the novice exclaimed.

"You wouldn't believe it," Kurik told him, swinging down from his gelding's back.

"Forgive me, Sir Sparhawk," the novice stammered. "You startled me."

"It's all right," Sparhawk assured him. "Did Kalten get back yet?"

"Yes, my Lord. He and the knights from the other orders arrived some time back."

"Good. Do you know where I might find them?"

"I believe they're with Lord Vanion in his study."

"Thank you. Would you see to our horses?"

"Of course, Sir Sparhawk."

They entered the chapterhouse and went down the central corridor toward the south end of the building. Then they climbed the narrow flight of stairs to the tower.

"Sir Sparhawk," one of the young knights on guard at the top said respectfully, "I'll advise Lord Vanion that you've arrived."

"Thank you, brother," Sparhawk said.

The knight tapped on the door, then opened it. "Sir Sparhawk is here, my Lord," he reported to Vanion.

"It's about time," Sparhawk heard Kalten's voice inside the room.

"Please go in, Sir Sparhawk," the young knight said, stepping aside and bowing.

Vanion sat at the table. Kalten, Bevier, Ulath, and Tynian had risen from their seats and come forward to greet Sparhawk and the others. Berit and Talen sat on a bench in the corner.

"When did you get in?" Sparhawk asked as Kalten roughly clasped his hand.

"Early last week," the blond man replied. "What kept you?"

"We had a long way to go, Kalten," Sparhawk protested. Wordlessly he gripped the hands of Tynian, Ulath, and Bevier. Then he bowed to Vanion. "My Lord," he said.

"Sparhawk," Vanion nodded.

"Did you get my messages?"

"If there were only two, I did."

"Good. Then you're fairly well up-to-date on what's going on down there."

Vanion, however, was looking closely at Sephrenia. "You're not looking too well, little mother," he said.

"I'll be all right," she said, passing one hand wearily across her eyes.

"Sit down," Kalten said, holding a chair for her.

"Thank you."

"What happened in Dabour, Sparhawk?" Vanion asked, his eyes intent.

"We found that physician," Sparhawk reported. "As it turns out, he *did* in fact cure some people who'd been poisoned with the same thing Annias gave the queen."

"Thank God!" Vanion said, letting his breath out explosively.

"Don't be too quick about that, Vanion," Sephrenia told him. "We know what the cure is, but we've got to find it before we can use it."

"I don't quite follow you."

"The poison is extremely potent. The only way to counteract it is through the use of magic."

"Did the physician give you the spell he used?"

"Apparently there's no spell involved. There are a number of objects in the world that have enormous power. We have to find one of them."

He frowned. "That could take time," he said. "People usually hide those things to keep them from being stolen."

"I know."

"Are you absolutely certain you've identified the right poison?" Kalten asked Sparhawk.

Sparhawk nodded. "I got confirmation from Martel," he said.

"Martel? You actually gave him time to talk before you killed him?"

"I didn't kill him. The time wasn't right."

"Any time is right for that, Sparhawk."

"I felt that way myself when I first saw him, but Sephrenia persuaded the two of us to put away our swords."

"I'm terribly disappointed in you, Sephrenia," Kalten said.

"You almost had to have been there to understand," she replied.

"Why didn't you just get whatever it was the physician used to cure those other people?" Tynian asked Sparhawk.

"Because he ground it to a powder, mixed it with wine, and had them drink it."

"Is that the way it's supposed to be done?"

"No, as a matter of fact, it's not. Sephrenia spoke to him rather sharply about that."

"I think you'd better start at the beginning," Vanion said.

"Right," Sparhawk agreed, taking a chair. Briefly he told them about Arasham's "holy talisman" and about the ploy that had gotten them into the old man's tent.

"You were being awfully free with the name of my king, Sparhawk," Tynian objected.

"We don't necessarily need to tell him about it, do we?" Sparhawk replied. "I needed to use the name of a kingdom a long way from Rendor. Arasham probably has only the vaguest idea of where Deira is."

"Why didn't you say you were from Thalesia, then?"

"I doubt if Arasham's ever heard of Thalesia. Anyway, the 'holy talisman' turned out to be a fake. Martel was there and he was trying to persuade the old lunatic to postpone his uprising until the time of the election of the new archprelate." He went on to describe the means by which he had overturned the white-haired man's scheme.

"My friend," Kalten said admiringly, "I'm proud of you."

"Thank you, Kalten," Sparhawk said modestly. "It did turn out rather well, I thought."

"He's been patting himself on the back ever since we came out of Arasham's tent," Sephrenia said. She looked at Vanion. "Kerris died," she told him sadly.

Vanion nodded, his face somber. "I know," he said. "How did you find out?"

"His ghost came to us to deliver his sword to Sephrenia," Sparhawk told him. "Vanion, we're going to have to do something about that. She can't go on carrying all those swords and everything they symbolize. She gets weaker every time somebody gives her another one."

"I'm all right, Sparhawk," she insisted.

"I hate to contradict you, little mother, but you're definitely *not* all right. It's all you can do right now to hold up your head. About two more of those swords is all it's going to take to put you on your knees."

"Where are the swords now?" Vanion asked.

"We brought a mule with us," Kurik replied. "They're in a box in his pack."

"Would you get them for me, please?"

"Right away," Kurik said, going to the door.

"What have you got in mind, Vanion?" Sephrenia asked suspiciously.

"I'm going to take the swords." He shrugged. "And everything that goes with them."

"You can't."

"Oh, yes, I can, Sephrenia. I was in the throne room, too, and I know which spell to use. You don't have to be the one who has to carry them. Any one of us who was there can do it."

"You're not strong enough, Vanion."

"When you get down to it, I could carry you and everything you've got in your arms, my teacher, and right now you're more important than I am."

"But—" she started.

He held up his hand. "The discussion is ended, Sephrenia. I am the preceptor. With or without your permission, I'm taking those swords away from you."

"You don't know what it means, my dearest one. I won't let you." Her face was suddenly wet with tears, and she wrung her hands in an uncharacteristic display of human emotion. "I won't let you."

"You can't stop me," he said in a gentle voice. "I can cast the spell without your help, if I have to. If you want to keep your spells a secret, little mother, you shouldn't chant them out loud, you know. You should know by now that I've got a very retentive memory."

She stared at him. "I'm shocked at you, Vanion," she declared. "You were not so unkind when you were young."

"Life is filled with these little disappointments, isn't it?" he said urbanely.

"I can stop you," she cried, still wringing her hands. "You forget just how much stronger I am than you are." There was a shrill triumph in her voice.

"Of course you are. That's why I'd have to call in help. Could you deal with ten knights all chanting in unison? Or fifty? Or half a thousand?"

"That's unfair!" she exclaimed. "I did not know that you would go this far, Vanion—and I trusted you."

"And well you should, dear one," he said, assuming suddenly the superior rôle, "for I will not permit you to make this sacrifice. I'll force you to submit to me, because you know I'm right. You'll release the burden to me, because you know that what you have to do is more important than anything else right now, and you'll sacrifice anything to do what we both know must be done."

"Dear one," she began in an agonized voice. "My dearest one—"

"As I said," he cut her off, "the discussion is ended."

There was a long and awkward silence as Sephrenia and Vanion stood with their eyes locked on each others' faces.

"Did the physician in Dabour give you any hints about which objects might cure the queen?" Bevier asked Sparhawk a bit uneasily.

"He mentioned a spear in Daresia, several rings in Zemoch, a bracelet somewhere in Pelosia, and a jewel on the royal crown of Thalesia."

Ulath grunted. "The Bhelliom."

"That solves it, then," Kalten said. "We go to Thalesia, borrow Wargun's crown, and come back here with it."

"Wargun doesn't have it," Ulath told him.

"What do you mean, Wargun doesn't have it? He's the king of Thalesia, isn't he?"

"That crown was lost five hundred years ago."

"Could we possibly find it?"

"Almost anything is possible, I suppose," the big Thalesian replied, "but people have been looking for it for five hundred years without much success. Do we have that kind of time?"

"What is this Bhelliom?" Tynian asked him.

"The legends say that it's a very large sapphire carved in the shape of a rose. It's supposed to have the power of the Troll-Gods in it."

"Does it?"

"I wouldn't know. I've never seen it. It's lost, remember?"

"There are bound to be other objects," Sephrenia declared. "We live in a world with magic all around us. In all of the eons since the beginning of time, I'd imagine that the Gods have seen fit to create any number of things with the kind of power we're looking for."

"Why not just make one?" Kalten asked. "Get a group of people together and have them cast a spell on something—some jewel or stone or ring or whatever?"

"Now I can see why you never became proficient in the secrets, Kalten." Sephrenia sighed. "You don't even understand the basic principles. All magic comes from the Gods, not from us. They allow us to borrow—if we ask them in the proper fashion—but they *won't* let us make the kind of thing we're looking for in this case. The power that's instilled in those objects is a part of the power of the Gods themselves, and they don't sacrifice that sort of thing lightly."

"Oh," the blond man said. "I didn't know that."

"You should have. I told you about it when you were fifteen."

"I must have forgotten."

"About all we can do is start looking," Vanion said.

"I'll send word to the other preceptors. We'll have every Church Knight in all four orders working on it."

"And I'll get word to the Styrics in the mountains," Sephrenia added. "There are many such things known only to Styricum."

"Did anything interesting happen in Madel?" Sparhawk asked Kalten.

"Not really," Kalten replied. "We caught a few glimpses of Krager, but always from a distance. By the time we got close to where he'd been, he'd given us the slip. He's a tricky little weasel, isn't he?"

Sparhawk nodded. "That's what made me finally realize that he was being used as bait. Could you get any idea of what he was doing?"

"No. We could never get close enough. He was up to something, though. He was scurrying around Madel like a mouse in a cheese factory."

"Did Adus drop out of sight?"

"More or less. Talen and Berit saw him once—when he and Krager rode out of town."

"Which way were they going?" Sparhawk asked the boy.

Talen shrugged. "They were headed back toward Borrata the last time we saw them," he said. "They might have changed direction once they got out of sight, though."

"The big one had some bandages on his head, Sir Sparhawk," Berit reported, "and his arm was in a sling."

Kalten laughed. "It seems that you got a bigger piece of him than either one of us realized, Sparhawk," he said.

"I was trying," Sparhawk said grimly. "Getting rid of Adus is one of my main goals in life."

The door opened, and Kurik came back in carrying the wooden case containing the swords of the fallen knights.

"You insist on doing this, Vanion?" Sephrenia asked.

"I don't see that there's any choice," he replied. "You have to be fit to move around. I can do my job sitting down—or lying in bed—or dead, probably, if it comes to that."

The movement was but a faint one of Sephrenia's eyes. She looked for the briefest instant at Flute, and the little girl gravely nodded her head. Sparhawk was positive that only he had witnessed the exchange; for some reason it troubled him profoundly.

"Only take the swords one at a time," Sephrenia instructed Vanion. "The weight is considerable, and you'll need to give yourself time to get used to it."

"I've held swords before, Sephrenia."

"Not like these, and it's not the weight of the swords I'm talking about. It's the weight of all that goes with them." She opened the case and took out the sword of Sir Parasim, the young knight whom Adus had killed in Arcium. She took the blade and gravely extended the hilt across her forearm to Vanion.

He rose and took it from her. "Correct me if I make any mistakes," he said and started to chant in Styric. Sephrenia raised her voice with his, though her tone was softer, less certain, and her eyes were filled with doubt. The spell rose to a climax, and Vanion suddenly sagged, his face turning gray. "God!" he gasped, almost dropping the sword.

"Are you all right, dear one?" Sephrenia asked sharply, reaching out and touching him.

"Let me get my breath for a minute," Vanion said. "How can you stand this, Sephrenia?"

"We do what we must," she replied. "I feel better already, Vanion. There's no need for you to take the other two."

"Yes, there is. We're going to lose another of the twelve of us any day now, and his ghost will deliver another sword to you. I'm going to see to it that your hands are free when it comes." He straightened. "All right," he said grimly. "Give me the next one."

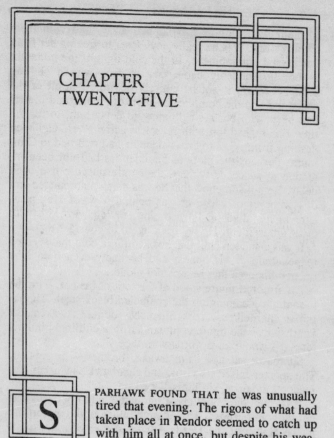

CHAPTER
TWENTY-FIVE

SPARHAWK FOUND THAT he was unusually tired that evening. The rigors of what had taken place in Rendor seemed to catch up with him all at once, but despite his weariness, he tossed and turned fitfully on the narrow cot in his cell-like room. The moon was full and it cast its pale light through the narrow window directly into Sparhawk's face. He muttered a sour oath and covered his head with his blanket to hide his eyes from the light.

Perhaps he dozed, or perhaps not. He hovered on the verge of sleep for what seemed hours; but, try though he might to slip through that soft door, he could not. He threw off his blanket and sat up.

It was spring, or very nearly. It seemed that the winter had been interminable, but what had he really accomplished? The months had slipped away, and with them Ehlana's life. Was he really any closer to freeing her from her crystal entombment? In the cold light of the midnight moon, he suddenly came face to face with a chilling thought. Might it not be entirely possible that all of the scheming and the complicated plots of Annias and Martel had been with but a single aim—to delay him, to fill the time Ehlana had left with senseless activity? He had been dashing from crisis to crisis since he had returned to Cimmura. Perhaps the plots of his enemies had not been intended to succeed. Perhaps their only purpose had been delay. He felt somehow that he was being manipulated and that whoever or whatever was behind it was taking pleasure in his anger and frustration, toying with him with cruel amusement. He lay back again to consider that.

It was a sudden chill that awoke him, a cold that seemed to penetrate to his bones, and he knew even before he opened his eyes that he was not alone.

An armored figure stood at the foot of his cot, with the moonlight gleaming on the enameled black steel. The familiar charnelhouse reek filled the room. "Awaken, Sir Sparhawk," the figure commanded in a chillingly hollow tone. "I would have words with thee."

Sparhawk sat up. "I'm awake, brother," he replied. The specter raised its visor, and Sparhawk saw a familiar face. "I'm sorry, Sir Tanis," he said.

"All men die," the ghost intoned, "and my death was not without purpose. That thought alone doth comfort me in the House of the Dead. Attend to me, Sparhawk, for my time with thee must be short. I bring thee instruction. This is the purpose for which I died."

"I will hear thee, Tanis," Sparhawk promised.

"Go thou then this very night to the crypt which doth lie beneath the cathedral of Cimmura. There shalt thou meet another restless shade which will instruct thee further in the course which thou must follow."

"Whose shade?"

"Thou shalt know him, Sparhawk."

"I will do as you command, my brother."

The specter at the foot of the cot drew its sword. "And

now I must leave thee, Sparhawk," it said. "I must
deliver up my sword ere I return to the endless silence."

Sparhawk sighed. "I know," he said.

"Hail then, brother, and farewell," the ghost concluded. "Remember me in thy prayers." Then the armored figure turned and walked silently from the room.

THE TOWERS OF the cathedral of Cimmura blotted out the
stars, and the pale moon lay low on the western horizon,
filling the streets with silvery light and inky black shadows. Sparhawk moved silently down a narrow alleyway
and stopped in the dense shadow at its mouth. He was
directly across the street from the main doors of the cathedral. Beneath his traveller's cloak he wore mail, and his
plain sword was belted at his waist.

He felt a peculiar detachment as he stared across the
street at the pair of church soldiers standing guard at the
cathedral door. Their red tunics were leeched of all color
by the pale moon, and they leaned inattentively against
the stones of the cathedral wall.

Sparhawk considered the situation. The guarded door
was the only way into the cathedral. All others would be
locked. By tradition, however, if not by Church law, the
locking of the main doors of any church was forbidden.

The guards would be sleepy and far from alert. The
street was not wide. One quick rush would eliminate
the problem. Sparhawk straightened and reached for his
sword. Then he stopped. Something seemed wrong with
the notion. He was not squeamish, but it seemed somehow
that he should not go to this meeting with blood on his
hands. Then, too, he decided, two bodies lying on the
cathedral steps would announce louder than words that
someone had gone to a great deal of trouble to get inside.

All he really needed was about a minute to cross the
street and slip through the doors. He thought about it.
What would be most likely to pull the soldiers from their
posts? He came up with a half-dozen possibilities before
he finally settled on one. He smiled when the notion came
to him. He ran over the spell in his mind, making sure
that he had all the words right, and then he began to mutter
under his breath in Styric.

The spell was fairly long. There were a number of details he wanted to get exactly right. When it was done, he raised his hand and released it.

The figure that appeared at the end of the street was that of a woman. She wore a velvet cloak with its hood thrown back, and her long blonde hair tumbled down her back. Her face was lovely beyond belief. She walked toward the doors of the cathedral with a seductive grace and, when she reached the steps, she stopped, looking up at the now fully awake pair of guards. She did not speak. Speech would have unnecessarily complicated the spell, and she did not need to say anything. Slowly, she unfastened the neck of her cloak and then opened it. Beneath the cloak, she was naked.

Sparhawk could clearly hear the suddenly hoarse breathing of the two soldiers.

Then, with inviting glances over her shoulder, she walked back up the street. The two guards looked after her, then at each other, then up and down the street to be sure that no one was watching. They leaned their pikes against the stone walls beside them and ran down the steps.

The figure of the woman had stopped beneath the torch flaring at the corner. She beckoned again, then stepped out of the light and disappeared up the side street.

The guards ran after her.

Sparhawk was out of the shadows at the mouth of the alley before the pair had rounded the corner. He was across the street in seconds and he bounded up the steps two at a time, seized the heavy handle of one of the great arched doors, and pulled. Then he was inside. He smiled faintly to himself, wondering how long the soldiers would search for the now-vanished apparition he had created.

The inside of the cathedral was dim and cool, smelling of incense and candle wax. Two lone tapers, one on either side of the altar, burned fitfully, stuttering in the faint breath of night air that had followed Sparhawk into the nave. Their light was little more than two flickering pinpoints that were reflected only faintly in the gems and gold decorating the altar.

Sparhawk moved silently down the central aisle, his shoulders tense and his senses alert. Although it was late at night, there was always the possibility that one of the many churchmen who lived within the confines of the cathedral might be up and about, and Sparhawk preferred to keep his visit a secret and to avoid noisy confrontations.

He knelt perfunctorily before the altar, rose, and moved out of the nave into the dim, latticed corridor leading toward the chancel.

There was light ahead, dim but steady. Sparhawk moved quietly, keeping close to the wall. A curtained archway stood before him, and he carefully parted the thick purple drapes a finger's width and peered in.

The Primate Annias, garbed not in satin but in harsh monk's cloth, knelt before a small stone altar inside the sanctuary. His emaciated features were twisted in an agony of self-loathing, and he wrung his hands together as if he would tear his fingers from their sockets. Tears streamed openly down his face, and his breath rasped hoarsely in his throat.

Sparhawk's face went bleak, and his hand went to his sword hilt. The soldiers at the cathedral door had been one thing. Killing them would have served no real purpose. Annias, however, was an entirely different matter. The primate was alone. A quick rush and a single thrust would remove this filthy infection from Elenia once and for all.

For a moment the life of the primate of Cimmura hung in the balance as Sparhawk, for the first time in his life, contemplated the deliberate murder of an unarmed man. But then he seemed to hear a light, girlish voice and saw before him a wealth of pale blonde hair and a pair of unwavering gray eyes. Regretfully, he let the velvet drapes close again and went to serve his queen, who, even in her slumber, had reached out with her gentle hand to save his soul.

"Another time, Annias," he whispered under his breath. Then he went down the corridor past the chancel toward the entrance to the crypt.

The crypt lay beneath the cathedral, and entry was gained by walking down a flight of stone stairs. A single tallow candle guttered at the top of the stairs, set in a grease-encrusted sconce. Careful to make no noise, Sparhawk snapped the candle in two, relit the fragment remaining in the sconce, and went on down, holding his half candle aloft.

The door at the bottom of the stairs was of heavy bronze. Sparhawk closed his fist about the latch and twisted very slowly until he felt the bolt grate open. Then, a fraction of an inch at a time, he opened the thick door. The faint creaking of the hinges seemed very loud in the silence, but Sparhawk knew that the sound would not carry up to the main floor of the church, and Annias was too caught up in his personal agonizing to hear anyway.

The inside of the crypt was a vast, low place, cold and musty-smelling. The circle of yellow light from Sparhawk's bit of candle did not reach far, and beyond that circle, huge expanses lay lost in darkness. The arched buttresses which supported the roof were draped with cobwebs, and dense shadows clotted the irregular corners. Sparhawk placed his back against the bronze door and very slowly closed it again. The sound of its closing echoed through the crypt like the hollow crack of doom.

The shadowed crypt extended back in unrelieved darkness far under the nave of the cathedral. Beneath the vaulted ceiling and the web-draped buttresses lay the former rulers of Elenia, rank upon silent rank of them, each enclosed in a leprous marble tomb with a dusty leaden effigy reposing on its top. Two thousand years of Elenian history lay moldering slowly into dust in this dank cellar. The wicked lay beside the virtuous. The stupid bedded down with the wise. The universal leveler had brought them all to this same place. The customary funerary sculpture decorated the stone walls and the corners of many of the sarcophagi, adding an even more mournful air to the silent tomb.

Sparhawk shuddered. The hot meeting of blood, bone, flesh, and bright, sharp steel were familiar to him, but not this cold, dusty silence. He was not sure of exactly how to proceed, since the specter of Sir Tanis had provided him with few details. He stood uncertainly near the bronze door, waiting. Although he knew it was foolish, he wrapped his hand about his sword hilt, more for comfort than out of any belief that the weapon at his side would be of any use in this dreadful place.

At first the sound seemed no more than a breath, a vagrant movement of the stale air inside the crypt. Then it came again, slightly louder this time. "Sparhawk," it sighed in a hollow whisper.

Sparhawk lifted his guttering candle, peering into the shadows.

"Sparhawk," the whisper came again.

"I'm here."

"Come closer."

The whisper seemed to be coming from somewhere among the more recent burials. Sparhawk moved toward them, growing more certain as he did so. Finally, he stopped before the last sarcophagus, the one bearing the name of King Aldreas, father of Queen Ehlana. He stood before the lead effigy of the late king, a man he was sworn to serve but for whom he had held but little respect. The sculptor who had created the effigy had made some effort to make Aldreas's features look regal, but the weakness was still there in the slightly harried expression and the uncertain chin.

"Hail, Sparhawk." The whisper came not from the sculptured form atop the marble lid, but from within the tomb itself.

"Hail, Aldreas," Sparhawk replied.

"And dost thou still bear me enmity and hold me in contempt, my champion?"

A hundred slights and insults leaped into Sparhawk's mind, a half-score years of humiliation and denigration by the man whose sorrowing shade now spoke from the hollow confines of his marble sepulcher. But what would it prove to twist a knife in the heart of one already dead? Quietly, Sparhawk forgave his king. "I never did, Aldreas," he lied. "You were my king. That's all I needed to know."

"Thou art kind, Sparhawk," the hollow voice sighed, "and thy kindness rends mine insubstantial heart far more than any rebuke."

"I'm sorry, Aldreas."

"I was not suited to wear the crown," the sepulchral

voice admitted with a melancholy regret. "There were so many things happening that I didn't understand, and people around me I thought were my friends, but were not."

"We knew, Aldreas, but there was no way we could protect you."

"I could not have known of the plots which surrounded me, could I, Sparhawk?" The ghost seemed to have a desperate need to explain and justify the things Aldreas had done in life. "I was raised to revere the Church, and I trusted the primate of Cimmura above all others. How could I have known that his intent was to deceive me?"

"You could not have, Aldreas." It was not difficult to say it. Aldreas was no longer an enemy, and if a few words would comfort his guilt-ridden ghost, they cost no more than the breath it took to express them.

"But I should not have turned my back on my only child," Aldreas said in a voice filled with pain. "It is that which I repent most sorely. The primate turned me against her, but I should not have listened to his false counsel."

"Ehlana knew that, Aldreas," Sparhawk said. "She knew that it was Annias who was her enemy, not you."

There was a long pause. "And what has become of my dear, dear sister?" The late king's words came out as from between teeth tightly clenched with hate.

"She's still in the cloister at Demos, your Majesty," Sparhawk reported in as neutral a tone as he could manage. "She will die there."

"Then entomb her there, my champion," Aldreas commanded. "Do not defile my slumber by placing my murderess at my side in this place."

"Murderess?" Sparhawk was stunned.

"My life had become a burden to her. Her sycophant and paramour, Primate Annias, arranged to have her conveyed in secret here to me. She beguiled me with wildest abandon, wilder than I had ever known from her. In exhaustion, I took a cup from her hands and drank, and the drink was death. She taunted me with that, standing over my nerveless body with her flagrant nudity and her face contorted with hatred and contempt as she reviled me. Avenge me, my champion. Take vengeance upon my foul sister and her twisted consort, for they have brought me low and dispossessed my true heir, the daughter I ignored and despised throughout her childhood.''

''As God gives me breath, it shall be as you say, Aldreas,'' Sparhawk swore.

''And when my pale little daughter ascends to her rightful place upon my throne, tell her, I pray thee, that I did truly love her.''

''If that, please God, should come to pass, Aldreas, I will.''

''It must, Sparhawk. It must—else all that Elenia hath ever been shall be as naught. Only Ehlana is the true heir to the throne of Elenia. I charge thee, do not let my throne be usurped by the fruit of the unclean coupling of my sister and the primate of Cimmura.''

''My sword shall prevent it, my king,'' Sparhawk pledged fervently. ''All three will lie dead in their own blood before this week sees its end.''

''And thy life as well shall be lost in thy rush to vengeance, Sparhawk, and how will thy sacrifice restore my daughter to her rightful place?''

Aldreas, Sparhawk concluded, was far wiser in death than he had been in life.

''The time for vengeance will come in its own proper order, my champion,'' the ghost told him. ''First, however, I charge thee to restore my daughter Ehlana. And to that end I am permitted to reveal certain truths to thee. No nostrum nor talisman of lesser worth may heal my child, for only Bhelliom can make her whole again.''

Sparhawk's heart sank.

''Be not dismayed, Sparhawk, for the time hath come for Bhelliom to emerge from the place where it hath lain hidden and once again to stir the earth with its power. It moves in its own time and with its own purpose, and this is that time, for events have moved mankind to the place where its purpose may now be accomplished. No force in all the world can prevent Bhelliom from coming forth into the sunlight again, and whole nations await its coming. Be *thou* the one who finds it, however, for only in *thy* hand can its full power be released to roll back the darkness which even now stalks the earth. Thou art no longer my champion, Sparhawk, but the champion of all this world. Shouldst thou fail, all will fail."

"And where should I seek, my king?"

"That I am forbidden to reveal. I can, however, tell thee how to unleash its power once it lies in thy grasp. The blood-red ring which adorns thy hand and that which in life adorned mine are older far than we had imagined. He who fashioned Bhelliom fashioned the rings, also, and they are the keys which will unlock the power of the jewel."

"But your ring is lost, Aldreas. The primate of Cimmura tore the palace apart again and again searching for it."

A ghostly chuckle came from the sarcophagus. "I still have it, Sparhawk," Aldreas said. "After my dear sister had given me her last fatal kiss and departed, I had moments of lucidity. I concealed the ring to deny possession of it to my enemies. Despite all the desperate efforts of the primate of Cimmura, it was buried with me. Think back, Sparhawk. Remember the old legends. At the time my family and thine were bonded together by these rings, thy ancestor gave to mine his own war spear in token of his allegiance. Thus I return it."

A ghostly hand rose from the sarcophagus holding a short-handled, broad-bladed spear in its grasp. The weapon was very old, and its symbolic importance had been forgotten over the centuries. Sparhawk reached out his hand and took it from the ghostly hand of Aldreas. "I will carry it with pride, my king," he said.

"Pride is a hollow thing, Sparhawk. The significance of the spear goes far beyond that. Detach the blade from the shaft and look within the socket."

Sparhawk set down his candle, put his hand to the blade, and twisted the tough wood of the shaft. With a dry squeak, the two separated. He looked into the ancient steel socket of the blade. The blood-red glitter of a ruby winked back at him.

"I have but one more instruction for thee, my champion," the ghost continued. "Should it come to pass that thy quest reaches its conclusion only after my daughter joins me in the House of the Dead, it lies upon thee to destroy Bhelliom, though this shall surely cost thee thy life."

"But how may I destroy a thing of such power?" Sparhawk protested.

"Keep thou my ring in the place where I have concealed it. Should all go well, return it to my daughter when she sits again in splendor upon her throne; but should she die, continue thy quest for Bhelliom, though the search takes thee all the days of thy life. And when it comes to pass that thou findest it, seize the spear in the hand which bears thy ring and drive it into the heart of Bhelliom with all thy might. The jewel will be destoyed, as will the rings—and in that act shalt thou lose thy life. Fail not in this, Sparhawk, for a dark power doth bestride the earth, and Bhelliom must never fall into its hands."

Sparhawk bowed. "It shall be as you command, my king," he swore.

A sigh came from the sarcophagus. "It is done, then," Aldreas whispered. "I have done what I could to aid thee, and this completes the task which I left unfinished. Do not fail me. Hail then, Sparhawk, and farewell."

"Hail and farewell, Aldreas."

The crypt was still chill and empty, save for the ranks of the royal dead. The hollow whisper had fallen silent now. Sparhawk rejoined the parts of the spear, then reached out his hand and laid it over the heart of the leaden effigy. "Sleep well, Aldreas," he said softly. Then with the ancient spear in his grasp, he turned and quietly left the tomb.

This concludes **The Diamond Throne**
Book One of **The Elenium**.
Book Two: **The Ruby Knight**
*will cover the desperate search
for the long-lost Bhelliom
through far lands and strange adventures.*

ABOUT THE AUTHOR

DAVID EDDINGS was born in Spokane, Washington, in 1931 and was raised in the Puget Sound area north of Seattle. He received a Bachelor of Arts degree from Reed College in Portland, Oregon, in 1954 and a Master of Arts degree from the University of Washington in 1961. He has served in the United States Army, has worked as a buyer for the Boeing Company, has been a grocery clerk, and has taught English. He has lived in many parts of the United States.

His first novel, *High Hunt* (published by Putnam in 1973), was a contemporary adventure story. The field of fantasy has always been of interest to him, however, and he turned to *The Belgariad* in an effort to develop certain technical and philosophical ideas concerning that genre.

Eddings currently resides with his wife, Leigh, in the southwest.